Delightmares

By Michael S. Gatlin

1.

See it Coming

Driving I-40 West was green trees and hillbilly towns full of methamphetamine teens and paranoid bible-thumpers with locked doors and loaded rifles. American flag monkey on the back of each timid voter. Every few miles an enormous two-hundred-foot cross rose from some manicured lawn, off the interstate—as if the believers needed a Tower of Babel to prove their faith.

What was that? Some sort of Small Messiah Complex?

It was April 1994. They had found Kurt Cobain's body, and the radio was full of Nirvana. Grunge was dead. A generation slammed on the brakes. Suburban kids across the galaxy had lost a star—a shining light went out in their rebellious lighthouse. A beacon went silent. It had nothing to do with me. There will always be new music, new stars, and new voices for kids to cling on to in hopes of shining brighter than their dull parents. There shall be no mourning for the completed cycle.

Nashville was large and welcoming—cowboy city lights and average American denim. I pulled into a Denny's parking lot and met Kramer at a booth in the back and ordered black coffee.

Kramer S. Lydon was a friend from high school. He came to Vanderbilt University to study the letters of dead men. I couldn't afford school—financially, emotionally, spiritually or academically. I couldn't sit in another classroom for anything—poring over the lesson plan, letting my boy age to man, in quiet obedience to the norm.

"Whatcha been doing man?" And other boring conversations ensued.

Starved, I ate the rest of his leftover french-fries like a vulture—the pickle, tomato and lettuce too, each discarded vegetable dripping with the fatty pink juice of a long-vanished mayonnaise-drenched hamburger.

We talked and talked, and my nerves cramped from the coffee—free refills—*no cream or sugar for me*, and a shit in the bathroom.

He told me all about his intentions of being an artist, a rock god, a poet. He regaled me with stories of being on stage and soaking in the lights and the applause. My eyes burned. He was a short man and I guess somewhere in the recess of his mind he needed the adoration of strangers—an audience—groupies and admirers, fawning critics—to prove something to himself, or the world, or the people he met, as extensions of his parents… I don't know.

Needing desperately to prove to the world that you don't need a ladder must suck if you're afraid of heights.

I grew tired of listening to his ambitious plans of becoming a rock'n'roll messiah with no message—but I pretended rapt interest in his words because I needed a place to sleep and had little money.

Eventually his stories blossomed interest in my mind, as he told me of a group of young men and women—poets and artists and deviants, the lot of them—who belonged to The Church. *The Church* was short for The First Interplanetary Church of the Immaculate Deception. The Church was a group of punk poets and social misfits who started their own religion: Plaguism.

It sounded fun.

Later in the evening, on Vanderbilt campus, I met Mark and David and Paul and John and Mathew and Peter and fifteen other black and white Anglo-Saxon boys with Christian names and wealthy families and nothing going for them but the bland vanilla existence of following the rules and taking orders and turning in assignments and everything in the world that I was running away from.

No one stood out. I can't remember a single word shared between us, nor would I be able to pick any of them out of a police lineup—powder blue button-up shirts and khaki pants—baggy, unfit—each of them in baseball caps and tennis shoes.

These were the future lawyers, bankers, and congressmen of my generation and they were original as dirt. I drank their whisky and smoked their weed and entertained them with stories of my rambunctious yesteryear. It was easy. There were no girls to impress, and none of them held my interest, so I feigned sleepiness early.

The cement floor of Kramer's dorm room was freezing. I laid out every article of clothing from my duffel bag and made a nest. He was too homophobic to share his bed with me—and rightly so—who knows how amorous I would've been with his small frame in the middle of the night?

"Tomorrow, I want you to meet somebody."

Whatever.

I've slept in worse places. I've lied to innkeepers and lain with donkeys and dogs in unclean stables where virgin kings without placenta were born from angelic promises. I've slept in vehicles, on piss-stained floors, in creepy beds with stinky, greasy sheets and unknown occupants moving about in grimy ecstasy unknown to me.

I've known many redneck waterbeds.

Morning broke me. We headed to Centennial Park where dark sunshine and rainbow-black swirled chaos with art.

Kramer introduced me to Jas. "Martin Hemlock, this is The Pope of the First Interplanetary Church of the Immaculate Deception—His Assholiness The Pope Jas, the First and Last…"

The Pope bent back, to the side, internally, awkwardly gracefully— "ALWAYS, MAYBE, SOMETIMES and NEVER!" He shot out his hand, fingers dangling from paw, brandishing an ostentatious ring, painted gold/plastic bejeweled—apparently for me to kiss.

I grabbed his hand and pulled him in close.

"Martin. Pleased." I spoke and squeezed firmly, probably crushing his bird skeleton hand too rough—but he was paper tiger butch and could take a punch—you could tell—no one that skinny sticks his chin out that far without being able to take an ass beating. I kissed his ring.

His frail body limply jerked into my larger frame. I sniffed around his face and neck as if I were a canine remembering his scent.

(Impress upon them.)

"Well! Take it all in, boy!" Jas exhaled smoke in my face.

I let him go and reached my hand out for the other one, the younger sultry one, the less dynamic, more subdued one…

"Martin."

"Christopher…"

"Everyone calls him Pookie," Jas interrupted.

Pookie was Jas's live-in boyfriend—a ghost waiting to happen—a bright red mop of badly-cut and misshapen hair exploded from the top of his head and accentuated his plump gummy lips. A torn and tattered shirt spilled over his pink Lydia Lunch t-shirt hanging on his thin and battered frame—a martyr for the mosh pit—bright yellow pants and bible black boots—mascara, and black fingernail polish—a whip-it kid with orbiting eyes.

"So, what's The First Inter-dimensional Church of the Whatever Deception all about?" I quizzed the kid in the camouflage pants and black priest shirt with white collar, calling himself The Pope.

"Stupid shit!" Pookie answered.

Jas's head whipped towards him with chicken speed. "Of course, it's stupid shit! It's *religion*!" He clucked. The last word secreted licorice emphasis—corrosive saliva and throat cancer.

"Yeah—well, fuck ALL religions!"

A reptilian ease, coiling in preparation for strike, Jas retorted, "You know, Chuckie believes that Blasphemy's the ultimate expression of the divine."

"Who's Chuckie?" I asked.

Jas splayed his fingers on his cocked skinny chest— "Why sweetie—he's our *Lord* and *Flavor*—He's God!"

I laughed. Nobody else did. There was a pause while the four of us smoked young cigarettes and sized each other up. I dug these cute rebellious rapscallions and their goofy religious/blasphemous trip. It was new. It was exciting. It was exactly what I'd been looking for—the post-atomic hard-bop of America. I, too, was desperate with madness and fumbling for the formula.

"You want to take some acid with me and climb this tree?" Jas asked me.

"Some?"

Jas laughed uproariously— "Why don't we start with one?"

In for a penny, in for what's in the safe.

Jas pinched a small square piece of paper in filed and polished fingernail talons and held it out to my mouth. I tried to dodge his advances and grab the wafer with my hand, but he jerked his hand away, and corrected my insolence with a waving finger in my face. "No, NO, nO! I am The *POPE* and you must accept the Holy Communion on your *tongue*. This is the body of our Lord and Flavor *CHUCKIE THE PLAGUE!*"

He was so fucked-up and dramatic, totally serious, (possible genius?) a wonderful joke—why not? —free acid and an Alice adventure through the Looking Glass… I stuck out my tongue and let this strange stranger place a laced piece of paper, containing an unknown dosage of some unknown mind-altering substance, on my tongue.

Upon reflection I guess it could've been any kind of drug he was offering me, but at that age—what the hell?

Careful consideration often leads to missed opportunities.

When going full throttle through life, scrutinize parsimoniously.

Kramer and Pookie weren't into taking acid in the middle of the afternoon and climbing some tree in some park, on earth. They had their own little party elsewhere—Kramer with some teenage Sylvia Plath in high heels, wobbly on the chair, but no real strength in the noose— Pookie with two girls in a band together—tongue on wet and muscle to give.

In the enormous oak tree, I scooted along the branches rubbing my fertile crotch on the trees, spreading my scent—letting the animals know that I'm everywhere. I felt my teeth sharpen, my nails harden, my dick stiffen, my mouth snarl. I was lycanthropic muscular distortion, bi-polar transformation—primitive metamorphoses. I licked ants from the tree and laughed—a moment of clarity.

How savage was I willing to become?

I became totally the here and now (there and then). I was a tree dweller. I stretched out like an arboreal Christ on sturdy branches and wondered where the Roman Soldiers were—totally prepared for the nine-inch nails. I laughed the thought away, knowing I was too selfish to ever be a martyr.

Homo habilis concerns came on. I began to wonder how I'd make a fort… A small nest of torn apart branches, for my sleeping here this evening. I'd need a canopy to sleep in, when the fatigue came. Perhaps I'd need a mate—a young college student studying anthropology beneath a different type of tree…

(In the jungle, I am an impaler, not an impala.)

Jas too, it seemed, wandered around the tree with bizarre connotations of holy discovery. I wondered if I should fight him for supremacy of the tree—really start my territorial pissing now. It seemed that maybe I shouldn't, that this performance would be rude, seeing as how we'd just met, and it was after all—his acid.

Hours later, we proudly fell from our leafy heaven in a cloud of post-angelic laughter. Kramer and Pookie were long gone. There was no impartial judge to our madness. The sun was beginning its descent.

"Do you have a car?" Jas asked.

I led him to my car. It was a triply painted burgundy 1980 Honda Accord. Sloppy polka dots and runny ribbons of vermillion and crimson… There were many designs, shapes, portraits, and graffiti coating the old, reliable four door sedan. It was painted the night before I left town to join the carnival. A year prior, I'd traveled across Canada in the Conklin circuit working for Bungee USA. We'd assembled, operated, and disassembled a large reverse bungee jump ride known as the ejection seat. I'd traveled from Vancouver to Quebec City working from city to city as part of the most celebrated team of carnies on the circuit. That, of course, was another story…

Jas enjoyed the mailbox letters on the driver's side door that read *The Mystery Ship* in black and gold. "I knew you were a Plaguist the first second I saw you," he said.

"What's a Plaguist?" I asked.

"Oh… A follower of Chuckie The Plague—a believer in the dogma-free truth that absurdity shall be the whole of the law."

"Oh. Okay." What else could I say?

It was dark. We'd been tripping for six or seventy hours and the acid had mostly worn off, but the distortion of the senses was still present. It was time to plan. Jas wanted a ride somewhere.

We drove to Fun Bar to pick up Pookie.

The band was between sets. The bar was well-lit and loud with chatter. Pookie dripped cool like Popsicle: purple cherry, orange banana, short red shorts and yellow shirt and purple socks pulled high, blue suede shoes, green fedora—every color of the rainbow—end of the rainbow—lecherous golden chains—leprechaun semen fertilizing a dangerous serpent in his spiritual glow… Perpetual lost boy half chub…

He'd seemingly made a complete transformation, not of just wardrobe, but of personality. He was happy, bouncing around the establishment seemingly knowing everyone in the place—or meeting them anew. He was in his element—drunken puppy sighs of laughter and '*buy me a drink*' batting flatterlashes.

First impressions are important and he made them around every turn—every corner—*hi, how you doing—let me get that for you—me too—I know*—Anti-social Butterfly whispering across the playing field on gilded gossamer wings—saying prayer to every invisible airy fairy queen in the mix—*Love your dress—call me sometime—I know I haven't had that much time*—Time. tIme: tHe fReQuEncy of events. TIme: irReVerSible succession. TiMe. We all need more time—a lifetime to do the things and people we want. WaNt: desire, wIsh… wAnt: craving, UrgE… WANT like spiritual graVity spinNing my attraction/repulsion receptors in a *mad* frenzy… EAsy to WanT, Lust, Urge, Get oFF, stay gone, high on the flavor…

Life—there in that bar—buBBling up in hashish tar pit sickness—thick and erect for aTTention… Every wink of the eye, smile, and curled lip around straw drinking drink…

Cigarette spark—blow away from your face—*pleased to meetcha:* —snaps her gum—That was Echo. She wore overalls and wife-beater/tank-top—real farmer-john hipster with no point to prove but every prick. Big mouth and small breasts, piano key teeth and guttural laugh—a holy toilet for the sacred bodily fluids of the aroused—thirsty for cock and cum and pussy and reaction and power—*that was me—that was me who made you cum—I'm special*—typical adolescent Scorpio desperation—anxious for approval, appraisal, praise—needy—all the time *look at me*… Great in the sack—a pain on the temporal plane—unless God. Oh god, another Scorpio egoist with no bend in the bamboo typhoon, no negotiation in the peaceful wartime treaty, all stick it in me, stick-to-it, and me, me, me…

She made me sick instantly—all bubble and twitch—need and desire—all-consume—multiplicity in her every response—*I want this—but I want the other thing too*—a real gross representative of the consumer sapient beast wrecking the Earth with their devastating vacuum of desire.

(I don't mind the destruction of the environment, but I protest the hypocritical path to its legislative deregulation in politics.)

There was a fight. Jas didn't like one bit what was happening in his reality.

I knew nothing. I was infantile mass absorbing the scene. I gulped my lemon soda down instinctively knowing it was time to flee—*nice to meet you—you too—have a pleasant evening—I'm going to take this crazy bastard home*—screaming curse words, glass breaking, alerting security.

It was time to leave.

Jas and Pookie had a fight apparently. I don't remember what about, if I ever knew. I only felt it was time to flee the scene with this newly-introduced-to-me maniac in tow. I guess Pookie and Echo had a thing?

Rollercoaster roads sparkled effervescent laughter as we turned from street to street and somehow obeyed the traffic signals. Where was I? Who was this mad man? Does anything matter in life? How far could I take this? Where were my boundaries? Was I some angelic deviant of the unsatisfied urge, or some devilish devotee to an endless crave?

Another wave of the acid…

There was a gift granted by the gods when youth tried itself out in unknown territory—luck, fortune, strength, wisdom, early retirement—at a reasonable speed. Never mind the electric jellyfish dripping neon tentacles across the windshield—turn the wipers on—a dead bug smear—made worse with the last of the windshield washing fluid…

I spat on my left hand and leaned out of the window—cleared away a sixteen-inch diameter to see through and didn't lose a mile an hour—*mama don't let your babies grow up to be cowboys*—sang Willie Nelson on the radio—*let them be doctors and lawyers and such*—he was a drunk lying bastard. Mamas raise them cowboys on buckwheat pancakes and whisky tits and trips to the mountains and boyhood rifles and boyhood killings—a 22 slug through the heart of a bird, or the throat of a deer. Teach that little bastard to gut his kill and filet the fish too—fend for itself—the best way an animal can learn.

"If I have a kid—it's going to be a Fucking CowBoy!!" I screamed at the top of my lungs, out the window, where my mind was.

Jas paid no response—he drifted in a psychodelicate plasma-fabric of timelessness and void—the wave of mutilation that pixies sing about in tiny voices from past lives. There was nothing holding him to the here and now (there and then.)

He held his head from the window like a dog and let the wind redden his eyes, dry his tongue, whip his hair, wipe his mind from his mind—ultimate glory—self-aggrandizing the gratifying luxury of nonsense.

There shall be no thing that is greater than me.

Was that the sentiment I want to express to the world?

Welcome to S.P.A.M. Manor.

SLAM! The door shook the wall and the other two walls.

Jas changed from sluggish companion to instant host, "WELCOME!" He sang in alto aria with squeak and slur.

I took a tour of his home. It was small. I'd been in bigger trailers, much bigger trailers. Hell! I'd friends with doublewides.

To the far right—eight feet—was the Master Bedroom. A full-size mattress blushed behind sheer chiffon drapes stapled from the ceiling, spilling across his bed to the floor.

On the wall, a David Bowie poster, that he wished he looked like, hung over the bed.

Dreams made the whole place stink of youthful significance.

A bookshelf divided the bedroom from the living room. The bookshelf was full of every book you should have read before me: Burroughs, Poe, Lautreamont, Schopenhauer, Nietzsche, Camus, de Sade, Rimbaud, Henry Miller, Hunter Thompson…

The brain is stretched into a bizarre mathematical formula. Fibonacci, da Vinci, Pythagoras, Erdos, Euclid, Newton…

(Where am I? How did I get here? The person I came to Nashville to see, I am no longer interested in, because *this* person is much more interesting—this deviant spiritual leader.)

I would go to the ends of the earth to avoid the fat middle.

The red sofa against the far wall was the favored spot of the house. It faced the door, the door that was slammed upon our entrance.

Jas usually nestled in the corner of the red sofa, by the kitchen, his skinny legs scrunched against his bird chest, heels against ass, knees under chin—ready to pounce from his position like a feline huntress should anyone need anything, or when the door shook, rattled, and rolled of the secret Plaguist knock…

If he had facial hair Jas would pluck the hair from his face with precision filed nails. He had some disease. He said he knew the proper word for it—trichotillomania, I think it was…

He had to feel pain—had to feel, had to feel pleasure, had to feel, feel pressure and release, preferring disease to ease and impossible to please. He had to be physically always engaged with the planet. This was why he had such fondness for pills, narcotics, marijuana, alcohol, nicotine, ('which is also a stimulant, don't forget!' I can still hear him say)—sex, fighting, slipping and falling, the following day's bruises and cuts—and the swollen tender places…

I never once saw him sit on the other sofa.

The other sofa was a black leather two-seater which divided the living room from the kitchen. In the corner of the sofas was a filing cabinet acting as a table with paisley-patterned material draping over.

The kitchen was the darkest place in the apartment—always—even right after we cleaned it. It was NEVER cleaned. There was movement in the sink. Dishes and cups piled high to the faucet, noisily resettled after the disturbance. The crime scene was alive with mushroom trolls and cockroach mutations that I was sure were grotesque and poisonous. It was an abysmal black crusty mess, a clutter of moldy growth.

I searched the cabinet for a clean cup and found only a Pyrex measuring glass, sixteen-ounce size. I turned on the faucet and drank from the odd vessel.

"Funny, that's what Chuckie drinks from," Jas chirped.

"Cleanliness is next to Godliness," I said and rinsed out the cup, before putting it back on the top shelf above the stove.

The restroom was tiny, lit only with a red heating lamp and containing only a tiny walk-in shower with a moldy shower curtain and a toilet to piss in. Green and black fungus and actual mushrooms blossomed all around the outer perimeter of the shower floor. Only a gray dirty spot stood where feet were presumed to stand, safe from the encroaching bacterial growth.

Between the tiny standing-room-only restroom and the tiny standing-room-only closet was the sink: brush your teeth, comb your hair, shave your face, and check out the mirror-mirror on the wall and gamble on who's the fairest of them all....

The tiny living quarters were impossibly small—four-hundred square feet.

This was Jas's home—a small efficiency apartment in the projects of North Nashville that he and his boyfriend, Pookie, had decorated with care and flair, transforming the bitty shell into a tripper's paradise lit by many Christmas lights.

Surprises kidnapped the eyes around every geometric bend. Reflective tinsel dripped from metal shelves. Small toys glittered in unsuspecting crevices. Candles burned and dripped wax from a candelabrum that rested upon stacks of bibles on the table between the two couches.

Jas plopped a cassette into the stereo, *In on the Kill Taker,* by Fugazi. It was sexy punk, bursts of energy and learned chord progression... Every instrument fit and tuned...

S.P.A.M. Manor was named after a group of poets and artists that Jas not only belonged to but helped form. They were Super Pimps At the Mall—a galvanized group of punks, goths, junkies, and drag queens—who believed they could sell anything—including themselves. They performed poetry on stage, with fake blood, cap guns, live mock crucifixions, simulated sex, anything that would provoke.

Like everything Jas did, S.P.A.M. was loosely founded in reality but steeped in mythical importance—like building a cathedral of iron on a river of butter infested with crocodiles made from churning the cream of the sacred cow's lactation with reptilian thrashing... A tasty impossibility but nonetheless dangerous.

We stayed up for hours—laughing, drinking cheap wine and smoking from a beat-up plastic bong that was broken in a hundred different places and glued back together again. It smelled of industrial strength epoxy and the fumes were inhaled with the smoke to increase the buzz.

Interestingly enough, we discussed comedy and who we thought were funny. We talked about George Carlin the most, but also Richard Pryor and Sam Kinison, Andy Kaufman, Red Foxx, Bill Hicks...

What!? How did this crazy leather queen have such comedic knowledge? And what was I doing at his place on the outskirts of town?

"Hey maaaiihn," he slurred trippy. "I studied cAAAHHmcdy looOOong before I studied anything eLLLSe!" Jas seemed to proudly/shamefully admit this adolescent truth with his syrupy southern evil-scented accent and eyes open wide.

"Me too, man!" I responded enthusiastically, showing my age— "I filled up notebooks with jokes and routines as a kid, years before song lyrics and then poetry…"

"Oh god!" Jas exhaled a splayed fan of fingers across his bird chest. "We're stereotypes!" He shrieked with dramatic distaste. "*We're chicken shit comics who wanted to be rock stars—but couldn't si1ing*—and then became *pOoEets.*" He bowed his head in dramatic showmanship as he said the last word with licorice teeth, wine-crust lips, volatile toxin and throat polyps. His long, black, curly hair wildly escaped his scalp like medusa serpents biting the angelic air.

I'd found a champion to the same ideals I'd been cultivating. I'd found a true American original, undaunted by the-way-things-are-in-the-world, an unfiltered batch of Tennessee whisky, a pure expression of the human mutant—alive and unafraid to die, to live, to blast off.

The sun came up—but it was impossible to tell—a heavy velvet comforter acted as permanent blinds covering the one window in the apartment. It was eternal night.

I passed out on the red sofa, and then stayed for three and a half months.

2.

Keep it Coming

All my dreams are the same: Me not there.

The next day Jas and I drove to Plague Central—where I was to meet God and understand Plaguism better and maybe score some acid and…

Loaded on drugs felt like home to me.

Why not join a cult and disgrace my ancestors? There was nothing that made sense to me in the real world—the world of credit and debit and mortgage and loan, twenty years of school and forty hours a week, a career, church, offspring, fast food and television reruns… Spectator sports, domestic beer, shopping malls, middle age pitfalls…

Plague Central was our destination. It was a creepy, shadowy drive— fibrous, arching limbs full of rustling leaves covered our path. The drive gave me shivers—like maybe murderers lived back there—every horror movie—masked villain point-of-view watching the fresh faces drive up in innocent delight—no idea of the consequences—of the final curtain… Close-up on heavy steel weapon, like an axe or a machete, rusted with blood—hiding a deformed face beneath mask, torn overalls and work boots, a sublime figure of fitness and evil… Catastrophic demented hard-on…

It was so goddamn dramatic.

We got out of the car. Chuckie smoked a cigarette on the second-story landing of the duplex known as Plague Central. "Who THE HELL IS THAT!?" Chuckie screamed from the balcony.

"Hey Chuckie! This is Martin!" Jas introduced us in screams.

I observed Chuckie's misdemeanor demeanor—tough and easy, greasy black jeans tucked into black motorcycle boots, black leather jacket and no shirt—random body hair—well built. He wore a long thin Mohawk from a balding head and sported extremely bushy sideburns that made his face look twice as large. He wore black sunglasses that wrapped around his eyes.

"What's happening?" I lamely asked the Lord.

"WHAT'S HAPPENING?" Chuckie seemed to be mocking me, was mocking me, "I'll tell you what's *happening*—*EVERYTHING'S HAPPENING!*"

Chuckie's tone changed from corn syrup to corn on the cob, "Hey Martin—are you a FAGGOT?!"

"HELL NO!" I protested, a little too loudly probably.

"Well, you're awfully *pretty* to NOT be a FAGGOT! —HELL! —I'm not going to believe you're not a FAGGOT until you come up here and Suck MY DICK—and DON'T LIKE it! —Haw! Haw! *Huck!*" His laughter transformed into coughing. He lit a menthol cigarette, and everything was Kool. He spit phlegm over the edge. "Well, come on up *motherfuckers!*" He was now a joyous and loving god.

I'd been studying him from the car, hoping I wasn't being dragged to some horrible detention center where I'd be forced to star in some terrible porn movie—prison showers, cops and robbers, cops on robbers, cops on cops—Billy-club sucking and getting fucked… I didn't want to act in anything serious… I was a silly nineteen-year-old, a long way from home. Home? Nevermind.

I lay to rest no more where my head had fallen before.

"Come on!" Jas motioned for me to follow him. I did. What the hell—right? I mean: in for a penny, in for the GDP of Bolivia.

Plague Central was surrounded by woods and had a private charm to it, a serial-killer den of craze and horror. These guys never had any trick-or-treaters, never any break-ins, never any trouble with the law, and they threw some of the wildest parties I'd ever been to.

We walked up the long, blue, wooden stairs loosely clinging to the side of the brick building and chipping with ancient paint—every step wobbly. The door opened by the magic of God's hand. Their home was dark and dank—much like S.P.A.M. Manor—dusty and gothic.

Rokusaburo didn't look up from his Nintendo driving game. He played Pole Position on a giant tube television from the seventies, the kind encased in wood with doors to cover the screen, only the doors had been ripped off the hinges and the hinges were sharp and distorted towards the viewer as if a mighty hulk force had ripped them easily from their puny home.

The house was full of smoke. We stood in the kitchen while Chuckie handed us each a 25oz. of Kiwi Lemon MD 20/20.

Delicious.

Gross.

"Wow, what kind of bug is that?" I had to ask. The thing was huge, yellow and black, and scurrying across the countertop.

"Hell, I don't know man. But if you see any *spiders*, don't kill 'em! They eat the *other* buUUugs." Chuckie had a cool hybrid accent—half California stoner/half Tennessee trucker, slurring his words sarcastically and laidback—eyes invisible behind black glasses.

A saucer-sized spider scurried across the countertop and pounced on the odd bug. The spider paralyzed the parasite and wrapped him in a suffocating cocoon to preserve his insides, which were slowly being digested by the spider's venom and melting into fine syrup to suck out later. The spider dragged the package away.

"That's Dave, man! He's our favorite spider!" Chuckie informed me excitedly of their prized arachnid that had evolved to a land predator. "Yeah man! Rock and I caught these small BUuuUUGS man—and wounded 'em *just enough*—you know—then dropped like A HALF a drop of liquid LSD on 'em and—fuckin'—threw the bugs on the spider webs." A quick hit of cigarette. "Man! The spiders went right over and paralyzed 'em and fuckin'—wrapped up their catch in cool spider silk." Chuckie drew mightily on his cigarette and exhaled smoke as he talked without burn or interruption— "Well, not two hours later the spiders were spinning these NON-*geometrical* webs all over the place 'at were fuckin'—clumsy and no good for catching flies whatsoever man! —Now they seem to *live* in the crevices! That one 'ere's, Dave, he's our favorite—look how BIG he is!" Chuckie looked on in delight, a ruby smile across his oily face.

The spider was indeed big. You heard each of his eight legs as they tapped against the laminate countertop and the silk of the cocoon as it was dragged out of sight.

"That is fucking fantastic!!" I offered.

Jas got to the point. "Chuckie, Martin wants to hear the genesis of our church."

"Well, hell! Why haven't you already told him?" Chuckie wanted to know.

Jas defended himself in wrongly accused squeals. "Because, I don't know which *VERSION* of the *true story* you're telling now." He hissed sarcastic laughter through yellowing teeth.

"All of 'em! Hell—if you don't fertilize the truth with enough nonsense, it'll never grow!" Chuckic lit a cigarette with his cigarette and stuffed the old one out in an ashtray overflowing with hundreds of cigarette butts. His actions were fast and confident, sure of their every move.

"There's no official story?" I asked.

"Well, I'll tell you the truth." Chuckie seemed serious.

Jas cackled like a manic rooster. He laughed and laughed, as did Rock, done with his video game and drinking a beer from the fridge.

Rock was a menacing looking punk rocker, with bulging muscles, black and partially dyed blood red Mohawk, spiked bracelets, eyeliner and missing teeth. He lived in the other bedroom at Plague Central. Chuckie joined in the laughter as if realizing that that was the funniest thing ever uttered.

"Seriously," Chuckie continued—more laughter. "I'll tell you Mar— I'd been tripping for LIiiIKE *forty-five hours straight* and—fuckin'—I was trying to get some sleep—you know—when—fuckin'—I heard this voice—and I looked down to see what I could see—and it was one of my old dirty socks, squirming around on the ground trying to talk to me. It was like a demented *sock puppet*, yellow-stained and crusty from a week in one of my boots—fuckin'—the damn little thing told me to start a RELIGION." The barbecue potato chip crunch of his words was raspy with cigarette tar and vocal scar.

"The sock told me that I was *God* and that I was EVERYWHERE, the *circumference* and NOWHERE the *center*—told me that I should BECOME Chuckie The Plague and lead others from the promised land of *lies* to the full-of-shit plane of truth."

Chuckie exhaled two taurine streams of smoke from his flared nostrils and extinguished his butt. "That's the fucking truth right there." He wadded up his empty cigarette package and pulled a fresh pack from his tiny saddle bag that he wore on his belt, beat the package of cigarettes, opened the cellophane and removed a fresh fag. He turned to look at Jas as he lit his smoke. "Or anyway—that's how I'm selling it today."

Jas cackled demon rooster screams that split everyone's ears—a real soundtrack to the cinema scene tickling my questionable fears.

I laughed right along with my new friends. "Did the sock give you dogma?" I asked.

"HELL NO!" Chuckie The Plague blasted. "That shit's easy—there IS NO dAHggMUH! —We have NO established doctrine OR set of beliefs! —We believe ABSURDITY shall be the WHOLE of the *law.*"

"That's absurd." I smiled. I've always appreciated the abstract and absurd, the surreal and the twisted, the off, the demented and the mutated—the marginal, the original.

Chuckie spoke through smoke. "We have dialogue with the divine. We have interest in the eternal and the supernatural. We don't give a *shit.* We've come to GRIPS that human behavior is an ABSURD *fucking* joke and the *meaning* of life is the LABEL you apply to it—since there i'n't a fucking MEANING to life!"

I laughed. He had me. He'd built himself into a religion and recruited followers. His effort was unique in its minimalism and correctness. Sign me up. I wanted to learn more about their showy know-nothingness—their grimy rationale—their palpable mystery, palatable history, babbling hilarity and acid-high sincerity.

"Here, smoke this," Jas said to me with a lungful of vapor leaking out from his mouth, like canary feathers from a guilty cat.

Accepting the blue porcelain pipe, I asked, "What is it?"

"Marination." Chuckie said.

"What?"

Rock obliged an answer. "It's like marinating a chicken before a feast—and the feast will be when you DIE and GOD will *eat* your *brain*—so, like, burst a few BRAIN CELLS! Get a little *loosened* up—GOD doesn't like a rigid brain man! *Understand?!*" His voice got louder and more and more stressed.

Jas exhaled an enormous plume of smoke.

I hadn't noticed but Rock had been inching closer and closer to me. He now stood right in front of me with his arms crossed.

"Are you trying to intimidate me?" I asked.

Chuckie and Jas howled with laughter. I wasn't sure at whom.

"I'm waiting my turn, man," he said with salt and vinegar lips quivering.

Oh well—what the hell? What else was there to do in life but what everyone else was doing? (Stupid teenage peer pressure.) There was a certain age in which to try everything. In for a penny, in for the piggy.

I sucked.

What marvelous understanding this. I now believed in a god who wanted me to drink and do drugs and try to dement myself—MARINATION he said for his consumption—for it had been writ—that Chuckie The Plague would consume our brains upon our death and become mad with Creutzfeldt-Jakob Disease and rush the White House in hopes of detonating the thirty nukes we've aimed at thirty hostile locations...

Amen.

Absurdity shall be the whole of the law.

This was the only dogma of The First Interplanetary Church of the Immaculate Deception.

The genius of that statement blossomed anthracite roses in the cavernous infinity of my mind. I awoke to the joke. The façade of the temporal existence melted in sebaceous oozing, like Godzilla semen dripping from toy skyscrapers.

My mind constellated with countless galaxies of thermal jewels, ultraviolet, nuclear reacting, each precious star of my endless mind a nucleus of its own life-giving system. Infinity was within me. I decided to become baptized a Plaguist at once.

(Note: As an infant, I was baptized Irish Catholic by my drunken father and stoned mother. I did not choose this ritual to happen upon me. My own blind defenselessness worked against me.

As a prepubescent pre-teen tween, I elected to be baptized Southern Baptist, the denomination of my maternal grandparents. I felt the brainwashed need to be born again and have the sins of the world washed away from my virgin body and soul. The man who baptized me was a red-bearded preacher who was having an extra-marital affair with my mother. I found out by reading her diaries. I was often left home alone, and curious about everything.

My decision to be baptized, to be born again in the name of Jesus Christ the savior, was to show the congregation that I was good and fearless before them on their spot-lit stage. Jesus Christ was a grand figure, but the written words of the Messiah have been forged and I have heard no heavenly voices.

I was corrupt before I entered high school. When the Southern Baptist congregation bowed their penitent heads in holy prayer and asked that the collection plate, being passed around, gather enough money to have the lawnmower fixed, I flipped my stance altogether on their absurd practices. I didn't want to belong to a religion that had to beg for money to fix the lawnmower—I mean, hell—let the damn grass grow, or more powerful—plant a garden, grow vegetables and feed the poor, like the redeemer you worship—but a manicured lawn says so much more, doesn't it? Anyway, that's when I stopped listening altogether. I was thirteen and no longer a head-bower. I received stern looks from certain parents who, while sneezing or coughing, opened their eyes and spied me looking around the meek congregation, disobedient to prayer. The one sneezing or coughing was always female, and searching the congregation for wretches like me, so she could tell her children not to play with me, wise choice though it be, me with lighters, wicks, and jars of gunpowder.

Maggie Gobert didn't close her eyes either. In fact, I caught her stealing money from the collection plate—for cigarettes and gum. She was never my girlfriend, but she did give me my first blowjob behind the rectory while the meek begged for providence in the chapel of lies.)

It was opium we smoked, a good-sized ball of it. I had three hits before I made myself stop.

These young men, these Plaguists, were each one fallen symbols of the fiery heaven. I wanted to belong to this group of outlaw geniuses. I saw potential in their art, and in their heretic display of original self. I wanted to know what made them tick. I was rainbow poet in search of a dark cave to bury my soul in. I wanted to dip my yellow in the blackest thoughts. I wanted spots and stains on my green and blue, more scars on my red and orange, and a permanent shadow for my sacred gray brain. I wanted ruckus of the spirit and pure identity.

I was baptized a Plaguist in the spring of 1994. I was one of the original twelve Plaguists to have recognized Charles Theodore Plague as God. In fact, when he told me he was God, I had no cause to not believe him. I asked him for no more proof than one of the chimpanzee tribal members who recognizes their leaders by the ruckus and splashing about, caused by the athletic body of the new sun-king.

To be baptized, I lay stiff as a board on the floor while reciting the sacred words and being splashed with holy malt liquor (Colt 45) by The Pope.

"*I once could see but now am blind.*" This was the beginning of the oath we took.

I once was found but now am lost. We continued to mock "Amazing Grace" because every Plaguist existed in a state of disgrace, which meant bacteria in your holy water: blessed be the potty mouth: whatever.

T'was disgrace that gave my fear heart. With a simple twisting of the words, we now implied that our weaknesses had become strengths while continuing to blaspheme the revered hymnal.

I once was free but now must pay the cost. 'Cause there ain't nothing free in this world.

Colt45 malt liquor, the holy piss of God, shook from the three Plaguists' hands and I was drenched with liquid gold—a pure and right ceremony had taken place, and I was now a Plaguist. I leapt from my spot on the floor and grabbed the bottle from Jas's hands. "Don't forget to bless the inside of me too, Pope!" I demanded and guzzled the suds from the bottle.

"ALL RIGHT! Here's to Martin, everyone!"

I raised my bottle with these maniacs, and the three wise-asses shouted in unison, "SUuuUUCKING MY DICK!" It was the official Plaguist toast.

"So, what are you?" Rock demanded—Rottweiler square with muscular bent, showing sharp fangs, a deep demonic voice of coal and gravel—punk rock, hard cock, fist first, fuck you, and always in boots.

"Angel of Death." What the hell did I know? I wanted to be different, stick out.

There were a handful of Sain'ts already. Sain't Rock, Sain't Dominic, Sain't Holly Cost. There was a church concubine also—Sain't Marybeth, but there were no angels—and staying true to form, I nominated myself for that lofty role.

I was Angel of Death in The First Interplanetary Church of The Immaculate Deception.

"What are your duties?" Rock asked.

"Well, first I declare Martial Law on the resurrected." I had no idea how to respond, so I made shit up on the spot. "I'm not talking about your medical miracles and defibrillated. I'm talking last rites given, mourned and grieved, at least twenty-four hours in the box. If you're resurrected after being clinically dead for twenty-four hours, then you're a zombie, and it's my job to make sure you're eliminated. Also—virgin births. It's my job to abort all fetuses conceived virginally."

Chuckie declared that lesbian types afraid of penises who became pregnant through in-vitro fertilization lost their virginity when the fertilized egg was placed back inside the uterus. Her future progeny takes her virginity from her, for she has been violated by the procreative act. The children born of this union were sacred oedipal symbols to the church...

Rock liked about half of what I had to say. "Bullshit!" He blurted out— "You're the fucking Plaguist Cookie Monster!" He turned away from the conversation and stormed from Plague Central. The room shook when he slammed the door.

"Don't listen to him, Martin. He has no authority beyond the conspiratorial realm. You make your own path as a Plaguist." Jas blew off the Tasmanian devil.

"Yeah—you have nothing to worry about—unless Rock starts to think that YOU are a conspiracy." Chuckie twanged. He and Jas shared a laugh, a cackle and a hack. I wondered if I should be afraid.

3.

Coming Up with a Plan

Jas invited me to stay with him for a week or two. "We could buy some acid wholesale, sell it by the hit and split town with solid cash." Chicago, he said, was sure to be the next literary town. He regaled me with stories of these genius poets he knew there—and if I was half the poet Kramer had built me up to be, the four of us should have no problem owning the microphones all over town.

Jas hit a nerve. He found the gold vein of my vain mountain. What juvenile and ignorant eyes! I was so ready to bring a new energy to the literary world! A new generation of writers! We'd be like the beatniks! My heart fluttered like a little girl who genuinely wants to be a princess for her seventh birthday. I was a sad sack of shit with a plastic tiara and a magic wand made of cardboard and aluminum foil, a pink flammable tutu and an imagined birthright.

Jas told me he could get me a job waiting tables. "Do you think you can carry a tray?"

"I never have before. But yes!"

Jas laughed and swaggered cheetah-killer to the kitchen and reached behind the fridge where he happened to have a drink tray hidden. Jas handed it to me. "Walk around the apartment carrying these two glasses of water." He put two glasses of water on the tray. He called everyone he knew.

We had a party.

BANGBANGBANGBANGBANGBANGBANGBANG!!! The
front door rattled, and the wall shook. I thought for sure the door would
smash from its jamb.

"The secret Plaguist knock!" Jas blurted and leapt to his feet and
opened the door. God walked in with a grocery bag of Cisco malt liquor,
kiddie flavors, 20%abv—a strange neon-colored syrupy sweet beverage
with the slogan "Takes you by Surprise." Hahahaha.

"Welcome Lordy!" Jas gushed and squealed with zeal.

"I didn't know what type of fireworks to bring, so I thought 'ese here
kiddie drugs oughta do the trick," Chuckie gurgled smoky cool.

Jas and I laughed at the large gothic cowboy in black leather
motorcycle gear, greasy denim and red bandana around his throat like a
Cartwright, like Lee Marvin, like John Wayne—like a roughneck gangster
on the cinnamon plane… "Put those in the fridge and have Martin bring
me one on a tray with a little napkin."

Jas halfheartedly looked around the room. "Oh, I don't think I have
any bar naps Chuckie."

"Well, tear up some paper—you sissy poets are bound to have at least
a few notebooks lying about the place—fuckin'—you can't learn to do 'is
job HALF ASS—you got to learn to put the napkin down and the whole
NINE YARDS. Get me an ASHTRAY, too, goddamn it!" God plopped
down on the red sofa, in Jas's seat, and lit a cigarette.

I brought him an ashtray and located a stack of typed poems on
paper. I went to the fridge, put a dirty glass of grape flavored Cisco on
the tray and walked to the sofa. I put the piece of paper on the table and
the neon sugar booze on the faux napkin.

"It's got writin' on it!" Chuckie said.

"It's a questionable establishment," I barked back, foot forward, chest
out—not to be outdone by someone's words… Even if it was God.

"Well, hell! Bless your little heart for being so tolerant. And would
you look at that—a free poem."

BANGBANGBANGBANGBANGBANGBANGBANG!!!

Jas strolled over to the door in mid-laughter. "Well, hello ladies!" He
spun fluidly and made swift introductions. "Martin, this is Marybeth, and
Minx." He hissed a sibilant snake tongue behind his joker grin teeth.

"Hi, pleased to meet you," repeated. I'm going to stare at you briefly
and absorb your essence—I hope I'm pretty enough for this not to be
too uncomfortable for you—I need to smell your nervous sweat and
stink—your natural pheromone and temperament—I need to watch your
nervous smile—or morose lack of one—your shining eyes and your

fiddle fingers touching your hair—where you sit—if you prefer to stand…

I needed the attention of every young attractive boy and girl. Either I want to fuck you or it's off-putting.

Jas splayed his fingers towards the gloomy kitchen. "There's Steel Reserve and Colt45. You know we ARE here today to help Martin learn to become a proper server—you should order whatever *you want* from *him*," so pretzel thin and salty hard was our perfect host…

oOoh really—and feminine smiles—*we'll take a black cherry Cisco*—gothic chicks who detested the status quo, the shallow pool of tepid genes that humans were spawned from, the hypocritical moral code—invaluable and unbelievable—mascara, tattoos, dark lipstick and black fishnet, Minx in corset and heels, Marybeth barefoot and in mini dress.

"Here you are, ladies." I placed copies of typed poems, face down, in front of them and placed their drinks on top as napkins.

Minx was the first to ask, "What's this?" She took her drink and flipped the napkin over.

"Napkin."

"Am I supposed to read it?"

"No, it's to sop up liquid mess."

Jas cackled; Chuckie laughed very loudly. Minx grabbed the paper and the beer. She guzzled, then read out loud, "Fire from the belly—head full of gold—gross and exaggerated. I plunged my fists into the guts of the world and pulled out the sausage and the sauce. I was stark raving mad and laughing like a clown, licking the lavender tendons with lupine tongue and wondering how fat I could get if I ate the whole thing." There was an odd silence. "Did you write that?" Minx asked.

"Yeah." I pretended to be meek, like I wasn't showing off how talented I thought I was.

"We're going to have to have a talk when everyone leaves," Jas said, suddenly seriously, almost sternly, no flamboyant emphasis, or exuberant lisp, dark and deep, like I'd stepped on his blue suede shoes or fucked his boyfriend in the ass when he only gets head…

Marybeth picked up her drink and flipped her napkin over. "Wants young lovers to astound you, surround you with wit and clever narcissism, running away from home and two-dollar solipsism, wants a fine selection of meats to be hung in your smokehouse, wants to delouse your body with the hungry tongues of mute lovers who know only your pleasure." Marybeth smiled blowjob lip-gloss up and down my body, slowly, like I'd have to prove my poetry by performance—proof was in the pudding darling—consistency was only good for batter.

BANGBANGBANGBANGBANGBANGBANGBANG!!!

Jas pranced to the door and swung it open drunkenly, though he was performing and far from drunk— "Everyone, this is Apophenia Pareidolia and her boyfriend, Leonard."

They were the only Non-Plaguists there, but soon that would change and there would be yet another baptism.

Apophenia, little wonder with beak nose and birdlike legs, powerful face of tension and beauty—slender waist and uncomfortable laugh—the scene was too perfectly freaky for her. She fell in love with everyone at once. I saw it happening—her astonished look at everyone's wardrobe, the macabre setting of the apartment and everyone's nestling into it like birds in a nest—a cute boy, me, behaving as waiter in exercise for job, and big ole God himself with his silver Scout skull woggle around red kerchief and no shirt.

Leonard was a sixteen-year-old runaway and cocky and pretty and lucky enough to catch Apophenia's eye, and The Pope's eye—because what lush-mouthed sixteen-year-old runaway hustler doesn't catch the eye of the tiger?

"Leonard, why don't you come help me find some music?" The Pope fished perfectly.

"Cool," the boy said dope-headedly and sauntered over a few steps to the edge of the bedroom where the devil sharpened his pitchfork and ironed his silk red costume in smoky hisses of laughter—*where are my cigarettes?* Always lighting up.

I brought Apophenia a can of Steel Reserve.

"Thanks."

"No napkin for Apophenia?" Chuckie asked, totally aware of every scenario unfolding in the tiny efficiency apartment and having fun with his environment.

"Oh yeah." I put a piece of paper on the table, poem side down. I shot Chuckie a quick glance, but he was unreadable in thick dark sunglasses, even in the dimly lit smoky apartment. God's eyes were not to be seen. His sensitive orbs were hidden behind dark cybernetic style armor. Anyway—I love that she didn't bother to pick it up and read it— and more curiously—no one bothered to mention that there may be some poetic masterpiece under there.

BANGBANGBANGBANGBANGBANGBANGBANG!!!

Jas swished away from Leonard and opened the door in a heavy swing.

"Dominic! Come in, honey! Martin! This is Sain't Dominic, head of Public Relations in The First Interplanetary Church of the Immaculate

Deception!" Jas took a deep, almost comical breath. "Dominic! This is Martin—The Angel of Death in The First Interplanetary Church of the Immaculate Deception."

There was general amusement by all of the girls in the room, how dramatically he introduced us with proper titles and seriousness of rolls—his swishing, his sassing, his matter-of-fact tasking, his batting kewpie lashes, his basking in the merest smiling light from the stagehand audience.

"Can I get you anything?" I asked.

He knew the game, but more importantly how to play it. "You know man, I would *really* love a *clean* glass of water, thanks." I loved how he said *clean*—like he knew that I would have to wash the dish in this horrible crusty mess of a living space—and how he said thanks, like if I was going to do a job, I'd better be prepared to do it all the way—so gracious, so courteous, so cute with his springy curls and decorative flare. The man always had on earrings and rings and bracelets and smiles and attention for you… Another Gemini flirt-with-disaster.

Dominic McCoy was born and raised in Nashville. He was twenty-three years old and almost always smiling—a giddy bouncing funboy. He liked pills, politics and pussy. He liked to get dizzy, fuck, and discuss U.S. foreign policy. He couldn't believe that anyone would be a republican, a democrat, a Jew, A Muslim, a Christian—couldn't believe anyone would be gay or straight. Dominic liked pretty young boys as well.

"You know, I can see why Jas lets you stay here, I mean, I too want to put my dick in your bottom." Dom bit his bottom lip. He wore long curly hair and mascara, had muscles, could fight, loved jewelry, and talked confidently.

I didn't know how to take this introduction. "Nice to meet you, too, but I do all the dick puttin'." I smiled and winked at the curl-headed funboy, then fled to fetch his water.

Jas screeched bantam laughter and mocked his new nemesis, me. "*Dick Puttin! —Sounds like a FUCKIN' Country Western Nom de Plume!*" Every phrase was emphasized with black alacrity and sudden death. Every sentence was poetry.

Everyone laughed, and we had an audience.

"Well, as long as you don't dick puttin'—where I dick puttin'—we'll be fine." Dominic's voice lowered as his feathers ruffled.

Attempting to flirt, I challenged him. "How about that pretty ass of *yours*? You dick puttin' that?"

Dominic's tone changed to violent alpha challenge— "Let me tell you something smartass, if you ever dick puttin' or anything to do with my ass, I will KICK Your ASS up and down the damn sidewalk."

"Easy Dom," Jas purred.

"I get it—I'm not your type—let's just be friends." I smiled and offered him water from my tray, in a pyrex glass with ice.

"Goddamn right!" Dominic barked, and then sang in laughter, his voice cracking. "What's this?"

"Pyrex—last clean glass in the house," I chirped charmingly.

All the girls were amused and laughed at our exchange. Dominic noticed the response from our performance and when he finished sipping his water, he smiled and put his arm around me. "I see how we could get in a lot of fun trouble together." He laughed and we became instant friends.

BANGBANGBANGBANGBANGBANGBANGBANGBANG!!!

"It's ROCK!" Jas screamed.

I approached the maniac with the attention of a server. "And for you sir?" I asked.

"ARE YOU FUCKING KIDDING ME?! What the hell's this?!"

"We're training him, Rock." Jas soothed the manic bastard blitzed out of his mind on a handful of acid. "He's never served before, so we're having him walk around with drinks on a tray for everyone. It's to his benefit, really."

"Goddamn it! Someone get me a beer!" He screamed. "AND COCAINE!"

I brought the shouting lunatic a forty-ounce bottle of Colt45. It was in the center of a tray. "Would you like a napkin, sir?" I asked, pretending I knew how to be snooty.

"NO, I DON'T WANT A FUCKING GODDAMN NAPKIN!!!" Rokusaburo shouted. I don't think he liked me very much at first—but then I got to know that that was how he was with everyone—and still—I don't think he liked me very much at first.

BANGBANGBANGBANGBANGBANGBANGBANGBANG!!!

Jas pranced to the door and flung it open to reveal Pookie and Echo. The Pope didn't say a word, he flitted away from the corridor, shunning nose in the air. He left them to shut the door and introduce themselves to whom they did and did not know. The Pope stopped and looked into Marybeth's eyes. He leaned into her and kissed her, passionately, tongue in the mouth, hands all over the curvature, two concupiscent sybarites embracing each other like neutron stars aching for biological fission—oh the sadness of nonlinear human failure to divide into two, become more than one, all by yourself…

Leonard was impressed with Jas's performance and that mattered most. The host of the party possessed power over place and time—and *to thine own self be true*—written over alchemical laboratory entrances and whispered into the perfect infant's ears—a spell cast on the placental beast—be true to thine own self. Above the alchemist laboratory an inscription read *I Am*. The center of the universe was you. Do unto others golden—shower them with love.

"May I bring you anything?" I asked the hot young couple, smutty, bubbly, colorful and jubilant with the scene.

"I'm already drinking a beer and so is she (pointing to Echo), but you can put these in the fridge," Pookie said to me pleasantly, as if he wasn't sure if I was the competition or the enemy or both or neither—if I was tethered, how weathered, if I liked it with a feather (I do).

I did as I was told and took one for myself because he brought dark German beer and that was my favorite and filling, especially when I haven't eaten in two days, and honey-sweet like the old European beer. The Christian monks and conquering warlords knew how to steal and tweak a recipe. I guzzled one and tucked another one in my cut off blue jean's front pocket for later.

BANGBANGBANGBANGBANGBANGBANGBANGBANG!!!

Jas swished to the door, stepping over sitting bodies, resting legs, intermingling guests, intertwined making out Plaguists, with exaggerated prance and totally phony strut, everyone laughed. He opened the door to the unknown world and in came Reverend Killjoy and Chef Hiccup. They were introduced. Chef walked right past me. He didn't say a word, he handed me a box of wine, a wooden box, a proper box, an interesting choice, 3 liters worth. He nodded his head and then made a b-line toward Chuckie and sat down on the stained red loveseat.

Reverend Killjoy handed me a tube of plastic cups encased in plastic wrapping. "I understand you're the sommelier this evening," she said stone cold and without emotion.

"I am. I'm assuming you'd like this chilled a bit, perhaps put in the fridge until it turns to a cave temperature, 56 Fahrenheit—and while you're waiting you would like a glass first?" I invented myself upon every new moment/movement.

"You're going to do fine. Where did you say you were going to work?"

"With Jas," I answered.

"Oh god, at that horrible restaurant?"

"I've never even been there."

"You're gonna hate it."

"Can I do it wasted and still make money?" I asked.

"Of course."

"Then I'll tolerate it."

We all had such high hopes—such self-esteem—such big ideas and such grand schemes—I was thinking poetry on a stage—drifting across the prairies and the planes—living in stinking conditions, debasing my senses, exalting my purity, finding the rhythm and the pulse. Reverend Killjoy was thinking I should be smart and hustle the pretty, bring in two hundred a shift at some money restaurant where they are serious about dining and wine. But we were too young to care, too high to die, too invested in the dark side of the force to care about the Jedi reality…

I'd rather die on the path than stray from its boundlessness.

"Would you like a glass?" She asked.

"Do I need your permission?"

"I like you already. You seem challenging. I have Asperger's syndrome so if I seem weird or like a CIA agent—it's because I'm genetically deficient."

"ASS BURGER'S!" Chuckie shouted from the love seat, four feet away.

"Don't slice the pie chart that way, sweetheart. What you are is mutated—and all the great ones are. How the hell else are you going to have evolution?"

My eyebrows rose in laughter, but I remained politely silent. Kathryn did not move a muscle. Perhaps the good spies have some sort of emotional disorder that allows them to remain unreadable, emotionless, cool under fire, able to beat a lie detector, and tolerant to pressure. Perhaps she *did* work for the government and was attempting to infiltrate the cult of Chuckie. That would've been funny, since she was brought into the church BY Chuckie.

Hours passed. The room burst at the seams with Plaguists and Plaguist groupies and it seemed that everyone in Nashville might want a taste of this offering—this spiritual mumbo-jumbo.

I went outside to take a piss.

"Hey MAYuungn! Why don't YOU have a TRAAAAAY with you?!" Chuckie shouted from the rubbery corner of his mouth. He was outside with a smaller group of Plaguists, each large and dark and clad in leather and shades and boots, each drinking Steel Reserve and smoking.

"I'm on break."

"Bitch! It's happy hour! Ain't no breaks! Now get your ass back in 'at house and get me a beer!" He seemed so militant and serious.

I ignored God.

"Hey motherfucker, don't make me call *MAN-uh-gement!*" He yelled in black cotton-candy concern that I may not be learning in the appropriate fashion.

By then I was pissing leprechaun rainbows over the ravine. I turned and aimed my arching piss in their direction. "Sure thing—customer's always right!" I shouted and walked toward the gnarly men, a hot yellow stream of urine leading the way.

Chuckie chuckled.

Rock snarled.

Punks scattered.

I slowed my pace, because neither Rock nor God moved an inch. How serious was I? What were the stakes? —It was as if maybe a dare— or an invitation? It was hard to tell with these psychosexual rapacious maniacs. Would I gain friendly points by making their blue jeans hot and soggy with my boy-urine or would it be an insult and result in my broken bone—face and body? (*I got a broken face—uh huh!! Uh huh! ooOOO!*) Tempting. But I waited until my pee subsided and I was no longer a urinary delight.

"You're no angel of death," Rock said, satisfied with his result in defeating me.

"Maybe. But either Urine or you're out."

God coughed a snickering hiss in my laughable direction.

I shook the piss droplets from my cock, slung it back in my short shorts and felt a drip from penis tip down my thigh to my knee. A wet blossom on my cut-offs, impossible to hide. Overanxious, as always. I got so excited. I really did. I went blue with ozone and couldn't wait to blackout in space. Let's chase the day with whiskies.

No one else wanted a beer, so I talked with Pookie and Echo in the kitchen. It was dark, but Pookie knew where the candles were hidden. He knew where everything was located. This used to be his home. He flip-flopped in slow motion, carefully from one group of Plaguists back to us in three rubbery steps, interjecting timely in two different conversations, opening a box and coming back with a candle in tow. He shoved it into an empty beer bottle, perfect fit. He lit it. The kitchen flickered. He stretched like a cartoon superhero through several realities all without losing his place in our conversation.

Pookie and Echo were awkwardly cute as a couple— (angry slow-learner's make incompatible jigsaw pieces and compartments fit together with forceful fists)— clumsy touching and a lot of it. She had a hick laugh and buck teeth, a giant mouth and corn cob drawl. He had a bulbous nose and big eyes and big ears and all around darling mousy charm.

"From now on, I'm calling you King and Queen Neat-oh!" I said loudly above the music, drunkenly from fun sport and in the spirit of a budding Plaguist.

They loved the idea, and before I knew it, he had his arm around me, and she ran her fingers through my hair.

"Barkeep!" Jas summoned me, saving me from some orgy in the kitchen.

I excused myself from the mating cephalopods.

I handed Jas a Colt45.

I walked back outside.

Chuckie said to me with sarcastic support— "I don't know how well you'll do at *Grazing Saddles*, but you'd make one hell of a barmaid in a biker-bar, buddy! Alls you gotta do is git cher self a fuckin'—little leather halter-top and cut them shorts off 'bout HALF-WAY up! *HAR! HAR! HAR!*" He laughed/shouted/coughed with a cigarette still in hand, putting it out and lighting another. John Wayne kind of smoker, four packs a day. Hardcore nicotine suck.

Jas passed out.

I was the last one up with Rock. He was wired, snorting bump after bump of cocaine from the back of his thumb and offering me none. He had a wild look in his eyes that suggested unrest, unease in his psychic fabric. He looked like a man who had wires welded accidentally crossed. He seemed hopeless in his mad pursuit of life, but this was his beauty, his charm. He seemed as if he could ram his hard prick through brick cement, as if he could slam his face into said cement and chew his way through to the other side, gnawing the rough stone to dust. He had the war face of a man who'd seen combat and never come down from the experience. He was the guy you wanted on your side in a fight. "Hey man—wanna play the market?" He asked me.

"What the fuck is the market and how do you play?" I said this with a thick tongue and double vision. I was ready for the big collapse.

"It's a POOL, man! It's goddamn, like an OFFICE pool you know? —There's like fucking HUNDREDS of dollars in this pool and it just keeps fucking GOING and going—GROWING and growing you know what I fucking mean?"

"I do not," answered I, lost.

"All it costs is a dollar, and you can go as many times as you want. Each GUESS is a dollar and if you guess RIGHT—then you get the whole POT! You win the month's BOOTY! Alls you got to do is fucking PICK the stock market NUMBERS at the closing BELL, and if at any time this MONTH the bell closes at the number YOU guess then YOU collect the pot."

"What happens if *nobody* guesses the number?"

Rock looked at me stone cold and said— "Well then, *genius,* I get the money! Why the *fuck* do you think I'm running this racket?"

As soon as the words came out of Rock's mouth, a loud but distinct cackle could be heard from the bedroom. I thought Jas was asleep but perhaps he was honed into the scene, absorbing my willpower, my stamina. I was on high. I wouldn't be defeated this night. Hell yeah I'd play. I reached into my pocket and pulled out a dollar bill. "Give me twenty-seven twenty-five!" I had no fucking clue what the stock market was. I'd barely even heard of Wall Street or the Stock Exchange. Words like 'finance' and 'economy' did not sink into my poor drug-addled, sexfiend, teenage brain tissue.

Rock ripped the bill from my hand but did not like my answer. "Do you have any FUCKING idea what would happen if you were right? It would mean that not only OUR economy but the whole fucking GLOBAL economy has COLLAPSED, and we're ALL in dire straits! Do you have any idea what a FORTY PERCENT loss in our economy overnight would mean?! It would mean total fucking APOCALYPSE!"

Jas continued to cackle from the bedroom. He coughed loudly. He had a dramatic fit of coughing that forced him from his bed. He pranced through the living room to the restroom in seven svelte steps.

I fished into my pocket. "Here's another dollar. What was the closing-bell at yesterday?"

Rock consulted his notebook— "3652.54"

"Put me down for 3721.23"

He ripped the bill from my hand. "That's a much smarter gamble. You learn quickly. What did you say your name was?"

I barely had time to say my name before he interrupted me. "Mar..."

"I'm kidding Cookie Monster—I don't really care what your fucking name is. Thanks for the two bucks, now I can afford gas to get home." He leapt up from his seat on the couch. "Tell the Pope I had a blast, and good luck with your ballet or why-ever the fuck we were here for tonight!" The door slammed behind him. He generally behaved as a human hurricane, gushing out the door with mythic force.

I heard the toilet flush. Outside, I heard Rock's motorcycle start, rev and roar off into the night.

Jas sat down on the couch with me and filled the bong. He lit, sucked, and passed. I sucked and passed. Repeat... "So," He coughed out a little smoke, but held the remainder of the hit. He released the rest of the smoke as he asked the big question— "Whadja think?"

4.

Grazing Saddles

Jas introduced me to Jodi, the general manager of Grazing Saddles.

"Jodi, this is my cousin, Martin."

"Hi Cousin Martin," the fat underwater sea creature gurgled at me.

It was all happening too fast for me not to be playful. "Hi, Aunt Jodi."

She wasn't fond of my joke, but she was a pleasant enough woman. Jodi Maison was large: robust, big-bottomed. She had large breasts and a belly like a Paleolithic Venus of Willendorf. She had salt and pepper hair that fell to the first fat fold in her neck and wore a sweater though it was ninety degrees outside—and red-rimmed glasses that threw everything else about her appearance off. I liked that, her odd, red-rimmed glasses.

I lied with smiling eyes and told her all about my previous experiences at local restaurants, careful not to mention any nationwide chains that she may be familiar with. It's important to dodge the questions before they're even asked.

Jodi asked me during the interview— "What were some of your duties over there at—um—*Bill's Big Beef*—did you say?"

I launched in at full speed, not knowing where I was going but talking fast, relying on my unconscious knowledge— "Yes ma'am, Bill's Big Beef, over there in East Knoxville off Straw Plains Pike—um—let's see—we had to marry the ketchup bottles and roll silverware." I repeated the four phrases that Jas taught me.

"Well, that's good to hear." She studied me for a few minutes and then decided I was at least eager enough to try out. "When can you start?"

"Um—tomorrow?"

Jodi removed her red-rim glasses as if to *sense* me more than *look* at me, to really see what she could see. (Good luck!) "Fine," she said, putting on her glasses. "We'll start you off on lunch, can you be here at ten-thirty?"

"Sure."

"Good. Take these menus and learn everything you can by tomorrow."

I started work fifteen minutes late—an inauspicious beginning to be sure. Jodi warned me how much she adored promptness. I promised to never again be tardy. I knew I was lying. She had some old tart named Virginia show me around the place. I had a nickname for the old sot instantly.

Clown-Face Virginia spoke with a slow witted drawl—a southern-battered corn syrup— "'Is here's thuh wade stayshun—where we roll thuh silver—a hunert pieces—no x'ceptions—you gotcher salt and paper shaykers rite-chair and the extry salt rite-chair in 'is cabinet rite-chair." Her skin smelled of alcohol vapor and bacon sweat.

She kept saying 'rite-chair' instead of 'right here'. I was used to this dialect—the southern-fried chicken clucking and hog calling of the Appalachian Anglo-Saxon… But more fascinating was the amount of rouge she used on her pale chubby wrinkles that brought too much attention to her drunk hung-over inability to gauge tint, space, or layer.

Her lips were a mess of candied cherries eaten hungrily. Disastrous amounts of red lipstick were applied with the DTs. Her four decades old fingers shook like rickety pistons in an antique engine as she applied globs of tar to her gray and decaying eyelashes, transforming her blink into a car crash. The eyeshadow was 'Summer Sky' and she used the whole horizon.

She looked like something all the children used to aim at in the carnival—a balloon sprouting from her head, each squirt hoping for a burst—circus punk hairdo—frizzled and stringy, brushed too much, waiting patiently for the high-school baseball players to wind up and knock her over.

I barely listened as she showed me around the place: where to find the ketchup, where we kept the kegs of iced tea—sweetened, and the one bucket of unsweetened iced tea and how to make the sweet tea and where the sugar was stored, how much to use: gallons—where we kept the lemon wedges, and how many seconds you're supposed to wait before asking the bottomfeeders would they care to see the dessert menu, which I later learned from Jas to put on the table as you remove the entrée course, because those fat bastards almost always want dessert, and if they think they don't, change their mind and sell, because every dollar you sell is another dime or, if you're really lucky, two.

Clown-Face Virginia continued— "Now ya always got to remember to go in and out through the right-sided door only. Don't never try to go in *nor* out of the left-sided door never. Ya might getcher self hurt." She wasn't the most eloquent of monologists, but she got her point across.

I had never worked in a restaurant before, but it was true—I had been *in* them and imagined trays of hot food splattered everywhere if not for this simple rule. Clown-Face Virginia showed me to the kitchen and introduced me to the chefs.

The chefs looked like the gnarlier of the staff—loud, tattooed animals with the radio up and a taste for cutting meat in their genes, sharp knives in their hands, and fire by their genitals—hot oil spitting at them from skillets and hands that seemed scarred and meaty like a villain's claws.

Clown-Face Virginia kept showing me around the place. "Now 'is is Cindy and 'is hears Brett—'ey've both been here forever, so you know, feel free to ask 'em anything."

I was so fucking hungover I'd already forgotten their names. My head was caffeine racked and light—airy. I followed Clown-Face Virginia around Grazing Saddles learning the ropes. I took my first order and sized up my new career.

The people that waddled in and out of there had enough oil in their bellies and arteries to fuel clean-burning lamps for the whole state for centuries. They oozed and seeped rich butter fat from their shortening skin as if their liver was protesting its job. They stank of rotten flesh trapped in folds of fat and unwashed skin, the gas of processed food and neglected assholes. They would've made vampires vomit.

Obesity was worse to me than being a drug addict. Often a heroin addict would live longer than a salt and sugar junky. Also, even with the fear of AIDS—I'd rather fuck a junky than a stinky fat chick.

Superficial down deep, like Andy Warhol.

"Hi, may I take your order?"

"Can we have more sweet tea, please?"

"*I hope you enjoyed your evening and y'all come back to see us real soon.*" This was the mandatory closing line, which never got old to the customer, not even as it was being said simultaneously three tables down.

I walked around Grazing Saddles pondering how to start my life as a drug dealer. How did one approach a potential buyer? I supposed talking about DOING drugs was a sure-fire way to spark an interest. I introduced myself to the thirty-year-old waitress, seasoned and slutty Crystal, and started on slow about what a crazy party it had been. Aren't they all when you're young enough to lose weeks, stay up for days, count the minutes until the next one…

She told me that she hadn't had a crazy night out all month, but that she was excited about going to a Fun Girls concert with her best friend.

I told her what fun I'd had at the last Fun Girls concert all loaded up on acid.

She loved the story which I was giddy and vague about because it was an obvious lie. But anyway, she bought two hits for ten bucks, after asking if I might know where to score a couple of hits.

That was how one begins selling acid—by talking about it. *Hey, you know what's fun? Acid. And I have some for sale.* There was no perfect crime, but selling drugs to partiers was close.

Our plan was going smoothly. But we sold the few hits Jas had in reserve. We needed more acid.

5.

Coy Boy Ploy

It was always dark in Nashville. I saw the daylight only on the lunch shifts. I sold hits of LSD to this crazy waitress named Janice for six bucks a hit—and to the busboy Adam for five bucks a hit because he was cute, younger than me, and knew how to keep his mouth shut. Besides, he smoked me out before every shift we worked together.

Adam lived with Clown-Face Virginia, and everybody felt sorry for him. Of course, he had a place to live that wasn't his father's (abusive) and he didn't have to pay rent. He didn't have to cook or clean, and he got his dick sucked whenever he wanted, so long as he'd fuck the sweaty pig occasionally. He described it as *raping a wet baby hippo.* I didn't know how he did it: pretty Adam with the long black hair and feminine features, the soft white skin and thin limbs, victim of a thousand abuses because of his frail beauty. He liked punk rock and skateboarding and weed, like every disenfranchised teen with more anger than dream.

We hung out only once at S.P.A.M. Manor. He left soon after Jas's endless boasting about his quality of dick-sucking.

"I couldn't help it. He was so fucking beautiful. I couldn't stop talking about sucking his dick. I don't know what's wrong with me," Jas sang with his high-pitched feminine voice—and that cackle!

"You're a dirty penis-toucher!" I yelled at him.

"Funny, that's what Rock calls me, a *dirty penis-toucher!* —Well, anyway—here's to dirty penis-touchers everywhere."

Of course, I had to join in— "*Sucking—my—dick!*" We dueted. It was the official Plaguist Toast. It was (is) not uncommon to hear the words

SUCKING MY DICK booming from a roomful of Plaguists in celebration of whoever was being saluted.

"Well, now what're we going to do?" The Pope asked, following the question immediately with a laugh.

"Measure our poetry dicks?" I asked.

"Reach under the sofa," Jas suggested.

I did. There was a stack of newspapers. I removed the top one. It was a copy of *The Nashville Scene*—he graced the cover—in mid-sentence—kneeling on stage, creasing his silk suit—hand reaching out to the victim/lover audience, fingers flexed and curled up like a cracked actor searching for the Hamlet meaning in the ghost of a skull—sunglasses responding to the camera in sparkly darkness, reflecting the starlight from the flashbulb—mouth twisted open in hot wordy moment.

What were the words, I wondered, that evaporated from his mouth like dragon fire?

I was impressed. Before I ever heard him read a word, I knew he was a competitor. "Read me something," I challenged, throwing the paper on the table as if passé.

"Oh! I don't READ. I *recite*." Jas flashed, rubbed his naked nipples with his palms, slid his hands to his sides, his elbows forming wings. He searched for, found, and lit a cigarette. He cleared his throat with a cough. He looked me in the eyes to capture my silent attention, and he began his rapid machine gun fire, fluidly letting out the music of his soul with reptilian certainty, mammalian urge, and an extraterrestrial intelligence unbeknownst to possibly even him. He slithered around the room backwards with his eyes closed and his head bowed and tilted.

Jas Swank was a poet with exquisite skills and iambic marksmanship, with nuance, music, and vision in his delivery, raw animal salt, and sticky bloody teeth that have bitten into the Holy Bible and ripped out a section of tissue… Old Testament.

His adjectives were colorful costumes for his painful dreams and delightmares. His verbs were atomic weapons ignited by a passion and disgust for life simultaneously, intertwining about the crux of his story like caduceus serpents, and the point of his story was YOU who might be listening—YOU who might be willing to join him in intimate occasion—YOU who might be the one true one to evict him from himself—YOU who might be willing to buy him a drink, offer him drugs, congratulate him on expressing his genius so eloquently… Coagulating with him your milk into curds for his holy cheese.

I won't pretend to quote from his lengthy poems. I would do him no justice in that department.

"Fuck you." was all I could say to the master. He was better than me. He had it—the quality of his language, the depth of his vocabulary, the inter-playful double-entendre of his awkward phrases... I admired his style.

"Your turn." He blew smoke in my face.

"Well, I have to read, as I haven't bothered to memorize my lines."

"Do it!" He raised his glass to toast the air and swallow.

Unprepared for the interruption before I even began, I stumbled for the beer and toasted him and took a long healthy pull from the bottle.

I jumped in: "I believe in the reality of every illusion / come to every conclusion. / I exist separate from every opinion. / I'll argue any point / and accept both sides of the story. / I decide right and wrong on a whim / skim the surface / plunge the depths / come out of the water dry / in rewound film fashion / pouring the splash back onto surface..."

"Stop!" Jas closed his eyes and shook his head and quickly walked away from the sofa. He paced away from and then immediately back to the sofa. "OKAY! I WAS NOT expecting you to be that good!"

He was so fucked up and dramatic, and I wasn't mature enough, or street-wise enough to decipher how much was acting—how much of his grandiosity was urge to feel me up/down/around/in and out, and besides, I was very flattered to have someone's attention on this craft I'd sought to harness, let alone someone of his importance in the small community of writers I was aware of.

It went like that for a few hours as we serenaded each other with our poetry and prose, sentenced one another to a life of audience. I'd exhausted nearly my entire catalog and he seemed to have been scratching the surface—though who knows?

It's always a gamble when deciphering a deviant.

I had no idea of the time of day or what day it was. I didn't know if I still had a job or if I was now a drug dealer by trade—or poet rather... I enjoyed the single moment—the perfect time and place where the dropped bottle rocket could go in any direction.

Eventually, it grew quiet.

The acid had worn off and we were properly stoned on weed and wine. I was ready for a nice nap on the loveseat that was eight inches shorter than I was tall.

"Martin." I heard The Pope say from his bed.

"Yes?"

"Sleep with me."

"No."

"Martin... I won't do anything you don't *really* want me to do."

"No."

"Martin?" He gently asked, almost pleading.

"Yes?"

"I used to have a twin brother—his name was Eric—and he…" Here the performance took a fascinating turn—a truly deviant mind was baking in that kiln oven head of his. "He… He died—and we used to sleep together when we were little… And…" He tried to water his eyes with method acting but failed… "Sometimes I can't sleep because of the anxiety."

Here his voice shifted again to learned scientist. "Twins often experience separation anxiety beginning in the school years when they're forced to open their intimate community to newcomers—and often throughout their life, leading to severe depression and even suicide in some extreme cases."

He was using everything in his arsenal to get me into bed with him. His voice shifted again, back to morose and lonely. "Sometimes it helps me sleep if I can hear… If I can hear someone breathing beside me."

It was lame, but I got into bed with him anyway. It felt good to stretch out on the full-length mattress. I hadn't been in a bed in weeks, more than a month. I'd slept in some rather rough places and traveled through some rather strange areas of the state getting here.

I was almost asleep when I felt his soft cool hand on my belly, his warm breath on my neck. He knew where to rub and where to breathe. I was almost in a dream, and it didn't matter who seduced me. I was aroused. I was erect. I was ready to explode. He gripped my cock and stroked. I reached over and grabbed his as well. It was hard and almost as big as mine. I stroked the new instrument and wondered briefly what the hell I was doing. I was in a trance. The snake charmer had succeeded. He had me. He bit my neck, and I came all over his hand and my belly.

I crash-awoke from the dream and felt disgusted by my performance. I turned and faced the wall and fell asleep as fast as I could. I left the sticky goo on my body—a habit of mine—and didn't bother going to the restroom. I was the worst gay lover in the history of the sport. I'm sure I snored.

(Note: The act seemed to unlock some secret memory. I was five years old, and my best friend and I used to build furniture forts out of sofa cushions, blankets, pillows, well-positioned ottomans, and chairs turned upside-down.

We had a game that he initiated where we'd play family. He'd be the wife and I'd be the husband. It was my job to take off his pants and kiss his bottom. I never became aroused, if memory serves, nor do I remember having any sexual realizations or confusion. It was a game.

We continued to play the game in secret hiding places. One hiding place was his brother's closet. His brother caught us naked. He told his parents. My family moved the following month. The details arc fuzzy— the faces are impossible to concentrate on—I remember a green and yellow basketball jersey of his brother and bushy brown hair, a headband and some free weights in the closet—but no face, no nose, or eyes—and no words. What sentences were used to express the disappointment in our behavior, our sport and deviancy? I have little recognition of the specifics. I remember the whiteness of the boy's ass but not his face. I remember the fronts of both of our houses on Bryarcliff Road.)

The next day, I said nothing to Jas of the previous evening's events. I drove us to work. We worked our shift and sat at the bar and had six or seven drinks. Neither of us wanted to revisit the scene of the crime. We needed the company of the *random other*—our co-workers.

Scotty the Bartender was a fat, bearded Quebecois who loved Hockey, action movies and French Poetry. Everything in his life moved fast, his actions, his language, his women. I learned nothing else about him while Jas and I drank at the bar in our honorable silence.

Jas introduced me to David Squared—which was really two dudes, both named David, and both dressed exactly alike. *Hi. Hi. HI. Hi.* Intrigued by their get up, I gave them my attention when Scotty the Bartender slid down to chat up a young lady about a blowjob he was missing.

The Davids were the same size and each had straight, bleached blond hair. They both wore red velvet bell-bottom slacks, black patent leather police shoes and white v-neck t-shirts. They had their eyebrows plucked alike and both wore violet contacts. They both had botox done to give themselves 'bee-stung' lips.

One David was having rhinoplasty to have his nose shaped to look like the other David, and the other David was getting otoplasty to fix his protruding ears to look like the first David. The Pope hated that, as he had a thing for boys with Dumbo ears—but the Davids were on a mission to look like one another—to fuse their physical likeness together and become one entity.

These two fascinated me endlessly—this LOVE that they spoke of— this LOVE that they deemed so much a part of who they were that they COULDN'T IMAGINE EVER being apart! This LOVE that they were together on was so forced and tragic I couldn't imagine the odds of finding someone with the same mental condition as you. Is that what true love is? —Being with someone who resembles your disorder the most… Or the least?

"Thorry if we thound funny our nothe ith runny," the David closest to me said.

"Well, you better hurry up and catch it," giggled Jas to the closest David to him.

It was strange—David Squared was to be treated as one person, a single entity.

What really annoyed me was how forced their demonstration of love—totally melding into one another. When we study, when we shower, when we sleep—I literally don't know whose leg I'm washing, or which of us is peeing—we're so the same person.

Apparently, they always dressed the same, acted the same—always the creepy closeness. They fed each other, maneuvered four limbs for two faces, drinking from the other's cup in hand, smoking from the other's cigarette in hand. They were a regular fucking circus act.

Jas left with David Squared and I couldn't imagine the erotic taco meat he was crunching, the cookie sandwich filling he was squeezing himself into—but it made me smile. *Oh, you guys are the most in-love people on the planet? Well, I just gotta see this!* I can hear him wink with a flick of his overnight wrist.

I had S.P.A.M. Manor to myself for the first time. I ran around naked, drinking, smoking, ejaculating on the holy mirror. (Note: The holy mirror was a 48x18inch mirror coated in a thick white film of the ejaculated semen of Pookie and The Pope, proof of their narcissism, a substance formed from their work.) I squirted my semen on the mirror, because there was no paper towel, toilet paper, tissue paper, napkin in the house. Bang! A nice long milky laser right in the middle. Why not defile the holy object? I did look cute when I came.

6.

Missionary Proposition

I was becoming a poet—finding my own voice and rhythm, my own tenor and alto—sharp and flat—crescendo and crash—my own bash the skull—burst the piñata—spew forth the violent truth—let the imagined words pour from my lips like honey—drip into your ears like song.

The door knocked. It wasn't the secret Plaguist knock, which was a chaotic rockNroll thrashing against the door with fists and boots, but a polite knock, a casual knock. Jas answered.

Two young men in white short sleeves and hand-me-down neckties stood at the door and smiled. "Hello sir. I wondered if you had a minute to listen to the good word of the lord and savior Jesus Christ," the older, bolder one inquired.

Jas smiled grandly and thrust open the door. "I would love nothing more than to hear you boys preach the gospel!" He shut the door behind them, and I felt his teeth sweat.

They were shocked by the interior of S.P.A.M. Manor. It was written on their blushed porcelain faces. Cute as a button introduced himself. "My name is Zachariah, and this is Caleb." He introduced shy and quiet, who raised a timid hand in attendance. "And we'd like to share the good news with you."

"Why?" I asked—knowing the answer, but anxious to hate.

Caleb squeaked. "Well, sir, Mathew 16:15 tells us to go out into the world and preach the gospel to every creature."

"You gonna evangelize to the bugs in the walls and the snakes in the grass?" I asked with too much sass.

"Now Martin, if these boys want to swap spiritual stories, we should let them go first." Jas hinted to me.

They ignored Jas's implication of barter.

Naïve little boys eager to impress their worthiness upon their heroes. This is prime recruiting ground, chemical urge anxious to aim and explode the self-outward: military, missionary, athletic competition, smelling sexy for sex. I have golden sunshine in my pocket.

"If they have ears to hear." Zachariah shined new plastic on his just grasping the theme.

"Are you nervous about proselytizing in this neighborhood?" I asked Caleb.

"Not with the lord as my shield," Zachariah answered for both of them.

The Pope warned— "Be careful you don't wind up being a Saint Sebastian."

"Who was Saint Sebastian?" Caleb squeaked.

Jas lit a cigarette. He wiggled in his comfortable sofa seat and skin like an awakening pupa. "Saint Sebastian was a converter of religions. He turned pagans into Christians, and when he turned the wrong people, they shot him full of arrows, and those arrows went through whatever lord-shield HE HAD and made himself a martyr—and you know what the WORST part about being a martyr is?" Jas sibilated.

"What?" Caleb breathed.

Jas smiled and hit his cigarette again for dramatic effect. "You don't get to stick around and enjoy it." Exhaling smoke. "You can never be sure it ever really happened."

"You'll know when you get to heaven," Zachariah quipped.

I interjected— "That's what the radical Mullahs tell the eager men in the village to get them to blow themselves up for Allah."

"That's different."

"It's the same," I challenged.

"All right boys, let's not get into that!" Jas looked at me sharply and then sweetly back to Zachariah. "Why don't you give us the good word? Here, have a seat," Jas pleaded, pointing with two ladylike forearms to the black leather sofa. "Would you like a beer?"

"We don't drink." They both sat on the black sofa.

"Oh, that's right!" Jas snapped his fingers as he pranced to the fridge in one antelope leap.

Zachariah sat perky ass on the cushion with straight spine and feet firm on the ground, hand on one knee, other hand around the bible. He watched Jas bring me a beer.

"Well sir, I believe god has a plan for us, and I believe it's important for each and every person on Earth to HEAR that plan—and have the opportunity to reject or accept god's plan." Zachariah was bent on getting his message out to the world.

"What makes you so chosen to speak for god?" I couldn't help myself, sucking suds.

"Well sir, I've met the Mormon standard of worthiness—by remaining chaste and repentant…"

I interrupted. "Wait a minute! How can you be chaste *and* repentant at the same time? What are you sorrowful for—being so innocent?"

Jas spazzed a cackle and released a snorting hiss.

"Sin can be in the heart. I've had lust in my heart, and I've asked for forgiveness, like you can ask for forgiveness for *your* sins," Zachariah dared.

We played air chess— "That's mighty presumptuous of you—I mean we just met."

"MmmmmMMM!" Jas mumble-squealed to himself as he lit a new cigarette.

"Let he who is without sin cast the first stone," Zachariah tried.

"Are you asking me to hit you with a rock?"

"Okay boys! Pissing contest over—back to your corners. And Mar, you shut up!" Jas was tired of listening to me eagle screech their chickadee glee. "I want to hear more from Zachariah."

He obliged— "God's plan for you is simple—it's for you to be more like Him. That doesn't mean he expects you to be PERFECT. He knows you won't be. BUT he does expect that while you're here on Earth you try, to the best of your ability, to be more LIKE HIM and that you learn and grow from your mistakes."

BANGBANGBANGBANGBANGBANG!!! The secret knock scared the shit out of Caleb. He jumped four inches in his seat. Jas smiled. He leapt up to get it.

"What's going on motherfuckers?" Chuckie burst in with malt liquor and a dark grin.

"Well speak of the devil, it's *GOD!*" Jas shouted. We three Plaguists shared a very wicked laugh. "We were talking about you! Zachariah, Caleb—this is Chuckie Theodore Plague—He's OUR God—these spring chickens were saying we should be more like *you*."

Caleb wasn't looking too well. I could tell he was nervous and frightened, and this delighted me. I wanted to punish him for his beliefs. I wanted him to feel grief for being so weak. I hated how dominant and cruel Christians were in the land of my birth. I didn't want to be special. I wished for a world of open-mindedness. I was cruel, yes, but I wanted a strict transformation from the way that it is. I was an outcast. I wanted more outcasts. I wanted complete societal collapse.

Zachariah stood his ground. He believed his faith was being tested. This is the internal workings of his mind that I imagined. He believed that if he could convert some of these venomous heathens then he would have a special place at the throne of his lord and savior centuries dust. "To be more like God we must choose Good," he proclaimed innocently. "Goodness leads to happiness and helps us become more like the heavenly father." Zachariah was very well-versed.

"I bet my heavenly father can beat up your heavenly father," I sassed like a bitch on the playground.

Three Plaguists laughed.

Zachariah persisted. "In the Old Testament it states—*Let us make man in our image, after our likeness—and give him dominion over every other living creature on earth.* Can you imagine a better gift, than to be like god and hunt and fish and cultivate the microbes in the ground?"

Chuckie wasn't interested in their conversation. "Do y'all really believe all that Joseph Smith Jr. shit—that a fuckin' ANGEL showed him *sacred* TRUTHS on *golden* plates that he uh—fuckin' transcribed with a seer stone? You believe all of that?"

"Well, we believe in the teachings of the American prophets..." Zachariah asserted.

Chuckie was firm— "Answer the fuckin' question."

Startled, Caleb answered, "Yes. We believe in the teachings of Joseph Smith Jr."

Chuckie lit a cigarette and scooted me over from Jas's seat on the couch. He sat down and stared at the boys through dark wrap-around sunglasses. "I grew up a Mormon out west—and I never did my missionary work because by the time I was eighteen, I was in the Army, and by the time I left the Army, I knew what god was."

"What's that?" Caleb asked with dry mouth and breathlessness.

"Well, you're fuckin' lookin' at him—man the killer, man the thinker!" Chuckie said matter-of-factly. "In fact, Biblical scholars are coming out in droves with claims that Jesus of Nazareth was—fuckin'—a propaganda invention by the Roman Empire as psychological warfare against the warrior Jews who rebelled daily against the ruling class. Can you imagine two thousand years of culture being shaped by a Caesarian placebo?"

Jas and I laughed.

"Maybe we should be going," Zachariah suggested.

"Well, how rude! You little darlings come barging in here and want to talk about YOUR religion, yet you won't stay and listen to OURS?" A sweet psychosis sang in Jas's inflicted sentence.

Zachariah tried to object— "Well, that's not really how we do things…"

"Oh, but it's how WE do things!" Chuckie reassured the young man.

"Can I have a glass of water?" Asked Caleb, soaking wet around the collar and under his arms.

"Sure, sweetie!" Jas pranced to the kitchen for a glass of water.

"And a beer!" God shouted.

Jas pranced back quickly with the drinks. I was left out of the service. This was common—me the competing alpha, clearly not a potential lover. I leapt up and miracled a beer of my own.

God popped open his Steel Reserve and took a good pull. "Ahhh!" He lit a cigarette, exhaled very quickly and talked suddenly and very fast. "You see boys, when I was high as hell on about ten thousand micrograms of lysergic acid diethylamide, an ant told me that I was God. He waved his antenna around and around and communicated to me telepathically. He didn't like *fuckinnnn'* chew letters through his mandibles or nothing like that, but—I got it. I understood. I'm God. I was tuned into the universal truth. I understood everything, fuckin', why we were all here and what was going to happen."

Jas was on his knees, squirming on the carpet to speak, to show his flair and prowess to those two young boys who apparently so easily took to religion— "Yes!" He stood up and made a fan with his skeletal fingers which he raised from his arm and pointed to the sky. "And with twelve years of acing Catholic school, I couldn't refute his revelation." He smugly laughed to himself and found a cigarette. He soberly continued. "But I'll tell you both, there's no more spiritual person than Chuckie here."

"Do you guys go to church and listen to sermons or do anything for the community?" Asked Zack.

Chuckie and Jas laughed and laughed. I smoked and watched, wishing the end to all major religions.

"We have Radical Vatican right here at S.P.A.M. Manor," Jas said, laughing. "Hell—SERMONS!?" Jas gargled and pointed to Chuckie with his thumb. "Every word out of this man's mouth is *SCRIPTURE!*"

Those two young cherubs had no idea what to make of this pock-scarred monster, this punkRock queen with leather wings, his thin sunglasses and greyhound face, manic, marred, beautiful, radiant, mad.

Caleb put his dirty water glass down on the table and spied the bibles stacked one on top of the other, on their spines the translations: Fireside Study Edition, King James Version, The Latin Vulgate, the New International Version, The Book of Mormon, The Good News Bible, The Picture Bible, all covered with wax from a slowly dripping candelabrum that rested on the stack of bibles.

Caleb lost all his color. He grew pale specter green, a milky camembert. We all saw it coming and none of us did anything to stop it. He threw-up all over the bibles. "I'm sorry!" He vomited again and then whimpered, frightened. He ran to the bathroom. He vomited in the toilet. We heard the spewing, splashing chunks and streams.

God heard this and was pleased—a ruby-slipper smile crept across his zombie monster face.

Zachariah felt uncomfortable, for the first time. I saw it in his shifting seat and stealing water from his sick friend. He was the perfect little missionary, who unfortunately knocked on Jas's door that afternoon.

"I'll wait 'til your friend returns to finish with my little improv sermon here," God said slowly with gummy gravel in his smoky voice.

"I think we should be going," Zachariah said firmly.

"You're going to make your friend ride his bike immediately after spewing chunks? That ain't the type of compassion I expect to see from you Christians. Aren't you supposed to lead by example? Now come on, we listened to you tell us how we should be more like the god you imagine. Now listen to us tell you."

Caleb returned. "Can I get another glass of water?"

"SURE," Jas swooned, chest out, and pointing down to the stack of bibles. "But no more vomiting in my toilet! If you're gonna heave burger—do it on the bibles like you did the first time." He laughed like light-loafered Lucifer and leapt to the kitchen.

Jas handed the boy a glass of water.

Caleb was genuinely upset about the mess. "I'll clean it up!" He offered weakly.

"I'm already on it, sweetie—you sit there and relax. You need to get your strength up so you can run like hell when we open the door." Jas laughed immediately after uttering the sentence.

He put on a show of cleaning up. He wiped the table around the bibles where pieces of food and pools of bile dripped. He wiped up the mess on the floor. He walked away with the rags. He came back, sat down and lit a cigarette, sure to leave the half-digested beans and the cheese on the bibles. A single gooey black bean slithered down the stack of bibles, leaving a stringy trail of cheese and bile.

"ANYWAY!" Chuckie continued. "We PLAGUISTS believe that absurdity shall be the whole of the law, that there's NOTHING sacred WORTH a *damn*, and that we should SUPPORT mutation by spreading *disease*. Every word's a *virus*, every thought's a *tempting offer* and the ONLY way to live is to burn. We believe in everything and nothing. We know no score, settle no debts, and go as fast as we can."

"How can absurdity be the whole of the law? What law?" Zachariah quizzed.

"Exactly! We're all out here making up shit about ourselves to FEEL better—so I say unto you, DO IT in a FAR-OUT and *cool* way! It's not a matter of WHAT you believe, but HOW you believe it!"

Caleb lost his cool. He'd vomited on bibles, and they had not been cleaned. "I have to go!" He cried. He wept. He rocked back and forth on the black sofa gripping his pant legs. "I can't do this anymore! I have to go home!" He sobbed in gross hysterics.

I smiled from ear to ear. My witness of their disintegration was evilly pleasing to me. I was proud to see them ignite into nothingness at the first sign of stress. It made me feel more confident in my choices on this spiritual path of darkness and distress. Did this make me evil? Perhaps. But I'd seen enough destruction in the name of misunderstood idols. I wanted rebellion and revolution, spiritual and social, death to the systemic bullshit that milks the people for the machine.

God pointed to Jas and then to the front door. Jas sprang into action, opening the front door. Zachariah helped his friend out of the apartment. Jas called after them, "Put me down as VERY Interested but NON-committal!" He cackled and slammed the door.

"Oh yeah. I almost forgot," said Chuckie. "Get dressed, we have a show to do in a few hours."

Jas laughed. "Oh my god! When were you going to tell us?"

"I was going to tell you ten seconds ago when I just told you—now get your shit together, get dressed, get whatever shit you want to read or recite together and don't worry—fuckin'—we have an open bar this time. Jane said we brought so many customers last time that this time the readers could drink all night for free, so there's going to be a lot of us. Even Rock's going to read something. I want to hear something special from you too, Martin," God demanded.

I was schoolgirl-giddy to have attention from this burly shit-kicker everyone called God.

7.

Tickle Your Fancy

Chuckie informed us we had to spill our seeds in the seediest place in Nashville. We were to pick up Dominic for this holy mission and meet Chuckie and everyone else at Jane's. We had a show to do, but first we had a mission from God to complete.

The next thing I knew the three of us were cruising through the World's Largest Bookstore which was a deceptive name really, because it was not a bookstore in the traditional sense of the word. It was a pornographic retail store full of enormous dildos, pocket pussies, vibrators, handcuffs, inflatable men and women and sheep and pigs… There were rubber toys that I couldn't imagine being inserted into any human cavity without surgery—fat, rubbery, fist-sized dildos that I couldn't get my hands around. I felt like a toddler masturbating my babysitter with that thing in my hands.

Jas could tell I was a little uneasy about being in a place like this. "Look Martin, if you can pull out your prick and jerk off in an establishment like this, then you can read your poetry on stage with us."

"Wow! Why?"

"Because it's a fucking *SHOW*! —That's why you have to memorize your lines! Because the only reason people care what the fuck's coming out of your mouths is because it's coming out of YOUR mouth! —Because of the crazy fucking monster you are! —Now come in here and behave like a Plaguist by cumming into one of these booths!"

He was right, of course. But I was more nervous about remembering my lines than I was about all these homo-trolls in pink polos strolling our stink and solo—noticing that we were all going into booths separately.

Jas went into one of the booths first—of course, the one the furthest away from the entrance, where the real shadows linger without penumbra in the numb darkness. It was like *Night of the Living Dead* except these zombies wanted cocks—lots and lots of cocks.

"Hey man, you want to share a booth?" I couldn't believe Dominic asked me this.

"All right." I couldn't believe I answered in the affirmative. I'd never done anything like this before. I was not only going into some pornographic viewing booth with another man, but it seemed that the whole store knew about it.

"What do you like?" He asked me, after locking the door and inserting the tokens into the monitor.

"What do you mean?" I was a little nervous—I mean—what the hell did he mean?

"Gay—straight—lesbians—animals?"

The last option confused me. "They have animals?"

"Hell no! That shit's illegal man—god—are you into that kind of thing?"

I couldn't tell if he was teasing me or serious. "NO! —But I mean shit! —I'd look at it once!" — (pause)— "Because if that's what *people* can do—I want to know about it. Wouldn't you?!"

"Hell yeah! But that's not my *thing*!" He looked at me suspiciously.

I had no idea what to suggest— "Put on the lesbians—who doesn't like lesbians?"

"Fags!"

"Jesus Christ! Well—what's your *thing* man!?"

"Oh me? I like it ALLL." Dominic smiled at me wonderfully, finally letting me off the hook of his joke.

Then a penis made its way into our booth—male human penis in its late thirties with some questionable scratches and an evil eye that winked the gangrene blues. Dominic smacked the penis at once with the back of his hand. "Hey, get that fucking thing out of here buddy! We don't do shit like that for NOTHING!"

The penis retreated. The man in the next buddy booth punched the plywood wall in frustration.

"Hey man, put your hand over that hole while we do this, huh? —I hope you can do it with one hand."

"Really?" I was completely flaccid.

"Yeah man—we got to cum for the lord." Dominic was on a mission.

I remembered then—something so absurd I thought to myself, how could I ever not go along with it? —Jas, I, and Dominic all promised to spill our seed for Chuckie in the seediest place in Nashville, and left The Pope to decide where that place was going to be.

And here we were—the World's Largest Bookstore which wasn't a bookstore but a cave for insatiable psycho hard-ons, hard-pressed for violent fellatio through anonymous wooden walls—which were thin enough, by the way, to hear every porn score and every gagging old man reflex, every roughhouse jailbird throat fuck with coughing cum and mucous gag…

I felt the hard-ons trying to get in through the cubby holes, the prick touching the palm of my hand. I heard them knocking on the doors outside the booth adjacent to our booth.

The muffled voice of the potbelly predator— "Hey buddy—c'mon—give another guy a chance."

I think they delighted in touching the palm of my hand with the tip of their penis. I switched walls and hiked my boot up to the hole. I had two free hands now. I turned my attention to the movie. Two lesbians were ass fucking the same dildo and it couldn't have turned me off more.

"Great idea man!" Dominic did the same thing, switching walls and putting his boot-heel to the glory-hole on the other wall. We faced each other. He changed the channel. We watched some young teenage couple have sex on the monitor—something that got us both hard. I was jerking normally with my left hand and Dominic caught a glimpse of my practice. "Hey man, put your hands together like this—make your palms a vagina—see—like this?" He showed me how.

I made a vagina by stretching my thumbs and forefingers.

"There you go, now fuck that!" Dominic looked at my cock— "Nice penis, by the way."

"Um—thanks." I had no idea how to respond to such a statement. "You, too..?" —I wasn't raised that way—I don't know…

He kept spitting on his hands where he'd made the vagina. "You don't want to fuck a dry pussy do you?" —He laughed and spit—another spit, some of the saliva missing his hands and going on his black jeans, and my bare legs. "Oh god!!"

"What?!" I hoped it wasn't a stroke.

"Oh god!!!"

"Really?" I hoped it WAS a stroke.

"OH GOD!!!!"

I hoped he had good aim.

"CCHHHHHUUUUUCCCCKKKKKKKKiiIIIIIEEEEEEEE!!!!!!!!!"
—A fire extinguisher has less of a load than Dominic. Semen shot in streams everywhere. I wondered if I shouldn't have worn my rain slickers and brought an umbrella. The semen flung to the top—icky baby goo dripped like snotty stalactites from the ceiling of our booth.

"UH!!" I did my best to dodge his raining ejaculation.

"Yeah?!" Asked Dominic enthusiastically—which didn't help.

"UuuuUUH!!!" I gave it all I had. I closed my eyes—the cheerleaders were lined up with open mouths like altar boys and the altar boys the same—why not, it seemed fitting to imagine such an atrocity in such an (un)holy place.

Nothing—it wasn't going to happen—there were big homo dicks trying to get into my cubicle. I couldn't concentrate. I couldn't ejaculate.

I failed.

But I lied— "UHHHH—UUUHHHH !!!" I shook and convulsed in the corner which was black and invisible like a galactic hole, "CCCHUUUUUUUUUUUUUUUCCCKKKiiIIIIIEEEEEEEEEEE!" I screamed. I betrayed my Lord's commandment with grace and ease and enough grease to fry my kernel of truth to a crisp.

Dominic laughed behind me. I wonder if he knew I'd faked it.

"It's too bad there's no Kleenex in here, huh?" I pretended to shake off my dripping penis, and I flung some imaginary goo into the corner,

"No shit, tell me about it."

I did, however, love this credo that Jas dreamt up as an article of faith—when having an orgasm one must scream the name of their Lord. I enjoyed hearing Chuckie's name screamed out in the night—or day— knowing that someone had discharged the divine sauce. Jas screamed the loudest,

"ChHHHHHHUUUUUUUUCCCCKKKKKKKKKKIIIIEEEEEEEEEE E!"

Dominic and I laughed in the booth hearing him scream, and the porn video on the monitor went out, because we were out of tokens. "Well, we've done our part for the Lord," Dominic gleefully chirped with cute irony.

When we opened the door to the buddy booth/porn cubicle, I felt like a Beatle or a Rolling Stone stepping from the dressing room with no security. We were mobbed by fans of the illest repute, all pawing and grabbing at us, touching our faces and our bodies. There were maybe fifteen or twenty middle age homosexual mustaches slobbering over us like zombies. "CAAAHHHCK!" you could almost hear them groan in hungry despair. Dominic grabbed one of the trolls and slammed him against the wall.

I figured it was time to bust our way through the gaggle, so I grabbed someone's wrist and bent it back, tripped him to the floor, which scattered some of the polo pretenders back a bit. Dominic pushed another guy out of the way, and we made for the door.

The dark hallway was packed with gawkers and rapists, anxious for the slightest fondle. They would've sucked the sweat from our aromatic armpits had we been willing to let them. (We should've charged them a fortune). I followed Dominic out and Jas was right behind me. We all pushed and shoved and punched our way free of the gauntlet of groping fingers and mustaches, some even so brave as to reach for our crotches with wrists of shaggy red hair and gold watches, sweaty walrus mouths, glasses and bald heads. I palmed a man in the face and pushed him over a bin of expired dildos. He fell right to the floor. It was a real scene— quite a commotion. We ran the rest of the way out of there.

We jumped in the Mystery Ship and drove away fast, spitting gravel against the front door which opened for a moment by a few in a daring pursuit of the three of us laughing our asses off.

It was getting late. We figured we might as well head on over to Jane's and start drinking tequila beer gin wine to prepare ourselves for the plunge into being the center of attention. Jas was right. I'd survived that terrible scene—reading poetry on stage seemed like a joke after that. What was there to be nervous about?

8.

A Nonchalant Au Chante

Inside, sticky steps made noise as we peeled our boots from the sugary residue of the never-cleaned concrete floor. Dim lights were made dimmer by a dense fog of cigarette and weed smoke. The top of the stairs revealed no haven, offered no refuge, opened to no luxury. It was a dank pit. The stage was immediately to the left and the bar was immediately to the back. Random tables and chairs cluttered the area in front of the stage, as if arranged by drunken Dadaists.

This was Jane's.

I followed Jas to the bar, a three-sided bar, the back wall had a door to the kitchen where dishes were sometimes washed, food was sometimes made, and all the time people fucked and did drugs.

We sat in the very back, in a large horseshoe booth. Chuckie greeted us with a greasy smile and dark sunglasses—impossible eyes—a raise of his glass— "What's going on, motherfuckers?!"

"Nothing more than parading about in our normal glorious form… Martin here jacked off at The World's Largest Bookstore and screamed your name doing it—and we totally got chased out of the store by like a MOB of Zombie trolls in search of our brainy COCKS!"

Chuckie lit a cigarette. He watched us sit down coolly and launched back into his sermon. He was on a bent about the overreaching powers of the U.S. Government.

"Man, these motherfuckers over here are so afraid of the government taking their fucking GUNS AWAY!! Fuckinnnnnn… AIN'T NO NEED for ANY fucking MODERN GOVERNMENT OFFICIAL to give a shit about taking your GUNS away. Look what they did at RUBY RIDGE! At WACO! They don't give a shit about how armed you are! They care about your constitutional flex to worship in any way you want, that's WHY they went after Karesh!" Chuckie hit his cigarette, exhaled excitedly and continued. "Fucking Weaver lost his son to a sniper because of a fucking bench warrant! How the fuck that didn't result in a COMPLETE and *total* million strong protest at the fucking FBI HEADQUARTERS I'll never know. Motherfucker was a green beret. — Besides, you ain't never gonna protect yourself from the government with GUNS, with thugs and crazy people, hell yeah, arm yourself to the fucking teeth. GUNS are *cool*. Our military's for overseas shit, oil interests, South American freshwater, and mineral flats. At home we're taxed and squeezed by laws written by the donor class and made into law by the Senate Majority. America's now a bureaucratic bank with an army. The local police will only get more and more militarized, and the banks are going to become more and more stingy, and the bureaucracy is gonna keep on doing what it does best, drown you in paperwork and keep you registered, and watched." He took another hit of cigarette, a small one, a fast rabbit half one and spoke as he exhaled. "Not GUNS! If they want you, the government's going to get you with tax evasion, economic warfare, financial regulation…" He smiled a fraction, as if enlightened with the punchline. "They only go after nuts in LARGE GROUPS who start their own *religion*!" He smiled a manic welcome…

"MARTIN!" Chuckie shouted at me.

"Huh?" Where had I been? What glory the acid. "WHAT!?" I shouted tough and loud.

"Don't go too far away on your trip—there's a SHOW to do."

More Satanic Satori from our Lord and flavor… The timing was impressive—Chuckie saw my head float away like toddler helium with no string attached—and he reeled me back in. Testimony to the genius of that man!

Rock burst in from nowhere, landing in the booth with a hard right buttocks and a Hazzard County slide into God. His shoulders slammed into Chuckie's shoulders as he smacked his hand down onto the table edge to catch himself from going further. Everything he did happened so impossibly fast and seemingly reckless.

"Well, hello, snookums!" Chuckie said hilariously, not budging an inch.

I laughed. He caught me off guard. I had no idea this large industrial machine of a man-God could use such cuddly cute language. Perhaps I'd stereotyped him, and therefore limited his omnipotence—a terrible thing to do to a God—like Christians with their philosophies, Jews with their severity, and Muslims with their rituals.

No God should need you.

"Yes! Hello puddin'! I see that you're out of beer." Rock grabbed an empty beer mug and a half empty pitcher of beer. He poured the beer mug full to the rim and then guzzled the contents from the pitcher while we all laughed.

Then he was gone. The pitcher was drained, and up he sprang to run to the bar. I watched through intoxicated vapors Sain't Rock slam the pitcher on the bar! Demanding attention and getting it!

Marybeth slithered in and took all our attention away. "Nice night for an evening," she said quietly, but we all heard.

Yes, it was.

She held a cigarette holder in her ladylike fingers splayed on a warm pedestal arm. A yellow and white widow's hat from the roaring twenties sat cocked on the side of her head, the white lace covering her eyes to her nose. She was plump with a pose and smelled like a rose. She ran her toes up my shin, under the table. I almost fainted.

"I'm dying to come over and practice my sermon," she purred to The Pope, and winked at me.

"Hell yeah! Are you almost done with that thing or what?" Chuckie demanded dandily.

"It'll be ready in a couple of weeks," she lauded back at him luxuriously.

"We'll let me know, so we can tell everybody," proposed gentleman God.

Apparently, Chuckie had ordered that anyone who was to be a Sain't had to give a sermon.

I secretly hoped he'd tell me I had to perform one as well. I was so needy—greedy for lusty leers, drunken peers, pretty queers, everyone's little eyes on me, ooh attention!

There were no lights to dim, but the applause came upon his entrance to the stage. Dominic was the evening's master of ceremonies. I saw why he had to change. He wore assless chaps, naked underneath, and a black leather vest, naked underneath. He wore pink rabbit ears on his head, and a pink bunny tail on the small of his back. He wore pink bunny slippers and a smile that couldn't be stopped. His long dark curls bounced above his shoulders, his long and strong neck, almost alien, perma-puckered cupid lips and bold black insect eyes. He was an unclaimable prize, easy to be had for one night, but impossible to contain. His left arm was covered in tattoos: the lifespan of a demon from fetus to beast, three stages of eerie cool captured in ink on his pale white baby flesh, worked out and strong. He had an intelligent stoner's mad laugh as if every conversation was a dictation of the absurdity of it all.

Dominic held the microphone like a rockstar. "I tell you man—I'm the doubting Thomas of the group," Dominic admitted. "I don't believe a word of their bullshit lies—but neither do they! —That makes me a Plaguist Extremist! —I have to preach the word of my non-believing faith!" He giggled to himself and then shrugged to us, the audience.

Dominic did a playful bunny bounce from one end of the stage to the other in three Olympic standing long jumps.

"You see how silly this shit is?" He asked. "We believe that God is Chuckie the Plague—our *friend* who washes dishes at The Quicksilver and teaches us that the government is a bank with weapons, and absurdity shall be the whole of the law." He thought for a moment and had great stage timing, "Jesus! I better stop this, or I'll convince myself that HE IS GOD!"

We laughed. There were more of us than I had been introduced to. Seventy or eighty Plaguists filled the room. I assumed we were all Plaguists. Perhaps many were being introduced to Plaguism that evening.

We were growing.

"What can I say? I was born to be a butch bunny," Dominic teased.

Everyone laughed and hooted and hollered *more*.

"Doesn't my ass look fantastic in these chaps?" He teased us more.

Jas whistled and woo-hooed and ran to the stage with a two dollar bill waving in the air.

"Hey, fuck you, Pope! I got the stage."

It was true—The Pope did have to be reminded when it was someone else's turn to be paid attention to. Jas tucked the bill in the crease of Dom's assless-chaps anyway and accepted the applause all the way back to his seat.

"The First Interplanetary Church of the Immaculate Deception," continued Dominic, "is clearly a church without boundaries, without doors, without a Corpus Christie, a Yogi Hindi, a hardened martyr, a pardoned felon, every one of us—fit for the electric chair!"

The three Plaguist tables erupted and cheered.

Dominic became enraptured with his bunny spirit and hopped around the stage— "I am speaking for the Church tonight because Chuckie asked me to." Hop, hop, hop… "I'm a Plaguist. I believe it *matters* more HOW you believe something than whatever that fucking thing *IS*—"

Dominic turned and bunny-hopped back in the other direction. "I'm a Plaguist and that gives me the greatest excuse in the world to be the biggest fuck up imaginable. There's no telling how high you can climb when the standards are below sea level."

The crowd erupted with applause.

Dominic continued his sermon— "We believe Holy Communion's the consumption of the flesh of our lord. Of course, we believe that Chuckie's flesh is made of LSD25 so when we take the host—the wafer is soaked in Lysergic Acid. —Also—if his urine's any indication—his blood's mostly Colt 45, so when unscrewing a cap you're performing a holy ritual. THIS is called SUB-SUBSTANTIATION!"

Dominic giggled. "You see how silly this shit is? I mean that's what's great about what these guys are doing—creating their own church and pointing out the absurdities of every other religion. Did you know as a Plaguist it's against their faith to believe in their own teachings?" More giggling, "Who ever heard of such a thing?"

Pookie showed up at God's Table, and with him the first grand wave of acid washed over me like salt water on a slug, crippling my spine and central nervous system. The fear. I lit a cigarette and couldn't stop from crying. I wasn't sad, the saline gushed from my eyeballs as if gripped with panic spasm. I sucked up the snot. Pookie looked right at me.

"What's wrong, baby?"

Through clenching teeth, I muttered the phrase— "It's kicking in."

"Oh god! Well, good luck soldier, see you after the battle." The giggle snort. ("HunH!")

I couldn't believe how different he looked. He wore bright yellow jeans, which I think he dyed that day, because I remember the palms of his hands being yellow. His nails were painted bright blue. His shirt was tranny porn-star small and glittered bright orange, cut off at the arms, and about eleven inches long, which accentuated his exposed midriff and flat belly with many different types of long necklaces, a random mix of gold, hemp and crucifix, each worn under his shirt and trickling across his flat belly. The shoes were bright green, and his hair was bright red. He seemed to be a walking commercial for Rit Dye. He looked perfectly ridiculous, a hideous angel with a special glow.

I could barely speak because of the acid, so I blurted out clumsily, "Colorful!" It felt like my teeth, tongue, lips and hair were all being directed by some unique individual source. There was very little communication between my working parts. I struggled to maintain.

Jas and the girls busted out laughing.

If it moves, try to eat it.

If it grows, try to eat it.

Mind the teeth and talons.

Mind the poison.

"Yeah, I felt like standing out tonight! Knowing you goth fuckers would show up in predictable black and olive green," Pookie said with gigantic eyes and cherry rubber lips, hair pinned back with bright purple clips, taking sips of my gin and tonic and looking into my dilated eyes. "Can I have the rest of this since you got an open bar?"

"Yes." I never knew if I was the mongoose or the cobra, but I did enjoy the hypnotic sway and dance.

Pookie was off, but there was a mist of rainbow colors in the space that his body once occupied. I began to really trip balls.

Jas climbed on stage next and let out a loud terrifying scream to get everyone's attention, and man, the whole place went quiet. Jas paced like a nervous animal in a cage, waiting for the trainer to slip up and leave the lock undone. He squealed and he growled, and he said the prettiest things. Euphoric wax dripped from his hot candle mouth and splattered on the messy floor with instant solidification. He moaned and he slithered, and he seemed to have spiritual orgasms as he held himself and fell to the stage in holy anguish, hand outreached for providence and gripping ghostly air.

He had grace and style, Ziggy Stardust superpowers, lithe and lightning, gazelle and wintergreen. He was the freshest thing on the scene, the way he made a sentence sing with his low gravel hiss and high pitch scream. He was song and dance—pace and prance and take up the whole fucking stage. Jas was romance and rage—a rocket in a cage with blast off and tear right through the bars. There were no perimeters. He could say anything. I watched and listened and read and discovered that though I wanted to write like him, better than him... I could never perform like him. I could never swivel my silk hips and purse my whore red lips with predatory eyes and theatrical thoughts— "a holocaust of honky-tonk cocks," I had no idea what he was referring to, but he looked great, and the poems sang and lit up from his mouth with electric spittle and high on drugs...

The crowd roared and cheered him on—and indeed he was a poet superstar if ever there was one.

Next it was my turn. I was holographically teleported to the stage if I remember correctly. I paced and shouted and yelled because I didn't have the slightest fucking clue how to follow that dramatic spectacle. Slowly my poem came back to me—I had chosen to memorize one, only one, for this special night, and recite it live on stage. I had never done this before. I was nervous.

"*Do Castrated Boys dream of weeping mothers?*" —That line got a few laughs—but that wasn't its purpose—I wanted to dive down into the depths of psychoanalysis. I wanted to be the Jacque Cousteau of the unconscious. But I was also enamored with the absurdity of it all— "*Do broken down cars always crunch so loud—is it getting hot in here to you? Would you like some of my priceless ice-cream?*" —I recited my questionable poetry like a madman, an unseasoned rookie—fast and anxious—like I couldn't wait to get every word out—

"Do dreams of flight provoke urgency to land? Do dreams of water remind you how to swim? Do dreams of fire wake you?" —By now I shook, shivered with nauseous excitement— "Is man more ape or angel? —Is it 'neither' that makes him special? Is he? —Is nature accountable for the flaws of man? —Does he have any? What about woman? Is she more mother or lover? Is it neither that makes her equal? Is she? Is she prepared to be accountable for a civilization spent? Shall we start with ours?" I was lost now—I didn't know where I was in the poem—I improvised— "Haven't we chosen to manipulate for advantage instead of harmonize with the pulse? —Doesn't genius just love a vacuum? Aren't some of the best ideas incomprehensible to the dispensable? — Aren't some scenes just for nativity? —Do flames have pity? —Would you—if you could burn—don't you?" —That was enough for me. I put the mic in the stand and took my seat amongst my company of Plaguists and weirdoes.

It seemed hours later.

Where was I? What had happened? How much acid had I eaten? I remembered taking a piss somewhere, but then what? The lights seemed lower and there was a band on stage now. Were we opening for a band?

Pookie handed me a gin and tonic. "These guys rock!"

I was shocked for several reasons. I didn't remember getting up from the table. I stood by the bar, and that I was doing so without a beverage in my hand, which I'd been informed was free for anyone who performed on stage. "Thanks." I responded to the beverage and whoever might have handed it to me.

"Don't thank me. They write all their own songs." Pookie laughed.

I didn't understand his joke. "Huh?"

"Nevermind. Listen, we should hang out sometime. Are you and Jas, like, a thing or whatever?"

"What? Hell no!" It hadn't occurred to me that the whole town would naturally assume that we were lovers. Well fuck—whatever—what a realization to have with a head full of acid in a town you just moved to. I soon lost that thought, with a laugh and a truly didn't care—passing through—in search of only one thing—the source of that mad cackle and those lengthy poems of his.

On Stage:

Lingus was a trio of young women who played haunting melodies with eerie sounds that shivered the ghostly spines of the music gods. The song seduced me away to another time and place, everything was so romantic, so gothic, so Byron and Shelly—so Rimbaud and Verlaine—so Mozart and Salieri.

Harriet played the violin beautifully and Echo purred over the drums like a pussycat rockNroller slamming the sticks against the animal skins and sweating from her tongue like an alpha bitch—and Ready—Ready with slow cello bow, slow southern drawl, and handiwork, easy on the eyes, easy on the ride, first to fifth in a week and a half. Madness. Molasses. They were three beautiful young women in their twenties, (Though I think Echo might have been the youngest, my age, nineteen) —blasting the beautiful sounds from the instruments which they'd all mastered to that point—to make me misty-eyed, half-chubbed, and wondering who to do.

Chirpy pop whistle applause.

"GOD! How good was that song?" Pookie threw his seven-pound arm around my neck, and I felt the heat from his skin, the slimy sweat, the desperate disease and the clingy needs of a lost boy on the ever-hunt for that certain Pan. I was not that Pan. I was boy becoming man.

I threw my ten-pound arm around his delicate neck and squeezed tighter than I should've but wanted him to know that I was on the verge of no longer being gentle with my strength.

We raised our glasses and whistled and woo-hooed for the band and I could tell that I made him a bit uncomfortable, and that he got off on the sensation of his own discomfort. He was my type—beautiful, unknowable and disposable. I wanted to be seen the same. I wanted to be at least *in the game*—a piece, a player, a pond, a king. I didn't care— well actually any other piece than those two because my best quality is— reckless determination to seize opportunity. I reckoned myself a bishop.

"Do you think Ready is hot?" He asked me.

"Hell yeah!" I youthfully declared.

"She thinks you're hot."

"How do you know that?"

"Everybody does," he purred.

I was raised by lonely daring.

The music was over. We applauded and hooted and hollered.

The joke was coming to me—the hilarious punch(in-the-gut)line—the Zen moment of clarity where it all makes sense—and here it was—*my god look at her dress—it's so short and her ass is so round—I bet her pussy can get very wet—I bet she knows how to enjoy a hard dick*—Ready. She was the Cellist for Lingus—a dark mutt—Western European and Negroid—peanut butter skin, caramel almond eyes, intense black corkscrew hair and a look that pierced the fabric of existence—a confidence supreme—that did not need a thing—Daughter of the Fire God—a self-worth priceless—an ego unsatisfiable—wild—feral—I couldn't stop looking at her—fuck the meaning of life—I had to have her.

At the Lingus Table: "You know Marybeth and Echo," Pookie said. "This is Ready." Pookie planted a serious kiss on Echo. She wore overall-shorts and a muscle shirt opened to the gut. She had small breasts and wore no bra, and when they kissed, Pookie shoved his hand in her shirt and fondled her nipples. She, in turn, grabbed his throat and kept him in check by squeezes.

Ready sat beside Marybeth and Pookie sat beside Echo. I pulled up a chair beside Pookie.

"Martin Hemlock, the Angel of Death, huh?" Ready didn't seem too impressed.

"Yeah." I was instantly smitten by this flinty kitten.

"Pretty harsh—why do you have such a badass title?" She wanted to know.

I stumbled over my ill-prepared statement. "It's—uh—more to do—with the understanding of God's *dark side*—necessary reaction for every *action*."

"You mean he has a light side?" Ready taunted.

"Would you like some beer?" Echo asked me. She must've noticed the empty glass I clutched.

"Yes, please." Where did I get this glass? What used to be in it? Was it gin? There was a lime there—I liked beer with lime and gin ice.

"Take some." Marybeth was cool as shit—the Plaguist concubine and ready for all types of action.

I did. I drank and bummed a cigarette from her royal smuttiness. Wasn't she just at the Plaguist table? How did she find me way over here?

This again.

This timeless parade of senselessness. Time out of place—not that I MIND—trying to keep track of where I was.

Harriet and Dominic were in their own little world at the bar. Harriet was the violinist and main songwriter for Lingus. She was also Dominic's girlfriend. He continued to wear the bunny ears and I don't know if it turned her on, but it did make me stare longer than I normally would. Also, he had a fantastic ass.

Pookie patted me on the arm and leaned over the table. "We should all hang out!" Pookie smiled and nodded with wide eyes and a grateful look.

"You like him, don't you?" Marybeth looked at Ready as if she was disappointed. She looked at me, up and down. "Yeah—I mean, he's cute in a goofy, untried man kind of way… Uh..!" She seemed exhausted and looked back at Ready. "Can I be there when you first fuck him?"

"Can I watch too?" Pookie asked me—half serious/half mocking Marybeth/half willing.

"Ooh! Should we have an orgy for your guys' first time?" Echo suggested.

Everyone laughed at us. I figured I might as well go along with the attitude but keep my alpha status. I looked directly into Ready's eyes. "How long do you think we can resist each other until they lose interest?"

The three egged us on in unison. "Oooohh!!!"

"Excuse me." Ready seemed agitated as she asked Marybeth to give her some room. "I have to go to the restroom." She looked at me disgustedly and at the rest of them too. I wasn't used to the prudishness.

She was gone a few minutes, and I mentioned a shot and slid off to the bar. I avoided the bar and headed for the restroom. I went downstairs. I waited for Ready to come out.

She came out.

"How much of a head start do we have to your house before they wise up?"

She looked at me with smiles, charmed by my surprise. "God! Probably hours!" She pushed me against the wall and kissed my tongue raspberry sparks.

The Lingus house was a cute three bedroom with the garage converted into a recording studio. They had a pool in the backyard, which they paid to have kept clean. The kitchen table and chairs were mismatched pieces from various thrift stores. Dirty dishes were piled all over the place. None of the girls were very domestic. They were artists, musicians, creative free spirits with no interest in routine or chore. They owned no vacuum cleaner, no feather duster that wasn't used for sex, no Windex, no Pledge, no polish of any kind.

The kitchen, dining room and living room were community rooms full of notebooks, chairs, instruments of every stripe—a saxophone on a stand, a small drum kit, several guitars, portable podiums dripping with sheet music, snow-cone microphones on stands or prostrate on the ground sprouting cords that snaked aimlessly and in coils—shoes, random articles of clothing, overalls and hats—gloves and empty bottles of wine everywhere, flowers, most of them dried or dead.

There was a sweet fiery smell—as if unattended scented candles had burnt a plastic sconce to the ground and almost the house. Sexy teenage danger and introduction to ecstasy—it felt angelic to be handed such sweets.

Ready closed the door to her bedroom behind her and pushed me onto her bed. She straddled me and kissed me with soft plum lips. I rolled her like a gator and grabbed her soft wiry hair and sucked on her earlobe. She breathed heavily and let me. I unsnapped her bra with my free hand and felt down her warm cappuccino spine to her sloping café latte rump. I thrust my hot fingers into her panties and felt her cool ass. I squeezed. She breathed… In. I stuck my tongue in her ear and made sure she felt my massive erection between her warm legs where the volcano erupts. I felt the moisture of her excitement between layers of denim, panty, and millennia in the making.

Genes were becoming perfect. Interracial breeding helped in weeding out the old and brittle DNA strands. Fuck racial purity, the smartest dogs were mutts, and the prettiest, and most fucking capable.

"I want you inside me." I couldn't believe she was capable of such a cliché—but she was only twenty—and besides, in the heat of the moment, we can't all be poets. She desired it, urgently. She needed it.

She went into my pants like a jewel thief, crowbar on the glass, unbuckling my fly. Smash! A soft fast hand to the cock to feel the diamond pulsing—and my god was it pulsing, aching to be free, used, handled properly. She jerked my cock a few times, and then pushed up from me and stripped my pants from me—pulling out the prize and lunging her body down, devouring me like a small Japanese kid in a Coney Island hotdog eating contest.

I teased the tip of the head of my cock about her bushy pussy, her pouting clit and labia lips. I threatened to thrust. I felt her drip with excitement on my flesh. She couldn't wait another minute, but I wouldn't let her. "Do you have a condom?" I asked in hushed teasing, strong young hands on her hips, fingers almost touching as they went around her tiny waist, for support and gravity control. I was hydraulic amusement ride about to happen.

"Un-huh," she breathlessly squealed, as soft as a baby mouse.

I lifted her off me and onto the floor beside the bed. She reached in the darkness to the drawer. She never let go of my arm and hand as she reached out into the darkness and opened her bedside drawer. Quickly she tore apart the condom wrapper and put the rubber in her mouth, then went down on me, covering the tip of my cock with the rubber. Suddenly acknowledging her sexual prowess, she was very happy I insisted upon a condom.

(When considering sexual protection, remember: the young and the pretty haven't festered yet.)

I woke up in Ready's bed, naked and dazed. I kissed her sleeping cheek and crawled out of bed. I found my shorts and shirt, where *thank Chuckie* a single cigarette was left in the pack.

In the morning-twilight backyard, Pookie joined me. He smoked his own cigarette. "Badass! You hooked up with Ready—now we can hang out around here all day while they practice—they have the best video games."

"Cool."

Dominic joined us. He didn't smoke cigarettes but wanted to hang out with the guys and maybe rib me a bit for hooking up with Ready. I felt as if I'd rushed for two thousand yards and won the Heisman Trophy, "How was it?"

I told him. Everyone laughed. We smoked and soaked up the early April sunshine that spilled on our exposed chests—three young gods immortal in the backyard of the conquered sirens. The conversation found itself on politics.

Dominic loved to go on tirades about the government. "The problem is systemic—the system's been rigged—we're living in a plutocracy run by greedy little bankers born without compassion or empathy and have only me, me, me in mind and are FUCKING this country—imprisoning our young and capable men and women with, on one side an institutional debt in the form of college loans and on another a rigged prison system that abuses its power and uses racial tension to produce slave labor!"

If he was handing out pitchforks and torches, I would've stormed the gates with him. He was infectious—he went on and on about the shape of things in the world—claiming to have solutions for solving the solvency problem in the country—assuring us that those jobs would be not only saved but created. He didn't believe in a communist state or even a socialist one—but believed in a heavily regulated capitalist market—the free market was a myth, we were told—there was nothing free about it—it cost to be in it, it cost to play—you could win it all or lose it all on the curve of a dime.

"I have to go." I put out my cigarette.

"No, you don't—besides, Echo's making pancakes for everyone." Pookie winked at me.

I stayed for two more days.

9.

Sermon on Mounted Televisions

Jas and I were summoned to Plague Central. Rock and Chuckie had already been up for thirty hours tripping and building this large square monkeybar type structure. Twelve feet tall and made of iron bars like a geometric cube of squares.

"We're gonna fill this thing up with televisions—and then Rock here's gonna give a sermon!"

More acid. We loaded into Rock's truck and drove away.

The wind was Mozart Requiem in D Minor. It burned to keep my eyes open. I did not care to hear a goddamn thing but the music in my head. I held on tight to the back of the truck as Rock swung it around corners wildly, roared it down backroads violently, speeding, screaming from inside the cab to Jas, sucking a cigarette or cackling.

God tried to light his cigarette while cupping his hands around the flame, not holding onto the truck but surfing the steel Ford flatbed as Rock floored it down Charlotte Avenue, afraid of no Cop. We hadn't committed a crime yet, so we could be as reckless as possible.

"FUCK! That took FOREVER!" God yelled as he popped up.

BANG!BANG!BANG!BANG!BANG!BANG!BANG! Rock gave the secret Plaguist knock from the inside of his pick-up—which meant that it was time to settle down and be discreet. It was almost time to break into houses.

We picked a house at the end of the subdivision. We parked right in the driveway. Rock went to the front door. He pulled a glass cutter from his pocket and cut out a 4x6 windowpane by the front door. The glass fell forward, and he caught it. No sound of breaking glass.

He'd scouted the house, it occurred to me. This was a plan. We were doing something that had been carefully thought out.

He reached his hand in and unlocked the door.

We crept through the house silently. We were after one thing only: televisions.

I was nervous. I was anxious. I ran to the bathroom and shit my brains out.

"Don't Flush!" Chuckie yelled and laughed.

TTTTHHHHPPPPTT! PLOP! The water felt cool against my sweaty ass as the shit made a splash into the small fresh pool of water that starving African kids would kill to drink from. I wiped and buckled up.

I wondered about the shit in the toilet. Was my DNA in that loaf of brown excrement? Should I really leave it for evidence? Would the homeowners merely flush out of embarrassment and shame— humorous—or of disgust of the smell and the thought? I bet the wife would. Was that sexist? I was still learning who to be. Could the man of the house be a detective, a doctor? You could bet that he may be a fan of detective shows on television. Would he fearlessly bend down among the refuse and go in for a sample? Was my DNA even on record? Was there some large database that had everyone's DNA on file? Everyone in the western world anyway—*not every Somali pirate could smuggle a salami through customs—but some could.* I didn't remember shitting for the police.

I didn't flush.

The adrenaline coursed through my body like electricity, I was Electrophorus, an electric knife fish. I was a satellite dish picking up every signal. I heard in color, using echolocation I heard the movements and the dance of my comrades in the house.

I opened the medicine cabinet and found a bottle of Vicodin, a heavy prescription. I opened the bottle and carefully emptied the contents into my hand. All but two pills did I take, the angels share—sorry sweetheart, if it's really an emergency—this should get you to the clinic or wherever your connection is… I stuffed the goods in my cutoff jeans and joined the crew. I went to one of the smaller bedrooms and carried a 24-inch television to Rock's truck.

One must choose the right drugs for the right crimes.

We broke into several houses in this fashion, stealing only televisions and whatever I found in the medicine cabinets. My pockets were full of Tylenol, Advil and Motrin.

By the third house I was anemic, shitting blood and vomiting. I was sick with rush. It was bone-rattling fear and excitement: undulating fat tissue, helium-headed gag reflex, uncontrollable muscle spasm, and shivering central nervous system. I desperately wanted each new house to be the last house we hit.

We scored nine televisions in that third house. Nine. I didn't know how many people lived there—but it was very Stepford Wives, very X-Files, very 1984 and Fahrenheit 451. The omniscient eye demanded their attention in every room, (except the bathroom—which was probably why I felt such a rush there—shitting my brains out and drooling).

We snuck out of the house like church mice. We were shadows in the evening, ridding homes of their televisions.

Chuckie and I squatted in the back of the truck, which was stacked to the brim in televisions, boxes and boxes of televisions, as we crept along at exactly the speed limit. Three dozen plus television-sets sat in plastic crates perfectly suitable for a mission like this. I marveled at the planning. These were soldiers after all, I reckoned, prepared for battle.

"You SEE Martin?" Chuckie started with a bellow. "A TV in every Goddamn room! The FAMILY room, the KITCHEN and ALL THREE bedrooms!" His wild sideburns fluttered a long downy mess in the muggy breeze. "Can you imagine the alienation that family must go through!?" He bent down to light a cigarette between thick strawberry lips, grimacing unknowable eyes behind large black sunglasses, and stood back up. "Fuckin'—what a way to spend your life huh, staring at a box of idiots?!"

Chuckie banged on the window of the truck. He informed Sain't Rock and The Pope that it was time to do another dose. He nodded at me as he ate his four hits of acid. I hadn't been down in a day and a half. I pulled out the aluminum foil packet from the breast pocket of my black snap shirt and consumed the flesh of Chuckie The Plague our Lord and flavor.

You can exist in one hour the entirety of your being. You can laugh in concrete spasms of heavenly delight. You can know everything and nothing simultaneously and forget everything instantly. Nothing will give you access to eternity. You are, after all, human.

We lined the large skeletal cube with planks of wood, creating a makeshift bookshelf around the perimeter of the cube—when loaded, the visible four sides of the cube would be television screens. Rock hooked up the electrical plugs of each individual television set into an outlet strip. Each outlet strip was plugged into other outlet strips until he had them all into one, plugged into an extension cord and snaked to the garage where he had many generators.

The TVs were on with the sound off. Rock enslaved them to a universal remote. He turned the volume up. A strange white noise rumbled.

Rock climbed to the top of the strange stage and held the bullhorn to his mouth. "WHAT'S UP MOTHER-FUUCCKEERRRRRSS!!?" He shouted.

A rapturous applause filled the air.

I looked around. Who were all these people? There must've been a hundred and fifty people in attendance. Plaguism was catching on. Or perhaps it was a con all along. Maybe I wasn't one of the original twelve like I'd been told. Maybe the first hundred were told they were of the original twelve. Maybe I was catching paranoia from Rock? Is that shit contagious?

Sain't Rock stood atop the cube of mounted televisions and surveyed the scene. Two hundred plus Plaguists scattered around the dirty yard, drinking, smoking, talking, yelling at him, flipping him off—joyous ruckus of the unbridled spirit. "ORANGES are NOT fruit! They are a conspiracy to rename the COLORS, man!" Plaguists laughed. Rock snarled.

"Beware the MIDDLEMAN! Beware the CAREFUL plan! Beware the EASIEST way! Beware the pricing guns at grocery stores, they are extraterrestrial BAR CODE stampers, and YOU ARE NOT what you eat!" Rock took a mighty gulp from his can of Steel reserve.

I looked around the yard, thirsty as hell, with nothing in my hand, and no one I knew personally in sight. I sauntered to the garage, where I knew of a cooler of beer.

"Beware the bargain! COUPONS are laced with a POISONOUS cocktail of birth control and LAXATIVE! Beware the GROCER! Beware the COOKIE peddler! The Keebler Corporation keeps its elves enslaved in trees, MAN! Those little fucking elves are FORCED to churn out billions of cookies, magically a year! They FEED on chocolate like hummingbirds, man! They're speed freaks! Caffeine and chocolate really jazz up the little bastards and they work with lightning SPEED, MAN!"

Rock guzzled his beer, crushed the can in his hand and threw it out into the audience. He bent down inside the stage and pulled out another can, cracked it and guzzled. Everyone cheered.

He was truly a mad showman—standing on the top of those monkey bars containing three dozen television monitors each blasting a different channel—none of the channels coming in clearly at all, with no cable connection and no antenna, the images were mostly static—but that was the beauty…

Rock showcased a rare moment of clarity: "Some say all religions and mythologies stem from the schizophrenic inner voices we mistook for the supernatural, or from outside our senses. Research suggests homo-sapiens were shocked into intelligence—as evolution works at two speeds you see, SUDDEN BURSTS and *slow stasis!* Fifty-three percent of the planet earth's population identify themselves as Christian, Jew, or Muslim—as descendants of believers in the four-thousand-year-old schizophrenic Abraham's wild hallucinations! I can tell you definitively that MOST of the people on EARTH have it dead wrong about GOD! There's no benevolent murderer, there's no omniscient side chooser, and there are no favorites in nature's game of survival."

Rock switched from philosopher to lunatic.

"Beware the Supersize! The extra cheese! The two-for-one! The value meal! The drive thru! Blessed is he who Charcuteries! Who cultivates, plows, and weeds! THE GOVERNMENT ALLOWS CORPORATIONS to patent SEEDS! Soon it'll be human GENOMES! THEN you'll *TRULY* be *COMPLETELY* OWNED—bought and sold! MONEY *Loves* SLAVES!"

Sain't Rock continued— "Ronald Fucking McDonald is a CHUBBY CHASER and wants to FUCK your MORBIDLY obese cousin 'cause he digs her FAT SMELL and wiggle waddle!"

The crowd cheered.

Hooting and hollering praised him from the ground.

"The molten center of the EARTH is responsible for our GRAVITY, man! They're stealing our GRAVITY! They're building skyscrapers that'll soon disassemble and float into space with the rest of us if we don't stop them and their corrupt fucking ways!"

Putting on a show is the Plaguist way.

"We'll be wobbling out of CONTROL! Our magnetic waves'll be altered! We MUST hold onto our molten center! Keep the nickel in the center! KEEP THE NICKEL IN THE CENTER!"

He went sideways a step and, with a speed and power I didn't think possible, he kicked in a television. It imploded into the cube. He leapt from his tower stage; fifteen feet high. He landed like a soldier, rolled and sprung to his feet. He chanted into the megaphone.

"Keep the nickel in the center! Keep the nickel in the center!" He shouted repeatedly, running around the yard getting in people's faces and screaming. He had had enough of being on the stage. Then one hundred and fifty people began chanting in unison with him— "Keep the nickel in the center!" —An unholy chorus of comedy rang out in the night.

The roses in the distance howled a murderous perfume. The moon winked at me, waxing and waning, disappearing and reappearing full. Stars shot themselves from the sky over and over, a race through space of glittery fire.

The sermon was over, and the televisions blasted in the noisy night. There were a hundred and fifty Plaguists in attendance, mostly in leather jackets, jeans and boots despite the eighty-degree Fahrenheit and seventy percent humidity.

Someone had a pet panther which turned out to be a housecat. One gothic chic had a giant Iguana on her shoulder—another had a pet black and white rat on her shoulder. It stood up on its hind legs and grabbed her raspberry sorbet hair and sniffed the fumes from the dye job and got high...

God approached me and said— "Not every molecule in the universe is jazzed about its existence." But I had no response to that as I was sure then, that he wasn't talking to me. He looked me in the eyes—firecracker green/blue sparklers fizzing and dripping the teary acid high ...

My molecules were, each one of them, jazzed about their existence. I was ecstatic about who I was. I had bluff and confidence, a carnie stink and no stem connecting my fruit to root. I was a rolling stone gathering enough moss, to gather the antheridia to explode.

The Plaguists knew who they were. They were aware of the path they were setting for themselves: dishwashers, truck-drivers, forty-year-old waiters in tablecloth restaurants where service is appreciated, chefs, thieves, murderers, arsonists, political and religious revolutionaries— every one of them: gorgeous souls enlightened about the bullshit rules and standards of society.

"Should we go back to the manor?" I asked, wobbly with warm brain.

"Not yet." Jas lit a cigarette, inhaled, exhaled and then said, "Okay, let's go."

It took us a half an hour to walk sixty feet to The Mystery Ship. We delighted in everything from a muddy rock to a lizard I'm not sure wasn't a twig. We laughed and we laughed and by the time we got to the car, the sun was up, and the day had begun. The rooster was done cock-a-doodle-doodling and strutted around the hen house, cock of the walk.

"Can you drive?"

"I can't believe I'm not asleep."

"Here take this."

"What is it?"

"Well, duh, Martin—it's speed!"

I took the pill, and we sat In the caR for a few mINutEs and I had A rEspIRatoRy attack and felt my hEaRt speed up like a kettle drUm. "I need a beer."

Jas pulled two from his jacket. He cracked me one. I took a long healthy pull from the can. "All right—it'll be a miracle if we get there— but let's see how close we get."

"Now you're talking."

I started up The Mystery Ship and sped off.

10.

War Torn

That night I met Uncle Bill. He occasionally visited his only nephew in the projects and sometimes bought marijuana—his only connection to that world.

Uncle Bill was Jas's mother's brother. He was a Vietnam vet, and I will forever wonder what his chemical balance was like before the war, because after the war he was a trembling wreck, on the verge of suicide and stinky with the paranoid gas of a disheartened and beaten animal. He'd seen tragic and horrific things, Apocalypse Now tragedies that no teenage hillbilly should be drafted to see. Rice and oil—the alpha male's needed for protection of the clan—but man—how far do we have to advance our weaponry? —How tortuous and inhumane do we need to be?

I called him Uncle Bill too—every one of Jas's friends called him Uncle Bill. He had a gray and auburn beard that seemed dried and unmanaged, like his mangy scalp that was hardened with dandruff and unwashed grease. He wore olive green fatigues and a seven-inch hunting knife on his belt—army boots and floppy safari jungle hat. He always looked sad—that worried kind of sad that's been to the edge of the universe and seen one terrible god and turned frightened eternally— damaged soul—war torn soul in a fragile body—soft with blood and knowledgeable of death.

He was divorced, of course. His daughter barely spoke to him. He lived in a tiny cinder block dormitory style room for the mentally disabled, and for veterans of foreign wars. His home smelled of camphor, liquor, cigarettes and cockroaches. I was only over there once and felt bad for declining the chess game invitation. We were (always) in a hurry.

He had a typewriter on a small kitchen table that he typed bad poems on. He listened to the classical radio station, smoked cigars, and drank cheap beer in a state of despair/disrepair that I never wanted to imagine for myself. Anyway, I wrote better poems then at that age—then again— maybe he did too, when he was nineteen.

The lights were fluorescent, and I didn't know why he didn't own a lamp instead. Perhaps he did. Perhaps he was a man who had night terrors and trashed his environment upon waking. Perhaps he was a destroyer of lamps and couldn't find one to withstand his three-a.m. assault.

Tchaikovsky was his favorite. He liked the Russians and The Austrians—the big boys of what he called Classical Heavy Metal— Wagner—flying Viking raids for the honor of Valhalla, wolves chasing the sun and the moon—dragon slayers, magical amulets and supernatural beings of awe and wonder. (I had that and then some.) We listened to all my classical cassette tapes—the operas of Bach, the symphonies of Beethoven, the clarinet compositions of von Weber—the works of Mussorgsky, Prokofiev (esp. The *Fiery Angel* which is also an amazing book) and Sibelius.

Chess was another favorite pastime of his, a fact that allowed us to spend more time together. Every two- or three-weeks Uncle Bill would stop over to buy weed from Jas and play me in chess, requesting that I play some Heavy Metal (classical) recording.

One night we got shit roaring drunk and stoned, or well anyway Uncle Bill did. We warned him that the weed we had was extra strong and to go easy on it, but he was in a particularly randy mood, especially after I beat him three games to none—the best of three becoming the best of five and then me not wanting to play at least four more games. People had come and gone through the S.P.A.M. Manor porthole that night and I'd barely gotten a chance to say hi to any of them, too locked into the black and white checkered battlefield.

Uncle Bill didn't listen to us and got apple pie high in the sky. I didn't remember how we verbally got to where we were exactly—I remembered vividly the snot and sputum and bubbling saliva issuing forth from his facial openings as he cried and wailed and begged us never to go to war.

I must admit I was taken back a bit by the hysteria and the general weirdness of the moment, but I've been around crazy my whole life, and had seen much worse. He hugged us. He made us join hands and pray to

Chuckie, a point that was not lost on me. Was he respecting Jas's beliefs or was he that much of a Plaguist? (I was later informed that he was a Plaguist fundamentalist—someone who knows deep in their hearts that absurdity is the whole of the law and therefore has no problem ACTUALLY praying to Chuckie.) I had nowhere to go or be, so I decided to ride the crazy train all the way to the station.

"…AND I HATE YOUR GRANDFATHER FOR THAT HORRIBLE THING HE DID TO YOU!" —More tears—more liquid mucous discharge—more shaking and wailing. "You know if you were _MY_ son I would've killed him. I can't believe your father did nothing! I'm so sorry, Jay!"
It was odd hearing Jas called Jay. Uncle Bill was the only one who ever did—even his mom, dad and sister called him Jas, and yes, I met all of them, too.

Jas told me the whole story—apparently at the age of five, he sat down on his grandfather's Santa Clause-costumed lap and found his first Yule Log. His grandfather instructed him to remove the erection from his trousers and to put it in his mouth. Jas was informed that this was the way to truly get what one wants for Christmas, and to be sure to swallow the savory goo—that's how you knew the wish would come true—unless you told anyone—then you may never get what you want for Christmas.

The ugly part of the story, besides its truth, was that Jas's grandfather actually got young five-year-old Jas what he wanted for Christmas—and then again, the next year—and the next year Jas told his younger sister how to get what she wanted for Christmas as she'd been told that no way in hell was she getting a pony. Jas loved his sister and wouldn't have minded at all if there was a pony in the backyard. She didn't believe him, and so asked her horrified mother. Jas lied when asked and was watched like a hawk. His Scorpio mother followed him everywhere, and when her father-in-law refused to open the door, she kicked it in. Of course, Jas wasn't traumatized until a couple of years later—when it occurred to him what had taken place. It's amazing how liberating sexual trauma can be— also how isolating.

One of Jas's more famous poems around Nashville in the beginning was his Santagram which he wrote about—driving to New York wearing fishnets, black leather jacket, army boots and little else, parking wherever and finding the Macy's Thanksgiving Day Parade. The idea was to mingle with the crowd in a non-suspicious full length raincoat, and then, right when Santa's float was at its peak television time, run up to the float, undress, and hop aboard the Christmas float, remove a pistol from his jacket and put a slug right through Santa Claus's melon—red plum sauce leaking from the gunshot, staining the fake white beard—the screams of greedy little children, confused cameramen and then either suicide or gunfight with the police. He was undecided on that. I always championed gunfight—because suicide was too easy, and way less dramatic. Anyway, that was a pre 9/11 world, and besides that, I doubted he could have gotten through security even then.

That was how I learned about Jas's traumatic past—though he often made sly remarks about molestation and sucking his grandfather's dick— it was always hard to tell with him—HOW much of the story was exaggeration and how much was terrible truth.

Pity for him? None. Nor would he want any. Jas was a man of his own making, he'd say—and I'd agree.

We finally convinced Uncle Bill to calm down and drink enough beer to come down from his weed high and be able to drive home, which he did after another calmer hour. He was a fiasco of a man, barely wobbling on unstable legs—but an openly loving and generous man.

He probably would've been a big success with the women if he was a little more selfish and knew how to prey on those overly motherly childless liberals who have yet to find a human to let her nurse them to the grave. The important thing about being crazy was you got to know HOW to be crazy. It's why homeless men can't steal their way to the top, because they don't know how to be crazy. What was that? Ego?

11.

Sacred Cow Tipping

After another lunch shift at another bumpkin-fried trough, I decided to take a shower and maybe a nap at S.P.A.M. Manor. I had my own set of keys, so I didn't even knock anymore—I went right on in.

A naked boy lay face down on Jas's bed. The body was pale, unmoving, seemingly lifeless, flat on his face, arms unresponsive. The round ass was beautiful and pointed up in the air. I shut the door behind me at Rock's barking. "SHUT THE FUCKING DOOR!!!"

Jas looked nervous on the red sofa, smoking and not talking.

"You got somewhere else you need to be?" Rock was terrifying in his stare me down.

"I can come back tomorrow."

Jas didn't look up at me. Rock snarled and nodded his head a single time for my exit.

I shut the door behind me. Warm spring air warned me to stay away from the area for twenty-four hours. I had nowhere to go. Should I get back on the road? Head west? North? Was that a dead body? It felt chilly. I got in The Mystery Ship quickly and she started on the first go—which was always a miracle. Should I visit Ready? Lingus was playing in Knoxville and gone for the weekend. Fuck.

Nashville had her magnetic talons in me, piercing the skin, gripping the bone, keeping me here (there)—I didn't want to be anywhere (else). I got in my car and drove away—toward the city—no Emerald City—no New York City—but tall with banks and communications offices—

square yellow office-lights kept on by the cleaning crew and the overachievers.

I didn't care if that was a corpse, I wouldn't tell on The Pope. I was never there—Well, I was there—but I never saw a body. I would lie to a judge and jury—'cause I cared about him—and I didn't care about the corpse—if that was a corpse, or the corpse's family.

How did the killing occur, if anything occurred? Did Jas strangle the boy with a pastel chiffon blouse hardly worn anymore? —Choke the life right out of the confused teen bug-chaser with his bare hands, angry at a god that still won't listen when warned?

Did he poison him with strychnine tea? Too many Percocets? Was the boy's death recreational? Accidental? Homicidal?

I didn't care.

Was Rock wearing an apron and latex gloves for butchering purposes? Was the kid about to be hamburger meat? Didn't know or care.

There was nowhere for me to be. I had five hits of acid from the day's leftover inventory so I ate them and decided to drive around downtown and see what I could see.

Too high to drive, I walked around the city. I said hello to several people who seemed to recognize me—downtown Plaguists—one engaged me in conversation about the Pope. I laughed and answered in unintelligible surreality.

"Cool. Cool. Yeah, see you later." The disappointed freak figured I was stoned, or asshole, or both and split my scene clean, leaving just me.

"Synchronized moments lead us to believe we are purposeful in our conduct but that does not account for the barometric pressure of our desires." I'm sure I thought it meant something. I didn't care. The frivolity of existence is proved in the living. The illusion is real. Exercise life.

The temperature was warm. I felt fine, feral, and fecund—free, frolicsome, fucking fantastic. I was lost to the walking, all the neon lights bending, warping, blending—warbling in teary eyed unfocused hallucinations. I wasn't going anywhere—I was exercising the mind and body, the heart and soul—contemplation while observing the world through altered senses.

Self-mutating the grand design was a fun sport.

I walked for a while, staggered, swayed, I wandered around downtown Nashville aimlessly trying to understand humanity. What every lonely nineteen-year-old should do with a head full of acid and nowhere to be. Where was I?

This again.

This belligerent bent on self-seduction, where can I stumble adored? What doors could I knock? And have unlocked? What strings could I pull, that sing? What abyss could I wink at?

Hours later I found my car. The streets were empty. I drove around aimlessly, occasionally catching myself sitting at a red light only to watch it turn from green to yellow to red over and over a few times, before driving on. Or was it the acid? Difficult opossum with gumdrop bottom… That piranha kind gubernatorial of succulent drug.

I parked in a lot and wandered around town with a backpack full of spray paint and an aim to spread the good word of Chuckie The Plague. I spray painted *God Will Eat Your Brain* all over Nashville—on brick walls, on sidewalks, on asphalt, on lamp posts—I had several different nozzle tips for size and penmanship.

Gigantic four-foot letters on a bridge—*God Will Eat Your Brain*—tiny three-inch letters on a fire hydrant—six-inch cursive letters on steps—up and down the whole city—leading to churches, court houses and condominiums. *God Will Eat Your Brain* spelled mostly correctly forty-seven times in two hours.

Four hours later my fingertips were jet black. If I got stopped: guilty. I decided to go back to my car and drive thirty-five mph to the other end of town. The sun was coming up. I guess I'd successfully killed a few hours and wondered briefly how The Pope was doing. Fuck him. He needed his peace and quiet—whatever his situation.

Twenty-four-hour refuge? Waffle House. Black coffee I could afford and a booth in the back with my books open. The waitresses were sympathetic to the student when the place was empty—but get your ass out of the money-making booth when the place gets busy.

"More coffee, hon?"

"You know it, mama." Playful was always better than polite.

Looking around the interior of the Waffle House at six in the morning is to gaze at the underbelly of a beached demon shark, silver pale flesh of trucker arms from cut off flannel shirts. Insomniacs sip coffee and stare with raspberry eyes at the pecan pies, hash browns, and cups of orange juice as herpetic waitresses chomping gum ask them, "That be all, hon?"

Sad nods from trucker hats with mesh backs and patches on front with words like LIBERTY… Keep the change, take a toothpick, walk tiredly out the door and into an unforgiving dawn of pink, two thousand miles in sixty hours, thirty cups of coffee and a forty-dollar blowjob, ephedrine, caffeine and nicotine, ex-football dreams, bloated ex-cheerleaders, debt cheaters and free-loaders—hordes of bad social decisions.

I fell into the sanctuary of my words. I scribbled in my notebook as if I was writing a major thesis. Not one nothing resembling cohesive structure: —*cranberry dishwashers were spinning disco music in peanut butter brains of apes trying to escape their cholesterol.*

The big sweaty chef came over to me after peaking over my shoulder at my composition book. His voice was deep and bottomless. "Excuse me." He was enormous, three hundred pounds—each sweaty Elvis sideburn heavy enough to cover a young cancer boy's bald head. His name was Hank and he asked me if I knew how to write poetry.

"Yes, I do."

"Well, tell you what—you write me—say—LIKE—two or three love poems to my girlfriend—you know—from me—don't be too fuckin fancy or nuttin." He laughed and snorted at me, as if I was supposed to gauge his intelligence upon our first meeting— (In fact he was quite insightful. I knew right away to use third grade grammar.) He continued— "Well, shit—if I think they're any good—your next meal's on me. Of course, you can have whatever you like this morning—if you write me somethin' for my girl. Her name's Charlene."

I agreed. I wrote poems to his girlfriend Charlene—and for the effort I had two scrambled eggs with cheese, hashbrowns with onions and cheese, raisin toast, apple butter and sugar with my grits.

I hadn't been that full in a year.

He took care of my bill right on the spot.

It seemed my luck had changed. I was a working poet. I had found a way to earn actual money from my work— (free food is currency when you have no cash). Needless to say, I went to Waffle House about forty more times during my stay in Nashville and got more than half those meals for free. That big sweaty Elvis cook took care of me every time he was working. He explained in graphic detail the nasty sexual things Charlene rewarded him with poem after poem.

The Mystery Ship started right up—always a good feeling as sometimes there was no gas, or luck in the starter. I drove around early morning Nashville and pondered the Country Music Mecca and the insane inner workings of The First Interplanetary Church of The Immaculate Deception.

I couldn't stop thinking about the naked boy on Jas's bed—was he dead? Was Jas a murderer? Was this a ritual for the Church? For the Pope? Was Rock there to dispose of the body? Could that have been me?

Could it still? The challenge didn't scare me—what a fantastic way to go—sexually murdered in the poetic slums of Nashville.

That corpse had a great ass. I wondered if Jas fucked the dead boy. Did the boy die with Jas's cock in him? Could The Pope feel the body temperature gradually lowering on his cock? Was he ever in danger of losing his penis to rigor mortis? Had Rock ever had to saw him out of a young man before—the Jaws of Life chopping the dead pelvis into pieces, so Jas could remove his swollen and sphincter-clamped upon hard-on? Was Jas an expert now? Did he know exactly what temperature to ejaculate before final stiffness? I hoped there would be no smell when I arrived back at S.P.A.M. Manor. How could you not be proud to die at a place called S.P.A.M. Manor? Of course, you'll be written about—whoever you are.

I finished reading Henry Miller's *Time of The Assassins* and watched the sunset on my third day up in a row. My brain could stand no more information. I needed sleep. I got on Interstate 40 and got off at The Dickson Rest Area. I knew I could get two legal hours and maybe four to six if I got lucky.

I got five. Energized, I drove back to the Waffle House. Sweaty Elvis wasn't there. I ordered only coffee.

I drove to Lingus House to see if Pookie was there. Ready entertained me briefly, scowled at me, scoffed my appearance, then took mercy. "Would you like a shower and a nap?" I almost wept with joy at the offer.

She didn't join me in the shower like I imagined, but the water was hot, and the soap was feminine fragrant, the shower itself was clean, there was light to see the body. She didn't join me in the bed, or anyway for the minute it took me to totally pass out.

It was the next morning when I awoke. Ready wasn't in her bed. I wondered what bed she was in, then realized maybe it wasn't my business.

What was I doing? Was this a love interest? Was this just fantastic sex and whatever I had to do or say to keep it going as fantastic sex? Am I a manipulator? I knew love wasn't on the table. Did I admit that? Is that an important part of the deal? "Look, you're sexy as fuck and I want to taste you and smell you and conquer you and be inside you and explode all over you, but I might disappear forever next month, so let's understand the future is mine alone." —Was it best to be a lyricist and either rap or sing about your intentions and diamond core ego?

Jas wasn't home when I arrived back at the Manor. It had been three days since I saw that body, still fresh in my mind, but being autopsied and erased as I lit some candles and sniffed around. There was no smell of corpse, though I had to sniff twice to be sure, because we were wild and dirty animals. Perhaps I'd imagined the scenario. For sure I would never ask about it. I would never ask what went on that night and whatever happened to whoever that was. Some moments disappeared from the record if you let them. History was written by the winners. Better parties were thrown by sinners. We were all beginners. I shoved my face into the ass sweat of the couch and went to sleep.

Late afternoon was my morning. I was surprisingly lucid.

Did I care that Jas might be a homicidal maniac? No. The greater the man, the darker the depths the soul must plunge to resurrect itself. I had no illusions about right and wrong on the planet earth. At seventy miles an hour, cheetah claws Achilles heel of gazelle, fangs find throat in the dust, and suffocates the life of the pursued for nourishment of the body—whiskers feeling the pulse slow and die in the subcutaneous throat. What if man needed to do that to nourish his soul?

What if serial killers behaved without guilt and their exploits were celebrated? —Say they were free to express their dark spirit to the world in truly fantastic ways—and the truth of God was revealed a little more.

Embracing the illusion of life was walking through fire unburned, a hundred prostitutes' eyes carved from their living skulls and sewn to your gown.

Maybe I was a sick freak and I had found a gang of sick freaks to belong to. I laughed out loud. What if that was the best you could do in life—belong to a group?

One of my favorite movies as a child was Lone Wolf McQuade— starring Chuck Norris as the Ranger who works alone and hates his partner—and of course, he has a fucking pet wolf and drinks beer from a can and doesn't take shit from anybody, not even kung fu himself, David Carradine— (who died years ago of autoerotic asphyxiation) —And in this one scene they buried him in his truck and he's beaten and worn and drinking a beer and then he finds a secret gear in his truck the bad guys don't know about and a nitrous tank shoots out blue flames and he drives his bad ass truck out of the fucking ground. Since I was eight years old, I've always been a Lone Wolf. Nobody's badder than Chuck Norris. The other day, I saw a pair of nunchucks made of hard plastic: two Chuck Norrises in nun drag as the hard weapon.

Pop culture gives me hemorrhoids.

I turned off the television and lit the bong.

Time to go out and look for a job.

12.

Isalma-dama-ding-dongs

Plaguism truly was designed to be a church for all—hell, if you believed any of this shit, then you're more than welcome to join our absurd crusade. The more the merrier—strength in numbers: let's make a complex system!

There were Jewish Plaguists that had given up the commandments of Moses for the suggestions of Chuckie and made jokes about the acid being kosher because it was blessed by the lord himself. There were Christian Plaguists who denounced their submission to man's interpretation of god and started partying with god embodied—Chuckie The Plague. (The 'The' is capitalized because it is short for his middle name, Theodore.)

Nashville was quite cosmopolitan. There were Plaguist Sikhs who shaved their heads in protest of man's interpretation of what God wanted us to do with our human appearance. In fact, Balkar opened one of the first tattoo/piercing joints in the world owned by a Sikh and gave free tattoos to lots of my friends. I didn't get a tattoo then. Rat-a-Tattoo was the coolest tattoo parlor in town.

It seemed one thing that attracted people to Plaguism was the fun it made of religion. Chuckie was hilarious and knew how to spin the belief system of any of the major religions and could even make fun of Jah, which was what converted Peter from Rastafarianism to Plaguism. I and I is I am that I am.

No one was excluded. Everyone was a Plaguist—even the Hindus who believed we were Hindus—we believed they were Plaguists.

Plaguists were born, not made. You came to us—the mountain didn't go to Mohammed, and yes, we had a few Muslims who had converted to Plaguism. We gave them their ass as direction to pray to five times a day as they seemed reluctant to drop the routine and seemed also quite comfortable in that position. Chuckie laughed and laughed as Jas suggested it to Ahmed and Mohammed.

(Note: How strange is it, that in Islam it's strictly forbidden to blaspheme the holy name of Mohammed, show any image of him so-ever—yet every third Arab boy is named something-something Mohammed something?)

Ahmed Rafiq and Mohammed Tanvir worked as Busboys at Chagrin's. They were both Bangladeshi and Muslim. Mohammed was twenty and his uncle Ahmed was twenty-four. Ahmed was clean-shaven—but Mohammed was attempting to grow a full clerical beard, but it was wispy and showed his youth.

Apparently, the boys had given Jas a ride home from a particularly profitable lunch shift. I had the day off since I'd quit and was on the sofa reading *God Bless You Mr. Rosewater,* by Kurt Vonnegut and listening to *Loveless* by My Bloody Valentine, because I am I and I.

The daylight was blinding but Jas soon shut the door and the darkness resumed.

"Beer?" Jas asked the boys.

"We do not drink," Ahmed answered for him and his nephew.

"Good Muslims, I see," Jas retorted.

"Yes. Obedient to the law."

"The Sharia law?" I asked.

"Yes."

"The far right believes radical Islamists are attempting to undermine the United States with their radical Sharia law," I fished.

Ahmed bit— "Yes, they are very ignorant. They believe we want to whip the drinkers and the gamblers—beat women openly in the streets, practice Polygamy, and all sorts of crazy nonsense that's simply not true."

"What is true?" I asked.

"We believe in the purification of the body and the soul—we abstain from as many vices as possible—drugs and alcohol—prostitution, gambling, and eating pork. We pray five times a day toward Mecca—where we will one day make a holy pilgrimage—and during the month of Ramadan we fast during the daylight hours."

"Sounds like your religion demands a lot," I suggested.

"But it offers a lot," Mohammed spoke up.

"Like what?" Jas was curious.

"Freedom from sin—peace of mind—healthy living." Mohammed smiled, dangerously sexy.

"Well, OUR god offers a lot as well—like gas money—free beer and chili on Tuesdays—proof that the world's absurd—and as many menthol cigarettes as one can stand to smoke!" Jas proclaimed.

"You have a god that does all of this?" Mohammed asked.

"Why yes! He's the dishwasher at The Quicksilver—Chuckie Theodore Plague! God!"

"And what proof do you have that this man is a deity?" Ahmed demanded.

"The same that you have of your god being legit," Jas quipped.

"May I have a cigarette?" Mohammed sheepishly asked. He'd grown nervous in the company of this wild man and his strange friend.

"Of course!" Jas sang, handing him one.

Mohammed took the light from him as well, ignoring the peripheral scolding he received from his uncle.

Ahmed was more curious, however, of the religious undertones and knowledge of his host. "You belong to a cult?"

"Well! Technically I AM a cult unto myself—and technically I'm a cult leader—but no—I DON'T *BELONG* to *ANYTHING*." Jas laughed.

"That's very confusing," Ahmed protested.

"Well, everything is until you understand it," Jas toyed with the boys.

"How is one to understand a law based entirely on absurdity?" Ahmed asked wisely.

"Exactly," Jas congratulated him. "Want to join?"

"I am devout," Ahmed declared.

"Well, so am I!" Jas stated. "Only my religion doesn't have any DAWG-MUH!" He laughed; a hissing tongue stuck out to the piercing.

"Then what's the point?" Mohammed asked.

"Well, like you—freedom! I've inoculated myself from the effects of sin by partaking in activities in life that are deemed sinful by a partisan congress. My free will's unencumbered by puppet-strings, ungoverned by rule or regulation—I am anti-society and the most popular belle at the ball."

"It doesn't sound like you plan on a long life," Ahmed mourned.

"Well—why live tomorrow if you're not gonna live today?!" Jas replied as if it was the simplest truth of all time and completely indisputable. He located the bong. "Bong rip, anyone?"

"Definitely," I didn't even need to say.

Ahmed protested the drug use. "I'm feeling very uncomfortable and would like to leave."

Jas blew a huge jet stream of smoke toward the boys. He coughed and coughed and had a mini-fit, face reddening, fist covering mouth dripping saliva and shivering as I pried the bong from his death-grip coughing, coughing...

"I would like to stay." Mohammed took a stand.

Ahmed insisted. "You are my ride home, Mohammed, and I would like to leave."

Blowing out a large stream of smoke, I coughed once and lit a cigarette fast to offset the tender lung feeling. "I can give you a ride home."

"That's not a reasonable request."

"Man, it's no big deal. Where do you live?" I passed the bong back to Jas. "I've got to run a few errands anyway—you know, go to the bank—buy and sell some drugs—see a girl about a blowjob and all sorts of shit you guys aren't supposed to do, maybe eat some bacon."

Jas cackled.

"I cannot accept," Ahmed properly declined.

Turning on the charm, I smiled. "Look man, it was a joke. I have a few things I got to do all over the city—tell me where you live. I can drive you anywhere."

I drove Ahmed home, got lost, decided to drive around until I saw the tall buildings downtown and drove toward them. I decided to pay Chuckie a visit at The Quicksilver. The place was packed with groupies, like always. It was impossible to get a table or a seat, so I slid into the back and found my way to the sink, where Chuckie washed dishes.

Chuckie was in a special place, high on acid and lucid with the universe, fluid and perverse and talking a mile a minute, sometimes in verse. "I have faith in TORQUE! I have faith in the FLAVOR of a TEASPOON of SALT! —I have faith in the COMBUSTIBILITY of *gasoline!* —I have faith in GRAVITY, sunburn, heartbreak, LOVE, the frying temperature of a *corndog*, the *towing power* of an F-150 Ford Pickup, and the CORROSIVE element in CONGRESS!"

"How do we fix the Democratic system?" I asked.

"Make. *Lobbying.* ILLEGAL! —Term limits of TWO for ANY government official elected By THE PEOPLE should be mandatory. If you draw a lifetime pension, it has to be your ONLY source of income, or you forfeit it and that yearly wage should never exceed MINIMUM WAGE. There should be no incentive for your job more than the LOVE OF IT!"

He had such Motorola rockabilly oil keeping his pistons lubed, that his aura oozed out of him like summer butter. He sweated profusely and seemed tense, clenching his teeth and flexing his muscles in acid shivers.

"Self-brainwashing?" I suggested.

Suddenly calm and cool like he wasn't shuffling two decks of quantum entangled tarot cards. "It's important to shuffle the filing system of your mind every once in a while, —lest ye forget that ye are but a simple organism in a complex universe."

"Mind if I have another beer?" I asked, lighting a cigarette.

"You know where the fucking TAP is! Have as much as you *like*." This was the generous and biting tone of Chuckie Theodore Plague.

"You should know I was born with a powerful thirst," I had to admit.

"Well, quench it motherfucker!"

I did indeed. I drank and we (he) talked about Plaguism. I asked him about the pineal gland.

"It's the fucking third EYE man! The pineal gland produces MELA-TONIN which regulates your *circadian* rhythms—so like—fuckin'—when you fuck with your twenty-four-hour cycle with DRUGS and *shit*—or fuckin'—SLEEP DEPRIVATION or whatever! THEN you experience the DIRECT link to *me*—every acid trip that one of you naughty monkeys take is a phone call to me man!"

"Are you trying to save humanity with this message?" I asked sardonically.

"Humanity simply refuses to mature. The Politicians are criminals and egocentric divas with no interest in truly serving the public—and fuckin'—the public's an obese apathetic *moron* that prefers to watch stock car racing than taking to the streets and racing themselves!" Chuckie hit his cigarette hard and stubbed his butt out in the tray.

"Rednecks making two thousand left turns," I joked.

"YEAH! I'll tell ya Mar, fuckin', every FORM of government can only go SO FAR before it gets *revolted* on—you know what I'm sayin'? —It's like—fuckin'—even this country was founded on principals of REVOLUTION—and I'll tell you something—the founding fathers believed we should have a revolution every couple of centuries or so. It's meant to make sure the POWERS THAT BE don't become too *corrupt*."

Chuckie had a thing about the founding fathers, the principles of Democracy, the revolutionaries who defeated the royal crown and established their independence with military, cunning, and expert geniuses to draft their declaration.

"Do you think we'll ever see a real revolution?" I asked him.

"See one? Shit! If I don't see one by the time I'm fifty, I might have to START one!" Chuckie lit a cigarette. "THESE assholes can't even recognize when they're fucking PARTY'S BEEN HIJACKED by fascist corporations' man!" Chuckie finally hit the cigarette—but it was out—so he took the time to light a new one.

"Where's the fuckin' Pope anyway?!" Chuckie blared.

"Giving some Muslim kid the Korantidote."

"Well, bless his little heart. You know what I don't understand about—fuckin'—ABSOLUTE religions Martin?" Cigarette suck.

"What's that?"

"Fuckin'—leaves no room for the future! —How the hell can DEVOUT Muslims be astronauts, man?! How the hell are they supposed to say prayer five times a day when your fuckin'—*circumnavigating* the globe every NINETY minutes? From what I understand, Salat lasts about six minutes—which means a THIRD of your time is spent PRAYING—never-fucking-mind—how do you prostrate yourself in ZERO GRAVITY! How in the hell are they supposed to point their *blessed* little heads towards Mecca from SPACE?!"

He had me in stitches—enlightenment in laughter. The world moved slower, and I moved faster.

"Religion should not BIND you to a PLANET! —Fuckin'—as far as I can tell—Plaguism's the ONLY true path to salvation." What a smirk Chuckie gave.

"The only?" I asked.

"Well, the only one I'm pitching!!" Chucky roared with laughter "Anyway—who the fuck *REALLY* needs salvation? What does anyone want to be saved from? Life? Death'll do that. That's your job—to prepare the Plaguists for Death, Angel. Hell! Maybe you oughta write a Plaguist Book of the Dead."

Chuckie stared into space again. I stole one of his cigarettes. I had my own, but I was pinching pennies. Fucking menthols.

I finished my sixth and poured my seventh and played Alien Sex Fiend on the free jukebox that Chuckie had fixed and all the Plaguists knew about.

"Fuck it! Let's get fucked up and do fucked up shit! Let's mutate the truth until it SUITS us—excite the pituitary gland to *excrete* as much of the juice as we can handle and then a little bit more." He laughed and hacked. He lit a cigarette and calmed down.

"When will we know when we've had enough?" I asked, playing the straight man.

"When they find our corpse." Chuckie smiled at me.

13.

Sermon on the Fiery Plane

Meanwhile, back at S.P.A.M. Manor, His Assholiness Pope Jas tried on outfits and needed my advice. I rested on the sofa, head on one arm rest, feet dangling beyond the other arm rest, cigarette, beer and James Dean cool.

"You look like a fool," I said.

He stormed off. He looked great, but I knew the blue boa to be a mistake, flammable, and easily tripped on. I wasn't trying to be his mom or anything—I could see his outfit spelled disaster. He was too skinny for a wife-beater—he was borderline emaciated, Christ-like in his rib-show. He looked good in black leather jacket and no shirt.

"Much better."

"Huh?! What do you think?" His jeans were ripped and shredded and tucked into purple leather Doc Martins. He even twirled, a little like Michael Jackson, like a gay Nazi soul singer. He stood on his toes, wobbled, and then almost fell over. He loved the joke. I wasn't prepared to catch him. He caught himself. "You're about to see something tonight, baby!"

I pulled up the long gravel driveway and there were already twenty or thirty cars there. My inclination was to not be blocked in, so I pulled into the grass and drove around the cars to get away from the possible block in. There was no way to avoid the soupy mess.

At last! I found a break in the rows of cars and made a run for it. The problem was that the run was up a muddy dirt hill and no matter how I gunned the gas and dug the tires into the mud—I perpetually slid back down the small embankment. Finally, I was stuck. I couldn't move the vehicle in any direction. "Here we are!" I turned off the engine and clapped my hands.

Jas laughed and lit a joint and stumbled out of the car in high Plaguist fashion. I did the same, but it didn't matter. It was his night. He was the lone star this evening.

We were there to celebrate some sort of Plaguist holiday. I forgott which because there were so many and none of them had specific dates—well, a few did, like Unhallowed Noon which occured on the second to the last Thursday of the month before the first full moon after the vernal equinox, and complicated as hell to remember, and therefore seldom celebrated. Anyway, our reason for being at Plague Central that night was an entirely different reason. Jas was to perform a Holy Sermon.

Jas wandered off. I found a beer and then like a moth found the fire pit. Chuckie and Rock constructed a cinder block rectangle around a small but growing fire.

"What's up motherfuckers?" I asked, probably sounding a bit too much like Chuckie, emulating him as I would a new role model for my behavior soup, the broth of which I was making—letting things stew, letting the recipe brew.

"DID YOU BRING ME A FUCKING COOKIE?!" Rock screamed at me.

"No, Rock. I'm not the cookie monster—and if I was, then I'd be eating all the cookies."

"APPARENTLY YOU HAVE NOT HEARD THE *SHARING SONG* BY THE COOKIE MONSTER!!" Rock screamed again. His face was twisted with spasm and moist with sweat. He was gacked out of his mind. He was amusement ride malfunction. He was spark and twist and zip out of control.

"Should I come back?" I asked.

Chuckie instructed me. "Bullshit! Grab a few of 'ese cinder blocks and start stackin'!"

"You're building the stage around a fire?"

"Well, duh! It's the goddamn SERMON on the FIERY PLANE! He's got to give it on a stage set aflame." Chuckie spoke fast and fierce.

There was no hole in his logic. I saw why he nominated himself God. I picked up two cinder blocks and helped the team. Back and forth, like hammer and sickle. I drifted away in thought while performing this task.

(Note: I remembered building forts out of cinderblocks when I was a kid, a tween, a lean, mean twelve-year-old hunter and destroyer of the enemy's forts. I built strong muscles carrying those cinder blocks from the late-night construction site to the deep of the woods.

My friends and I stole bags of cement and mixed buckets full of water from the stream, deep in the woods behind my grandparent's house. We made a simple c-shaped design. The structure was impossible to destroy. We caked mud all over it—put a tin roof on it, pilfered from behind old man Johnson's house. We covered the roof in sticks and mud. We felled trees and put them in front of our fort as if they'd fallen by design. It was laborious work and took us the whole summer—but when it was complete, it was the perfect place to run away from home to—to hang out in the rain and snow.

The clubhouse represented freedom from authority. It was a prepubescent libertine experience. I found old Penthouses magazines and Hustler magazines down by the dump. I smuggled these to my secret fort and taught myself how to masturbate. I unbuckled my trousers and shoved my hard cock into the mossy ground. It was cold and damp, but it gave way, and I imagined steam coming from the dark soil as the heat from my youthful erection excited the elements and energized the planets. Young cum flung. I fucked Mother Earth, and she loved it.)

Back at Plague Central, I laughed to myself as I grabbed the last cinder block and put it into place. Ours was a temporary structure, no cement.

Rock grabbed a large 4x8ft sheet of one inch plywood, birch, fire treated. He placed it onto our 4f tall cinderblock platform. There were three and a half feet on either end of the stage where the fire could breathe and burn away the fire retardant and really latch onto the wood.

Flames spurted out of both sides of the platform dramatically.

"Well, what do we have here?" Jas at last pranced to our accomplishment.

"YOUR STAGE!" Rock snarled and ground his teeth.

Jas cackled and almost threw his neck out as he jerked back in surprised pleasure. "Well," he southern belled in marshmallow whisper. "Do I at least get a microphone?"

Chuckie handed Jas a cheap bullhorn.

Jas cackled again… On high, never die, live forever, all trees are Jesus…

He held the bullhorn like it was a .45 and he had the papal bull in his sights. There would be meat on the table tonight, and horns to drink the wine from, wail the song from.

He jumped up on the stage from a weak running leap that almost busted his knee, but grace was not always judged on form. He guzzled from his 40-ounce Colt45 and sounded the alarm on the bullhorn. EEEEEEEEEEEEEEEEEEEE!!! The siren rang out deafening in the bat dung night.

Plaguists cheered. The noise caught me off guard. There were over three hundred and fifty people in attendance. I looked around the yard and recognized a couple dozen or so faces, the rest were new to me, Plaguists and Plaguelings with young alert faces eager for something different to happen—anything.

Jas took another fast swig and then spoke— "I am His Assholiness POPE JAS the First, Last, ALWAYS, MAYBE, and NEVER of The First Interplanetary Church of the Immaculate Deception!"

There was thunderous applause from the loud maniacs littering the yard.

Jas boomed into the megaphone: "Amen! Hail Chuckie!" He drank from his beer. "All Plaguists live in a state of *disgrace*! And—there's NOTHING more *disgraceful* than PRIDE! So be *proud* of your *disgrace*! Be *proud* of your *shame*! Mostly be proud of MY DICK—that I hope EVERY one of you shall soon *SUCK*!"

He let the bullhorn fall to his side as he raised his beer bottle to the crowd in salute, then guzzled the content.

"Now I'll share with you—The Parable of the Rapable:

"BLESSED is he who allows the kingdom *cum* into his earthly body for the *pleasure* of the *other*. Blessed is he who SUCKS the Pope's *dick* and believes in his fallibility. BLESSED is he who finds the secret heated spot on the Sain't and strokes the throbbing place. Blessed is he who WELCOMES the *orgasm* into the world. Blessed is he who has MOUTH to *suck* and THROAT to *massage*, SALIVA to *lubricate* and *hands to assist*. Blessed is he who *spreads* the other cheek!"

Plaguists hollered and cheered and threw empty beer cans at the stage, all of which missed Jas.

"Blessed is he who gets sticky knees in dank places—who unzips and slides down behind the driver's seat. Blessed is he who tickles and teases—who pauses and pleases the no need to rush. Blessed is he who Blushes for the kingdom of Chuckie is a place of nerves and warmth."

"WWOOOOOOOOOOOOO!" Screamed some turned-on Plaguist.

"Woe to you who refuse the sexual advance. Woe to you who aren't laughing now—because soon you won't be able to! Woe to those who heed the sermon, for theirs is the con of another man!"

More applesauce applause.

"Our sentiment is Discordian! There is no aim! There is no Dogma! There is no God, and his name is Chuckie the Plague!"

"Hail Chuckie!" Twenty or thirty Plaguist yelled simultaneously.

I observed Jas as an audience member. I did not have what he had. He had star power in his starboard motor and willing prance in his port motor and man, did he hum, did he really take off. He became a character of his own invention: himself.

THAT was the holy act: becoming what you have willed to be, forming from your inherited mass/mess, with tools of your environment, a rare and perfect being: an individual.

"Consume yourself with flame, lose yourself to passion. Go FUCK yourself!" He screamed to the mad midnight masses.

More applause. Butter whore molasses.

Jas beamed at the effect his amplified voice had on the particles in the air. He continued into the bullhorn. "Article of Faith number nine! — Before fooling others, we must first learn to fool ourselves!"

The crowd went nuts as if they couldn't wait to be fooled, tricked into living, tempted to take the first step to their own personal eternity, seeking not reward but reality, not reality but reward… Jas continued. "I wouldn't be here tonight fooling you people—if I hadn't been suckered into this religion by my own *manipulative* willingness for being SUCKERED!" He let out a tremendous cackle that woke dogs and roosters all over the county.

"All drugs are HOLY! We consider ALL mind-altering substances SACRAMENTS! They fuck you up, man! Anything that marinates the brain is fucking HOLY as far as Chuckie is concerned—'cause as we all know—GOD WILL EAT YOUR BRAIN!"

Slaughter the cause with more applause.

The fire rose up the sides of the stage, higher and higher, brighter and brighter, orange tongues licking the air, urgent to turn the earth into ash.

"MY God is the one true —LIVING, *full of shit* GOD and we know this because having faith in BULLSHIT is *easy*! Why test God with something as pitiful as the truth? Would you ask Mohammed to pose in a photograph with you? Would you ask Moses how many mushrooms he ate before he saw the burning bush? Would you hire the best trial lawyers for Christ the criminal?"

He drained his 40-ounce bottle and threw it into the crowd. "Another!" He shouted as if he were Little-Boots, the Italian baby emperor.

Some kid brought him another. The kid looked not yet old enough to drive.

"Wanna be baptized on stage?"

"Sure." You could almost hear the satanic Beaver Cleaver chirp in his voice.

Jas pointed to the stage floor. Damn, it must've been hot.

The kid lay with his arms by his sides, on the stage: easy religion cinnamon bun, like Sunday school.

"Now—repeat after me. —I once could see but now am blind."

"I once could see but now am blind." The boy closed his eyes.

Jas enunciated theatrically, "I once was found but now am lost."

Repeating, "I once was found but now am lost."

Jas raised a triumphant fist, "T'was GRACE that gave my **fear** heart."

"T'was grace that gave my fear heart." The boy exhaled scout's honor.

The Pope continued, "I once was free, but now must pay the cost."

Repeating, "I once was free, but now must pay the cost."

Jas doused the boy in the beer that he had recently seized from the boy himself. The boy shot up like a light and grabbed the bottle from Jas's remaining grip. He poured some beer into his mouth and handed Jas the bottle and jumped off stage with triumphant fists and little arms raised.

Everyone cheered.

Jas drank the remainder of the bottle. He tossed it off the stage. "More!"

Three young Plaguists rushed the stage offering him more booze. He took all three, setting down two on the stage.

He guzzled a third of the fullest, freshest, and coldest of the three bottles.

The stage was really catching fire now. The flames licked his boots. "Watch out for zombies! They're after your brains! You must save your brains for God! God will eat your brain! Through the digestion of your brains through Chuckie's intestines will you reach salvation—which is SHIT!"

Jas drained and threw another bottle from the stage. He picked up another one.

"Plaguists are anti-EVERYTHING, including anti-*Plaguist*! We believe ABSURDITY shall be the WHOLE of the Law!"

More guzzling beer. I could tell he was getting tipsy. The flames leapt and ignited some of the hanging rips and tears in Jas's jeans. He swatted them out with his hand. The left side of the stage caught totally on fire. The oxygen really stirred up the charcoal and the flames shot up beside him. He looked like a suicide—a holy Joan of Arc, untied but no less willing to crisp her bacon for the right kind of future.

"If you can't stand the heat, hold still while I light this cigarette off ya!"

Flawless cause applause.

Jas got down on his knees and felt that the stage was hot with his palm but stayed in his squat contemplating the time he had left until total stage collapse. He went to the edge and lit a cigarette from the flame of the stage because he knew it would have a dramatic effect.

It did.

The crowd roared and roared with wild screaming and shouting.

"The future ain't what it used to be!" Jas guzzled beer. "Annihilation of the un-working model is the only way to get one that DOES work! Let's even the odds. Who out there has weapons grade plutonium? Weapons grade anthrax? Weapons grade ANYTHING?!"

The stage blackened and cracked. He had nowhere to go but off—he leapt like a gray rhebok from the lioness flames that licked and tasted and threatened his warm leather boots... He landed safe in the arms of several adoring teenage fans of the fantastic...

The fire devoured the stage at last, collapsing the wood into its welcoming mouth. Cinders shot hot sparks into the air that danced about the compound. Jas was long gone but the words of his sermon lingered. *We will all burn. Our greatness will only lead to decay. You cannot preserve the flesh.*

I wrestled with his subtext, his suicidal pleasure fest. He seemed destined to singe the ground he walked on. Jesus may have walked on water, but Jas's footsteps ignited the forest floor. I was in love. I knew I couldn't satisfy him sexually because I couldn't give myself to him in the way that he desired. An unsatisfied man would collapse—no matter the pretext. These were the laws of physics. My time at S.P.A.M. Manor suddenly seemed limited.

There was something growing here. There was a real scene I hadn't quite anticipated. I couldn't count all the Plaguists. There were hundreds, seemingly twice as many as attended the *Sermon on the Mounted Televisions*. There was much ruckus and applause when The Pope leapt from the stage. I wondered if it was possible to start a religion for real—to write holy books and worship the self into heaven.

I spoke to the old drag queen libertarian Sain't Ruby Ridge on our popularity.

"Well, there's a lot of disenfranchisement in modern society. Religion has failed us by building cathedrals and mega-churches while ignoring the needy, Government has failed us by kowtowing to special interests. Education has failed us by becoming a business more interested in Athletics than Academics. The core problem's the Bottom Dollar. We're a greedy lot. Insatiable sins from a prudish birth. We devolved from sun gods to royalty, from holy men to scoundrels, and on and on down… From babies to skeletons."

The conversation became too much for me. "I got to go find The Pope," I blurted, dizzily squiffy.

"I understand, honey. You go run along."

I found an unopened Colt45 and unscrewed the cap. I tossed the cap aside. I guzzled and walked. I soon found Dominic and we talked politics and law. He was studying law. *I didn't know this. Yeah, in his fifth year, sure to graduate this term and pass the bar. Really? Yeah man, we're going to have a Plaguist lawyer in the family.* That sounded like a recipe for getting away with murder.

"Do you have, like, political aspirations…? Do you want to be, like, a congressman or a senator or a judge even?" I didn't really know how to proceed with the news that Sain't Dominic, Head of Public Relations for The First Interplanetary Church of the Immaculate Deception, was about to become a lawyer.

"I don't know, man!" He smiled giddy gummy. "I wanted to go TO, and FINISH law school so that I would have a better *understanding* of our legal system." He sounded like a natural born politician.

"Is there an office you'd say no to?"

"Well, I'd have to debate the circumstances."

"I mean in general."

"You mean would I ever say no to running for the office of the Vice President of The United States, because of its title?"

"Yeah."

"No."

"You'd be a great congressman."

"Do you think so?" He asked so sweetly and sincerely. "Because I'm worried about these tattoos on my arm." He pointed to his beautiful demon ink on his arm. "I'm worried about Pictures I KNOW I'm in doing fucked up illegal shit and there are other pictures I'M NOT SURE I might be in—and am probably in."

"Well, most everything's forgivable."

"I know, man. It's all kind of hazy and blurry when you talk about being ELECTED by the voting public to a JOB." Dominic took a deep breath. "You'll have to excuse me Mar, a second strong wave of Acid kicked in and I'm starting to lose the grip. I'm not sure how linear I will be able to… Keep up with you… Right now, because of the… Words that are coming… Out of my mouth and…. Are starting to… Sound like musical instruments being played… On fire and the… Hot brass are burning my lips… To kiss sentences with…"

"I totally understand."

Goodnight sweet prince.

"THERE THEY ARE! Sain't Dominic! And the Angel of *Death*!" The last word sarcastic spasm.

Jas introduced us to Rambo, the kid who was baptized on stage. Rambo looked fourteen. He swore he was nineteen. Apparently, he was acknowledged by the state to be Hermaphrodite and collected S.S.I. checks from the government and didn't have to work and usually had somebody pay his way while he saved money.

For a brief second the world seemed perfect. What type of backwoods pickup- truck hillbilly names his son after a Sylvester Stallone character? The poor boy's father probably thought he was gonna have some kind of rough and tumble hunter, some heavyweight footballer, fisherman, policeman, shit kicker, construction worker, tough guy. No. Rambo was a bitty fairy with glitter lips and porcelain cheeks rouged naturally. He was a precious cherub of sexuality, with long curly hair and succulent berry mouth. He had thin limbs and neck, like he didn't like to eat. He was five foot flat and ninety-five pounds maybe.

Dominic walked away.

"Okay!" Jas looked confused.

"He has the fear."

"Got it!" Jas turned to Dominic walking away. "Hang in there, sweetie, all you got to do is get to sunrise!" He hissed laughter to himself.

Jas swiveled swiftly back to me. "Anywhere you need to be tonight besides S.P.A.M Manor?"

"Absolutely."

I no longer had a place to sleep that night. All right. I ate a bunch of Acid. It was the season for it. Time and a place: usually when you're young and discovering who to be.

I walked around the compound and met many people. There was Nao the Japanese Jainist who believed that it was absurd to draw an arbitrary line in the sand. *Why should I sweep the ground beneath my feet with a broom to avoid squishing insects where I walk, when I breathe in millions and millions of molecular organisms who perish in my hot nostrils and boiling entrails? Where should I draw the line?*

Questions which beg to differ.

Suddenly a bright light shone in my face. I surmised that these must be the extraterrestrials coming to abduct me aboard their spaceship. But this was no tractor beam—I could move. I put my arm to the light.

"Here's a gentleman I know from my hometown, Knoxville, Tennessee, Martin Hemlock."

I recognized that voice.

"Martin, can you give me your official church title and duties?"

"Official?" I asked the light. "Can we do something about these high beams?"

A filter came over the glaring bulb and I suddenly made out Kramer Lydon—the man I'd come to Nashville to see, to hang out with, and whom I hadn't spent a minute with in three weeks. He stood there pointing a microphone in my face. It all seemed very official.

"Do you care to share with the cameras your title and duties for the First Interplanetary Church of The Immaculate Deception?"

"Sure whatever—I don't ever need to be a congressman—I'm the Angel of Death in the First Interplanetary Church of the Immaculate Deception—and my duties are to abort all fetuses conceived without insemination—to kill all babies born of a virgin birth and to slaughter zombies—and that includes any body resurrected after twenty four hours of death."

"You're a mercenary."

"Sure," I replied, feeling a little uneasy about my title now.

"Can you tell me a little bit about your Lord and flavor Chuckie The Plague?"

"A little bit? Sure. He thinks he's God and no one can prove him wrong."

"Very good, thank you." Kramer smiled and nodded to the camera man to cut.

"What the hell's all of this?"

"Documentary on the Church for my senior film thesis." Kramer smiled.

"Aren't you a sophomore?" I surmised.

"I'm gonna spend three years filming everyone. See what happens."

"Cool, let me know how it turns out in three years," I replied, snarky blue.

Kramer flashed a grin and motioned for his crew to follow him along. Suddenly Sain't Taint of The In-Between was bathed in light and Kramer was in her face with a microphone question. I liked the surprise guerilla tactics Kramer employed on everyone—*Here I am/what do you have to hide?*

I walked in the opposite direction as the film crew, continuing my meeting of new Plaguists. Perhaps the only thing I had to hide was all that I am.

Sain't Tom Foolery oversaw all serious matters pertaining to the church—he had nothing to do ever...

Sain't Dickens Shakespeare was the patron Sain't of literature, and he was the first illiterate teenager I ever met. Couldn't read a lick. Dumb as dirt. We talked about baseball. He knew nothing about the sport.

Maybe the apocalypse that Plaguists were preparing for would be one they were planning on generating. Maybe the ease into their club and the seduction of their methods were designed to trick minds like mine, open to the ride, free of shame and pride, and ego blind.

Hours passed easily into dawn. The yard was littered with young bodies in various positions of sleep or rest, some shivering the speed away, some covered in their own vomit. A dozen or so people still paced the grounds, smoking cigarettes, mumbling attempts at conversation with other Plaguists, or themselves. I observed them all completely detached from any judgment so ever.

14.

Coming Clean

Ready and I slipped from the party to her bedroom. We kissed passionately and undressed each other. I kicked my shoes off and lifted my feet to me, taking my socks off with a mouthful of her tongue.

Naked, I kissed her mouth, her neck, her clavicle, her specula, her chest, her breast, her ribcage, stomach, bellybutton and pubis. I found her clitoris and lollipop licked the skin red with furious wet movements. I stroked and spit and sucked her juice into my mouth. I gagged on her abundant wetness. I swallowed her vaginal discharge. I lapped her up like a puppy—but this was no puppy love. This was gross exercise of the accomplishment.

Loving her never occurred to me. I was taking a break from love. I needed to sort out my place in society. I had prevailed in acing their early academic and social tests and after graduating their high school saw no reason to continue their line of reasoning. It wasn't me versus them—I could cohabitate peaceably possibly—but I could never buy into what they were selling.

Did she invest in me? Was our physical frolicking anything more than blissful- eruption of the pleasure sensors? I don't know.

My own system awaited epiphany and design.

I stroked her cheek with my finger. I pulled the springy wool of her hair. It bounced gingerly back into place. Her lips were puffed cupid innocent, and her cheeks were baby smooth. I leaned in close to smell her—lilacs, bergamot, spicy tuna and musk. I could've fallen in love with her smell, for sure—a lesson I took with me—finding the sweetest smelling plums in the garden.

There was no Eden free of damning temptation.

I leaned down and smelled the sheets—musky skunk and short rib—unicorn ass and mango chutney, rainbow wax and fairy blood. I was on my tiptoes as usual and sneaking off with my clothes in my hands. Ready was asleep in bed.

Outside Pookie smoked a cigarette.

"Don't you ever sleep?" I asked him. It was four a.m.

"Hell no! Too many dreams that know my name." He smiled and snorted a canine jester laugh my way.

"Got the hots for me?" I asked, pointing to the unlit cigarette in my mouth.

"Sure do. Can I touch your penis?"

I laughed to cover up any type of uncomfortable feelings I may have been experiencing. "It's a bit sticky with pussy juice," I said, I thought hilariously.

"Now you're just flirting with me."

How to fend off a Plaguist? But to be fair, Pookie was never a Plaguist. He never bought into any of it—hated the whole gang mentality of it all actually—thought it was a great big fuck off for originality—wanted everyone to be who they were outside of any arena—naked and in his mouth...

How to fend off a deviant?

"Are you hungry? How about I buy us breakfast?" I offered his offensive knight and already downed king.

I drove us to Waffle House. Hank was working, so I told Pookie to get whatever he wanted. He asked why, and wondered if I was a big spender.

"No." I told him the story of why I get to eat for free.

He was amazed. "This is the whitest trash story of poetry I've ever heard." He laughed and he laughed and shook his head. I was happy to have his attention.

We got along like a house on fire. He was the first person I had met who was as interested in new music as I was. He knew all about the same bands I did, same record labels, producers and amorphous musicians.

That spring it was all about Tortoise, Breeders, Experimental Jet Set, Trash and No Star had just come out and it was all about Self Obsessed and Sexee—oh Thurston—with your unlucky lanky accountability... Stereolab, Hole had just put out Live Through This—and Doll Parts was the song... Flaming Lips, Tom Waits, and My Bloody Valentine...

Pookie told me the story about his first time being sexually harassed. He was thirteen-years-old and a rowdy kid like the rest of us, but only because he was bored with his lessons and smarter than his teachers, already sexually active and interested in everyone. He garnered a lot of attention, both good and bad.

He spent a lot of time in detention. It was a small school. There were times when he was the only student in the science lab with Mr. Lawrence the biology teacher.

"I might be able to reduce your sentence if you don't mind doing some field work," the smarmy teacher insinuated.

"What kind of field work?" Pookie asked with big marshmallow eyes, splattered with blueberry jam and round like sheep.

"I'm working on a science project at Vanderbilt University. We're studying the emergence of the male erection and its dominance in society. You would only answer a series of questions. If you're interested, we can begin immediately." The teacher offered him no emotion.

"I answer questions and you take time off my detention."

"That's correct. I will dock an hour for every set of… Twenty."

Pookie sensed that the teacher Mr. Lawrence had invented the number on the spot. He was very good at reading people. We shared this trait, him and me, emotional intelligence, psychological sensitivity, acute awareness of the room and its occupants.

You never knew when there was a wave of activity you might need to be a part of. You didn't want to get left behind when the party relocates.

"Are you a virgin?"

"No."

"Do you masturbate?"

Pookie hesitated.

"If the questions make you uncomfortable, we can stop at any time and I will still give you credit for the extra hour." The teacher was very sly.

"I don't mind." Had Pookie ever felt uncomfortable? He seemed to always be accepting of the moment, as a Zen Buddhist might, aware of the sensation and either altering it in some magical way or letting it be. "I do." Pookie wondered if he should clarify his response. "Masturbate, I mean. I do it all the time." He couldn't help a nervous giggle. The schoolgirl part of him sometimes took over.

"Do you fantasize about your classmates?"

"Yes, all of them." Pookie answered quickly and laughed a little as if embarrassed to admit the truth.

"I'm serious."

"I am, too."

Mr. Lawrence stopped taking notes. "Do you fantasize about anyone outside of your classmates?"

"Sure—sometimes I even think about ACTUALLY choking a chicken when I have my dick in my hand."

"You have to take this seriously or not participate." The teacher was being so...

"I am taking this seriously—I didn't mean to say chicken—I meant to say swan, like a young one, a soft baby one. I figure my cock is the same size as a baby swan's neck and I'll think about stroking the soft neck and the climax would be the bird's final earth breath—my ejaculation, the young animal giving up the ghost."

"No, you didn't," I interrupted his story.

"No, I did. I figured this guy's a freak and no way is he asking me kosher to my school—I figured I could say what I want."

"What happened?" I was truly captivated by his perverse story.

"The next day he brought in porno-mags and asked me to do it in front of him."

"You've got to be kidding me."

But the teacher was serious. "Yesterday you answered twenty questions and have had an hour removed from your detention. Today, if you'd like to participate in an experiment, I'll erase your final nine hours."

"Anything," Pookie answered prematurely.

"I have several different sources of arousal. I would like to time your performance and your orgasm and ask you to answer a few questions after climax. Do you think you could do that?"

"Sure," Pookie answered, and couldn't believe his luck to find a teacher who could utilize his strengths.

The serpent didn't offer fruit for free. His interests were in swallowing the heartbeat.

I had no way of knowing if he was telling me the truth or not, except for the conviction in his inflection, the pitch in his timber, the smile in his look-away. Anyway, I believed him. It sounded like something that would happen—weren't the slickest foxes chickens? I mean, didn't the most sophisticated pedophiles show up as teachers, preachers, priests, camp counselors, prepubescent beauty pageant contestant handlers, little league coaches, ice cream truck drivers, Mall Santa's, scout leaders, clowns...?

There was a beauty to the abused, an unpolished stone no ruby could compare to, glittering sediment, shy frightened smile and switchblade pocket...

Pookie was a puckish boy, a Peter Pan fairy with his hair in his face and no concern for the direction his feet were walking. He was a mystical savant, *duhmonic*, he was strut and swagger to cover up every no idea he ever had.

He was the coolest welcome. He had amazing grace and blessed virgin all over his orphan peepers, but tattoos that suggested he'd been in prison. On his arm was tattooed a smiley face ripped in half, the torn yellow face, bloody, exposing the skull beneath. The subcutaneous revealing of the smiley face—it was an image worth a novel, a symphony, a war.

We got along famously. We were getting to know each other. We were two fools playing poker, each holding five jokers. I wonder now how far we could've bluffed our way into nothingness. We were supreme emptiness searching for a hurricane. We were constantly looking to be blown (away).

I drove Pookie back to Lingus House. They were rehearsing in the garage. Pookie stripped naked and jumped in the pool. I did the same. The water was cold and shocking at first but then cool and soothing— like being born, I guess, or dying.

I swam laps and ignored Pookie's advances. I didn't want to frolic playfully like Alaskan otters in the gay wild. He grew bored and went inside. I swam fifteen more laps. I was on the swim team in high school because I wanted to fuck the coach, Jennifer what's-her-face.... I came in third place in the butterflies. There were only three racers, and I never fucked the coach.

I swam on my back and took it easy, letting the sun redden my face. The sun! The sun! I'd been in the dark too long. How much longer was I willing to miss the sun?

Shaking the water from I and I like a dog, I immediately put on my three-day-old boxer shorts. I hadn't yet done laundry in Nashville and owned few clothes. I was modest in the May sun. It was warm and felt good—seventy-five-degree sunshine on my shoulders like angel piss. Cock hanging well to the left. I laughed and smoked a cigarette with my eyes closed.

Ready asked me to stay. I told her I had to work and left. I forgot I didn't have a job, and wondered how I was going to get money.

15.

Ouroboros Remains

This again...

This drug again...

This distortion of the senses and bending of the lens. More acid, more weed, more beers, and cigarettes, and need—carnal need—human need to be loved... No... Not loved—adored, like a porcelain whore in a clown's curio cabinet, stiff and waiting for use—worshiped, wanted, needed, desired...

I was teenage sweat and a dare to show off... All sense of responsibility, blown off.

Some cute teenage runaway waif blew me in the bathroom—androgynous Andromeda, non-homogenous, astonish us with your beauty—my hands in short hair—baby fine—silky scalp, thin greasy neck and big ears... I stroked the unknown skull, my fingers, tendrils exploring the blind sea bottom... I didn't know who she or he was—didn't know where I was, or how long I'd been there...

I couldn't come. This only excited the mouth more. The mouth wanted to be expert-seducer, tutelage sucker, off-getting way-getter—way out here in the margins of the paradox—nervous systems all a go-go—synapses anxious for the firing—ready to get off, blast off, bang the drum loudly...

"You don't want to come?" Potty lips begged, wet and red.

"I don't think I can." I shoved my stiff prick back into my pants. The head of my cock hard against the belt buckle.

The mouth had a face which was pretty, and a body which was skinny—and lady parts—I saw her piss in the toilet. I was relieved somehow. Deep down inside my superficial abyss I always wanted to be straight. Too many jealous kids called my pretty face 'faggot'. Too many pretty boys I wanted to kiss, touch, feel, fell, put a spell on… To take over the world… But more interesting and puzzling were the girls, with their sinister whim, and mystical quim, hidden in perfect paradise, the ultimate prize when stripped down and anxious for connection, their apple eye, puncture pie, stunning I, and take it all.

I wanted them all—all the pretty faces—all the slender bodies, all the defining parts… Not the fattened weak, the vulgar over-mothered twats, and the father-encouraged brats… But the gnats near the rotting fruit circling drunk in sugar heaven… I wanted to touch the body heat with my fingers and mouth, feel the wet and the pulsing, the slippery opening, and the battle horn. I wanted secret saliva to consume, like Dracula blood, in soft-porn kissing, never missing the responsibilities of life— curfews, bedtimes, due assignments, growing up… Ugh…

This again…

This nowhere-serpent eating its own tail—this infinite moment—this full-circle, self-imploding supernova of numb erasure… I wobbled around the party… What party? Where was I?

Did it matter? Probably not. My hosts could've been murderous rapists or radical Islamic terrorists for all I cared—with hashish and booze—I would've gone on a cruise with a sweaty wealthy cougar if she got me high enough—or I would've fucked the farmer's earth with my fertile cock if the wrathful grapes fermented quickly enough for my refill.

It was a Plaguist party!

It was always a Plaguist party.

Leather jackets hung from broad shoulders of stinky men and women, each coated in various degrees of dust and grease (lust and ease).

Who held the lease to this place? Didn't matter. There had been too much swelling of the architectural membrane. The house was breathing. Did I need a priest or some Thorazine?

Lean teen limbs with high-beam eyes and no tan skin-show, swaggered past my sniff and stiff. I didn't lose my erection walking down the hall. I throbbed.

"Ha! The Angel's got a WOODY!" The Pope shouted as he swished by with some loose-limbed epicene, destined for the latrine with serpentine wiggle and swallowing giggle.

Angel.

I was the Angel of Death in The First Interplanetary Church of the Immaculate Deception.

It came back to me in hallucinatory waves of orange particles glowing Yellow fluid, kumquat bug splat green and neon bloody spleen...

I was a disciple of Charles Theodore Plague and I had agreed to help his motley band of punkrock misfits start a religion.

Where was I?

Oh yeah...

We were at one of the Plaguist houses watching another episode of the dOcumEntary from Kramer's mOst recent footage. He was my introduction to The Pope and by proxy all of Nashville. Kramer was airing his documentary in parts on public access television.

It must've been SaturdaY.

Plaguist Yoga.

MmNasty.

"Need help with that, baby?" Marybeth asked me as she grabbed my cock through cut-off denim pants and shoved a door open behind me—closed behind me. Dark, Naked, High, Throat around my cock, tongue on my balls, fingers playing my sides like a harpsichord—warm tears and sputum moistening my crotch.

This again...

This wonder—what day was it? How long had I been there—in that house? In that city? —Where was I going? What was I doing?

I was supposed to be there a week... Two at the most. It had been almost two months. I thought. Fun was being had, but I smelled the stale stain of myself in the confines of my current residence.

SatUrday...

Yesterday was Friday. I quit another job—SaTurday—Plaguist Yoga—I knew where I was! That's right! I was supposed to take more acid—I forgot—I was high on acid and forgot to take more... Acid...

I got pleasantly molested by the best of them. Sain't Marybeth gripped hard with both hands at the base of my shaft until I blasted steam-rocket into magnesium flame...

Light speed laser beams of sticky pearl milk.

I came and I came, stiff gyrating orgasmic seizure... We were here... A forever cum that lasted decades in the ether. I came so long that when I stopped coming, Marybeth was nowhere to be seen. She existed in dream and didn't clean me. I was sticky, nasty, beautiful, and full of adventure...

How many more times was I going to overact in that scene, before they cut me out of the picture altogether? And when would I meet the director? I was never off the set. I bet I could steal every scene…

This again…

This infinite spin—this quantitative naïveté—I had narcissistic tics that made Liberace seem drab… I wanted free-space and light-speed until fertile planet to slam into—I wanted dinosaur-killing gene-mutation—planet-slaughtering panspermia—intelligent sentient evolution—tender hairless babes again and again born from my thunder….

I was helping to start a religion?

Sure. Why not? I was well-versed in the spiritual. How to brainwash the masses? Start with their young, feed them drugs, then suggest you have a path to take far superior to other paths, especially the path of their parents and ancestors, "for mankind has come to evolve—so let's evolve together baby!"

It started to make sense. As soon as I ceased to believe in reality as a shared experience, I learned how to let go, and share my experience with myself first, then others…

SaturdAy?

Plaguist Yoga?

I felt the air on the tip of my sticky wet penis as my half chub threatened to peek out from beneath my shorts, cut too short probably. (I came. I finally came. Chuckie bless Marybeth.) My cock was temporarily satisfied and had released its capture of blood, finding a better position in my thin shorts.

I left a puddle of me in the dark room.

The den was littered with Plaguists passed-out in some awkward pose. Young bikers in new-leather curled in the fetal position (Aborted Prayer) —young skaters gripping the shag carpet, trying to ride the world spinning too fast (Calculated Obliteration).

A smile crept upon my teenage idiot face. Acid was a good choice if you wanted to get so fucked up you can't get fucked up…

(Myopic bipeds place spatial limits on the omnipresent—expect answers from gaseous vertebrates after praying to space.) How many thoughts crippled our inner editor?

The VHS tape captured us. Kramer roamed the party filming us all fucked up and glorious. We were all a part of Kramer's Documentary of The Church. Everyone wanted to do interviews. Anyone could be a Plaguist and be baptized with some awesome sobriquet like Sain't

Sebastian of the Archery Range—Sain't Mike of the Monosyllabic Response. There was no shortage of material.

Some postulated the possibility that we were nothing more than players in The Documentary and that was the only reality. Rock was enthralled with these notions, as Head of Conspiratorial Affairs he embraced every conspiracy, every absurd rumor...

Plaguism was the new cool—a curse really to a band of misfits who prided themselves on being contrarian. There was nothing worse to an individual than being accepted...

I was starting to think I'd never get out of Nashville.

16.

Sermon of the Holy Fool

Jas was in love. His chocolate wormhole eyes glistened eternal gratitude to the attractive magnet of perfect feeling.

I spent less and less time at S.P.A.M. Manor, as was everyone that season. The Pope was so insufferably in love... But I was invited to hang—and they had beer...

It was good to see Jas, my old friend of five weeks, that felt like forever. I tried to tease him. "Love is nature's only flaw," but maybe that's how I really felt?

"Oh Martin—I hope you find *true love* someday," Jas whispered drunkenly.

"Isn't all love supposed to be true?" I quizzed.

"No," Rambo inserted. "*Family* love's not always true, but it's LOVE none-the-less—genetic, obligatory, useful *love*." He usually sounded frail when he spoke, fragile fairy whisper thin—but this line of reasoning, love—he was certain of his place in earthly love.

I was not. "Is untrue, self-serving love, really love at all?"

"I don't know—I don't know what you mean," confessed the pristine epicene.

"I mean—if you're satisfying your tendencies and reacting favorably toward that which gets you what you want—are you really engaging in some *spiritual* connection with another human being?"

"Oh Jesus, Martin!" Jas exhaled smoke in my face. "Not everything's *spiritual*, some things are *emotional*—and the ultimate *emotional* expression is LOVE!" Jas was pretending flamboyance, but his jaws clinched, and his head lifted as he hit his cigarette like a strung-out starlet reciting improvised lines.

"Yes, but doesn't that emotional enlightenment or orgasm or whatever become spiritual?"

"Martin, when you have true love—everything else fucking vanishes—it's more than spiritual—with love there's no need for an explanation of any kind for any reason, so it doesn't matter what you're talking about." Jas spoke jittery and calm, unconcerned with how he sounded—certain he was correct in every syllable.

"Isn't that what mystics seek—that great spiritual enlightenment?"

Jas waved his cigarette around in lazy half figure eights, "No, no, no, no, nO! Love trumps enlightenment."

"Aren't we gonna be late?" Rambo asked sheepishly.

Genetic love? Maybe Rambo was right. I looked at Jas in my rearview mirror, his back against the passenger backseat window, legs behind me. Rambo leaned against his chest, feet behind me. Perhaps I was terrified of this type of intimacy, this connection with another human being. I wanted fresh air, speed beneath my wings, and learning to be a better human being. Christ! Did that sound corny or what? I was the type of asshole who would sell phrases to greeting card companies for any amount of money.

Where were we going? Oh yeah, Toys"R"Us: The warehouse toy store where kids realized how poor their families were. The Holy Fool had a show to do, and it was Chuckie approved and I was jealous as hell. The little prick got to do a show, perform a sermon, something I really wanted to do myself.

I finished my cigarette in the parking lot and let the love birds go in together. I needed a minute to clear my head—figure nothing out, stare at the clouds, confuse the darkness with my sunshine face in the yellow affirmation life-giving source.

Fuck it.

I stomped the butt with my boot and went inside, smoke pissing into the sky from my mouth.

One hundred gnarly gothic Plaguists stomped into the toy store smelling of smoke and booze and shit and unwashed skin and greasy hair, all stained with motor oil, blood, cum, and piss.

"Is everybody in? The Sermon's about to begin." Rambo almost lisped the limp words from his larynx. Little Jim Morrison, little Plaguist plagiarist, little Genet Rimbaud, Little gay Dionysian crucifix nothing! I couldn't believe I was being so hard on him in my mind—but perhaps that was part (all) of the attraction. Maybe I was "*getting him*" and therefore empathizing with The Pope's choice in mates.

"Welcome to the palace of plastic promises. Observe the sexist demarcations in color and function. These future gifts continue to warp the senses of the human child, which has no age limit."

I wondered if Jas wrote those opening remarks. It sounded a bit advanced for Rambo's thinking. I'm not saying he was dumb or an idiot, just not as advanced as The Pope, and therefore not literally qualified to speak that way.

He pointed to the pacifiers on the wall—the first thing in the store— "Learn first with the pacifier—move on to the thumb, the lollipop, the pencil, the cigarette and the dick. Suck! Suck! Suck! Because that's what life *does* to YOU!"

The curious, gruff, awkwardly quiet, hellion crowd moved in through the store, observing the bright colors and petroleum-based-products for themselves. Each leather punk blinded by the fluorescent lights shining obnoxiously from above.

The little kiddies shopping for birthday presents found themselves in the presence of Chuckie and his gang of misfits. All of the kiddies were in the presence of God: the kiddies strutting about the spoiled aisles with rich complacent parents terrified of their kids' screaming and whining— the unaccompanied kiddies dreaming of the plastic wonders wrapped in shiny packages too big to steal—the kiddies who learned to share and the selfish kiddies who grow up to run companies—all these kiddies were joined by several dozen leather-clad punks—some wearing spikes and chains—heavy metal rockers, dejected outcasts, rebels who called themselves Plaguists, stomping biker boots and reeking of smoke and oil.

The Manager called the police.

Nervous children kept their heads down and shuffled closer to mommy and daddy. The parents hurried their children's selections or dragged their precious progeny out of the store.

Some kids laughed and asked random Plaguists questions, wondering why they were in costume and were they going to a party, or were they filming a movie? Some were old enough to join, and they should be thankful The Pope was in love that month.

Rambo was on a roll near the Sesame Street characters, and plush, teaching teddy bears— "If you believe in *Anything*, you're an idiot! Hell, even Atheism's a *belief*! It's a safeguard against the responsibility of recognition! You cannot say that NOTHING is in charge, if YOU are not willing to be in charge! Don't let yourself convince you of *anything*!

We'll take care of EVERYTHING! All you have to do is not trust *anything* else—other than *Nothing!*"

Chuckie roared with laughter. He was a big fan of the Holy Fool.

In the action-figure aisle Rambo stopped for a moment, to gaze at the GI Joe abs on the well-sculpted miniature warriors and the mysterious shields and emblems they wore, the concealing ninja masks, the haunting gas-masks, the hooded monk samurais, the Mexican wrestler's mask, Batman's cowl, the Lone Ranger's secret identity protected, all secret, all mysterious, not wanting to be recognized for the gallant effort of violent retaliation to invasion of self and home. Rambo marveled at these champions of the pedestrian, these heroes to society with weapons and skill set to dismantle the most challenging threat.

Jas handed a starry-eyed Rambo a battery-operated microphone.

Rambo spoke into it, his voice cracked with feedback. "The only sin is Conformity! Become a Plaguist like everyone else!"

Plaguists cheered.

Moving along to the ball aisle, Rambo looked loathingly at basketballs that he couldn't dribble, and footballs that he couldn't kick, and balls that he couldn't dodge, hit, shoot, bounce, punt or score within any fashion—taunting him in their silent spherical geometry, their stitched perfection and oblong slipperiness.

He picked up a football and threw it very hard, as a small girl would throw it very hard, that is to say, without the form and grace of a practiced athlete. The ball *just* tumbled over the aisle wall.

The ball came right back over the wall of sporting equipment. The ball knocked into a section of Whiffle balls. The plastic white balls scattered all over the place, bouncing and sliding on the ceramic tiled floor. Rambo reacted to the tossed ball as if it were a hand grenade. He covered his face and body with his arms, standing on one leg and protecting himself like a flamingo. He looked ridiculously perfect. However, he did not lose composure regarding his sermon and continued in the ball aisle.

"There is no god but whoever says they are god. Whoever she or he says they are god, then they are to be believed as god. Our proof of god is the fact that Chuckie the Plague says he is God. He is the living God of the one true faith that happens to be also TOTALLY full of shit!" Rambo showed his little bottom to the growing crowd of Plaguists and shoved his thumb up his baggy-shorts ass as if he was indicating the shit physically.

We toy store full of Plaguists hooted and hollered and no longer cared about the impending ejection. We moved onto the remote-control car

aisle where Rambo looked in disgust at the vehicles. I wondered if
Rambo's father was some sort of off-roader, beer can redneck who liked
to tear through the mud in a 4x4 pickup truck with a gun-rack listening
to loud country music with arrogant prideful lyrics and no innovative
composition. Probably. This was no *radical* description of the average
lower middle class white person from Tennessee.

Emphatically Rambo kept the sermon moving. "There are no
Commandments! Only Suggestions! The first writers were politicians!
Every good Plaguist should know how to behave… Restricting No
Urge!" The meaning of the words heavy, but his breath was airy and
childlike. His performance gave an extra nuance of absurdity.

Plaguists went nuts, shouting and yelling! Agreeing with the sermon
with clapping and 'hell yeses'.

"Honor thy sloth and thy froth!" Rambo slurred.

More Plaguist Cheers…

We were in the girlie section, and wanting to skip it because it was
feminine, cutesy, girlie-girl, and very alluring to him, Rambo paused but
gained courage. He tried not to, but gazed longingly at the Strawberry
Shortcakes and Blueberry Muffins which were the names of these frui-
scented fairy people he clearly once so fondly loved.

I personally hated the girl aisles, all white silk and pink cotton candy,
dainty, rainbow dandy and glitter fairy. It stank of demand for diamonds
and imagination substitute. It was fluffy and starched, thin and
diaphanous, easily crushed, not durable. There was no interaction, no
remote control, no contest with defined rules and points, no rough and
tumble job description—make-up and tiara, vanity mirror and dress up.

"It's impossible to bear false witness! Nothing is true! Everything is
permitted! Reality's an illusion that subscribes to your willful bent! Fuck
'em if they can't live a joke! I want to dress up as a mermaid!" Rambo
shook out his long locks from his ponytail and sprang them from their
confinement with thin delicate hands. He found the most expensive,
most decorative, largest, most ostentatious plastic tiara and put it on. He
pranced to the next aisle.

We Plaguists cheered him on in full appreciation of his will to be
whatever he wanted to be. There is no partial freedom in life—you're
either bound by shame and fear and the trepidation to conform or you're
a total fucking original.

Ambisexually the board game aisle is mostly gender nonspecific. In
the board game aisle one can shop for one gift for every member of the
family—great for poor people who buy Monopoly or Clue or Candyland

for the whole family so that *something* is under the tree, and maybe we can survive as a family unit!

"Have yourself a lifetime—or you'll owe the bank more than you're worth!"

I watched Chuckie observe the police cars pulling into the parking lot. He interrupted the sermon and instructed everyone to buy plush stuffed animals. Four police officers entered the toy store and talked to the manager.

Forty-nine Plaguists demolished the stuffed animal department. The black and blue tattooed punks and anarchists stood in three cash register lines, each holding a brightly colored stuffed animal.

The lines moved slowly but surely, reaching to the back of the store. The policemen watched the orgy of cuddly commerce with bewilderment. There was no crime being committed. Everyone was purchasing a product. No one was loitering.

"May The Beastly Bunny shit rivers of chocolate on your good luck heaven!" Rambo screamed, effectively ending his sermon. He was prepared to buy the microphone and tiara too.

Everyone laughed.

It was as if some little bastard had been playing with a Ouija board and summoned this macabre parade.

Jas and Rambo piled into The Mystery Ship. I drove the lovers over to meet Minx.

17.

Passion of the Beaster

Minx was a downhome goth—her black hair had dyed streaks of neon green. Her thin lips were black with lipstick. She wore a gingham skirt and leather corset, black motorcycle boots, and an apron. She lived in the middle of nowhere. She was the only daughter of an only daughter and the inheritor of forty acres in the middle of nowhere between Nashville and Murfreesboro. Chuckie had taken to spending more and more time out there. The house wasn't on a hill, so it didn't look down upon the three-mile gravel driveway, but it didn't expose its inner workings either.

The gathering was discreet, as discreet as three hundred Plaguists could be with a ceremony taking place.

Everyone was there. Literally every human being on Earth was there. Her property could hold it, and seven billion people showed up. You were there and everyone you know was there. I'm sure you remember, but I'm going to retell the story my way—*yeah?* —Like Frank Sinatra, like Sid Vicious, like a lonely narcissist invested in the Word.

The cross was eight feet tall. It was made of sawed branches of the largest tree in the yard—the old oak. The upright limb was twenty-two inches in diameter. The cross beam was fourteen inches in diameter. Minx, now Bishop Minx, cut fitting forms into the upright and the beam and bolted them together. Next, she wrapped the corners with wire and rope. She planted the cross into the ground using a Post Hole Digger and a little cement. She wanted to make a monument of her mockery. The cement dried. The crucifix was firm.

Chuckie and Rock were each armed with Stanley Sharpshooter TR150 Duty Staple Guns. The admission to the party was one plush animal. Now coming from the Sermon of the Holy Fool, everyone had a pink pastel or canary yellow felt critter in its horny and intoxicated hand.

"MAKE SURE THE FUCKING TOY IS SECURE TO THE WOOD!" Rock instructed me as he handed me the stapler, having finished putting forty-seven staples in an eight-inch-tall stuffed Mickey Mouse.

We covered every square inch. I stapled my bunny head to the wood and one bunny ear through the loose fat of an orange kangaroo, another bunny ear through a gorilla's neck. I stapled the tail to the wood and one foot over the ear of an elephant weakly stapled to the wood. I handed the industrial stapler to Jas. He took it limply. "We're supposed to cover every square inch."

I heard him put only one staple into the wood with a grunt. "Next!"

Soon the crucifix was affixed with one hundred and sixty stuffed bunnies and ducks, teddy bears, and plush unicorns, raccoons, and panda bears, koala bears, kittens, and puppies—of every color and stripe. The bright and furry fluffy cross was covered to every tip in colorful plush fabric and shape of animal. The weird monument stood eight feet tall and five feet wide.

It was doused in lighter fluid and set on fire.

A toxic, oily smoke wafted into the air and swirled a bit as if Walt Disney was directing, then streamed away in ugly smog of gaseous sewage, a gorgeous black silk. Hundreds of brightly colored children's toys screamed in flames, melted in orange and dripped red fire. The Chinese-made toxic fairy creatures died on the cross for the frivolity of our amusement.

I was in awe, smoking and drinking and weeping from the joy of the moment.

Apophenia Pareidolia paraded in slow motion to my center of the universe— "You have a special that doesn't belong here."

"I have a special that belongs everywhere," retorted indestructible youth I.

"Well, if you don't put it somewhere special it's going to dissipate into everywhere and lose whatever special it had…" Apophenia Pareidolia with the told-you-so soul and spectral death glow that said alive for now—but not for long…

"What's more special, the eternal one—or the infinite many?" I played poetic chess with her more mature attitude.

"If you try to quantify love—you're not in love—and therefore know nothing of the subject." Apophenia had the hots for me—I knew it… I smiled uncontrollably.

"Maybe love is nature's only mistake?"

"Of all to accuse nature of you choose love?" She asked, confidently bewildered.

Chef Hiccup joined us then. He nodded his head up and down like a chameleon. "Wh-Wh-Hw-What's G-Go-going on-N-N?!'" He blinked when he jerked his head up and down. It was music and jazz and rhythm, and I liked listening to him speak and welcomed a conversation.

Apophenia Pareidolia said nothing. She wanted to observe us males in our social circle.

"Tell me Chef—what's your favorite thing to cook this month?"

"Oh! Oh! I'm glad you put a time frame on that—most people don't do that." He spoke quickly and didn't stutter. He was happy to answer. "Well, It's-It's-It's…This WEEK actually I'm only fucking around with things that begin with the letter B—I'm making a lot of Blueberry biscuits with beef brisket and Brussels with balsamic bacon and banana bread with brie."

"Damn!" I shouted, because I thought talking louder to him would help his stutter. "And you get paid to cook this stuff?"

"Yeah," he answered slyly.

"I've got to come eat where you cook."

"It's expensive," he reminded me.

I never went to his restaurant.

There was a ruckus. Well, the whole party was a ruckus, but then a wild animal was brought to the party.

Rock brought in a kid goat and led the frightened Bovidae to the party. The goat cried and wailed and dug in its hooves to prevent the coming sacrifice. Rock grew frustrated with fighting the animal and picked it up. It pissed all over him.

Hiccup grabbed the legs of the kid. Rock stretched out the neck and held tight the head by the small young male horns.

The goat pissed and shit all over the place, scared out of its mind. Chuckie chanted something low and baritone, almost subharmonic, paralyzing the goat into submission. Chuckie unsheathed a machete, raised the blade into the air, and then in two very quick strokes, hacked the head from the animal.

Rock raised the head of the goat into the air. "Kill your food!" He cried to the sarcastic night of worship. The decapitated head dripped blueberry syrup onto the dirt and torn long grass. The weird eyes with the horizontal pupils grew milky with death.

The boys butchered the beast—skinned him, gutted him, rinsed him off real good and Chef Hiccup went to work on the paprika rub—olive oil, salt and pepper. He got down on the ground and found the liver, the kidney and the heart. He threw the organs into a bowl. He next found a garden hose and inserted it into the large intestines and squirted out all the shit and bile. One or two burly Plaguists got shit splashed on their month-long worn jeans, but they didn't mind, unwashed leather and denim is sometimes better cured with a little shit and blood splashed on them.

Sausage. Chef Hiccup was making a Moroccan Merguez. He mixed mostly paprika with cumin and fennel seeds and coriander seeds and cinnamon—salt and pepper and more pepper. Delicious—a crisp snap when the teeth break the casing and a rich spicy blend of exotic and gamy flavors awaken the palate to the land of the Bedouin, land of the assassin, the hashish smoker, the twirling Sufi mystic, and the crazed devout.

I smelled it—the pile of guts where it had been opened and dressed—a foul-smelling lump of innards. The animal was run through with a spit rod and placed on a pit of cinderblocks.

It was May 15, 1994, Beastly Sunday.

Minx wore a Viking helmet she made with an old motorcycle helmet and enormous steer horns. I don't know how she held her head up, her thin, strong neck. She spoke into the bullhorn loud and clear, her good-buddy southern CB twang and confidence rattling our ears. "On this day the goat is slaughtered so we don't have to sacrifice our God to the rapacious community of man! We eat from the flesh of the ruminant, starving hillbillies feasting on this here Billy goat, because it's FUCKING delicious!" Plaguists cheered and stomped their boots and blew smoke up the ass of the night.

"Chuckie asks you for no sacrifice! No tithing! He sells you no indulgence! He offers you no eternal reward! He offers you this meal tonight not as sustenance for your soul, but protein for your body, flavor for your palate."

The chemicals from the plush stuffed animals soaked into the wood which fueled the cross shaped flames. Black smoke pissed in streams upwards cutting through the white smoke from the wood.

Minx was ebullient. "Spring has sprung and brought forth meat to eat and cocks to suck!"

"AMEN SISTER!!!" The Pope bellowed/screeched louder than the other girls giving thanks.

"The blood that flows tonight is for maggots to sup—it belongs to no deity, no prophet! No religion or spiritual program should be profitable! It's why so few Christians are Christ-like, because their comfort comes WAY first—and if you knock on their door asking for food—they'll call the police—have the state deal out their brutal blows at the taxpayers cost—because that loaf of bread still has a day left on it before the expiration date and won't that go in the trash?!"

Minx was red in the face, her blood black lipstick lips stretched around her throat in fantastic growl as she recited her sermon and ad-libbed, went off course, hit tirade on the automatic pilot and coasted into all our hearts.

"No church should own property that isn't a garden, creating food for the hungry. No temple should shutter its doors to those without shelter. No pastor should profit financially!"

There was an eerie quiet while Minx quenched her throat with Colt 45. She had us on hooks from her lines.

"Chuckie resurrects himself every morning. And some mornings I erect him myself, cock first into the world!"

A grand celebratory noise erupted from the hundreds in attendance.

Did we have enough minds and guts to start a proper religion? Did we need a martyr, a corpse on a crucifix, a geek on a glow-in-the-dark effigy of infinity? Did we need prophets in lions' dens, dehydrated poets hallucinating in lost deserts, schizophrenic sons of pharos, epileptic camel herders, bad carpenters, monsters of the obvious, unconscious demons, bland rituals, outdated prohibitions? Yes! It seemed we had all those things!

Minx continued her Sermon. "Farmers, pull out your hard cocks and shove them into the soil and stroke until you explode your semen into mother earth! Maidens, milk those cows, take those rugs out of your house and beat them—get the dust off! Wash your shit until you cum! Spring's here! Sweep your floors and then get down on them, covered in Vaseline and baby oil and wax those floors while fucking something fun!"

She threw her empty can of Steel Reserve into the crowd and miraculously a chilled new one was flung back in seconds. She caught it, popped it, and drank thirstily. What a sight.

There were three hundred people there—those who weren't already Plaguists were seduced into taking the sacred oath and became Plaguists.

I witnessed many beers sprayed onto lots of bodies—in the name of Chuckie.

The cross finally cracked. It had been on fire for hours. The left black arm hissed and fell to the ground in a shower of tiny orange particles. Sparkling glowing embers splintered and quickly withered to black chunks smoking in the warm sunrise.

18.

Violent Vellum

The air was hot and moist. The air was not so much humid as it was soaked with mist and grease. Dishes came up and were sent down on a dumbwaiter. Sometimes a bell would ring to let the dishwasher know they desperately needed trays of clean dishes. Chuckie rarely heard this bell. He could wash as fast as the entire restaurant could dirty and that was a lot.

It was an off time, not too many diners, but upstairs was jam-packed with Plaguists, groupies mostly, eager to get a glimpse of God, have a chat with our Lord and flavor. Damn, I felt special, walking in that dank kitchen with all the illegal Mexicans and quiet mice.

"Angel! I have a mission for ya!" He yelled after he lit a fresh cigarette, his first one in minutes. It was the first time he called me Angel.

"What's that?"

"Come by Plague Central tomorrow night and help me get rid of a raccoon problem."

"Why me?" I asked.

"Because you ARE The Angel of DEATH—and WE have to KILL it—and WE are going to make *vellum* from its SKIN—and YOU are going to use some kind of INK—that we'll come up with, probably squid or India ink, and a quill from a dead angel's wing—and write— THE PLAGUIST BOOK OF THE DEAD!"

I felt like a giddy girl finally being asked to the prom after years of rejection, wondering what to wear, who to call to share my exciting news, what new shoes should I buy? It was disgusting, but absurd and perfect.

I met the Lord in the backyard of Plague Central. He was in the middle of a dirt area rocking in a rocking chair holding two rifles in his lap, drinking Colt 45 and smoking. He wore his dark glasses of course, but amazingly took them off.

It was the first time I'd ever seen the Lord's irises circularly contracted showing a constricted pupil. They were green blue, blue green, sparkling jewels, dazzling pools of pale iridescent gems. They were beautiful, marvelous.

"Don't tell me I have pretty eyes. I hate that shit." He gargle-growled like a greasy gargoyle.

"Is that why you wear the glasses?" I asked.

"I don't suffer from vanity," he answered. "Here, take 'is here rifle!" Chuckie handed me a rifle, and a forty-ounce bottle of malt liquor. "You ever kill a mammal?"

I took the booze and gun. "I shot a dog, and a bird, and once I ran over a squirrel with my car."

"What did you shoot the dog for?"

"My grandfather made me do it. He had a chicken farm, and once the dogs get a taste for the chickens, they won't stop their hunger for those chickens, and they'll sneak onto your property and kill the fattest hens."

"Why didn't he get a bunch of roosters?" Chuckie asked.

"My grandmother couldn't sleep with all the crowing, so he only had one rooster. He tried to have two, but one would always kill the other."

"Ain't that just the fucking way it is?" Chuckie asked. "How big was the dog?"

"Bigger than me—I was eight years old and eighty pounds."

"You won't have any problem shooting a raccoon, then?"

"No. I guess not."

"You ever shoot a twenty-two?"

"I can operate this weapon."

(Note: The gun he gave me was like the one my father's father gave me. I shot out all the windows of an old door and lied when he asked me if I did it, though there wasn't another person around for a hundred miles. He didn't properly teach me a lesson about lying. He just scowled at me and never trusted me again. I've always been corrupt.)

A God outside of yourself is designed to grant your weaknesses forgiveness. If your God talks to you—obey or blaspheme are your only recourses. Choose wisely your defiance.

Chuckie and I went into the woods a few paces, behind the second row of trees, and cased out the garbage alley of Plague Central. Rock and God had pizza the previous evening and they emptied out all the trash cans in the place as well. The area was ripe with fermenting cheesy aphrodisiac and rotting vegetable goodness.

We waited for an eternity in silence. My acid-head full of dreams and cheeses, creams and diseases, memories like flashbacks to a cornfed beginning.

(Ten Years Prior: My father's father gave me a .22 rifle for my eighth birthday. I loaded the weapon carefully and crunched up the gravel road to the big wood barn. It was full of hay and cows and chickens.

The previous week I'd seen an enormous snake sunbathing on the side of the barn, and it scared the hell out of me—it's phallic leglessness—it's gravity defying act in slither, resting on the vertical wall of the wood. The reptile frightened my arrogance. I didn't know enough about the exotic vermin. I ran for the house without my feet touching the ground.

Now I had a gun. I aimed to kill that great slithering beast. It was not there. I searched high and low. I didn't find the satanic tempter in my garden. I sat and waited for the snake. He never came. My nemesis was a no-show. I was amped. I had a killer's heart pumping wildly in my chest.

There was a bird on the wire, chirping wildly. There were no other birds in sight. I don't know bird talk—I don't know if he was warning all the other birds that this was his territory and not to munch on his berries and worms—or if he was singing some pretty song for the girl birds to want to mate with him—not unlike a Leonard Cohen or a Ray Charles.

Taking aim at the tiny body, I didn't care why he was singing. I took a deep breath and held it. I let it out slowly, and fired the shot when the end of the breath came out. A blast of feathers antedated the bird's heavy pummel downward. The singing had stopped. I silenced the songbird.

I ran towards my kill in shock as waves of panic and terror swept over me. I'd sinned. I knew that immediately. I wasn't prepared to eat this animal, to slice open its belly and remove its organs, to pluck it and carve it and roast it. I wasn't prepared to feed this animal to another animal. I wasn't prepared to make arrow fletching or a writer's quill with the small bird's feathers. I wept openly.

Walking closer and closer to the bird, I prayed to the invisible bird god for it to still be alive. It was heavy in its wounded silence. The avian no longer sang. I cried boyish tears, fearing becoming one of the warrior elders—one of the cracked and strained aged men with weapons and cock, dirty talk and hard walk. I wanted forever young playtime and new wonder, new discovery upon each first step.

A rite of passage had taken place. Where were my elders to walk me through this ceremony, through this field of fire? I was alone with a gun, never having ejaculated, a fresh kill at my feet: too young. I brushed the lifeless avian onto a small thin board with another thin board. I took the bird on the board inside the screened-in-porch located twenty feet from my grandparents' house.

The screen door closed behind me. I took the bird in. I studied his little beak, his iridescent feathers and his tiny talons. I wept sourly. I hurt infinitely.

My father nursed a hangover watching Hollywood Insider and cursing those actors who made it and their lack of talent compared to his own. My father's mother read a romance novel in her mildewed and neglected room—three-hundred-pounds of wonderful person rotting in the company of men. My father's father was 'in town' getting drunk and whatever else he did—no one in the family knew… My retarded uncle clipped interesting stories out of the newspaper for his walk—in which he handed out various articles from the paper to various neighbors.

Spasms in my stomach clenched up my lungs and I could no longer breathe. This was the most upset I'd ever been—the first true feeling of guilt I'd ever experienced. It seemed I might die of grief from my terrible actions.

A miracle occurred. The bird became alive. I had grazed it with my naughty new bullet. The bird awoke with a start—startled, clipped and imprisoned. He chirped madly at me, and hopped around the small, enclosed screen room. He jumped and tried to fly but I'd hit his wing. He flew in circles and spiraled down. He was dazed and confused. He chirped and chirped and hopped like mad. He WAS mad. He was pissed off and frightened to find himself in such conditions.

No longer in the clutches of a grievous death, I sprung to life as well and jumped to the door. I opened it wide, but the bird wouldn't move. He looked at me and screamed at me, but he wouldn't hop away.

Deciding I needed to assist in his getting away, I took off my shoes and socks. I put my socks on my hands and slowly crawled to the bird. I don't know why I needed my hands covered to touch the animal. Was I afraid of germs? A peck on the fingers from the bitty beak? Sharp talons?

I propped the door open. The swing in the middle of the room was a heavy pendulum obstacle as I inched to the corner where the bird crept.

Eventually, the bird fluttered toward the door, hopped outside and struggled to a low-lying branch on the tree outside my father's window. I say my father's window—it was the rear window of my father's parent's house—the house he grew up in—his room—child man—momma's boy.

The bird screamed and chirped for two days straight, figuring out what had happened and really pissed off. After fifty hours or so, the bird grew strong and flew off to relocate to a place less populated with people. I prayed hourly for the health of that little bird and after a spell, my wish was granted.)

Now, years later, I had a .22 rifle in my clutches, and I was quiet in the woods with a headful of acid and a mission from God.

Chuckie and I heard the rustle. He came out of the woods a few yards upwind from us. He was a large procyon lotor with bandit-mask and lemur tail.

The gun was an extension of my will. My eyesight blurred with teary eyes, not for the sadness of the animal, but from the effect of the LSD. I could barely see.

The raccoon walked with a fat waddle hobble and before he made it to the garbage can… BAM! I put a bullet through his neck at two hundred feet. It was the best shot of my career. I had no idea how I made that shot.

"Nice Shot!" God shouted. Chuckie looked great with the twenty-five-pound coon dangling from his muscular arm and grip. Chuckie took the little bandit to the garage.

Rock had parts of motorcycles scattered everywhere on the concrete floor of the garage—tires, engines, seats, handlebars, crankshafts, all oily and metallic strewn about the lawn, under the awning, on the floor. However, Chuckie had previously cleaned a spot for this very activity. We were going to skin this dead animal and use his skin to make holy paper for me to write on. I was flabbergasted.

He handed me a knife and asked me if I'd ever skinned an animal. I wanted to lie but did not. "No."

He took the knife back. "Well, I'll show you once—but you gotta finish the job," he gargled, exhaling cigarette smoke with every vowel.

"Okay." My favorite response.

God shoved the jagged dagger blade deep beneath the raccoon's breastplate. He stretched the victim out onto the plywood resting wobbly on the basement cement. "Put your foot on the tail and don't let up."

"Okay." I did as I was instructed.

God held the pest by the front legs and pulled the hunting weapon down the animal's belly, opening it up to the blood and the spill. He stopped midway and nodded for me to take the knife from him. "Cut him to his asshole!" He held the front legs firm.

"Okay." I cut the nocturnal omnivore the rest of the way. Off Chuckie's further nod, I picked up the beast by the tail, and handed him out away from my body.

God reached in and grabbed the remainder of the guts. "Cut here!" He motioned to the diaphragm. I cut along the windpipe and the gullet, eventually freeing the entrails from the prize. Chuckie caught and dumped the innards into a bucket. The organs hit the plastic with a meaty splash and splat.

Next, God cut off the ring-tailed scavenger's head. He put it in a separate box for later—a later I'd never know—a secret he kept to himself. What did he do with that head? Was it more than a souvenir? Was there a sacred spell cast?

Our gods should (not) be naked and bowing before us…

He showed me how to cut along the inside of the legs and pull the skin back, making slicing motions across the membrane between the skin and the meat.

When the skin was free of meat, I asked, "How are we going to get all of the fur out?"

"We're going to soak it," Chuckie answered.

"In what?"

"A mixture."

"Sounds specific!"

"Uh—fuckin'—mixture of eggshells, baby powder, marble rocks, morning piss after a night of drinking too much by about twenty Plaguists, and some other shit, I'll send you the fuckin' recipe…" Chuckie glared soft lip smile and piercing beams from sunglasses.

"Is it an *exact* recipe?"

"Yes, it is *motherfucker*—the calcium carbonate in the eggshell, talcum and marble will act like an acid and help dissolve the hair follicles of the animal while keeping the skin elastic and ready for the next stage." Chuckie seemed more and more like a God upon each next thing that came out of his mouth. "Now, let's piss in that barrel over 'ere tonight. We need some fresh bile acids to assist in the project."

"How long's it going to take?"

"I don't rightly know Martin—this is my first Plaguist Vellum making."

Chuckie reached into the bucket of entrails. He held the slimy bundle of raccoon innards with one hand and dug around in the pulpy mess with the other. He strained a bit and then ripped free the prize. I wanted it to still be beating, but the heart was just a red lump of bloody organ. He tossed the remaining pink and grey matter into a waste bucket. It made a horrifying splattering *thump*.

"Trophy?" I asked.

"Something like 'at," he responded.

He took out his switchblade pocketknife and opened it with frightening speed. He sliced the meat. He was luckily cutting the slices thin—because he handed me a slice.

I didn't ask questions—I didn't ask if it was meant to be consumed, I knew it was meant to be consumed. But for what purposes—as a curse to our bodies for killing the animal, an ingestion of parasites... Or were we acquiring its spirit abilities by magical consumption... Would we be able to see in the dark now? Develop a taste for spoiling pizza and rancid banana peels?

I didn't get sick, but I did get sneakier, more nocturnal, quiet-in-the-gutter and in-love with other people's trash. Deep down inside I've always wanted to buy a trans-am and change my name to Bandit.

Several days later, I returned to Plague Central.

Chuckie handed me a bottle of black liquid.

"What's this?"

"Homemade ink."

"Homemade?"

"Marybeth and I burned a dozen bibles for the ashes—mixed a few shots of vodka in the mix to make slurry, Pope semen, etc.... We filtered out the clumps through her pantyhose. It's the sexiest fucking ink in existence. Did you bring a feather from an angel's wing?" He smirked.

I showed him the feather I plucked from a hawk wing I found on the side of the road, hit by a car and left for dead.

"Cool." He assured me and ushered me into the garage. He'd set up a small workstation for me. The raccoon skin was stretched and nailed to a large wooden board.

I lit a cigarette and drank from a bottle of Colt 45. I dipped my sky quill into the fiery ink and scribbled across the land skin. I wrote small. I wrote slower than I ever have. I couldn't rip this paper from its spiral cage and discard it in a can. If I screwed up—I would have to shoot another scavenger and eat its heart.

19.

Plaguist Book of the Dead

Amen. Life ends. Pallor through Rigor mortis sets in. The body decomposes. The Spirit exists in memory.

Never concern yourself with bursting supernovas or colliding galaxies. Souls come and go like gods do. Drink your wine and eat your pie and have an orgasm or three. We're all going to die.

What to do when you realize you're dying? Well, that's up to you— very much like your life was.

How did you do? How did you live?

Maybe you'll prefer death—it's not colder because there's no temperature.

Life is hot and cold. Death is constant. Comfort is nonexistent. Sensations are for the living.

Heaven and Hell aren't destinations. There are no punishments or rewards for obeying or disobeying any law, commandment, or deity.

The last sensation to leave your mortal being is your hearing. It's important to choose the right soundtrack to your death. Something with a loud beat is recommended if you'd like to dance into the afterlife with fire and fury.

You still have a will when you're dead—but again, how you manipulate your environment is up to you. How well did you will your life? How much did you laugh? How much pain did you inflict? Joy? Love? How extensive was your concern for others?

The virtuous don't become angels. Angels are terms we labeled supernatural agents of the heavens that were extraterrestrial travelers who gave us great architecture and mathematics, electricity etc…

Have faith in gravity, inertia and the laws of physics. When the supernatural occurs, have a drink and relish the witness. Miracles occur every day. Every breath is a miracle. But the source of these miracles does not have a face, a name, or a description of any kind. We call it Chuckie because it's funny, and you should, too. You should be in our all-inclusive club for deadbeats and mystical realists. You should become a Plaguist. Or not—whatever, it doesn't really matter… Nothing is real— and by proxy the greatest silly putty ever—interpret the infinite jest however you wish. We are all here to go, to be active in the pulse, to generate sensations, and experience this instantaneous trip.

20.

No Sain'ts Day

It was the middle of May. We'd been summoned to Plague Central.

Jas knocked; Chuckie answered. The light from outside singed the eternal darkness inside—smoke and dust and the rotting gas of dead rodents behind the walls igniting in the rare sunshine beam—darkness, stench, decay…

"What's up, motherfuckers?" God asked quickly and spun—up for a hundred hours without sleep—devising a plan. He was on the cracked black and badly burned sofa, carefully filling up small sandwich bags with five cigarettes each.

"Doing your bidding, oh Lordy," I said, imitating Jas in faux gay whine, I exaggerated a lisp and punched The Pope in his always leather jacket.

"My bidding?" Chuckie leapt from the sofa, already grabbing his crotch. "Well, get on this then bitch! It ain't gonna suck itself!"

"Thank You, you're into blasphemy," I responded in self-defense.

He let go of his crotch. "Ahh! Another prideful angel who refuses to PAY THE RENT!" God rolled his eyes.

"Well, you gotta hand it to him, Chuckie." Jas hesitated a dramatic breath. "The boy does dance well to new songs," The Pope sang.

God belched sauerkraut bubbles— "Well, Bless His Little Heart!" He changed tone and headed to the kitchen, spinning on his boot heel and stomping the linoleum.

Jas and I followed, confused and intrigued.

In the kitchen were twenty-five sandwiches in glassine bags, stacked neatly on the table.

"What's with the sandwiches?" Asked Jas.

"NO SAIN'TS DAY!" Chuckie blurted loudly. "Official Plaguist holiday where we behave charitable to those less fortunate than ourselves—which pretty leaves the homeless who have—fuckin'—been banned from the shelters, and bars."

"We're gonna drive around and hand out sandwiches?" I asked.

"I figured the three of us would do it—since no *sain'ts* are allowed to participate—and fuckin'—almost every Plaguist is a Sain't SoandSo—head of fuckin'—whatever."

God lit a Kool and handed me a Happy Meal box which had been spray painted black, inside and out. On the main panel, on a wetly glued printed-on piece of paper, I read the following:

The Seven Deadly Morals:

1. Chastity: Because too much semen in the system can drive a man crazy—and a woman's only truly happy if her pussy's getting pounded (clitoris licked). Every orgasm is heavenly. (Lust is only a sin if you don't orgasm the object.)

2. Shame: Be ashamed of nothing in your mind. The world needs wolves, worms, wind, and weed. Be neither proud of accomplishment nor ashamed of failure.

3. Ambition: The need to accomplish will only cripple your ability to enjoy time.

4. Charity: As a Plaguist, you should never be able to afford to give anything valuable away.

5. Altruism: You are impossible to remove from yourself. Seeking selflessness is a selfish act.

6. Satiation: Self-control presumes destiny wants nothing to do with you.

7. Piety: Because my living God is full of shit and reminds me of it reverently.

I was truly impressed with the seven deadly morals. I turned the box around, and found:

The Four Ignoble Truths: Buddha was a big fat liar:

1. Life is not suffering: Conscious awareness is not pain and agony but hilarious absurdity. 'The pursuit of ecstasy' is the drug users' motto,

but also the mystics' who seek to take in every particle of existence with a calm, but full breath. Don't worry about shit and have a good time.

2. <u>Suffering's source is circumstance</u>: Pity not yourself. If you're innately clumsy, try a career in comedy before taking on an auctioneer of fine china. If you're a bedwetting crybaby, date the stern. If you think life is suffering, then you haven't suffered correctly.

3. <u>Suffering's cessation</u>: Get over it. See truths 1 and 2. If you're the child of a suicide, take pride in your better resolve. If you're the parent of a deviant, write Plaguist on a shirt and send them off to wherever they play loud rockNroll—they'll be taken care of.

4<u>. The way leading to the cessation of suffering others</u>: This is the ignoble truth of the way leading to the cessation of suffering others. It is the Ignoble Eightfold Path:

I turned the box now one quarter, and find on the side panel:

The Ignoble Eightfold Path:
1. See.
2. Intend.
3. Speak.
4. Behave in accordance with will.
5. React to prejudice loudly.
6. Gain access.
7. Take every chance.
8. Afford every consequence.

I turned the box again.

The Ten Suggestions
(Fuck All Commandments)
Thou should do drugs and marinate the brain for a hungry God.
Thou should not obey any rules for the sake that they are rules.
Thou should accept no word as truth.
Thou should tug on Superman's Cape—'cause it's only an actor in costume.
Thou should not trust any elected official.
Thou should order the fried calamari.
Thou should not order the fried calamari.
Thou should listen to rockNroll at least once a day.
Condescend.
Thou should come up with their own ten suggestions.

Chuckie explained further. "I was at the liquor store buying a case of thunderbird when I saw 'ese fuckin'—stacks of vodka bottles and I bought 'em on a whim—and fuckin'—knew pretty *instantly* what I wanted to do. I did a little more shopping—stole these-here kid's-meals paper to-go boxes, and fuckin'—here we are."

Jas cackled as he read the box I had finished reading.

"Yeah, it took us all night to put the paper on the boxes 'cause alls we had was modeling glue and kept getting high you know—laughing and shit..."

"What's in the box?" I wanted to know.

"Fuckin'—cigarettes—sandwiches—cookies—a little juice box—a little bottle of booze, which I think is cool as shit, and uh—fuckin'—five of which will be dosed with LSD—and fuckin'—a packet of restaurant butter."

"What's the butter for?" I asked.

"Well—those that have been locked-up will know—you use it to jack off with—best prison lube there is—the others will ignore it or spread it on their sandwich."

I was overwhelmed. "This is genius!"

"Everything we do is genius, you moron!" Chuckie laughed a hazy cough in my face.

We three young men laughed loudly.

"Do you feel bad about secretly dosing the homeless?" I lamely asked Chuckie.

"Look closer!" He barked at me.

I looked closer—there was a small white sticker on each bottle that said—May Contain Acid.

More laughter—closer to insanity—bulletproof—fireproof—young.

Chuckie banged on the dashboard as I sped up to sixty miles an hour, acutely aware of the attention I received driving that painted-up automobile The Mystery Ship. Jas laughed and smoked a hash pipe in the backseat. We were on our way to pick up Reverend Killjoy. She was stone cold sober and was interested to go along for the ride and give out gift baskets to the homeless.

"Hello everyone," she said without looking at anyone, or rather, looking each of us in the eyes then staring off into space.

I played Reverend's mixtape she handed me—it began with Dead City Radio, William Burroughs + John Cale—*No More Stalins, No More Hitlers.*

We listened intently to Uncle Bill tell us of frightened pilots elevated to the highest positions based on abstract and economic factors… The song lasted under one minute, then *Jesus Built My Hotrod* by Ministry.

"STOP!" Chuckie yelled.

I stopped. He jumped out. He strutted big and tall up to some wino with a gray beard and skinny bones, and his company a younger bum with dumb luck and no shoes and offered them each a Plaguist happy meal. They thanked him confusedly and profusely, especially once they spotted the tiny bottles of vodka.

We drove on. I didn't know who was more impressed, me or the Reverend. I felt like I was charioteer to Krishna—a character-driven plot, a god-consumed pilot—a virtuous Vishnu charioteer—a part of something holy. *Rock Music* by The Pixies played, and I sprayed invisible happy pheromones into the air, hoping to get everyone **_off_** unconsciously…

"How many of the bottles are dosed with LSD?" The Reverend wanted to know.

"I'd say about *Five*."

"Out of how many?" The Pope wanted to know.

"TWENTY-FIVE!" God replied.

"Up to five people will be handed a wee bottle of vodka dosed with how much LSD?" Reverend Killjoy, the accused CIA agent pressed.

Chuckie growled— "About two hits worth—enough to put you in proper geosynchronous orbit with Earth But not take you OUT of it."

"Unless they're crazy," I interjected.

God spoke, "Well, if they're crazy, fuck 'em—or God bless 'em— whichever way it turns out to be—there might be a fuckin' amnesiac who gets the lucky bottle and remembers he's from two thousand miles from here and gets to go back home to his loved ones—or one lucky son of a bitch will go haywire berserk and slaughter some random family with an axe. You never know! —But putting crazy shit like this into effect is what the creator does—sometimes you have to encourage a little *frenzy*."

Jack Nicholson couldn't have read that line any cooler.

"Well, what if one of them does ax-murder their family? Aren't you worried about an autopsy and a possible link back to this experiment?" I asked with a paranoid tone.

"STOP!" Chuckie yelled.

Obeying, I stopped suddenly. *Scentless Apprentice* by Nirvana blasted from the car.

He jumped out of The Mystery Ship, ran this time, and placed a Plaguist happy meal on the stomach of a passed-out bum and ran back to the car. I was waiting, of course, in awe of the comedy of the cosmos. He shut the door. We drove off.

He spoke as if the conversation had been on pause for his performance. "No, I ain't worried. Fuck-n-hell! If there were security cameras around here these men wouldn't be able to drink so openly. This is the fucking ghetto. We're not actually SAFE in this neighborhood. But Art Ain't Cheap! No matter what religion you *belong to*, or magic you *believe in*—they all require some *sacrifice*. There's no *sure thing*—even *change* might one day become nil. STOP!"

I stopped and was worried. We were in a bad part of town—a derelict part of town, dark without streetlights. The shadows owned future corpses and crept along the safe place-to-hide in horrorshow fear. Another three happy meals were placed in the hands of pitifully downtrodden alcoholics. They muttered acceptance, but upon discovery of the booze all yelled *'thank you'*.

We drove around some more and I became aware of headlights following us.

"Someone's following us."

Jas lit a cigarette and positioned himself to see my rearview mirror. "Speed up," he encouraged my daring.

Rid of Me by P.J. Harvey blasted.

I sped up. So did the tail.

"How do I get to the Interstate?"

Chuckie pointed directions.

The tail followed me all the way to the Interstate. I got on the interstate. The tail did not. I guessed it was local thugs protecting their hood like Rottweilers, chasing away the suspicious element.

In various fashion we gave out twenty Plaguist Happy Meals. Some were left to be discovered by janitors, raccoons, or school children. One could never be sure when fate comes into play. I remember the spray paint graffiti on the brick wall of some store's alleyway: *if you ain't playin' fate, then fate's playin' you:* painted in sloppy yellow letters and barely legible, a secret language spoken only to the observant.

"STOP!"

Chuckie got out of the car. I waited.

Sex Sux by The Vaselines played on the tape. I loved this mix from the sexy Reverend.

"I'm pregnant," the Reverend blurted out matter-of-factly. It took a minute for the information to sink in.

"Congratulations." I looked at her pretty, pale face and dark-socketed eyes in the rearview mirror: she truly expressed no emotion about this fact whatsoever. She was impossible to read, not even a light flinch or a transparent twitch—no invisible cinch in her crow's feet, no clinch in her jaw, no slight pinch in the corner of her mouth.

"YOU KNOW!" The Pope hilariously blurted, "I always thought you women getting pregnant were the only reason we kept your kind around!"

"Huh?" The Reverend asked, curious as to how her announcement meant death to all females.

"I mean, if it were up to ME, I would DESTROY all women and have MEN give birth by symbiosis, like a *wet* gremlin."

I laughed.

"Shush!" He pointed a finger at me, fearing my participation in his monologue. "We could feed them with our consumption, a rich diet for the parasite, and they could grow too heavy and plop from our bellies." He sucked from his fag— "And like *birthing* wouldn't even cost you your *six-pack* 'cause you could easily lose the four-pound placenta on your gut like so much jellyfish foie gras."

I laughed more. He joined me. I thought he was a genius. So did everybody else. He was revered for his cunning words and citrus tipped kisses.

"AND THEN!" He announced with new cigarette, louder and more ready-to-burst-with-the-joke-so-please-don't-interrupt. "Our testicles could swell to enormous size and fill with milk, like tittie size, and to feed the next generation of our all-male/all-gay society we would insert our limp penises into the mouths of our boy offspring, and they could feed. SEMEN would be our life blood—literally." He sucked from his fag, exhaled and then laughed.

I was in stitches. I barely remember the story, but every word of it made me laugh. No one could be less serious than the Pope, even when he thought he meant every word.

Talkin' About The Smiling Deathporn Immortality Blues by The Flaming Lips played loudly.

The Reverend didn't laugh. She didn't bat a lash, pucker a lip, or swallow a word. She was still waters. Not even a leaf floated on her pond—no ripple of emotion on her undetectable surface. Glass. Cool. I wondered if she knew how to play poker, or had any interest in hustling the public, because with a straight face like that you could bluff your entry anywhere. Hell, probably how she got herself knocked up. How well did I know this Reverend chick? Was she alien? C.I.A? Was she a company girl?

Whatever. I thought it was funny. I think everything should be made fun of, including any dogma, or opera, anything holy, anything sacred and therefore profane. I long for the love of ridicule.

Chuckie got back in the car. I started her up. Don't you hate anthropomorphizing modes of transportation? Started HER up. It's always a feminine pronoun, or a female name, isn't it? Well, I for one would rather ride in a female, wouldn't you? Wouldn't you have rather been born of your mother than your father? What would that have been like, sucking your dad off for nutrients with no mommy around?

21.

Opening Up

I lay flat on my belly and closed my eyes. I reached out and hugged the bed. I didn't care what happened to me. I was naked and sexed, bare, relaxed and open. Ready poured baby oil on my ass and massaged my legs. She worked the young muscles, teased the tender tendons and tactile tissue. She used both hands on one cheek massaging the ball of my half ass and sliding her pinky up against my crack. The oil slipped in. I was lubricated. She continued, stroking and molding, massaging and teasing. My tired and sore dick was regretfully erect.

She stuck her pinky in my ass first. Slip! She took it out quickly and played with my balls. I throbbed. My heart pounded electroclash. My cock danced. She stuck her pointer finger into my ass. Whoop! Wiggled it. She took it out slowly, easily. I fucked her comforter, rubbing my hard-on up and down the soft quilting of her blanket.

A hot flash of pain electrocuted from the center of my back through my whole body. I clenched and released. She dripped violent wax on my back from a lit candle. I masturbated her bed spread with humping motions.

"If you let me finger fuck you—you can have my ass," she whispered a hot challenge into my ear.

"Okay." My favorite answer.

Sounds of rabbits sniffing violets rattled in the quiet of my peaceful head as she licked my balls and tickled my sides with her long fingernails. I was as hard as I've ever been. My heart galloped triple crown and my stomach filled with electric eels attacking rattlesnakes. Nauseous euphoria, caustic heaven—I was bent orgasmic and shivering. I clenched every muscle. My teeth clamped shut as if by electric stimulation of the Masseter muscle. I squirmed in ecstasy then clenched in an overload of sensory input.

She poured water into my asshole. It felt incredible, cold wriggling liquid licking my insides as she licked my outside. My God, she was getting ready to fuck me. I was too hard to come—too numb to feel where my dick was any more. She grabbed my balls and pulled them very hard. I thought I might pass out.

This was my first submissive position—I laid prostrate and waited for the prostate's fate. I could do nothing but take it. My heart raced, but my mind was remarkably calm, lucid, fluid, allowing the pleasure to come into me, the new sexual experience to blossom within me, a schoolgirl crush on whoever was doing this to me…

Ready operated on me, behind me. I couldn't see her café late skin with almond butter freckles and dark chocolate corkscrew hair. I couldn't see her cloudy Milky Way eyes and burnt marshmallow lips, soft hot sweetness of the orgiastic campfire song…

She stuck it in slowly and easily. The smooth long finger wiggled. It went easy to the first knuckle and then she slowed down, crept her strong cello bow middle finger into me. At the second knuckle I clenched. "Shhh!" She calmed me like a mother to her noisy child. I breathed in but not out and relaxed. She went further in, and I exhaled.

Slowly, expertly, with my balls in her mouth wet with pleasure and swollen with copulative energy, she pushed her long strong middle finger all the way into me, until her ring finger was flat against my balls and her pointer finger scraped my cheek.

Sucking and stroking my dick was the only way she could do this properly. The feeling was complete and total pleasure, every atom, every pore open to the sensation of this moment, this time and place with Ready.

Could I love a woman like this? Would I be a junky slave to her passionate embrace and destroy our artistic careers with want nothing but constant ejaculation and play? That was a worry.

She poured more oil on my ass and spent a lot of time on my balls, teasing, tugging, tickling, up to the shaft and a stroke, a stroke and the deep burn of her middle finger slowly inching into my rectum, a powerful presence, meant to be there. I was about to be fucked. I knew that, I felt her fleshy extension in my wet orifice. She dug around. She stretched and wriggled and slowly found her way out of there and then suddenly she was back in and deeper, my God, she could've given me an exam.

Deep inside me was her musician's finger searching my harmony and key. I whimpered a fractured lullaby of pleasure in soft alto moans and unsure baritone growls. She took it out and put it in me, so much that I no longer clenched. I relaxed and let her have my ass.

I came so hard it shot into my hair, and after a blow job and two proper fucks. She jumped on my back and put me in a headlock. I couldn't breathe. I almost passed out but came again and remained hard. I couldn't become soft. I was worried.

Ready squeezed the baby oil all over my backside. She put her ass toward me and her face on the bed. She reached her long slender arms beneath her and played with her pussy. She reached further and played with her asshole.

"Now. Shove that thing in my ass."

I was not interested in love. All the love I had given away in the past half decade had been mostly unrequited. My mother was in New York sobering up and battling her demons and my father stayed out all night getting drunk with the boys, coming home shit-faced sour and sometimes with a black eye or a smashed front fender and more than one time being followed by the police.

The girls I chose to offer my attention to were lost causes, beautiful bitches and a gothic ex-girlfriend of a suicide. I had nowhere to hide. I was vulnerable from the start. I wanted to melt off the bridge in a slow-motion snowstorm. I wanted to consume and be consumed, run away from home and join the circus—I wanted sexual ruckus and the nothingness of the touch-us to touch us.

I fell in love too easily like a cartoon unicorn in a four-year-old's fantasy. I fell for every misfit kindergarten shadow, every triumphant elementary school spectacle, every pre-teen anxious grumble—every adolescent acting out—every...

I dulled my blade on stone monuments. I waged war on windmills. I drove my buffalo over the cliff. I found comfort in drugs and alcohol and decided to invest property in the dream of being a writer. (How am I doing?) I invoked the external. I created a safe place to hide and invented myself omnipotent.

I was beginning to understand Plaguism—the belief that absurdity shall be the whole of the law. I understood what it meant, the following of THE IDEA of Chuckie The Plague: free of belief, containing no Dogma, no Commandments, No judgment day, no need of praise.

My loneliness helped form my religious views.

I loved my new brethren, my new familiars, my new lovers and competitors. But I had no intention of staying. I had a wild magnet inside of me lusting for new poles. I knew that sounded gay—but that was not what I meant. It was good to laugh at myself. I was tuning into the joke—the absurdity of it all—of man the gold miner on temporary terracotta… Half ape/half star child… Midnight dreams of Homo Erectus ancestors undergoing the treatment—extraterrestrial gene splicing…

All the worlds' myths danced in my head—Egyptian chimera, African spiders, American coyotes, Yeti, Nessie, The Jersey Devil, Asian Dragons, Aboriginal kangaroos, American rabbits, Hercules, Dionysius, and Atlas…

The drugs kept me incapable of linear thought.

I was numb from the love I couldn't give away. The love festered and rotted around me until it hardened and had to be chipped away at—which is where we were now—me doing this—now.

I was so free then—to explore anything I wanted—so long as it had nothing to do with love.

22.

Sermon of the Bi-Attitudes

Clip-clopity-clop swish-swish-swish-swish she entered through darkness to the obvious stage, cleared for this performance and the spotlight, set up for her. Marybeth was skinny milk in mad villain silk puckering neon cherry mouth—full down south, a snarling darling smoker too.

She went to the mic. The stand was low to the ground. She stroked the mic on the stand like a hard on. She tweaked the imaginary nipples of the man standing by. Everyone laughed. She turned the mic up and brought it to her face. She stroked and stroked the microphone and opened her mouth and pretended to be jizzed on by some ejaculating ghost. The stand got higher, the microphone closer and closer to her mouth, until she tightened it into place.

She licked her lips and began her sermon. "Lust is only a sin if you don't orgasm the object." Marybeth was drenched in red—dress, shoes, lips, nails and bow-in-hair. The dress accentuated her childbearing hips, the contours of her body like a rollercoaster.

I felt an electric spark as she shot me a look and then shot several other looks across us, the audience. But I didn't have time to recover.

"Pull my hair, pull me close, pull me down, pull my clothes off, pull your clothes off—let's do it skin-to-skin in intimate sweaty detail. —Let's fill each other up with our own fulfillment of each other. Let's make love."

"ANYTIME, ANYWHERE!!!" Shouted some loud Plaguist. Could've been anyone.

"What to do with life? Suck it, fuck it, kiss it, make it wet. —Lick it, stroke it, pound it, make it hard. —Take it, give it, open it up. What to do with the great mystery? Come to no too soon conclusion—play with it, explore it, get to know it, hunt it, wound it, fuck it."

"WOO-HOO!!!" Was a common interjection form us the audience, mesmerized by the experience, that moment, her legs, her dress, the syllable-express coming from her red choo-choo mouth.

"The positive and negative charges are equal opposites of the same energy. The negativity of humans is born at the same time as human's most positive. In this way we find emotional equilibrium in our collective unconscious."

The audience, stunned still, baited on an inhale, held total silence. You heard her hand smooth out her dress and her mercurial inhale.

"Relax the body, address the issues, knead the knot, massage the soft, pet the tender, open up the petals, bee buzz the stamen, collect the pollen, hum your symphony in the orchestral flower—make your honey."

Marybeth became the audience's muse then—every one of us listened intently to her smooth delivery and practiced potency.

"Bind your finger in gold and go forth with another—reproduce if you must, but be true to any dedication, or don't fucking take it." She cocked her head once more and again took a hit from her cigarette. "Now. Who wants to get nasty?"

Of course, we ejaculated in our pants and screamed our presence and gave aye-aye to whatever Ahab for whatever whale.

She sauntered across the stage and slowly looked us each one up and down. "Blessed be the hungry for my pussy—the thirsty for my sweat. I want to be salty with the earth of you. I will never lose my flavor, but you can lick me to death to find out." She sat down on a wooden stool and hiked her dress up, showing off an eight-inch switchblade in her red silk panties. She removed the blade and stabbed her dress. She pulled the sharp blade through the satin fabric all the way around her body, leaving the dress to just below her panties.

My God, when she sat on the stool and tucked the switchblade back in her glistening panties, I almost passed out with a smile.

"Blessed be those who moan—for they will be fondled with ever increasing delight." She hit her cigarette.

"Blessed be the myths we create in our exorbitant youth! Blessed be the cool we enrage with our flames! Rejoice! We are shaded from the blinding light of the world."

Jane's was packed with Plaguists. There were hundreds there, jamming the aisles, creaking the stairs, listening from downstairs, standing around outside in massive clumps and, of course, drunk and high in booths and in chairs. Everyone was quiet as we listened to the sermon of the church concubine.

Marybeth bit her bottom lip and stroked the microphone like a cock. She slowly stuck out her tongue and let it retreat. "Let no virgin god have the audacity to restrict your pleasure. Let no penitent head-bower break your pride. Let no merciless heaven-seeker condemn you to any sentence. The only prison that can contain you is the prison of your own mind."

She had us in the palm of her hand, drooling, oogly-googling, gawking, wet panties and hard-on. This whore of Babylon babbled-on about love and sex and orgasm and the wet needy greed for a cock and a cum to hear Chuckie's name screamed—his name soothing regal word of great inspiration.

"Spread the other cheek! Respond to your aggressor in confidence!"

Cheers. Goddamn there were cheers and loud whistles and bellowing howler monkey growls and deep guttural groaning obscenities. It was glorious rapacious restraint. Bridled passion.

Marybeth spoke with chubby cheeks and succulent mouth, eyes downsizing the audience to our knees. "Orgasm the object lesson. Caress the moral compass until it's corrupted by your lust object. Never object to an orgasm. To refuse an orgasm is to strain the universe. Fire the synapse! Race the heart! Lick my pussy until I fart!"

We erupted in applause, hooting and hollering and on our horny feet.

She disappeared into her adoring mob which licked her and kissed her to bruises. I saw her later—she was a wreck, but what a great show. She had such a shining glow. I'll remember it forever.

23.

The Baptism of Sain't Gabe

Immediately after the Sermon of The Bi-Attitudes, a young man in a wheelchair rolled up to Jas and squealed to him that he wanted to be baptized a Plaguist. Jas smiled and inquired more.

"Well, what makes you think you're qualified?"

The boy stumbled upon himself smiling and gasped a laugh—which was enough apparently, because Jas agreed to baptize him right then and there.

I came back from the bar to find Jas in full flight as spiritual guru.

"NO! Say it right! —I once could see but now am blind." Jas raised his eyebrows, eyelids, and mouth as if encouraging the struggling inflicted.

The face of the palsied boy contorted and twisted like a dying hamster. He spoke very fast. "I onst could snee but noW Am bLIND!"

"There we are!" Celebrated Jas by tossing beer on Gabe's greasy hair. (I found out later his name was Gabe. He was the brother of Sain't Jefrey with one f.)

Gabe squealed like a delighted toy.

"I once was found but now am lost!" Jas looked into those innocent and damaged eyes and smiled.

Gabe exhaled and inhaled spittle rapidly in three quick progressions. He was agitated, but courageous.

Gabe's eyes grew wide, and his jaws clenched and he breathlessly declared. "I Unst zZ LOST but noW Am FOUnd!" He exhaled and breathed heavily.

"Nope! Try again." Jas wiggled the can of beer in front of him as if a carrot stick to a donkey. "If you want to be a Plaguist, you got to get it right—I'm not concerned with your palsy—I mean: would you want to belong to a club that let in *any* ol' retard?!" Jas laughed respectively somehow, encouraging with his lacerating truthfulness—not giving an inch, treating equally.

"I ZXFOUNDUT OW M LOSHT!" Screamed Gabe in high squeals of delight and spittle courage. It was a beautiful thing to see, his wet and wounded single peacock feather—but its rise and shine…

"Well, congratulations, Gabe, you're a Plaguist!" Jas doused Gabe's head with his can of beer. Gabe squealed and opened his mouth, catching some of the liquid. He was truly having a party. Was this his first one? What happened? Did we convert a mentally handicapped person to Plaguism? What did that say about the rest of us? Were we sincerely all inclusive, or did it simply not matter one way or the other if you fucking considered yourself a Plaguist or not?

"Plagueeest!" Squealed Gabe, twitching his head from one side of the wheelchair to the other.

"Not just a Plaguist! A Sain't! You are Sain't Gabe of the Joystick!" Jas looked at me and smiled. He looked into Gabe's eyes, which couldn't be looked into, and declared as a creed— "Anytime someone has a problem operating their joystick, be it to operate a wheelchair, or man in a video game, or a man in general, they should pray to you—Sain't Gabe—Holy Sain't of the Joystick."

"WHEEEEEEEE! Sain't GAAAAh-AABBE!"

Sain't Gabe wheeled around now, operating the joystick with his chin. He spun around and around laughing and squealing. He pushed over a few chairs with his bruised and useless legs then hurried off to tell someone about his new rebirth.

Jas wasted no time whispering to me— "Do you know how many hours, how many nights—months—possibly years I'm going to spend masturbating to Sain't Gabe of the joystick?"

"All right: that's enough."

"It's not nearly enough!" He said loudly— "I mean! I bet he weighs *sixty-five* pounds. To lift him up and place him in the bed, —oh—his muscles so constricted and *tight*, TENSE and almost mummy-like, and that terrified skull that couldn't possibly know what I'm about to do!"

If one is to know no bounds, then one cannot escape their own villainy. To be free…

"Okay! We get it! You got the hots for the paraplegic. You have found a new low to sink to and wish to wallow in the stink for a little while."

Jas smiled smugly at me and breathed in delightfully. "You know Martin, in some ways—you and I are very different."

24.

Bubbles Blown

Meanwhile, back at S.P.A.M Manor:

I ate my sixth hit of Purple Funk or whatever the shit was called and couldn't smoke enough cigarettes, couldn't drink enough booze, smoke enough weed. Nothing affected my trip. The LSD took over the ride.

Became lost in a series of bubbles that formed from my soapy, drippy wand: blew perfect spheres of transparent rainbows and they slowly drifted in the humid haze of Jas's smoke-filled apartment. Watched as they delicately floated through the crowd…

Rock constantly popped the bubbles that came near him. Jas tried to catch them in his palm as if they were butterflies. Marybeth and Minx were mesmerized, too high to be otherwise. Chuckie and Dominic were discussing the earnest importance of being.

Imagined everyone was dancing in a sort of syncopated stasis telling one another where the brightest flowers were. Was the only one not dancing. Bees.

"Why are you not dancing?" The voice came forth in slow and deep ocean grooves, the speaker had the head of Marybeth, the body of Chucky and the legs of Jas.

Stood stoned with my mouth agape wondering if I should go to the hospital. Someone grabbed my hand and pulled me from the sofa—but once up, my body didn't function as a dancer, more like a quadruped made of wet clay.

Had issues with gravity. Stuck in the wobbly reality of an acid frenzy. Didn't hear music. Heard only the bizarre vibrations that buzzed all around me, from every direction, as if I had the metabolism of a hummingbird and was in fast-forward.

Nothing was stationary, every atom in existence was in flux and saw every particle, every proton, every electron, rapidly circumnavigating their nucleus. Saw the infinite universe.

Understood the mystical dance of the whirling Sufis, the planetary revolutions of the solar system, it all made sense now—life was in motion—be in motion—be active with spirit—use the energy that's been given to you—dance! Dance! Dance! —I danced to every song that had ever been recorded—and at once—thrust and jolted and basically spazzed out, jerking around like a victim of electric shock, but really feeling the spirit—and the music came to me—I comprehended what we listened to—it was The Pixies—the wonderful Pixies—Doolittle even— and yes—I did want to grow up to be a Debaser—a debaser of art and standard and morality… We danced and we ate more acid and basically everyone lost their mind.

Started freaking out. Ate too much acid. Someone suggested I take a Spleef exercise. Didn't know what that meant.

"Come here and I'll show you—" guided the Pope.

I followed Jas outside. We lit cigarettes and I watched as he smiled and stared at the sky, back to me, and back to the sky.

"Well?" I impatiently asked.

"Well, what?"

"What the fuck is a spleef exercise?"

"Well, first, tell me how you're feeling?"

"How am I feeling? I'm feeling better out here in the air and away from the catacomb aura of your haunt…"

Interrupting enthusiasm—quoting in gallantry: "Catacomb Aura of your Haunt!" He almost cackled out the phrasing of his mocked appall. "You better write that down or I will."

I felt the drug consume me in wonderful spasms of muscular happiness. I took it in the gut. I used to flex my stomach muscles, tighten my gut and make all the speedy acid twinges go there. Tense still— "What the fuck is a spleef exercise? Is it this? Being outside?"

Jas looked at me in superior seriousness. "Not JUST being outside, but taking big, delightful gulps of air and remembering who you are. That's a spleef exercise: take a moment away from the party to get a breath of fresh air and remember who you are. —Also, don't let the drug take you—don't let the high succeed in you surrendering all gravity— because it's a meaty fall!" Jas smiled and laughed and smiled wider and seemed to have surprised himself with his own eloquence. He laughed and cackled some more. It seemed he'd discovered who he was and, as always, gloated his Raven magic.

I took a deep breath and remembered who I was. Who was I? I was Martin Socrates Hemlock, poet, ex-carnie, teenager, captain of The Mystery Ship, and apparently Angel of Death in The First Interplanetary Church of the Immaculate Deception. I busted out laughing. What silly titles I'd accumulated. I was a long way from Esquire or PHD and, I think, in the right direction. I was who I was. I remembered those little freak outs and how easy they were to squash. I freaked out, calmed down, went back inside and had the time of my life. I enjoyed being a tamed psychotic.

The party shifted, and Jas and I were alone with our bubbles. We blew bubbles for hours, doing experiments with blowing cigarette smoke into the bubbles and watching as they popped and let go of their foggy ghosts. I had no recollection of anyone leaving that party, hours later blowing bubble after bubble, unable to stop. Horror! —We ran out of bubbles. This was a worse thing that could've happened than if we were robbed at gunpoint and tied up. I would've gladly given those cat-burglars every cent of our Chicago fund and what else they wanted if they would leave the bubble mixture. Alas! No robbers—out of bubbles. Fuck it—we drove to the all-night grocery store and bought two gallons of liquid dish-soap and a six pack of beer.

"Hey, you guys got any glycerin?" Jas yelled to the late-night stock boy.

I was curious. "Why, what the fuck does that do?"

"It makes all of the bubbles stronger, sturdier."

"How the fuck do you know that?"

The stock boy heard his question and scratched his head when he came over to greet us. "I don't rightly know—but I would guess it'd be in pharmacy."

"Why do you guess that?" I wanted to know

"Cause I ain't never heard of it before." He looked at me as if he was upset that he couldn't help us with the glycerin problem.

"Sounds reasonable—thank you for your time."

Amazingly enough, we found the glycerin, and we had sense enough to buy beer and cigarettes—which is no small feat at three in the morning tripping balls on six hits of kick ass acid and roaming a fluorescent lit grocery store of the most frigid kind—which is completely empty except the drunks, the cops, and the misfits, which were us.

Meanwhile, back at S.P.A.M. Manor, things had gotten out of control with the bubbles. We took coat-hangers and bent them with diligence and precision to form perfect bubble wands. We used dish-plates that we first scrubbed spotless clean, the first time we deemed it necessary to do so, amazingly clean, and poured them to the rim with a mixture of liquid dish soap and glycerin. We played outside for the first time—we made gigantic bubbles in the warm, humid, wee hours.

There was a technique to the process. One didn't blow these bubbles. These bubbles had to be coerced from their metal rings with a pull of the arm and a twist of the wrist, cutting off the flow and forming the bubble. The amorphous globules jiggled and jellied from the wand, gigantic and dancing in the humid evening. They had difficulty forming perfect spheres, oozing and bending heavy with their own weight in the dense air.

We paid attention to each bubble at first, amazed by the slick rainbow surface of the gelatinous shapes, playing strange games with gravity and balance—floating in front of our eyes for what seemed like hours. There was little to no wind, so the bubbles hung around for hours (minutes) before gently fucking off. I saw my own reflection in the perfect sphere—sixty inches across in the thick air—rise and float away into the starry ink.

We made more, more and more—for hours, and when the bubbles formed spheres and hung around too long, we blew on them with exerting force—rippling the belly of the bubble like the surface of a pond with a skipped rock—undulating waves of shape-shifting wobble on the unresisting bubble. The humid night was right for us. It was June—and we were on our twentieth or thirtieth trip together in under two months.

It was a miracle that humid weather—and those monstrous balloon-size bubbles quivering and hovering so—transparent mirrors of rainbow oil swirling slow hurricanes of colors and suds. The glycerin did the trick, really holding the soap fat together.

Soon, the sun came up, and we were still hypnotized by the levitating liquid circus before us. I assume people came and went through the apartment complex, left their homes, walked, rode bicycles, drove their cars and came back to their home throughout the day—but I was aware of none of them. Apparently, Rock and Marybeth came over to see how we were doing around five pm—but neither Jas nor I had any recollection of that reality. We were stoned and stuck in the land of the bubbles. There was no other reality except the importance of our mission to keep making these giant bubbles. I wondered if some wizard on the other side of town hadn't cast a spell on us as a sort of clown show for his children—as if these bubbles formed in magic were going to glide on over to the other side of town and entertain their party. I didn't care if that was the truth—I was getting so off—I would've blown those bubbles for Satan or Christ alike. —The sun went down.

"Did the sun go up and come down really fast?"

"Yes."

"This is the best trip I've ever had."

"Me too."

"We're almost out of bubbles."

"Well, we'll have to go get more."

I have no idea which of us said what in this dialogue reproduction, but I do remember that we shared a similar experience—a similar spiritual high—a similar sentient moment in our creative lives—these bubbles were the best work either of us had ever done as artists.

In the grocery store, we were experts as to where everything was. We walked with slippery confidence, leaving a trail of soapy footprints towards the pharmacy. We bought glycerin so many times the workers were convinced we'd found a new way to get high—home care for the liquid detergent—we bought four gallons this time. We bought some beer and some more cigarettes because we smoked John Wayne amounts of tobacco, and I put a little more gas in the car, because I wanted to make sure that we could get to the store if we ran out of bubbles again.

On the thirty-tenth straight hour of making bubbles, the humidity lifted, and the wind picked up. Now the bubbles were much bigger and more of them came from the wand at a time, because you could simply hold the wand at an angle and close the opening with a twist. The bubbles lifted chaotically across the playing field and as some of them blasted into the house window, I wondered if everyone inside was okay. I knew the bubbles had power and could go through matter. Jas was convinced one of the bubbles had cracked a tree limb off. He watched it fall to the ground.

We became worried, at first, that the bubbles might get sucked into the engine of a passenger jet and down the enormous 747, killing all three hundred on board. We tried to make this happen—thinking we'd been given clever weapons by some god concerned with overpopulation.

The Sun didn't come up this time. The day broke gray with clouds and rain on the way. The silver skin sky hung low from the calcium flesh—pale amethyst crystals drained of their magic—electric darkness brought us sparking shards of heat cracking—bellows of faraway thunder. The bubbles looked great with this backdrop. We let the wind have as many bubbles as we could coat the earth with.

The rain held off for as long as it could. The air was once again thick, charged with ionized particles—the smell of ozone and mushroom—the bubbles continued to form from our wands, some rising into the sky slowly, some carried off with the wind intentionally, depending upon the temperament of the afternoon.

The first few drops came, hitting our magical bubbles in the head, exploding their perfect formlessness. The bubbles popped heavily, letting out their oxygen and nitrogen and other gasses in slow, sickly motions— rainbows dying in heavy vomit of liquid soap, splashing onto the ground with a SPLAT!

One after the other our bubbles busted. All hell broke loose. The raindrops hit the pavement in a heavy curtain of hydrogenated pounding. It was impossible to make bubbles anymore. We watched as the blood of our babies foamed into pretty white suds, caviar of tiny white bubbles, frothing foam of fish roe. They formed on the asphalt, on the car windshields, hoods and roofs. A frothy floe of suds dripped from the apartment roof.

We'd cleaned a portion of the complex. The yellow tree pollen that coated most of the vehicles in our lot washed away, down the drain and into the sewer system, where hopefully more shit would be cleaned.

Inside S.P.A.M. Manor, Jas instantly changed into a towel and pranced around the tiny apartment like a satirical satyr insatiable for attention and yet ironically misanthropic. He breathed in, filling his emaciated frame to slender proportions and stroked his xylophone ribs. I heard them clink and plink like a cartoon soundtrack. "Well—I—need a shower—care to join me?"

"I'll wait my turn, thanks."

It was a shower that needed no soap. I was soaked from head to toe in Dawn or whatever it was—blue and green glowing syrup for doing the dishes—coated all over with these cleaning ingredients. It took forever to get the slick off.

I was glad Jas left the door open. It was nice to see, hear, and smell the fantastic storm. The house shook with striking lightning close by— rUmBLeD with thunderous sound waves forcing the air around us!.!..!!!

Billions of watery bullets shot from the heavens storming the earth— really giving it to the ground, suffocating her puddles and flooding her plains, soil saturated, unable to hold, spilling over, the Cumberland River already running high—washing away all the dead matter it can, to make room for new growth. I smoked cigarettes and stared at the rain for hours. It rained and it rained, and I wondered if we didn't unlock some mystical porthole to some alternate rainy universe, and that it might flood for an eternity and a half.

The rain cleansed the earth. I, too, felt a need for cleansing. My season of filth and degeneration coagulated my senses. I needed a spiritual scrub.

25.

Bottoms Up

There was now a Plaguist lawyer. Dominic passed the Tennessee State Bar Exam. He could officially represent us in court—AND WOULD! Jas had helped him study all spring. Now, he had passed. It was remarkable. The money and the effort were there all along—all he had to do was take it.

Bits and pieces of film footage—reels half-burned by the invading army and pieced together by future archeologists. Shredded and recollected film reels crisply rotting in the film canisters of my mind.

This was what I remembered—in spurts and waves... Dominic jumped on the bed, naked. He kept saying "Look at me babe! Look at me!" Harriet took photographs of him the whole time. He kept demanding to be looked at, while she looked at him through her camera and snapped photographs.

I was drunk.

I was curled around the toilet and unconscious. I learned later that Generalissima Mellisa developed a form of Plaguist Yoga by my being passed out on the bathroom floor. My position was called *The Porcelain Pedestal*. It was the embodiment of the place where all prayers were flushed.

I was hot and numb. The vomit came by force. My stomach muscles contracted in unholy cramping spasms. Streams of hot saliva, bile, and mucus streamed from my mouth to the side of the porcelain toilet rim. Seat up. My mouth was heavy and rubbery against the yellow crusted pee-stained rim. What pubic hair? What vile caked-on disease? It didn't matter. I found myself in complete surrender. There was no winning this argument. I'd gone too far. I'd drunk too much.

Bits and pieces: I remembered my arm going numb, after passing out on its soft savior from the floor, which was even more vile and excreted upon. The door would have to remain open. I was sprawled out, half in the restroom—half in front of the vanity mirror and sink in the itty-bitty hallway. I wouldn't let go of the toilet or let anyone move me. It was as if a spell had been cast upon me to remain in that spot, glued to it for punishment.

I heard the ruckus of the party. Laughter was prominent—mad, boisterous unforgiving laughter. It was, after all, a Plaguist party. I remembered wishing I knew what was so funny—though I knew what was truly funny—what was truly absurd—that we were allowed to behave the way that we did in the name of freedom, and that mankind had come to this. Logic dictated. Reason stood. The bottom-line and the punchline were what mattered in a capitalistic dystopia.

Chuckie's heavy motorcycle boots gripped my ribs as he snuggled up against my ugly with his still-standing champion stance. "What's going on, motherfucker?" He whispered in charcoal ember—immediately exhaling menthol cigarette smoke.

"FFfffllLLUUUggggGHH." I think something sticky and yello-brown spewed from my mouth in gravy chunks as I attempted to answer the Lord.

"Well—try to make your way over there to the shower and wash all of that funk and shit from your face and clothes before you make it back to the party," he said while pissing over my head and into the bowl, the splash was miraculous, a little bit on my hand because I was gripping the rim, and I remembered a sense of some warm mist in my hair.

I still couldn't open my eyes. I thought I might die. I tried to sleep. Rock was less gentle when it was his turn to piss in my porcelain god. I heard him laughing as the warm splashing went from the water to my hand and arm. I let go of the rim when all that urine rained down on it. My head fell and clunked heavier to the ground. I threw up behind the toilet. The smell was less pleasant than a month-old camel corpse on fire being pissed on by Bedouin celibates.

I felt a steel-tipped toe in my gut and imagined Rock's boot. Sure enough, "Get it all up motherfucker!" That insane tripper said, tense and jittery and loud as he bent low to my head and dug his boot into my belly.

I vomited again and sobbed. I had nothing left inside of me to give to the needy sewage. I was spent. I had no water to drink. There was no concerned loved-one by my side with a wet washcloth or a glass of 7-up with six ice-cubes. I was solo miserable.

I crawled into the fetal position and dug my head into a crevice underneath the toilet tank. I crawled my other half into the shower so that the door could be shut. The door was shut and for a couple of hours I heard violent and rowdy love-making. I didn't know who was who—what girls and boys got it on, what girls and girls with masculine voices, and boys and boys with feminine voices got it on. I heard someone say, "Eew—you got it all over him." I knew I'd been excreted on. I laughed a bit because I thought of my mother—who was in Alcoholics Anonymous and constantly talked about her hitting rock bottom—and I wondered how many people in her group had a bottom way higher than this—and I was just getting started!

The joke gave me strength to roll over to the shower. I summoned some ancestral strength and found the knob to turn the water on. The streams splashed down upon me with savage grace, hot laser beams that doused me free of the crust and crud and spores now growing on me. The vomit and pee and semen dripped from the top of my head down my face. I washed my clothes and wrung them out. I stood somehow, found my strength and held onto the shower nozzle like a punkRock microphone. I opened my mouth and let the hard water pressure into my mouth. I used the showerhead like a water-pick. I brushed my teeth. I soaped down and scrubbed my bits and pieces and turned the shower off. The steam rose from my body. I carried my soaked clothes back to the party. I figured I might as well be a showoff and impress my fellow Plaguists with my lithe, naked body and thick cock.

I opened the bathroom door and made my grand entrance, but the room was empty. The music still played, and the candles were still lit, but there were no people—no laughter—no happening of any kind. Jas was passed out in his bed with Rambo and Apophenia was passed out on the black sofa. Was she waiting for me? What had happened? What did I miss? Well, anyway, I was still alive, and that was more than something. I'd survived the bleakest moment of my existence.

I decided to go outside and smoke a cigarette. I put on my least soiled pair of cut- offs and opened the door. I was blinded by the light. It was early, eight thirty probably. The respectable people went off to work. I'd been at S.P.A.M. Manor for a couple of months now and I'd never seen any of these people. They were all miserable, and bleary-eyed, hating their futures, pasts, and present—hating me for being young and carefree, for making ruckus and keeping them up late, too afraid to call the police or say something to any one of us themselves. There was a middle-aged woman in a Dunkin Donuts costume, I'm sorry: uniform—she sucked a Marlborough 100 as she gave me the stink-eye and found the right key to unlock her 1986 Buick Regal.

I guess it was time to make the donuts—but what she would never learn was that it was always time to make the donuts. You had sacrificed your free time to a schedule—your existence was calculated and accounted for. That was why there was nothing good on non-premium television.

I sat in the Mystery Ship and started her up. Reverend Killjoy's tape played: *Creep* by Radiohead. At that time, it was their only good song. Who knew? Then: *Human Behavior* by Bjork. It occurred to me—that Reverend Killjoy's mixtape was no less than a masterpiece—an audio beacon of syncopated reasoning… There was a vibe she had her fingers on the pulse of the early nineties music scene.

It was time for me to steal the donuts.

26.

Chuckie Sightings

Sometime in early June, people began seeing images of Chuckie in various places around the city. The first Sacred Image of Chuckie (sic) that I saw in person was at the home of a local Plaguist everyone called Wingnutt. He was a bit batty and fancied himself a ninja.

"Here! Look—this is how to defeat four people who advance on you—like Lee does in *Enter the Dragon*. Here! Four of you—four of you bigger suckers—advance upon me!" —Who was he even talking to?

"None of you? Fuckin' pussies?! —I'm twice as small as any one of you."

Wingnutt must've gotten wind of a group of four who might like to advance upon him—maybe teach the young karate kid how true predators behave—because he decided to demonstrate the routine with ghost warriors tearing down upon him. He steadied his pose and flailed his limbs and contorted his body.

"Here! See? The first guy attacks a split second before the second one, takes the number one and smash him into number two—immediately breaks number three's nose with a swift punch to the face and flip the advancing number four—like this, here! Over your shoulder." He was in full flight, dancing some choreographed maneuver as if a cinematic professional, as if teaching young stuntmen to inherit his intelligence.

Wingnutt punched the air and kicked the wind. He flipped an imaginary attacker over his shoulder. "You can kneel on him quickly, crushing his esophagus and killing him instantly—or land on his head and knock him out with only slight or possible brain damage—in time to

KICK recovering number one, should he be able to—right in the head—or two quick ones to the chest." He was surprisingly agile in his demonstration. He seemed strong and powerful, as if he could do some damage in a tournament or a judged competition.

Exhausted from his speech and his fluttering about kicking and punching the air, Wingnutt took off his shirt and squatted down in the middle of the floor, breathing heavily and surveying the imaginary corpses and their possible further attack. He had everyone's attention.

I took the moment for comic relief. "That's the job you wanted four of us to sign up for?!"

Everyone at the party he hosted laughed.

He looked at me intensely and gained his composure. "I'm almost a NINJA, man!" He walked closer to me, looking nine inches up at me. "I bet you that it'd take you two hours to find me in this house!"

"Deal." I smiled jokingly—unprepared for what followed.

Wingnutt bolted from the scene. He sprinted from the living room, his performance area, and disappeared deep into the house. There was laughter and loud music and almost immediately fifteen conversations broke out around the house.

No intention of looking for Wingnutt entered my mind. He kind of creeped me out. His house was decorated with swords and staffs and strange weapons of all kinds. The music that blasted from the speakers was loud death metal—none of his neighbors complained. I later learned that he practiced martial arts in the front yard—including nunchuck theatrics, complete with hard breathing exercises and yelling, grunting. He let the neighbors know he was a force to be reckoned with.

I was in the yard speaking to Bishop Goldie Pawn about the finer points of checkers when a shooting star blazed across the sky in neon green. Others outside *oohed and awed,* so I'm sure it happened.

"Bless Chuckie!" Bishop Theresa Mothers shouted from her sitting boulder.

It seemed real. This was a real church to these people, these misfit punkRock lost boys, these genderfluid sexual deviants, these social outcast miscreants…

"Martin, come with me." Jas dragged me by the arm.

"What is it?" I slurred.

This again.

This territorial pissing the pants, and emitting seductive pheromones to the ghostly drones, and bisexual Betties and Buddies, off on my own with only myself to blame, fame….

We were off to some other portion of the party. I was hand-in-hand with The Pope, being whisked around the party, meeting Sain't Betty Bourbon of the sober response, Sain't Marcus Gravy of the Black Liberation Army, which was yet to be started, but sounded urgent, all the young melanin-rich young people being harassed by the police and the privileged...

Racism was timeless. The intelligence of a people could be measured in their empathetic response to those of another member of a different tribe in need.

It seemed everyone I met was a Sain't in the church—Sain't Donna Party head of Vegetarianism... She had the wickedest sense of humor. She also had the best cocaine. After ten minutes or forty-five? The high seemed like a natural place to be.

The closet door blasted open. Wingnutt bolted out from the closet, from under a pile of clothes like Eddie Munster in *Lost Boys* tearing up the bedding. He yelled and ran out of the room. Jas snickered to himself, and the girls were all ablaze with cackling.

Wingnutt ran around looking for me. He ran out of the bedroom for a few minutes and ran back into the bedroom. "I told you that you couldn't find me in two hours' time!"

"You're right. You win. What did we bet?"

"Oh shit! We forgot to bet!" He screamed in disappointment.

"Anyway, I'm very impressed. You are indeed a ninja." I kept my hands in my pockets as a sign of submission and meant what I said—the only way to fool anyone...

"Well, don't forget it," he said in a marshmallow threat and hot caramel scald.

It was a fun party.

Finally, Wingnutt brought out the butcher block with the pork chop bloodstain of the likeness of Chuckie—and "Eeeww!" and "AaAAAAHHhhh!" Accentuated the room perfectly. It looked like Chuckie with his always sunglasses and long bushy sideburns—puffed out and obnoxious—glorious and delightful—as any modern God should.

I wondered if it was fabricated—or make-believe—it's hard to tell sometimes—which way the arrow's pointing.

A week later, there was another Chuckie sighting. There was a big party over at Sain't Jedi Northup, Minister of Everything Star Trek's place. Apparently, the pan he placed under his Harley Davidson motorcycle to catch his oil spill showed itself a holy relic. When he removed the oil pan from the concrete, the residue left a black stain on the concrete that looked exactly like Chuckie—sunglasses, roundhead and bushy, bushy sideburns. Everyone agreed that this was another miracle, and we all drank beer and did drugs and tried to fuck each other.

That same week the most dramatic Chuckie sighting took place. I drove Chuckie and Jas to the speedway. Along the way, Chuckie insisted that we all drink some kind of tea he'd made from two different types of hallucinogenic mushrooms AND LSD. We had to make several stops along the way. Forty minutes passed and the effects of the tea hit me like a melted Crayola wave of Jolly Rancher juice, candy Starburst, rainfall Skittles.

We were finally on our way out to the speedway, listening to Last Rights by Skinny Puppy, and the galloping commenced. The noise was loud and ferocious. "Do you hear that, guys?"

"Yes." God was the calmest I'd ever known him.

"Hear what?" Jas perked up from the backseat.

"We're being followed," I suggested.

"By whom?" Jas asked coldly.

"No. We're being accompanied," God said.

I immediately understood what he meant. There were only three horsemen. The three of us Plaguists in the Mystery Ship were the fourth horse of the apocalypse—the red horse of war.

"When the Lamb opened the second seal, I heard the second living creature say, 'Come and see!' Then another horse came out, a fiery red one. Its rider was given power to take peace from the earth and to make men slay each other. To him was given a large sword," Jas quoted the book of revelation seemingly from memory.

"What do you say Angel of Death, feel like sparking the apocalypse?" He seemed to speak low and distorted, slow and as if with computer effect.

"Why not?" I responded, partly wanting to be cool—and partly unconcerned with billions of the population. How bountiful our resources would seem if the right billion people ceased to exist. But that was the kicker, wasn't it... You couldn't hand select a billion people...

This was on the minds of world leaders. This was why we allowed genocide in Africa, weak infrastructures in Haiti, starvation in China, and allowed Pakistan and India to have nuclear weapons. There was a saying in Washington—how can we get India to invade China? —It meant—how were we possibly going to feed all these people? There was no answer. Contagion was too dangerous—too threatening to the home soil, and therefore the self. Genetically modified crops created diversity loss, and gamble on the life support of one type of food, vulnerable to blight.

How did we shelter the masses, stop them from procreating like selfish, bored organisms? Where did we bury the billions dead? How did we keep the ecosystem clean of our rotting masses? The same could be said of our culture, and our collected psyche.

The white horse beside me ran in time with my car, thirty miles an hour on a back road, the flesh of the animal partly blurry, an occasional glimpse of the bony haunch of his rotting ham. The rider wore a crown of stars and a cape of Old Glory, seven red stripes, six white stripes, blood and innocence, thirteen rebellious colonies who stood up against the British Monarchy and defeated their oligarchy with bent on freedom and the pursuit of liberty, fifty white stars in a blue square of sky in the corner, neatly arranged, states like puzzle pieces on the map of the continent. The cape was decorated with a gold fringe because the conqueror understands symbolism and opulence.

His skeletal face oozed puss and bled maggots. He breathed fire onto the tip of his arrow, setting the sharp head aflame. He fired the glowing missile into the night. He tried to laugh, but his mandible became unhinged from the left side and hung there. He didn't try to fix it. He breathed more fire onto another arrowhead and flung it into space, continuing his will to burn the world.

From the passenger side window, the black horse appeared—the horse was dark and slick like oil spill, unstoppable like midnight. The rider wore a cloak of night and starshine, a cloak that rendered him virtually invisible. From his billowing cloak, clouds of locusts and cicadas were thrust into the jetstream behind him.

Famine was coming—a depletion of the people's food supply. There would be fewer cookies in the world—that's for sure—no more extra cheese. I welcomed the cycle. There was no nonhuman Satan.

In my rearview mirror I saw the green horse, glowing in the dark, hepatitis yellow. The rider was all bones, limp and dead on the horse, seemingly glued to the saddle, lifeless and unresponsive to the ride. In the horseman's wake the grass crackled brown and the flowers withered down: in the pale horseman's path a desolate landscape of pestilence.

The sign came upon us from nowhere. The giant billboard that oversaw some dilapidated industrial part of the city I'd never been to before. Over the years, the many advertisements weathered away. They plastered paper advertisements over the old ones until a thick book of plastered posters had gotten too heavy to add to. The posters advertised Mountain Dew soda pop, Copenhagen dippin' snuff, Tyson's frozen chicken nuggets, the local morning radio show, the largest local Baptist church, Hardee's steak biscuits, and The Grand Ole Opry—now, a Plaguist icon.

There were no words on the billboard now, no deals, no steals, no promises of bargains—penitence for indulgences—no times and dates and locations tempting the image of nothing…

The paper had weathered and torn to reveal the image of Chuckie, bushy sideburns, sunglasses and cowboy hat—a twist, but no less effective. But had the paper been expertly ripped or was this an actual apparition of the Lord, our flavor, Charles Theodore Plague?

The answer seemed irrelevant to God. "Holy Place!" He shouted as we got out of the car, laughing hysterically. The horsemen galloped away to continue their ghostly threat of revelation.

I noticed our destination was a cold, gray building in the middle of nowhere. The name of the warehouse had been spray-painted out, and with it the "e" in Warehouse—it now said War house. We were there to see an old friend of theirs spin records. The party was illegal, unadvertised, and so underground you almost needed a shovel. There was a five dollar cover charge at the door which we didn't pay—because God.

The War house was a giant, empty space—there were folding tables full of buckets of beer and ice—large tubs of beer and ice beside the tables, igloo coolers full of more beer, malt liquor, wine coolers. There were large trash bins slowly filling up with bottles and cans. There were no chairs, no place to sit. This encouraged movement. It was instantly my new favorite place. I loved the enormous empty space. Three kids on skateboards zipped by doing ollies and kickflips, emphasizing the vastness of the concrete haven. There were bizarre lights shining and revolving around from some unknown source that gave it the sense of a nightclub, but a cheap one.

The music was fantastic, all curated by their old friend. Cannon Milne was all smiles behind Buddy Holly glasses, and pompadour. He danced around while he searched for a specific song on the vinyl. He wore blue jeans with thick cuffs rolled up over black motorcycle boots and had a pack of cigarettes rolled up in his white t-shirt sleeve like a 1950s actor portraying a rebel.

He wore a wallet-chain. He was Lucky Strike no-filter, and Burma Shave. He had tattoos of dice, and redhead buxom ladies in blue bikinis on his forearms—sparrows, daggers and Turkish Eyes on his biceps. He was comb-in-pocket and always on form.

Cannon spun Rockabilly, Psychobilly, Punk Rock, and Industrial Goth. Mostly RockaBilly—upright bass and stray cat strut. He loved Demented Are Go, The Cramps, The Meteors, The Exotic Ones...

Chuckie danced. It was the first time I saw God dance. He did a vibrating fist and forearm thing in hydraulic pumping to the hardcore bass thumping and ruckus guitar of P. Paul Fenech and took one step to the left or right or backward in a sort of three-foot invisible box, every time the song went from chorus to verse or vice versa. It was odd and perfect.

I studied God briefly then studied Cannon—how long he'd let a song play, sometimes cutting Johnny Cash from three minutes to one. (*Come on—we all know the song.*) As a DJ, Cannon was innovative and fun to watch. He even mixed in a sprinkling of Public Enemy, some fight-the-power shit between Gene Vincent and Alien Sex Fiend, keeping everyone on their toes.

Cannon spun for two hours without taking a break. It was a real show. He mixed shit I would've never thought of, mashing Black Sabbath and Hank Williams—Bob Willis and Ministry. Chuckie danced the entire time, dripping with sweat and remaining in his invisible three-foot box. He behaved as a punkrock shaman. He oozed metaphysical understanding in his every wheezing breath.

The night was a total success. We drank for free because Cannon knew the nutty skinny thrasher who threw the party (his name I never knew) and was fascinated as hell to listen to Jas tell him about Plaguism. I got to know Cannon and saw why he was Jas's best friend.

We talked about Nashville. He'd been here all his life and was desperate to see more of the country. I was burning out and started talking about the Atlantic Coast and my mother in New York City, and how that might be my next step if Chicago didn't work out.

Things I would learn later: Cannon was a founding member of S.P.A.M. Cannon Milne was Jas's best-friend in high-school. They were in bands together, and when Jas was trying out his comedy routine on stage, it was Cannon who'd always attend. This was before the church, before the First Interplanetary Church of the Immaculate Deception, when Jas was a star in his own right.

Jas was the kid in high school who'd been expelled from Catholic School for fucking a teacher— "for an A plus" he'd tell the other school children that went to his public school, as they listened with rapt disgust to his story of bending the fat, bearded priest over the desk and sodomizing him, over last night's history papers and Jas's own special paper about Pope Julius III and his beggar boy lover.

The little listeners told everyone they knew about Jas's wild sexual escapades, insuring Jas a certain reputation amongst a certain community—one that he was used to—no big deal—except to the losers and loners attending that public school who'd never met someone so confident and so cocky, so cock-strong, so self-assured and righteous— kicked in the teeth smiling, bloody lipstick kisses blown as Jas hit the pavement—a clown from heaven—an indestructible faggot nerd.

Cannon had never met anyone who'd read the same comic books and listened to the same comedy albums—never met anyone who'd seen *Rocky Horror Picture Show* as many times as he had. They went every Friday midnight to The Belcourt Theater screening—in full costume, Cannon with hunchback and long stringy hair wig, Jas in corset and heavy eye make-up, dark lipstick and size ten pumps that made his childish ass have curves for once—Jas so German, so Anglo—not a single strand of negroid DNA in him—all conqueror, no native.

It seemed I had an ally who had interest in seeing New York. Maybe I could use that as a means of escape from the great city of Nashville.

27.

Double Super Crazy Motherfuckers

Apparently, Jas and Pookie were in a band together called The Double Super Crazy Motherfuckers. They were putting on a show at Freshwater—the beat-up old beloved dive bar where every stripe of musician performed. There were screen doors open to the summer wind. Clouds of smoke poured from the entrances like a house on fire.

I drank a beer in the back of the bar. I didn't know what to expect. I didn't even know Jas could play the drums. I didn't know he was in a band with Pookie, and I sure as hell didn't know they were ready to perform live on a stage. I'd been away from the scene for a few days, a night at Ready's—a night at Marybeth's—still unsure how I got there—a night at Sylvia's, the bartender from Chagrin's…. I was lost on purpose.

Cannon came over with a beer and a smile. He was always so gracious and happy to be alive. He had an infectious laugh, and bright eyes that seemed interested in everything you said. He was the penultimate playmate.

While we waited for the band to come, a huge neanderthal of a man walked in sporting a red button up shirt with a black band around one bicep. He had a shaved head with a swastika tattooed on the back of his head. He was followed by three more butch losers with similar garb, red and black, swastikas on their clothes and skin. They didn't seem friendly.

"Whoa!" I said to the obvious air.

"Yeah—I fucking hate Nazshies," Canon said.

"Nazshies?" I asked.

"Nashville Nazis," Cannon replied. "They follow the teachings of this impotent thug named Allen Polecat who believes in scaring the opposition into submission—probably because he knows he can't intellectually debate a single person in the world. He rallies big, moronic thugs who believe in the superiority of their own reflection, because they have no empathy, imagination, or complex thought process beyond eat, shit, and fuck. They believe they're right because they can fight—but wouldn't know what to do legislatively or financially if given the keys to the kingdom, couldn't govern a trailer park, let alone a country."

"Allen Polecat?" I laugh/asked.

"Sssh!" Cannon warned me. "These brutes will fight at the drop of a hat, and I, for one, would like to see this band try and get through a set of songs."

"Ha. Nazi skunks," I whispered.

Some hot girl interrupted us to say hello to Cannon. They hugged and had an intimate conversation, so I wandered around the back of the club.

I said hello to Chuckie and Minx, they said hello back and not much else, blushing and touching each other in cobweb secrets.

"What's up, Rock?" I tried to say coolly.

"My tolerance! Somebody buy me a beer!"

I gulped my last three sips and paid for two more beers. I had a fake ID I found on the side of the road, the guy in the picture barely looked like me, but I noticed mostly those checking the ID didn't really give a fuck. They looked at the birthdate and took the money. I bought a beer for myself and one for the maniac.

"CHEERS!" Rock barked in my direction and walked off. He always made me feel like I had a schoolgirl crush on him, the way I was always disappointed in his treatment of me. We were all such needy bitches.

Double Super Crazy Motherfuckers went on stage. Pookie looked great in a gold lame blouse and slicked back glittered hair. He wore bright red spandex pants and silver vintage platform shoes. He strummed his guitar like Pete Townsend.

Jas walked on stage wearing tighty-whitey fruit-of-the-looms and a chamois pink bathrobe, open, no belt. On his chest was a giant black swastika scribbled in magic marker. He scribbled on his upper lip with a marker to give himself a Charlie Chaplin/Adolph Hitler mustache. He cut his hair and straightened it and greased it down to look like Hitler. On the back of his robe was his name—FAGGOT HITLER—also in haphazard black magic marker. He picked up his drums and did an amazing solo. Pookie did an amazing guitar solo. They riffed. Apparently, they'd practiced songs together before I arrived in Nashville. They had plans on doing this show for over a year.

Jas was resplendent behind the drums with Bam Bam Rubble smashes on heads and cymbals. He'd found an exercise worthy of his heart. Now, not even smoking was going to kill him. In fact, he could probably afford himself another addiction if the band made any money. Unlikely. Too pure to the punk spirit.

The first song had no words. It lacked in scale, meter and timing—the rhythm was hackneyed and butchered, the chords shredded like government documents, the pitch off, and the notes nonexistent. But through the stumbling chaos and the tripping scales there was music. There was thunderous applause from the appreciative audience.

For the second song, singing did not help matters much. The words were unintelligible, and all the keys were off and fit no locks. Wounded bobcats in forest fires sounded more harmonious. It was glorious and perfect. RockNroll.

"You suck!" Yelled the enormous neanderthal Nashville nazi. Apparently, he was working on his review for *Rolling Stone* magazine.

"YeahyoufuckingFaggott!" Shouted the fattest, possibly slowest of the Skinheads there that evening.

It was always amazing to me how people who believed they were a member of a superior race could do so being a hundred- and fifty-pounds overweight, with receding hairline, red scaly flesh and bloodshot eyes.

The confrontational racist scumbag stood up and threw a beer mug toward the stage. It *just* missed The Pope, who everyone was delighted in seeing.

Rock witnessed this egregious act from twenty feet away. With a reaction instinctively fast—he leaned all the way back, like an Olympic athlete, and he threw his beer mug at the boisterous bully, before the bully's mug finished ricocheting to the stage floor. The heavy bottom of the mug connected with the boy's skull between the temple and the forehead, knocking him clean out. Blood from his head spilled across his swastika tattoo and onto the floor, as he lay unconscious and wetting his pants.

A fight broke out. It didn't last long. Chuckie, Rock, and two large Plaguists I did not know, but who looked menacing in leather, denim, and oil-darkened skin, chased the four other skinheads out of the establishment. None of them volunteered to stick around and take the kid to the hospital. They fled like rabbits, into the evening.

The ambulance came in a few minutes. Everyone expected it. The ones with warrants fled the fastest and in fact, very few stayed. I helped Jas and Pookie load their equipment into Pookie's van.

Pookie had a nineteen-seater—it was really a minibus as opposed to a van. I guess he liked the idea of driving a lot of people around—being the guy with the van, sure to be invited to SOME big event. He had the back two rows of seats taken out for band storage, so it was only a thirteen-seater now.

"Thanks, man! Wanna go to whatever hospital that gorilla is staying at and kill him?!" Jas cackled, hit his cig, sucked from his forty, and hit his cig again.

"What makes you think he's not dead already?" I baited.

"What do you mean? I didn't really see anything," Jas asked, alert and enthusiastically interested in a report.

"Well, if he dies, that's what you should tell the police." Was I the only voice of paranoid reason here?

"You can't say shit like that, tell us!" Pookie demanded.

I obliged. "Kid threw his mug on stage and just missed you, my friend, by three inches. Kid took the heavy side of the mug from Rock at full force from fifteen feet away. Kid hit ground and A LOT of blood came from his head and kid did not get up. Pete the manager led two orderlies to the body. Kid was bandaged tightly and taken away unconscious on a stretcher."

"WWWWHOOOOOAAAAAAAA!!!!!" They said simultaneously.

"Kid's either dead or has permanently scrambled eggs for brains for sure, concussion, probably definitely coma. You hope he's only out for a day or two, then amnesiac to the point of being his dumb old self."

Jas cackled, as if that was surely what was going to happen. "Wanna do it in the van, anybody?"

Meanwhile, back at S.P.A.M. Manor, Jas's moods alternated between moaning for Rambo who'd been missing for three days and celebrating The Double Super Crazy Motherfucker's one and only show, which lasted for about six minutes but had an actual casualty.

"He better not be off fucking a whole bunch of trolls!" He said angrily, referring to his boyfriend.

"Wanna go fuck a whole bunch of trolls?!" I asked.

He screamed defiantly to the universe. "NO! I want PURE LOVE!"

"No such thing." I took the stance.

"What do you mean?"

"Love is Nature's only flaw."

"ONLY FLAW?!" He squawked. "Oh! Martin. What kind of mother did you have?"

"An absent twenty-year-old—wrapped up in her own selfish needs," I said, reflexive pronoun use be damned.

"OH! We'd probably *get along*!" He posed, hissed laughter and bowed his head.

I blew smoke. "Without love, we would've colonized the moon already and possibly gone to MARS."

"Martin, without love, we would've never left the savannah!"

I scowled at the ceiling.

"You've never been in *LOVE*?" He asked.

"I'm 0-for-3." I snarled an unrepentant lip.

"Well, that's because you're a difficult bastard whom none of those pretty bitches could ever understand."

I instantly felt better and smiled, totally giving away my royal flush.

"Wanna make out?" He asked sheepishly, almost cutely, coyly, what little he could muster.

The door knocked. It was suspiciously formal in its authority and resonance. It was the cops. "May we come in?"

"I'd prefer you stand at the threshold." Jas opened the door wide. The light framed them with luminescent auras of holy dust.

"We'd like to ask you a few questions," the white one said. They might as well have been Officers Ponch and Baker from CHiPs.

"I'm all answers." Jas cocked his left foot up to his right thigh and stretched his arms up, palms against the door jamb, like Samson on temple pillars, blind and begging his lord just strength enough for one final push.

"Where were you on the night of the fifteenth?" Baker asked.

"Of WHAT month?" Jas asked belligerently.

"This one," Ponch snapped.

"I don't know what this one is."

"You don't know what month this is?" Ponch challenged him.

"I only know four months: winter, spring, summer, and fall."

Baker put his arm up in front of Ponch's chest to prevent the officer from rushing the witness. "All we want to know is where you were on the night of June 15th of this year, three nights ago." Baker's teeth shined bright in the door jamb, framed by the unholy entrance to our world of sin and degradation.

"Oh, three nights ago! You've heard!" Jas proclaimed triumphantly, sucked his cigarette and blew smoke into the ceiling.

I was stunned. So were the cops.

"Heard what?" Ponch baited.

"That The Double Super Crazy Motherfuckers played a kick ass rock show, and some dumb Nazi threw a mug at me. A hundred people saw him do it. When he wakes up, I want to press charges."

"You can't press charges, Mr. Swank." Baker set him up.

"Why not?" Jas demanded his rights.

"Because he's dead." Ponch brought it home, nailed the scene.

"Why are you here if I can't press charges?" Jas asked, cold and hot at once.

"We'd like to know if you saw anything," Baker asked coolly.

"Yeah, a large mug coming AT MY HEAD that I had to DIVE away from! And a couple of fucking EMs who wouldn't let me fucking kick the dirtbag who threw it as he was being carried away in a stretcher!"

"There's no need to get upset," Baker attempted to calm Jas.

"I have nothing to report," Jas said matter-of-factly.

"What about you, sir?" Ponch yelled into my lying on the couch pretending to read Genet's *The Thief's Journal.*

I, of course, ignored them, pretending total absorption into my book.

"Sir!" Ponch shined a flashlight in my face.

I flipped him off.

He tried to lunge in, but Baker held him back, confined to the jamb without probable-cause or search-warrant. Baker was always by-the-books, and on-the-record, Ponch was a hot-blooded Latino with a sexy smile and perfect teeth—good looks and excusable actions.

Officer Baker gave Jas his card. "If you think of anything," he said, knowing that there would be nothing.

Jas took the card and held it to his side, without looking. The cops got in their cruiser and split, like a banana. He watched them leave then shut the door.

Jas exhaled exuberantly. "WHHHhheeeeewwwWWwwwwWW!" He lit a cigarette then went to the fridge for a beer. He twisted and cracked and guzzled the contents. "AAH! FFUUUUUUUUCCKKK!" He sucked and savored and snorted his cigarette.

Jas paced and forgot all about Rambo, which was good. "This is serious! I mean this is uber-cool. Our show KILLED! But we have to be careful about talking about it because the cops are listening, Hell! They already know who I am! I hope they never figure out that Rock…"

"HEY!" I shouted.

Jas stopped pacing and looked at me.

"You should reconstruct the truth in your mind to fit the story you told those cops—and you should pretend that the cops are ALWAYS listening—because a MURDER has occurred, and they tend to go hardcore after those cases—unless you haven't seen prime time television lately."

"Be paranoid. Got it. The truly correct function in this environment." He looked at me, pleased. "Thank you, Martin!" He paced again. "Every word out of my mouth must be in accordance with the testimony I gave those television cops. I cannot stray from the path unless my friend gets busted. Thou should brother thy neighbor and keep his liberty sacrosanct!"

28.

Fireproof Ignition

I dressed as quickly as I could, looking for my socks—when I remembered they were in the car. I developed tricks, tics—I wore socks and boots everywhere I went—and they took time to put on and take off—so when I shut my car off in front of Lingus House—I took my shoes and socks off. I bought a roll of paper towels and a bottle of Purell to keep my feet clean—enough to not stink.

Grass and soil in my toes—that was the best feeling—wiping the real stink and gunk off in the grass and soil. I could walk on gravel and asphalt barefoot, no problem—and inside the home—humble and respectful like Buddha but fuzzy and comfortable carpet tickling the vestigial platypus webbing between my toes. I enjoyed going barefoot, walking with my natural gait—unafraid of hookworms.

How many more times? How many more times was I going to make that walk from my stinky beat-up car to her warm embrace? Ten? Fifty? Two? It didn't matter—one of them would be my last—and I knew this and did not feel sad or melancholy—I felt nothing—taking the fluidity of my passing through lightly—I sought no permanent solution to the way I felt about being a human being on earth, loveless, empty, and ready for anything.

High and drunk and sweating for an hour plus—thick numb cock no longer in need of coming—aggressive animal fucking. Biting, clawing, pulling, stroking, sucking, digging, licking, pushing, shoving, grunting, gasping, squealing, laughing, growling, choking, kissing, sniffing, sticking, wiggling, shifting and flipping over to do it again.

This again. This nowhere spin and do it again, through the motions, through the fiery hoops. This physical interaction with no spiritual satisfaction. This delicious friction and well lubed traction. Maybe I could have a career in pornography?

Out-of-breath cigarette and a few hours of sleep. It was always the same. I rarely stayed until morning. I didn't know why—perhaps it was my way of displaying my impermanence and the impermanence of any kind of relationship I could offer. Cold scientific data reaffirmed my antisocial suspicions. Love was not something I was interested in. I'd lost too much to that notion.

But in the yard, there was always Pookie.

"You should let me suck your cock."

"Why?"

"Cause I'm so good—I bet you'd let me fuck you in the ass."

"Why don't you just let me fuck you in the ass?"

"Okay."

Gross positions in fragrant vehicles of new discovery. We resembled what we were attracted to—it was a result of our narcissism. We wanted to get off. Bulletproof muscles of thrust and thunder—shaking The Mystery Ship violently.

an androgynous Adonis upon us
an underdeveloped eloquence
with the skin of fruit
still clinging to vine
I have seen his kind before
his tease and whore
shut up and kiss me
sarcastic mouth
impatient to find tongue
upon new wine
meat
urgent with his theatrics
and answers to questions
you shouldn't be asking
and
what's this you've kissed?
a hypnotic gaze in his eyes
inches
and silent from yours
what capacity his lungs
his breathing heavy and slow

one to your four
what rat-a-tat heartbeat
beneath his chest
masked in glass and stone
and made of neither
an interesting entourage
of riddles and pranks
a brilliant collage of butterflies and tanks
swimming in his empty belly
what feminine lava
dictates the movement
of his limbs
his torso
and neck
a divine playground
for the myriad parasites
with dry thirst tongues
some sexual organs
pained by pulse
and throb.

29.

Preacher Man on TV

I didn't remember falling asleep—a common tragedy to my season in hell with God and The Pope. My mouth was dry, my dick was hard, and the sounds of love making came from one corner of the room. Rambo grunted girly, gingerly, greedily... Jas cooed like a faun. I waited 'til they were finished, lit a smoke and went to the fridge. I drank a beer, took a piss, a shit, a shower, no towel, and when I returned Rambo was gone. I sat in wet clothes and finished my morning beer.

The night before was Saturday—Plaguist Yoga at Generalissima's house—where we Plaguists gathered to watch Kramer's showing of more of The Church Documentary on Public Access Television. Last night was all about The Fiery Sermon—and Jas enjoyed much fanfare and celebration as he adored the star of himself on television.

Now, Sunday morning, Jas sat cross-legged on the red loveseat/my bed, and rolled a joint. With the joint in his mouth, he flipped through the channels searching for the right sermon. It was Sunday morning, and this was his routine. He wanted to hear the southern self-righteous brothers babble on about Babylonian end times. It helped with his own performance, he told me—the cadence and timbre—the timing and rhythm…

It occurred to me that His Assholiness was more of a performance artist than a writer. What he had to teach me was how to perform, not how to write. Perhaps I could add some of his affectations to my own, but that was it—the rest of it was up to me—I guess there was a limit to what you can learn from your master.

It was Sunday Morning. We watched the preachers on television as we did every Sunday Morning. There was the red-faced fellow, with shock silver-white hair in an expensive Italian suit, who held the bible open to one of several marked passages—and the leather-bound gilded pages flopped open upon his palm and drooped over the edge of his prayer hand. He recited verse after verse—story after story with his eyes shut and that red face perspiring.

Jas changed channels. There were other men preaching across the dial, selling Jesus Christ the Savior as if it was enough that he was born the son of god. Poor storytellers shouted memorized passages and learned clichés. Some were good storytellers but easily convinced that nature was a miracle. They probably made the most money—in fact, some of them presided over live congregations in the thousands—mega-churches for mega-losers.

One of them mentioned us by name.

A fat shiny one with a stuffed three-piece suit and effervescent bald head. "Beware of False Prophets who come to you in sheep's clothing, but inwardly are ravenous wolves. You will know them by their fruits! Do men gather grapes from thornbushes or figs from thistles?" I enjoyed his rhythm, his mixture of scripture and lecture.

Jas cackled at the wolf in sheep's clothing on television warning of lupine wool.

The preacher man continued. "Now, Mathew asks us if we pick grapes from thorn bushes, and you might be smart, and you might be clever, and you might say, well, wait a minute, we do pick blackberries from thorn bushes, and don't they make a good cobbler?"

Jas laughed at the fat man on TV. I struggled with an acid hangover and every half an hour or so shot off into space again.

"They do, friends. Blackberries sure do make a great cobbler. The cobbler is how the blackberry is judged. Just as every one of us will be judged on that great judgment day. The question Mathew is proposing to us is, what kind of fruit are you?"

I even had to laugh at that one. Jas was in stitches. "Oh god! I hope someone's recording this!" He squealed in delight at the religio-comedy.

"Now, what does he mean, Wolf in Sheep's clothing? Friends, he meant be careful of whom you trust." The preacher was very matter of fact. "I believe we are living in the end times, and soon, we will be seated by the side of the heavenly father and bask in his eternal glory."

"Amen!" Appraisal came from the congregation.

The Preacher man on TV was a real fanatic or pretending to be. "There will be false prophets. There will be agents of the devil coming to steal away our children. We must protect them from these true predators of souls." He stared into the camera. "Friends they walk among us. Look at your public access television programming. Right here in our beautiful City of Nashville, there are a group of men and women who call themselves Plaguists."

The world suddenly seemed very surreal.

"I say unto you fellow brothers and sisters of Christ… That a great Plague is INDEED upon us—a cultural plague threatening to infect the sanctity of our way of life! Our holy moral compass is threatened! Our communal integrity is being compromised!" The preacher oozed sebaceous perspiration, soaking his thousand-dollar silk suit in sweat. He waved his gilded bible about and clenched his eyes tight to really show how passionate he was about making money as an evangelist.

Wordlessly, Jas turned up the volume.

"This past weekend, as I watched television and relaxed after preparing my sermon—I came across a disturbing program on one of our public access channels. It seems a group of young people, right here in our beloved Nashville, have started their very own cult. A group of NE'ER DO WELLS! A group of HEDONISTS! A group of SINNERS and BLASPHEMERS gathered around a young homosexual man calling himself The Pope and listened to his SATANIC blasphemy! These young men and women cheered on the defamation of our lord and savior JESUS CHRIST, and ladies and gentlemen—some of them I recognized as members of our very own congregation, young boys and girls in their formative teen years—OUR children—YOUR children—persuaded by the dark heart of these, these—PLAGUISTS! They called themselves, of all things! —Hoodlums! Thugs! Deviants of the basest sort! Lowlifes, ladies and gentlemen! These people, if you saw them, you would understand that THESE are the TYPES of people that must be stopped!" The preacher lowered his book and opened his eyes. "Sing us out Brother Thomas."

The choir began a booming rendition of *A Mighty Fortress is Our God*.

I expected a loud bantam cackle, but nothing. Jas sat there with his mouth open and the joint stuck to his bottom lip, dangling unlit, useless. He was in shock. It was all too much, really. He had not only been mentioned by one of his Sunday Morning enemies but vilified personally. I thought he was going to pass out. He looked at me bug-eyed and said in a dark whisper, "we did it."

30.

The Cadillac Crusades

Sain't Sunshine Amarillo was decked in black leather, black denim, black mohawk hair and black mascara. He was killed by some tiny-minded dickwad dumbshit Christian conservative in a Cadillac. He saved his friend Sain't Dynamite King, pushing him out of the way of the oncoming DeVille.

Apparently, there was a brawl outside of the IHOP, where the high school jocks and high school punks both sometimes gathered late at night to socialize and eat sugar bread. The fight went outside, where one of the jocks ran down Sain't Sunshine, crushing his body, breaking his bones, opening his skull and splattering his remains all over the asphalt.

The little bastard drove for a hundred feet with Sain't Sunshine's body under the chassis—cracking, splitting, opening, and expiring in a red raspberry parade of senselessness. He got away. No one knew who killed him.

Apparently, the fundamentalist little Christian scum was inspired by the preacher man on TV, and when he found out Sain't Sunshine was a Plaguist—he decided to fight him, and when the football playing, preppy Christian shit couldn't whip the skinny punk, he decided to run over him with his car.

Meanwhile, back at S.P.A.M. Manor, Rock handed me a Smith and Wesson Snub Nose .38 revolver. "If you see anybody getting run over by a Cadillac—empty this fucking thing on the driver."

I put the gun between my belly and belt buckle like I'd seen cool hitmen do in the movies. The weapon felt hard and cold against my cock and cutoffs as it slipped down my thigh. With lightning quick reflexes, I caught the gun before it hit the ground.

"You ever shoot a pistol before Angel of Death?!" Rock interrogated me.

"Yes—a 9mm automatic," I confessed, holding the .38 and examining it.

"Point and shoot!" He shouted. "Hold the gun strong and hold your breath when you fire off the rounds."

"Do you have any more bullets?" Jas asked coldly, still a little shaken with anger that there were young Christians in Cadillacs gunning for us because of our religion.

"No—that's all I found. But shit, get as many as you want—go to Wal-Mart, K-Mart, every where's got bullets for this thing—go crazy—you didn't get the gun from me." Rock turned from Jas to me and stared me down with a mania I'd never seen in another man and haven't seen since. "If you get caught and tell on me, Martin… I will fucking kill you."

"Maybe I don't want this gun, I reasoned.

"Too late—you own it." Rock stormed from S.P.A.M. Manor.

I stood staring at the gun in my hand as motorcycle danger revved outside. I prayed for no Chekhov formula. I feared murdering and being murdered. I knew my disposition to human life and wanted no part in being responsible for ending another. But if you put me in a situation where it was me or you, I would blow your fucking head off.

"Let's go," Jas exhaled heavily.

The Mystery Ship had been fixed and she ran good-as-heavily-used. I cruised slow and steady, as were the orders from Chuckie, and studied every person driving a Cadillac. There were long and low thirty-year-old Cadillacs, cologne drenched jerry curl powder blue Cadillacs. There were cherry red luxury Cadillacs, brand new showroom Cadillacs, with tinted windows and blue smoke sipping from the cracked windows. There were 8-cylinder, cruise control Cadillacs with tilt steering and power windows, cream colored chopped stock Cadillacs, Fleetwood Cadillacs, kickback Cadillacs with obvious license plates and thick mustache.

Sain't Dynamite King was in the hospital with a broken back and two broken legs. Sain't Sunshine was dead. The boys put up a good fight, and it seemed like they'd won, but the cowardly Christian pigs ran them down.

When Sain't Sunshine died, he became the first Plaguist to be murdered by a Christian. We knew we had a war on our hands.

Rock was out there in the evening on his motorcycle, hunting Christians in Cadillacs—following random black DeVilles in case they decided to run over some innocent Plaguist.

Chuckie was out there on his motorcycle as well, in a different part of town, doing the same thing—as was Dominic, Tommy, Rick, Scott, Wingnutt and Otis—and every other Plaguist with a pistol and a willingness to shoot to defend a member of their clan. Every war started this way, didn't it? —Food source, sex source—must protect where we slept tonight, where we were vulnerable in dreamtime…

I drove The Mystery Ship up one side of Nashville and down the other, searching for Cadillacs: black DeVille Cadillacs, recklessly driven teenage eldorado Cadillacs, freshly cleaned and nervously over-waxed Cadillacs, guilty little boy Cadillacs with murderous faces.

I was into it—I thought I might be able to shoot as many people as there were bullets in the gun, if they kept coming at me in pursuit of my hurt. The self and the self of your loved ones was what needed protecting. I was sure the driver of The Cadillac-ac-ac-ac-ac thought the same thing, a little more paranoid, a little more agitated, a little more ready to take the other guy out before he takes you out—never mind that he wasn't hunting you.

Whatever—people sucked. How should I have felt? Murders had taken place—lives had been lost and ruined—all because of what some Christian TV preacher scum said about my religion!

(Freedom of Religion! Don't Tread on Me! —But so help me god, if I see you worshipin' different 'n me, I'm'n'a fucking kick your ASS!)

Perhaps man needed a competitor, a better to best, a dragon to slay, a hero to worship, shiny pebbles placed in his path to show him the way from the unconscious forests into the open fields of consciousness where sunshine farts and bloody roses boil.

Sain't Bruce got run off the road by a black Cadillac, but also, he got a shot off—it hit the left blinker light and took out the bulb. Now we all rode around at night looking for a black Cadillac DeVille with a busted-out driver side tail light.

"How do we know the DeVille has a busted taillight?" I asked.

The Pope exhaled great smoke from a huge first hit of weed. "Fucking! Sain't Bruce Campbell Soup shot out a taillight when they clipped his fucking motorbike man! You know he has that HUGE bumper sticker that says God Will Eat Your Brain—and shit, I must've said that at least TWENTY Times during my Sermon of The Fiery Plane, which you know they saw on TV!"

"He got run over?"

"Oh man! I don't know exactly—but he got like four shots off and for sure—busted out the driver side taillight." Jas exhaled huge plumes of smoke.

Jas wasn't lying about Bruce being a good shot. He was a Ranger, Sergeant First Class. Many Plaguists were former military, disenfranchised from the Planet's number one employing entity.

(Note: ON THE PLANET EARTH: The largest employer of people is:

First, the United States Department of Defense: 2.86 million employees. Second is Walmart: 2.2 million. Third is The People's Liberation Army of China is number two with an estimated 2.18 million employees—McDonalds is fourth with 1.7 million employees. Fifth on the list is China National Petroleum Co.: 1.5 million. Make what you will of these statistics.)

Plaguism was the answer. That was clear to me. To attack these people meant you didn't have the guts or the brains to debate them. Soldiers went to the blind desert to kill the boogeyman and spread democracy, scavenge oil and mineral resources. They came back home to find filthy hospitals and no jobs, unsympathetic police, and a condescending populace.

"Thank you for your service," and no benefits.

The Plague was an antidote to the hypocritical bullshit being fed to us by Populous Control, or as most of you knew it: Mass Media.

Chuckie spread the word: Absurdity Shall be the Whole of the Law.

We continued to drive around Nashville looking for Cadillacs.

I became increasingly paranoid that having a firearm was somehow detrimental to our well-being. We weren't really killers. I mean, I'd slaughtered a racoon, but that wasn't a human—and for sure, I was a million percent more concerned with being caught and doing serious time in jail than I was about some shithead Christian named Chip, or Skip, or Kip, taking a slug in the throat and bleeding out his selfish meaningless life.

"We should toss the gun," I admitted.

"I don't know—I think I might like to keep it," Jas protested.

"It's a stolen gun."

"Christianity is a stolen religion," Jas dared with flippant wrist flung back. "What do you want me to do about it?"

I didn't have an answer. I thought he'd be too irresponsible to own a handgun. I told him, "I don't think you'd be any good at owning a handgun."

"What do you mean?" He squealed, offended.

"Suicide, jealous rage, explosive circumstance, nothing on television—I could imagine you blindly firing off a pistol for ANY reason and in ANY direction!"

Jas cackled with delight. "Oh, right!" He declared and provided a mock scenario in sarcastic slur. "Like I'm gonna be all—whoops! Seen this episode of Star Trek—time to shoot the lights out!" Then scrunched his face and shook his head. "Come on!"

"Yes! Exactly—I could see that scenario—but with a handful of Percocet in your belly and right after or during an aggravating phone call from your family."

There was a pause while Jas lit a cigarette. "Okay. You're right. This thing would be fired within a week." He took a hit and tried to hand it to me while I was driving.

"I don't want it either, man!"

"Well, what do you want to do with it?" He inquired as we drove out of downtown and into suburbia.

"I don't know. Bury it?" I asked.

"Bury it? We'll know where it is!"

As we contemplated what to do with the gun, a black Cadillac DeVille cruised up behind me and beside me. The windows were tinted black and impossible to see in, and they came down with a very quick speed. I was very observant. They looked like every other Vanderbilt student: young, dumb and full of cum. From their fists a mighty fury… Of eggs.

SPLAT! Split! Splat! Splatsplatsplat! SPLIT! Splatsplitsplatsplatsplat! Splat! Splat! Splatsplitsplitsplitsplitsplat! My windshield wipers caused a sunny side up streak of yellow sludge. Zero visibility. I slowed the car as best I could and put on the hazards. I stopped.

Jas leapt from the car and opened fire—BANG! BANG! BANG! BANG! BANG! Click click click. I watched the DeVille speed off into East Nashville.

Jas leapt back into The Mystery Ship, and I rolled the window down and drove with my head from the window to the nearest coin operated car wash. Neither one of us knew if anything was hit. I saw no glass or blood and heard no explosion.

We met Dominic, Rock and Chuckie back at S.P.A.M. Manor. Rock had chased some DeVille a few miles from the bridge, but it turned out to be a frightened soccer mom who raced all the way home to Belle Meade and her mansion built upon the grounds of a vast plantation.

"What about that preacher man on TV? Should we put a Fatwa on his head?" I asked Chuckie.

God responded— "No!" He sucked his Kool. "You either fuckin'— put a Fatwa on EVERY FUCKING MEMBER of a stupid thing, like the NAZIS did the JEWS, like I'm thinking about doing to *Scientologists*— or *none* at *all.*"

That was some reasoning I could get behind. I wondered if Salmon Rushdie agreed. Probably not—he would've had no career if not for the global fame and attention brought on him by Ayatollah Khomeini's Fatwa.

There was no god but Allah Muh Boolshet!

Was I on acid? Damn—it felt like I was always on acid—always high on weed and drinking whatever whenever I could—pills too—popping like celebration corn. I didn't think I went more than a day or two without dosing LSD and goofing off with these Plaguists. *Getting fucked up and doing fucked up shit*—was a sacrament to these people—and why not? I was suddenly now—ONE of these people. I was a Plaguist. I'd gotten the mortified stink of enlightenment like I wanted. My angel wings crispy barbecued and dipped in blue cheese sauce.

A pitchfork consensus. A semen coated mirror for the witness. The love from our community just missed us.

"Are you all right?" Jas asked.

Everyone stared at me. Reverend Killjoy, Bishop Minx and Sain't Marybeth had arrived and with everyone else were staring at me. "Huh?!" Where the hell was I? What the hell had happened? Was there really a fatwa on my head?

"Chuckie wants to know if you got a good look at any of 'em."

I addressed Chuckie. "Oh man—I don't know—The Average White Band—they looked like assholes at Vanderbilt—rich-kid airheads."

"We should burn Vanderbilt down to the ground!" Rock growled.

Dominic interjected coolly. "Vanderbilt is concerned with higher education which we need for our civilization to prosper, plus the university brings in a lot of jobs for our local residents, which means fewer people on welfare—and fewer taxes imposed upon us at the state level."

"Run for fucking congress already!" Rock shouted to Dominic.

Everyone started speaking at once: Rock listened to Dominic, Chuckie listened to Minx, both Reverend Killjoy and Marybeth listened to The Pope, as I pretended to. What glory glory, holy holy holy, hell yeah hallelujah, and ballyhoo sang themselves a song on that glorious stage of life in mythomaniac detail.

"Rock, you got to get rid of this thing for me!" The Pope demanded.

Rock took the gun, examined it, clicked open the spool and spun the empty chambers back with a click.

"So, The Pope emptied the pistol on the DeVille?" Rock interrogated me.

"All five rounds," I answered, apparently correctly.

"You counted?"

"Onetwothreefourfive." I showed him my fingers and thumb.

"You know why smart gun owners keep the first chamber empty?"

"Too many half-hearted suicides?"

Rock leaned in a little closer to me, suspicious. "Something like that."

Christians were attacking Plaguists and we needed a battle plan. Jas suggested we sue the Sunday morning TV preacher—but Dominic didn't believe we had Just Cause. He needed to win this case—not necessarily exploit it for publicity. He wanted to prosecute the driver, but first we needed to find him.

Chuckie decided that Dominic could no longer be head of Public Relations and a lawyer too, so he smartly gave the job to Marybeth, who relinquished her role of Church Concubine and thankfully accepted, to the chagrin of future Plaguists—you have no idea what you missed…

"Angel of Death, SOMEONE needs to die!" Rock shouted at me.

I was suddenly flush. Was I expected to murder?

God saved me. "Martin, I gotta strip you of your Angel of Death title and duties."

I'd been fired from a lot of jobs, been broken up with by a lot of girls, told to go fuck myself by a wide variety of people on the planet—but this—this losing face with God really hurt my feelings. "Okay." But how else to respond?

"From now on, you're going to be The Holy Scribe. Your duties are to record, in FICTION and in *fact,* the goings on of the church in ANY way you see fit."

"Who's Angel of Death?"

"I am."

"But you're God."

"Yes—and in being God, I'm also everybody and everything else. I'm The Pope, papal paupers, and every fat Mexican kid stuffing his face with jalapeño poppers." We all laughed at that line. "No one else can be The Angel of Death, though, except me—I'm God and The Angel of Death. I couldn't let you roam around with such a wicked cool title never having killed hundreds of people—especially during wartime—and we're at war."

"I understand."

"Do you?"

"You're a fan of my work." I smiled, teenage-hoping I was right.

"You're full of the right amount of shit." He smiled and grabbed my head and kissed me on the mouth, for about five seconds. I hoped he didn't have herpes, or French Legionnaires Disease.

I've always remembered that line—God telling me that I was full of the right amount of shit. It was probably how I wrote this book so freely. Coming to terms with your pitfalls and polishing them was the Plaguist way.

"I KNEW you weren't the Angel of Death! Fucking COOKIE MONSTER!"

"I'M NOT THE FUCKING COOKIE MONSTER!" I screamed. I stood up and took a step towards Rock. "I'm The HOLY FUCKING SCRIBE!"

Rock looked at me with eyes slightly larger than I'd ever seen.

I didn't need periphery to know that all eyes were on me, us—this—dramatic situation. "HOW I DEPICT YOU might matter TO YOU one day!" I tried to boom. I tried to express my anger. I did so with bright feathers, throat pouch, neon skin, with words instead of weapons, like fists, but I was a wordsmith and that had been my gift since lying to parents and teachers and preachers and principals and friends and lovers and neighbors and relatives and *strangers when we meet...*

Without missing a beat, he switched to cool-cat and spoke evenly. "Take it easy Tiger, I was pulling your tail."

It seemed I'd finally gotten the respect of Sain't Rock. He always saw right through me—knew I was no Angel of Death—no killer, no holy representative of the afterlife.

Holy Scribe he could buy, and from that point on, he was always cool with me.

The next night, there was an arrest. Justin Champ, 18, from Nashville, Tennessee, was arrested for the murder of Shelby Sebastian, 18, also from Nashville. Apparently, there were dozens of kids in the IHOP parking lot that night. High school kids. They all knew each other. The punks and Plaguists got together and fingered the little preppy football player, so desperate to fit into the normal dull, he'd happily kill any variation.

The boy's parents did a good job cleaning his car, but when the detectives checked underneath the vehicle, they found chunks of skull and tissue in the chassis, which they positively identified as containing Shelby's DNA. It seemed to be an open and shut case.

Justin Champ was exactly as you'd suppose him to be, with tanned skin, short blonde rabbit fur and pearly white Bucky Beavers that had never been chipped from fighting—manic bright eyes that had never been in trouble, never experienced consequence, never felt the fault of the self-falter—little virgin wanderlust who had been protected from the outside world by hovering mother—button-up tucked into khaki, hair gel, 5'9, almost there, needy to prove.

He was recorded as saying, "I'm a Ninja in my Cadillac," while he ran down Shelby Sebastian.

The heat cooled down. Plaguists were told the war on Cadillacs was over. But the threat was still very real. Fewer and fewer young people were converting to Plaguism. Could be we converted all the punks in the city, could be the heat from the preacher man was real, and kids were scared for their lives. Fear was such a useful tactic when you were preaching the gospel of love.

31.

Two Pairs of Shoes

Lingus house was on the other end of town. Driving gave me plenty of time to think. I won't tell you about the time I broke down and had to run across the highway to find help—or the other time I broke down on the highway and had to call for help—or about the times when nothing broke down—they were all the same—a time to smoke weed and listen to music and trip out on the city that was Nashville: plastic cowboy training wheels on a carousel horse—fat-bellied men tucking their shirts into blue jeans—showing off ostentatious belt buckles/not rodeo prizes—and clean cowboy boots that had never seen stirrups or waded through rainy puddles of horseshit.

I didn't feel like I would be a good addition to this environment.

Ready was beautiful. Her mouth felt warm and soft on mine. Her tongue was patient and cool. Her hands knew the right firmness to explore, the right strength to pull the clothing off. She held tight and let it happen. I squirted all over her curved caramel back after plowing her wet fertile fields—after moistening the clover with my fresh dew mouth—a finger first knowledge of the muscular clenching… Lubricated machine glory…

She had to practice afterward with the band. I was still horny and hungry, so I smoked cigarettes with Pookie outside in the yard and we chatted about the weather and the wayward winds.

"Did she tell you?"

She told me nothing.

"Lingus is going on the road next month. They got signed to Bastard Sloth Records."

"Who's gonna watch the house?"

"That's your first question?" Pookie sized me up as the opportunist I was.

"What was yours?"

"Can I come?" Pookie showed the opportunist he was.

"Are you going?"

"Of course, we're taking my van."

I thought about it, but decided to wait and see if Ready would even want me to go—dare ask me to join them on their adventure—and it was going to be an adventure. How could it not be—three hot girls on the road in a stinky van with drugs and Pookie and whatever other dudes? Maybe I didn't want to go.

Dominic stormed out of the house screaming. I couldn't make out what he was yelling about, but he was very upset. He picked up rocks and threw them at the house. No windows broke. Pookie yelled at him to stop, and he got in his face. I didn't even stand up. He could've thrown a flaming bulldozer full of cobras through the wall and I wouldn't have tried to stop him. I wasn't in love.

He yelled some more and stormed off ranting and raving.

"What the fuck was that about?" Pookie asked.

"I guess he's pissed," I offered an obvious retort.

He trotted after him. Later, I learned that he and Harriet had broken up. That he wasn't happy with her wanting to go on the road. He wasn't willing to join, either. It was over.

Bummer.

Plaguists were upset—but I was a newcomer—I was not invested in their relationship. I had my own concerns. I planned on staying at this house for a while—using it and S.P.A.M. Manor to balance off one another—not wear out my welcome too soon at either location.

I am reminded here of why I always had two pairs of shoes. My grandfather taught me to always alternate my shoes so that they would have time to air out. He taught me that this would help the leather last and prevent fungus from forming. My attitude was the same for these two addresses.

Ready never invited me to go on the road with them. I didn't offer to watch the house. It looked like I was down to one location, and really, how long could that last?

32.

Nashville Nazis at Dragon Park

This again…. This blissful spin, unable to focus, unable to balance, wobbling around some strange new environment—Dragon Park— named because of the presence of a giant sea serpent sculpture by Chilean artist Pedro Silva. The enormous dragon stood eight feet tall with brightly colored mosaic tiles all over the long body, huge triangles acting as enormous fins for the beast that appeared to be diving in and out of the concrete water. Several serpentine half circles with triangle fins decorated the park.

Dragon Park was a popular hangout and meeting place for Plaguists and local punks. It was a great place to hallucinate. I brought Jas there to give Pookie back a bong that meant so much to them, broken and re-glued so many times—like their relationship.

We smoked hash out of the red plastic bong and for the first time, I waved off the next pass.

"Yeah man, I'm pretty fucked up," The Pope admitted.

Several other Plaguists were there as well, getting high and laughing.

Our party was interrupted by a trio of Nashville Nazis. These grotesque slobs wore their black and red costumes like they were actual uniforms, clean and sharply pressed—black pants, red shirt, black suspenders, red boots—shaved heads—swastika arm bands—little cosplay jack offs.

"OY!" The largest, slowest one of them shouted. "You the little pussy who calls himself Faggot Hitler?"

I wasn't ready for violence. I could barely stand. I was ready to sink into the sofa and watch cartoons. But when life deals from the deck—you gotta play your hand. I stood up—and was instantly pushed down by the tallest of the Nazis. Adrenaline found a home in my blood. I popped up on my knees and lunged for his ankles. I knocked him over and grabbed his head and smashed it into the concrete. He kicked me in the balls, and I rolled over in starlight pain and suffering. I curled into a fetal position and gagged.

I forced myself to my knees and took a boot to the gut. I lunged again and my fist found home in the Nazi's guts. I punched him in the mouth. He fell backwards and smashed his head on the concrete.

Pookie showed up on his skateboard and blindsided the largest Nazi across the face, cracking his board and the mouth of the fuckwit. Three other Plaguists joined in and kicked the shit out of the Nashville Nazis. The three hate-filled scumbags were a crumpled mess of blood and torn uniform. A gunshot went off. No one knew from where.

Everyone scattered.

Pookie jumped into the Mystery Ship, and I drove away with spasms in my stomach and tears in my eyes. It was a horrific scene. I received no joy from the fight. Humans slamming each other across the face and body with fists was the most primitive form of expression I knew. A stick fight had more grace and form. Fist fights were for the unevolved, a type of gross human aggression that was a pathetic display of savagery and unwillingness to resolve any issue. Caveman battlefields for the ignorant and clumsy with words.

The word spread quickly across the Plaguist community. The Nazis had it out for us. Now we had two enemies, Christians and Nazis—it seemed they were of the same cloth—like 1939 Germany—the Nazis were overwhelmingly Christian. This should surprise no one who understands the religiously inclined. A belief was only as valuable as your disbelief in everything else. There was no love of a god without the hatred of all other gods.

33.

Love Leaves Scars

We were having goodbye sex. I didn't know that. She did. I ran my fingers over the scaffolding of her body, sliding my young fingertips along the curves and folds of her flesh, the architecture of her animal. Her large breasts hung down in my face as I tasted one, the left one. She rode me gently.

Hot tears fell on my forehead. I was confused. I'd never made a girl cry during sex before.

"What's wrong?" I asked.

She covered my mouth with her left hand. She looked at me sadly. She covered my eyes with her right hand. She sobbed as she rode me, sweetly grinding me, warm melting bee's wax on my pistil—hot sad tears on my chest and thighs. I couldn't see or speak, thankfully, she didn't have a third hand to cover my nose. I needed to breathe, at least.

Some memories lasted lifetimes—some sensations you took with you—a soul was something that was grown. I wished I knew everyone on the planet more intimately. Stay away from me.

She uncovered my eyes and was upset that she did not find sadness in my baby blues. "You don't even know me," she whispered.

I was mesmerized. I was glad she kept her hand over my mouth as she made love to me in waveless waterbed motion. Thick gelatin landscape, thighs squeezing my naked saddle. I didn't know what to say. I had nothing to say. My feelings were numb soldiers returned from battle.

My emotional currency was bankrupt. I wanted to try out the world without the pestilence of love. I wanted only good times and more objective human understanding. I wanted only the rhythm of the gods—balcony tornadoes—sexual intercourse with young beautiful other—ones—I wanted to come and come often and kiss and kiss often and get high and be high and write poetry in the dark with blowtorch words and blowjob punctuation. I wanted to skim the surface like a well-skipped rock, dizzy and swiftly across the watery plane. I wanted little splash and slippery sink—but far away from the source. I wanted to go far and be far gone.

She lifted her hand from my mouth. "What do you have to say to me?"

I spoke without thinking. "I wish I could say to you more than we have time for."

She leant across me and shoved her larger, right breast into my mouth. (To shut me up? This occurred to me upon reminiscence.) Maybe she wanted to shut me up—she shut me up with her motherly tit—and I sucked—and she gripped the brass railing of her bed and fucked me until my dick got numb and she fucked me more and more and cried no more over little old me and drove her clit against the root of my tree and found the maple syrup sticky-sweet.

"I don't want you to stay here tonight. I want you to let me fall asleep, and I want you to sneak out in the middle of the night. Okay? Like you always do." She looked sad. "Can you do that for me? Promise not to wake me?"

"Okay."

Her bed was so comfortable. I fell asleep. I dreamt of nothing. I woke up quickly with a start. She lay naked on top of me, head on my shoulder, arm on my chest. My left arm was asleep from the tension.

Gently placing her arm on the bedspread freshly abandoned, I knelt to retrieve the pile of my clothes. I closed the bedroom door behind me. I put on my boxers and shorts. I walked down the hall. I opened the sliding glass door.

Pookie was outside smoking a cigarette. Man, that boy had timing. I put on my shirt and shorts. My walk was elegant and staged, sublime. I had the stink of perfect sex on me.

"Have a good life," Pookie mumbled with a cigarette in his mouth, which he lit with matchstick and sulfur flick.

I joined him in a smoke. We sat on the bench. "You know—you never know—It's a long road."

"That should be a country western song," he suggested.

"What?"

"You know—you never know—it's a long road."

We shared a laugh.

"See you," was the last we said to each other.

I went to Waffle House for breakfast. Hank was there so I figured I'd squeeze out a meal. He was upset. Crystal had broken up with him. He asked me for the best poems of my life—to try and win her back. He promised meals for life and actual cash if it worked. I wrote two poems that almost made him cry and ate three eggs sunny-side up with pecan waffles, sausage, ham, and bacon and orange juice and coffee.

That was the end of that meal ticket. I didn't think any amount of poetry would be able to win her back. Once a woman had been scorned, usually the end was nigh. I decided to check in on The Pope.

Arriving at S.P.A.M. Manor, I found Jas bawling on his bed. More drama. Great. "You okay?"

"NO!" Jas sniveled.

The large mascara swastika melted down his birdcage. It had been days since he'd bathed. He smelled of alcohol in vapor form, escaping through a stinky human filter, acrid gaseous drunken skeleton of flesh. He moped around his apartment with his pink chamois bathrobe loosely dangling open, ugly umbilical ululations of his whining strings. Snot-faced and pissed off. He wore combat boots and tighty-whities, stained yellow with pee and crusty with semen.

"Pope! What the hell's wrong with you?" I asked/laughed. I hadn't seen him in days.

"The Pope's Dead!" Jas shouted in crystalline raspberry syrup. "Long live FAGGOT HITLER!!!" He slurred, drunk, mourning the loss of his newest loved one.

Sarcastic sinister suck it, "well, The Pope has a show to do."

Jas was sad, wore a mad mouth beneath shriveled wet nose and pouting eyes. "Nope! Nope! No more Pope! If I go on stage, it will here-to-fore be as Faggot Hitler." He spread his arms apart in faux celebration. Sad pink wings, useless and musky.

I challenged his vanity, the easiest mark. "The Church needs a Pope."

He took a long pull on his half empty fifth of Evan Williams. "Find a new one," he dared. The copper-tinted sour mash dribbled down his chin like a teething baby.

"How? What's The Church's policy on electing a new pope? Are we supposed to form a kindergarten of magpies? Who gets to be a magpie?"

Jas smirked. "I hate you." His mood changed from almost-made-to-feel-better to sullen-surrender. "Why do you have to be so—so—you? Get out of my house!"

I spun on my heels before the punctuation.

"No, wait!"

I continued my ever-spin and stopped after completing the full circle. I was a hilarious robot anybody.

"Stay and get drunk with me." Jas pranced to the fridge, opened and threw me a beer.

"You never needed to ask before." I smiled, attempting to reassure my new friend, who seemed like one of my oldest friends—for all that we'd been through in the previous months.

"He took everything," Jas moaned.

"What—like your heart and soul?" I sought to cheer The Pope up with sarcasm.

"Like our Chicago money, my solid silver cock-ring, all the weed in the house."

The beer felt cool against my fingers. "That's all the money I have to offer for rent."

Jas breathed wounded disgust and fired a bullet of a stare through my forehead. "HE LEFT ME!" Jas lost it again and wailed sorrow and grief into the dark kitchen corner of crusted dishes and cups.

"I got fifty bucks—want me to go score a bag?"

"Would you?" Jas squealed. "And cigarettes and beer and band-aids."

"What do you need band-aids for?"

"Later," Jas exhaled, prognosticating the inevitable.

I bought a case of pilsner. I scored an eighth of an ounce from Dominic and bought four packs of cigarettes.

By the fourth six-pack, we were drunk.

Jas threw a bottle against the wall, then another.

BAM! Whizzz—BAM! Whizza—BAM! Whii—SMASH! Whizzz—CHANGCK! Bottles zoomed around the room from every direction smashing into the walls.

"Hey, that one almost hit me, motherfucker!" I screamed, ready now to kick his ass.

"AAAAAAIAAIAAGHGGIIIIIGGGGGHHHHHHHH!!!!" Jas screamed and threw the bottles around the apartment faster and with more force. Bottles exploded and showered the apartment with tiny particles of glass, which became wedged in the fibers of the carpet so thoroughly and completely that they'd never be totally cleaned. "RAMBO!!! POOKIE!!! YOU MOTHERFUCKER!!!"

The nightmare went on for three more songs. It truly rained glass splinters from a torrential force. Jas screamed and cried and smashed every bit of glass in the kitchen. There were several cases worth of empty beer bottles whizzing by the tiny apartment and shattering in dangerous shards and dusty fragments.

As suddenly as it had begun, it was over. There were no more bottles to break. Jas was in the fetal position and crying. The floor glittered with sparkly shards of bloodletting glee—little diamonds of pain and misery—only a thousand-year storm would turn this glass shore into a sandy paradise.

I delicately brushed off the brittle crumbs from the sofa cushions and assessed the damages—total. There wasn't a vacuum strong enough to undo this wreckage. We'd need an industrial strength cartoon Shopvac—one that could suck up everything in the place—the debris, the TV, the sofa, the bed, the carpet, all our writings, the dishes, the floorboards, the walls, our souls, the world… It was a disaster.

I located my shoes. They were by the door. I brushed off the other sofa, to make a little walkway to find my shoes. It was a long process to remove the glass shards from my burgundy boots. Jas stopped whimpering and was in a post-apocalyptic blackout. I fished out as many shards as I possibly could, first by turning my boot upside down and smacking the heel, next with kid-gloves inching my fingers around the soles to retrieve any wayward particle. Satisfied—or rather impatient at last—I shoved my bare feet into the boots and cut my toes only five or six times—trickles of blood though—not pools.

I found a broom behind the fridge and swept up the transparent fragments in the kitchen.

"What are you doing?!"

"I'm fucking cleaning up your fucking mess, asshole?!"

"Well, stop it!"

I let the broom drop and headed for the door. I was out of there—sayonara—I couldn't take one more minute of the madhouse.

"What are you doing?!" Jas whimpered/screamed.

"I'm leaving!"

Jas crawled on his hands and knees through the sharp amorphous mess and slammed a bloody hand on the door, closing it on me. My hand stayed on the knob. "You can't fucking leave!" He squealed in desperation.

"Well, you have to let me clean *something!*"

"No! —Look! —Look at this place." He searched my eyes with manic depressions in his skull, tiny mad wormholes— "Look!"

I looked.

It was the wreckage of a Godzilla film coated in pixie dust. It was beautiful and horrifying. I truly didn't know what to do.

"You see?!" —He ran his already bloody fingers through the silica and quartz, making geometrical shapes on the kitchen floor. "It's temporary, I know that! But the best art's—the most spiritual—like the Mandalas of the Tibetan monks or the Cherokee shaman—here today—off your rocker. —Ha! HA! Ha!" He laughed, but in seriousness. He hunkered down on the floor covered with bits of boron and lime.

Jas was no longer crying. He was manic, focused on his new project— a bloodletting prayer to the destructive force. He said no more. He continued drawing on the floor—an intricate design, geometrically balanced and artistically pleasing to the eye. I watched him for a spell and walked to the table, where my notebook was open, and pen waited.

I picked up the wicked journal and before writing, gave it a mean and sudden wipe with the palm of my hand. Of course, the book was coated in glass and halfway across the page, great streaks of red blood coated the snow of the page—an auspicious beginning, to be sure. I wrote away, on the same bloody page, letting occasional red drops drip from my hand and pen spilling on the page like sacrament. I wrote more questions to the spirit of the universe:

Does your physical vehicle sparkle? Does your smile shine? Do you have a light to hide? Is your engine running? / Does it react to the lack of you with grace or sleepy bump? Does it fear the crash or anticipate it? —on and on I went with this poem—ending with What flavored intestines for that future tomb? I was scribbling and dripping blood forgetting all about where and when I was.

Jas came over to the sofa. He looked like a different animal—a soulless robot monster with dead batteries—drained and amazed—dazed and spent. "You're going to have to do me a favor."

"Yeah?" I was in no mood.

"Can you cook heroin?"

"No."

He plopped down on the black leather sofa beside me. "Sure, you can—it's fucking easy—all you do is put a little water in the powder and boil it."

"I'm not the right man for this mission," I assured him.

"Look, I can't use my hands, okay?" He showed me his hands, gnarled gargoyle claws of torn flesh and bloody glass. He'd been playing in his mess and fucked himself. Well, he'd finally done it. He'd crossed over to the other side.

I thought maybe he should go to the hospital to have the shards removed, but figured I didn't want to drive him, or wait for him, and he would probably refuse anyway— "Well, okay—but this is your suicide."

"You're going to have to shoot it in me, too. I can't even use a belt. —Can I use your belt? —Wrap it around my arm and put the leather in my mouth."

I couldn't believe the reality of what I was doing. I found it absurd that this sissy fucker who lost all my money, or stole it, was now asking me to shoot him full of a lethal drug. Well, the only thing to be sure— was that absurdity shall indeed be the whole of the law.

I poured the powder into a spoon and added a capful of tap water. I put the spoon over a candle and watched the crust dance and sizzle. I took a q-tip and a syringe from the medicine cabinet. I drew in the gunk from the spoon, using the cotton swab as some sort of filtering device, I think—upon instruction, I flipped my middle forefinger against the thin medical bone to remove the air-bubbles.

"Listen, if I die—this isn't your fault, okay—type up a nice suicide note for me." He looked at me with dead eyes and I thought of my grandmother.

(Note: My father's mother was a large jolly woman who cooked the best biscuits and gravy in the world and never had a face without smiles on it when we were together. I loved her dearly, more than any other. She slept in a different bedroom than my grandfather. They were not on the best of terms. I was the only grandchild of four boys. My father was the oldest. My father's mother was dying of cirrhosis of the liver. I visited her in the hospital every day after school. I drove to the hospital, and we watched *The Honeymooners* together. She was a woman who loved to laugh, who loved children and who loved life, when it was good.

Her last few months hadn't been good. She deteriorated. She lost a hundred pounds in two weeks. Her system corroded. Her liver leaked oil at a rapid rate. I helped the doctor change her sheets, which were thick and heavy—soaking wet with the oil expunged from her liver. They were yellow and stank of uncooked food. This reminded me of the baby shark I dissected a week earlier in biology class, thick with oil.

My father's mother's body was disappearing. Her face was sunken and sallow.

My next few visits saw her get worse. On my last visit she was screaming in pain. "Sweet Jesus—bring me home! I want to come to you SWEET LORD! I'M READY!! AAAAAAGGGGGGH! Please lord, I'm begging you!"

I heard her. It was the sound of life ending. It was the worst noise I'd ever heard. I didn't see how the staff at the hospital could experience such conditions day and night—the agony and despair of the dying—I could barely visit. Now my large, lovely grandmother was a screamer wishing for death in the last moments of her life.

"What the fuck are you giving her for her pain!?!" I screamed at the doctor at the top of my lungs with tears in my eyes.

"Relax, son. Let me check her files. Um—it says here… Darvacet."

"What?! That barely takes away my headaches! My grandmother's in *AGONY*! Can't you give her some morphine or something?"

"If it's not surgery related, I need a relative to sign the permission slip to give her morphine."

"Give me the papers!"

"It has to be an adult, son."

"I'm eighteen!" (*I'm a boy and I'm a man*) I showed him my driver's license. He wrote down my driver's license number and handed me back my wallet. He handed me the clipboard and I signed. I watched them shoot the morphine into her. I held her hand until all the strength was gone.

She never woke up.

I overheard her four sons, my father and his three brothers, at the funeral, angry, upset at that damn doctor for giving her morphine. They were sore as hell and wanted to investigate. I wonder if they ever did. I left town a few months later and never saw any of them again, including my father.

Anyway, she had no more life to share with you boys—her time had come—and if I killed her, believe me, I would do it ten-thousand times again because no one should go out in that kind of shit-storm of suffering.)

Now a couple of months later, I was pulling the needle out of my friend's arm, which was bleeding profusely, and his eyes were rolling back into his head and I was wondering how I should start the note. I wiped my prints from the needle and put the needle into his right hand. He could barely hold the syringe and I considered taping it there as if the detective on the scene was some slapstick keystone cop and wouldn't notice. I didn't know what to do. Was he really getting off or was he overdosing? I threw a glass of water on his face.

Nothing. I wondered if I'd have to grab him by the arm and shove a fork in an electric outlet—therefore creating some sort of Plaguist Defibrillator.

I decided to give it a minute, besides, I really had to pee. On my crunchy way to the bathroom, I took a look at his Mandala. The Mandala was beautiful, crystal clear and bloody, made from the exploded remains of Cinderella's glass slipper. He must've had a thousand cuts and scrapes. But damn, I looked at the beautiful mess, an exact moment when the emotional wound displays itself as a psychic scar. What witness! What time and place. I didn't want to take a picture. I didn't want to share this moment with you in its exactness. It was impossible to capture on film. It would be swept away, as it should, like every sandcastle and empire was destined to disappear. Nothing lasts forever. Enjoy each breath. It would all be over soon.

See you next time, spoke the bodhisattva. I wondered if there would be a next time. The road called me away. I felt it. I felt the need to flee was in me—I wouldn't last too many more days.

The gypsy in me. The grand magnet pulling me…

I pissed.

I came back and threw another glass of water on Jas's face.

"What the fuck?" He mumbled and that made me feel good that at least he was still able to draw breath.

Heroin was a scary thing. I never enjoyed it.

"Have a beer with me!" I said.

"Later…" He barely mumbled. He seemed to lose all coordination of his head—it fell on his chest as if he'd broken his neck and severed several tendons, as if his head was hanging on by a thread. He did, however, hold onto the needle now as if it were a cigarette. He dreamed the white dragon semen dream of junkie heaven and tried with all his might to raise his head. It stayed suspended at a forty-five-degree angle halfway between erect and collapsed.

I laughed and lit a cigarette. I took a hit and blew it in Jas's face.

That did the trick. He woke up enough to search for his cigarettes. He put the needle down and found his pack of cigarettes. "OW! —What the fuck?" Jas looked perplexed at his hands as he tried to hold his lighter. He suddenly remembered— "Oh yeah!" He laughed to himself in hoarse whispers and coughed and lit his cigarette from my friendly flame.

34.

Licking the Wounds

Jas soaked his hands in hot water for hours, using a steak knife to pry out the tiny pieces of glass that were embedded in his flesh. I could tell the water was hot because of the steam issuing forth—even in the heat of the summer. I boiled the water and drank a green tea while constantly refilling his water bowl. He put his hands in the water and yelped. He pulled his hands out, and focused himself with a deep breath and plunged his hands in again. It was this time that he used to pry the little chunks of glass from his hands—pain everywhere, not isolated. Crimson ribbons squirted into the bowl; tiny glass shards hit the bowl bottom with tiny, muffled dings.

The door was open. There was light in the room, one of only a handful of times that ever happened. I was happy that he'd survived his night of me shooting him up with heroin. He was stoned for hours, and I didn't sleep, making sure to blow smoke into his face nod after nod. FUCK! It wasn't fun, but it was informative, and I made a conscious decision to never shoot drugs.

What was worse than shooting Jas up with heroin? Pouring the iodine on his self-inflicted wounds. He screamed and he screamed, and he cried, and he shouted, and he gritted his teeth and breathed through his incisors and his face reddened and I didn't mind that he spit on my face. I knew the iodine annihilated him. Tears streamed down his radish red face, and you'd think he was having a baby the way he was exorbitantly breathing his Lamaze class training and push-push-pushing the watermelon through the lemon size opening.

The next day, I helped him to eat, drink and smoke but then he was on his own. He was a fright to see, inching his pained fingers along the lighter to try and light the cigarette that took seven minutes to pry from the pack and put in his mouth. He was like a wounded Dungeness crab with his limited pincers.

I angrily grabbed the lighter from him and lit all the candles. "These should last you until I get back."

"Where are you going?" He asked feebly.

"Breakfast!"

I brought him back an order of pancakes. I cut them up for him and poured the butter and syrup all over them. I taped a plastic fork to his wrist and despite his protests laid myself out on the sofa and fell right to sleep.

35.

The Burning Tree of Life

Jas and I both were unemployed, so we woke up and took acid. We decided to clean the house until the drug started to come on. It was a new day. We even cleaned with the door open—poltergeists and demonic spirits, love ghosts and benevolent angel corpses filtered out of the dark and dank pit of S.P.A.M. Manor in wavy gaseous spasms of released heat and disease.

I took a moment to step outside and feel the sunshine—hear the birds sing—feel the wind blow change. I smoked a cigarette and wondered how many more days I had left on my meter here in the country music capital of the world.

I swept and we put all the art supplies away, all the coloring books and notepads and crayons and pastels and paints. We put all the toys back in the toy box, except the yo-yo I'd forgotten about. I went on a mad yo-yoing spree, walking the dog, around the world, fast sideways action, upside-down. I forgot that I'd turned the water on to do the dishes. Jas didn't notice either. Apparently, the acid had kicked in.

"What's going on, motherfuckers!" Chuckie walked in and laughed. I hypnotized myself with a spinning yo-yo from a limp string and Jas ripped out random passages of one of his bibles and laughing. Meanwhile, the sink overflowed with water and suds: a horrible flood of water and soapy bubbles spilt over the counter, down the cabinets, and onto the floor. I looked down and noticed the kitchen floor looked like a winter wonderland. I ran into the kitchen splashing and sloshing.

Jas followed me, laughing. He ran to the cubbyhole closet and the enormous landfill of clothes. He pulled out every available towel, dirty or clean, and tossed them to me in the kitchen. "Put 'em on the floor man! We'll do like a whole *soaking* thing."

By now, Rock and Marybeth and Minx and Dominic had arrived and were marveling at our idea of a spring cleaning. "You guys got more acid?"

We did.

We dosed our fellow Plaguists and took a walk—leaving S.P.A.M. Manor to soak in soggy towels and neglected suds. S.P.A.M. Manor was in the projects of East Nashville—one of the poorest parts of town.

On our journey through the projects, we were stopped by a group of black and brown children, no older than twelve, some on bicycles. "HEY!"

We ignored them.

They got closer. "HEY!"

We continued to ignore them, but they were persistent. "Hey! Y'all worship Satan?"

Chucky had enough— "Hell no, we don't worship Satan! Do y'all?"

"NO!" They seemed to shout in unison as if that was a stupid question.

"Why in hell do you think *WE DO?*"

"Ain't them devil worshippin' clothes?" Asked the second grader on the bike.

"I don't believe there's such a thing—you ever seen Jesus worshippin' clothes?"

"Uh-huh—what my preacher wears." Young and naïve.

"But you ain't wearing that now—must mean you don't worship Jesus."

"Uh-huh! Yes, I do!"

"SEE? —you *cain't* never tell what someone does by what they *wear,* now CAN you?"

"No, I guess not," moped the newly enlightened ten-year-old—then suddenly sprung to life again— "Wanna see something cool?"

"SURE!" God yelled, startling the boy a bit.

"Come on!" He bicycled a bit, and his gang of merry boys followed him, and so did we.

The kids took us to the edge of the woods.

"Up that hill is a burnt-out house."

"All right then—we'll go check it out," Chuckie said. "You coming with us?"

"Uh-UH! It's haunted!" He turned his bike away and sped down the hill, and all the neighborhood kids ran after him.

We were left to climb the fence and venture through the woods to the top of the hill, all on our own. We had to walk through the woods a ways and up a fairly steep hill, but we came to a clearing. There stood the burned-out remains of a house. The lawn was manicured and well-kept, something I found odd and unusual. Who would do such a thing—a family member of the tragic fire? A real-estate agent who wanted to sell the property in good time?

What was fantastic about this place was that it was on a hill—a high spot in the neighborhood. It overlooked most of that side of town, and in the distance rose downtown Nashville. Standing like a lighthouse beacon on the edge of the property was a luminous tree with white and peach-colored blossoms, vibrating violent whites and pale oranges, neon yellows, and violent pinks, glowing like a Moses bush—a radiating magical life form. It felt as if this was it—the dangerous fruit tree from Eden—alluring, enticing, seducing us with her fruit and flower—her proof of power.

The tree burst into flames. I bathed in the supernatural warmth of the colorful petals—cherry tree? Dogwood? Peach tree? Impossible to know. Soft whites exploded with orange, yellow, and pink hues. I thought of Moses and Rumi and wondered what their wonderful drugs were like. What sixth century Hindu mystic wasn't a tripper with a fondness for mushroom tea and hashish?

It was the dosage that makes the tonic a poison or a remedy. Sixteenth century alchemists cured the Black Plague by inoculating the willing with tiny dosages of the Plague itself. In this way one was either the sommelier or a wino.

Perhaps the day was perfect. Perhaps the company was unparalleled. The drugs were the right amount. My every vibrating cell was lucid with its surroundings. The hair on my arms and legs tickled the skin on my arms and legs. I sensed pollen collecting on my cilia and wished I knew the secrets of the honeybee.

I was one with each and every one of my seven-octillion atoms. I was seven- octillion solar systems strong. The dancing of my body and mind and soul in complete harmony was the reason for this trip. I was meant to see with new eyes, hear with new ears, trip with a new purpose.

My heartbeat kept time with the second—sixty beats a minute. My plumbing ran smoothly, and my kidneys enjoyed the alcoholic workout. My toes were comfortable in torn leather boots with worn thin soles and broken laces. My eyeballs adjusted to the trans-dimensional vision. I saw the invisible creatures dancing and lickety-split swimming through green—everywhere—the grass, weeds, tree leaves and new fruit.

"I am that I am," Chuckie said to me, laughing as I walked to the tree. I was too high to speak. "REMEMBER—you are that you are…" There was mumbling and something… Something… Something…

I climbed the tree. I leapt, grabbed a limb and pulled myself up. I climbed higher. I scraped my leg and ripped open a finger, but I got to the top. I was consumed in the fire of the flowering fruit tree.

I could've climbed that tree to the sky. I felt like a leopard, a bear, a monkey, an orangutan, gripping her golden arms and hoisting myself up into her nest. I was inside the tree. The tree was alive and communicating with me secrets beyond my comprehension. I marveled at the velvety lips of her petals—the delicate pistil and ovule. I sang to her, and she caught on fire.

I held onto the tree and stared out into the city and all I saw were apocalyptic scenarios of cannibalistic desperation—a world on fire—skyscrapers of banks exploding, investment bankers and derivative traders thrown from their bloody glass offices as the rebels came to take back their country.

I saw into the future: a celebration of the burning in modern youth culture—everything caught on a hand-held device—more movie-makers than audience members—more writers than readers—more singers than songs, more guns than people, more bullets than rice, more desire and desperation than time…

My attention devolved from revelation to psalm. The ants tickled the bark on the tree. One little social insect strayed from the path and climbed on my hand. He climbed up my arm. I was very still and let this rogue Hymenoptera stray from his social order and find me, scout me, discover me.

I was warm. Was I food or eater? These were his questions. The ant moved the segmented funiculus of his antennae and gestured to me a type of sign language. I understood. I concentrated all I could with my eyebrows to communicate my passive aggressive response as uninterested in devouring them and absolutely destructive upon attempting to be devoured.

The ant crawled from me and joined his parade of fellow ants identical in appearance (to my eye), links only in a chain, useless in solitude. I wondered if this was Oscar, the ant who told Chuckie he was god. That was the genesis God was shopping that week as he continually explained his origin in conflicting mythologies and malarkey marmalade. Another dose of hocus pocus to focus away the real attention.

The fires are coming. That was the message I received. *Head east.* The orange and yellow and white and peach blossoms of whatever fruit tree that was bedazzled by my hyper-focused incoherence. The pale silver dollar flower pedals velvety pliability sizzled to my touch, the flowers burst into flames and fell to the ground in puffs of dusty smoke. The wind blew the petals from the tree then, not all of them, but a quarter of them—an enormous gust, a first heavy wind of changing seasons. The ground was absolutely littered with these delicate pedals.

I climbed down the tree and joined my friends, showering in the petal storm, visibility low, tiny errant petals blowing in our eyes—snowing. It was like snow. It stopped. The wind had stripped thousands of petals from the enormous fruit tree in twenty seconds of calming bliss.

"THAT WAS FUCKING COOL!" Chuckie declared for all of us. There was much laughter and shit I don't remember.

We followed some old gravel road down this hill that was covered in trash. There were plastic bags ripped open everywhere. It was impossible to drive up to it, really—even walking it was a tiny labyrinth of loosely strewn refuse. But I was a natural born scavenger. I had to look at everything. You never knew when a diamond was going to be lurking in that lump of coal. (The garbage dumps in Knoxville—that's where I found my first porno mags (age 13) —heaven of masturbatory bliss.) —I looked down on the ground and found this busted up fire-extinguisher case like it might have come from a school or some institution, with the glass walls busted and the extinguisher gone, but the dangling hammer on a chain remaining. I yanked the hammer and chain from the emergency box.

I played with the thing for a minute as we walked down the garbage hill and decided to give it to Jas. "Here," I said, smiling. "In case of emergency."

It was the loudest I ever heard that rooster crow in all my days of making him laugh. He cackled and he cracked and he choked and he repeated the joke out loud as if it was the funniest thing anyone had ever said. He repeated my phrasing— "in—case—of —eMURgeNncy! — HAI! KZHAI! KZHAI! HA! HA!"

His hands were still red and butchered from the glass shards, so I attached the little hammer to his cool punkRock jacket, somewhere near the handkerchief pocket, if memory serves, attached to the zipper with tripper magic-spell and perfect fit. Jas laughed and he laughed until Plaguists asked questions. "What's so funny Jas?"

"This!" He grabbed the little hammer that hung down from his breast like an absurd medal of honor. "*In / case / of / emergency*!" Jas said with extended syllables of every word, crunching his face to his body in honored adoration while pursing his lips and using his eyes to smile and twitter. He tried to break himself open, mimicking a good whack of that little hammer against his Auschwitz physique. I loved Jas for this reason. He was a natural born clown, no matter how down, up or sideways— always good for a laugh.

I wish I knew then that this was the last time I would ever see Chuckie alive.

36.

The Anti-Eucharist

Disbelief. Acceptance. Sadness, but not grief. Grief was for the mourning. Plaguists did not mourn. To be mournful was to be crippled by events. I was not distraught. I fought back tears but accepted the raw emotion of losing a friend.

It was important to live by your words. Death was not a time to mourn, but a time to celebrate. A cycle had been completed. A timeline had been created. We could close the book on the subject—finalize the last chapter.

Cold distant logic kept me grounded to the cyclotron of my centrifugal vacuum. I had a cold wall built around my impenetrable castle.

I never knew how Chuckie died.

There were many stories.

Jas didn't talk. He didn't say a word. He lit one cigarette from another, two packs on one match. He drank and wept and stared out the window as I drove us to Plague Central. There would be a viewing of the body and the ceremony—which Chuckie wanted everyone to participate in—every Plaguist in town was to view the sacrifice.

One hundred and seventy-three people littered the lawn. There were cars everywhere—parked cramped together—abandoned like Woodstock—no one had time to figure out where to put a hundred cars and motorcycles. As God would say, "Fuck it."

The sun set. A fire was lit in the humid summer pig sweat evening. God was naked, pale and lifeless. They tied him to a giant oak tree. I was in shock with the loss. Had this really happened? Was God dead? Perhaps he'd finally become unbelievable even unto himself.

Rock covered Chuckie's whole head in shaving cream. He seemed particularly out of it, wired and tired and mad at the world. He shaved God with a straight razor, tufts of hair crowning his head, enormous bushy Fillmore-for-president sideburns.

He smiled and cried at the same time. I couldn't believe it—a tear of sadness escaped that maniac's eye. He held up an old-fashioned seltzer bottle and sprayed Chuckie's corpse, washing it free of the shaving cream. There was slapstick schtick to the very end. Absurdity shall be the WHOLE of the law. Death was an absurd ending to life—a flame extinguished, relegated to smoke—mixed with the ether...

What did this mean for the church?

Chef Hiccup had a much harder go of it. His responsibility was the least enviable. He had to dress and cook our Lord and flavor Charles Theodore Plague. Chef raised the familiar machete above his head, and let it stand at attention, glinting firewood sparkle. He summoned courage from a cavernous vault inside his caveman memory and let the blade down swiftly—slicing through the chest, the belly, instantly blood and the blossoming of guts, down to the crotch...

Chef turned, wobbled, bent, stabbed the earth and fell to his knees. He winced and vomited. He sobbed and let out a terrific scream.

"AAAAAAAAAAAAIIIIIIIIIIGGGGGGGGGGGGGH!!!!"

He stood breathing schoolyard steam and snot bubbles. He plunged his arms into his friend, his motorcycle riding companion, his punk rock guru, and he shivered at the cool texture of his organs and fluid. Chuckie had been dead for twelve hours.

Chef dressed God, spilling his stomach, intestines, kidney, liver, and heart into a large cook-safe plastic bucket. He went at him wildly with a hunting knife, stabbing, hacking and sawing the connective tissue to remove his insides completely from his bony cage.

I couldn't stand to look anymore. I walked away. Most everyone had turned away at the first cut, but I made it 'til Chef removed the guts. I wondered if I had the courage and strength to open and barbecue the corpse of a close friend—even if it was their wish to have me perform this ritual. Perhaps that was the genius of Chuckie—teaching us not to be afraid of the task of life—the inevitable deterioration of our biological mass—the final goodbye to breath, and a journey to the long goodnight.

They kept his head on, as per his wishes. Rock held Chuckie's head back as Chef Hiccup slid the spit in his rectum and up his cavity and down his throat backwards and out his mouth.

The boys locked him on the spit, and Chef basted him. The fire was small, but flames leapt up a little and licked the flesh of our Chuckie who weren't no more.

That was enough for me. I couldn't watch it anymore. I walked around in a daze of confusion and nausea. Was this all for real? Had my mind become so distorted on my diet of acid and hash and opiates that I lived in a fantasy world and nothing I viewed could be trusted as real?

Sain't Donna Party walked by weeping. She was consoled by Sain't Holly Cost and Sain't Mickey Finn. They seemed sad, like maybe somebody had died.

God was dead. Redemption was now more expensive than ever—the price of our souls had inflated, and American immorality was at an all-time high.

Every four hours for the next twenty-four, Chef and Rock flipped the fat melting game. They made a cinder block pit, cinder blocks from the Fiery Sermon's stage, lined at the top with strips of rebar. There God rested with a spit up his ass, until it was time to flip him. A small pit of charcoal sat in the corner. Slow and low was the only way to cook mammal.

Chef had a few folding tables set up that worked as a makeshift kitchen as he sliced and diced vegetables and cooked things on many small, flat butane stoves.

Fat dripped from Chuckie's body and sizzled on the fire. I'd never seen him naked, but there he was, deader 'n hell with an eight-foot spit rod up his ass and out his mouth. They put the tin lid back on the pit and hid him. It was better.

Jas told me that God had died sitting on the toilet with his pants around his knees like fat Elvis, a coughing fit brought on an aneurism which found him collapsed stiff, cheeks on the cool tile floor… There was an unforced pause between the story and his heinous cackle of fuck-you-universe. I wondered if I alone hadn't been told the truth.

Cannon told me he heard God had died from bullet wounds acquired while in a gunfight, apparently standing up in the back of a pick-up truck firing guns in each hand and killing Nashville Nazis that he had long had a feud with 'cause he stuck a pie in the face of one of their girlfriend's for being a bitch at Quicksilver to Marcos the busboy who everyone liked on account of how hard he worked.

Rock denied this and told me THAT was a story, and that Chuckie WASN'T even dead—that he'd merely been ABDUCTED by aliens and would return in the year 2222. Never mind what my lying eyes thought I saw and everyone around me was saying. God wasn't dead—merely abducted. The body on the spit was somebody else.

Dominic swore up and down he knew nothing but had heard from various reliable sources that God died after inhaling a case of dust-off and literally froze his lungs.

It was good to have various versions of the truth. It was good for The Holy Babble.

(I wondered what would become of The Holy Babble. God had some of my writing that maybe I didn't have copies of... Was God the editor of this thing? I wondered who would finish the project. I hoped it wasn't me—I would have to re-write the whole thing. Suddenly, being The Holy Scribe seemed like a job, more than an absurd title. Well God—I hope this book does the trick—because it's all I have to say on your unglory.)

My heart hurt. It sank into my stomach and was devoured by ravenous piranhas. My head hurt. The throbbing tear ducts of my face exploded salty brine. Nowhere to run. Nowhere to hide. I'd abandoned the safety net of my hometown, my mother's parents' house. I was exposed to the predator world in shiny white fur and pale blue eyes, baby skin cock and locks of long curly hair tussling in the degenerate air.

Veterans of desert battles and meaningless wars strolled up to Chuckie's cooking meat. They were in full combat gear, packs and rifles, pants tucked into boots, beige fatigues. The first one grimaced, the second one laughed. It seemed they were on patrol. Their presence almost FREAKED everyone out until the word spread that they were Plaguist friends.

Chef Hiccup didn't acknowledge their presence, continued to baste the body in cranberry-orange barbecue sauce, in bacon-infused bourbon, in coriander-infused clarified butter. I imagined you only get one shot at cooking the Lord, so you better do it right. He chopped carrots and celery and onions and potatoes and peppers and radishes and garlic and talked to no one, made eye contact with no one. He was in a trance and mourning the only way he knew how, with a wordless knife and a constant chop.

I didn't speak to the soldiers, but I surmised they were in the shit with God. Rock had a playful engagement with the biggest, meanest, unshaven, and dirtiest one of the fellows, some shoulder grabbing and chest punching, back slapping and hair tussling, like grizzly cubs in the Kodiak.

Chef Hiccup went out of his way to send God off right. He served smoky tomato compote with the thigh meat. Chunks of his kidneys, intestines, and buttocks were ground with spices and set into the casing of his intestines to create a large sausage, which was dipped in a corn batter and deep fried like a corn dog.

The scene was more festive than morbid—most of the Plaguists didn't seem too disturbed to be chowing down on the cooked flesh of their dead friend. Perhaps I wasn't as hardcore as I pretended to be. I was nauseous, ill-coated, slime molded, green-faced and swerving with the wobbles. I had trouble communicating with people. How could this be right? How could a dead God's last wish be for his friends to consume his flesh for spiritual purpose? (Cue sitcom laugh track.)

Was Chuckie's body being given to me—to partake of him in remembrance? Was I some sort of Judas for not eating the flesh he put forth before me? Was I some sort of Plaguist betrayer? Wouldn't that be keen?

Yes, of course—I was to betray Chuckie by writing about him, by spreading MY VERSION of his gospel. But I was a fucking Plaguist and no one told me what to do, least of all whom GOD!

I got a beer from the keg and Marybeth looked up at me and walked away. She was upset. Her friend was dead. They knew each other before Plaguism, like a core group of people I knew here. I was a bit of a cultural carpetbagger, new to the scene and adopting it as my own, however—I was always treated with the utmost love and respect by these glorious monsters and their anti-mediocrity blasphemy.

Minx stared into space, half-heartedly tasting Chef Hiccup's *God Sausage Corn Dog*. Her lips barely parted for the yellow bready coating, and she seemed to force her teeth down and into the firm and squirting meat of her ex-boyfriend. She wept.

I went to her. "Get you a drink?"

"He was always such a good-tasting man." She rolled the dog in balsamic mustard splotch on a Styrofoam plate and crunched down harder, full of a new hunger this time. "That fucking chef can cook, huh?" Her mouth quivered, crumbled. Her thick mascara ran black rivers down her pale cheeks.

"You bet." I failed to console her.

She walked away—the cooked stomach of her ex-lover dangling on a stick from her hand and dripping mustard on the grass as she roamed aimlessly around Plague Central.

"Now THIS is a funeral!" Jas paraded up to me with a 40oz bottle of Colt45 in each hand, a cigarette in one hand, a joint in the other. Here was a man I would've bred with an octopus if I was Dr. Moreau. A homo-cephalopod with wriggle all at once, eight hands to be occupied with bottles of booze, smoking devices, free hands reaching curiously, tempting fondles, perpetually slinking around for feeling something good.

The acid didn't seem to take. I couldn't get higher than my shock at Chuckie's passing and our cannibalization of him. "Yeah, what a way to celebrate, huh?"

"God wanted to show how tasty he is."

I noticed Jas said God instead of Chuckie. I didn't think I ever heard him call Chuckie God, in fact, but refer to him as *our Lord and flavor* as a deeper dig to the jest. Was this The Pope's way of dealing with this tragedy—and more so—was this the Plaguist way of dealing with life itself—developing a stage persona and becoming that act?

How long did I want to be The Holy Scribe of The First Interplanetary Church of The Immaculate Deception—or Captain of The Mystery Ship, or Martin from Knoxville?

"I'm stuffed—I couldn't eat another bite," I pretended. I tried to walk away. He followed me.

Jas looked at me with don't-you-dare eyes. "Well, you have to save room for the grand finale."

I couldn't imagine what that could be. "What?" We continued to walk.

"Well, you know—God will eat your brain—unless he goes first, and then you shall eat his."

"There was a second part to that?" I asked, astonished.

"You never heard that?" Jas asked—eyes ablaze with devilish knowledge.

I prayed to the corpse of Chuckie that his Pope was joking. I knew he was not joking. Luckily his attention was distracted.

Marybeth tried to comfort Minx. Minx sobbed violently. "I'm all right! I loved his guts so much!"

The Pope knew what to say. "Would it help if I added commentary, darling?!" He pointed to the bloody oak where a pool of Chuckie's insides still sat. "How about? —Oh, I don't know—THAT took guts!" Jas hit his cigarette and snarled his face in a sad explosion of tears. He joined the girls and they all hugged.

Three blind witches in a Shakespearean tragedy around the bitch's brew. What future held this time and place? If this was fiction, there would be a subplot here—but this was memory—and memory served the master—and I was no slave, least of all to my own inner mastermind.

Wayward Plaguists roamed listlessly around the yard, some with heads bowed, in shocked silence—some whooped it up and laughed and yelled and reminded everyone what Chuckie would've wanted—but nobody knew what Chuckie would've wanted—besides us eating him.

Kramer didn't attend. There would be no film of this gruesome act—this last act of defiance, this testimony to Plaguist aversion to seriousness. I couldn't imagine how many arrests and ostracizing sentences would've formed from the showing of a hundred or so young people drunkenly devouring the flesh of our Lord and friend.

I didn't care. Most of you were wrong about life and death and the balance of risk and reward. There was no system more valuable than the one you invent for your own existence.

God was dead. How did he die? Was I supposed to invent that too?

What book of Revelation? What welcomed Armageddon? What Second Coming? What zombie resurrection? What flash of light in the sky welcoming him into heaven? What three-day rainbow from his dying hut?

Sain't Boyardee was a heavy-set redhead fellow who oversaw financial wisdom. According to Chuckie, who baptized him, Chef Boyardee was a man of impeccable skill. "*Nobody could feed a family cheaper or tastier.*" Sain't Boyardee raved about the deliciousness of the prepared God. I didn't know what to say, so pretended to agree and walked around Plague Central talking to random Plaguists, most of whom I'd never said a word to. Who were all these people? What were they going to do now? Did I care? How much longer would I participate in this farcical romance?

I took no part in the tasting menu—I tasted not one mini-rib meat taco with cilantro, lime and crème fraiche—not one pickled phalange or ass-crackling—not one barbecue kidney empanada or deep-fried blood sausage roll with Swiss chard and garlic—I didn't try the grilled fatback watermelon salad or the many steaks of arm, leg, breast…

Chuckie wanted the chef to carve him up nice and as close to the bone as possible—you could graze if you wanted to—venture up the spit where Chuckie rested lifeless and basting over a tiny fire, smoke pouring from the cinder block pit when the tin roof was peeled back to reveal our buddy's corpse.

Fuck! I'd never lost a friend before. I'd lost elder relatives and seen suicide enemies rest in pillowy caskets of eternal rose silk slumber and soon rotting lumber, but I'd never cared for someone so much that I wept at their passing. Of course, I had never seen anyone treated like a rag doll meat puppet, let alone God! Here was God, cooked to extinction, emptied of his language and response, his sensory kingdom and fleshy feel-good center, melting fat on the coals.

XXXXXZZZZZZZZZTTTTHHHHHHHHHNNNNNNNNN!!!
The tiny saw sang as it sliced open Chuckie's hairless and roasted skull.
He sat upright in a chair slumped empty and useless and looked at us
with eaten eyes and face, the remains of a God consumed. His body was
mostly skeletal, dripping tendon and cartilage, all flesh and fat gone.

I was in too deep. I'd taken one too many chances and gotten off on
going too far, and here I was too far again—out there—surrounded by
people cannibalistically consuming my God like 1.2 billion Catholics
every Sunday. A yucky Eucharist happening, and prepared by an
excellent, award-winning chef. There'd be no transubstantiation for us
Plaguists, we would consume the body of our Lord. Forget the wine and
wafer, nothing tastier than a God you can put in your mouth and
swallow… My God, I would love to hear his dick-sucking response to
that last line.

The party spread thin as the fortieth hour approached. Plaguists left
the party early to be responsible for their jobs and families
(blasphemers!), many more passed out in various Plaguist Yoga positions
around the yard. That left forty or so of us standing in a circle around
Chuckie. Chef sliced the brain into thin slices, the gray matter speared
with appetizer toothpicks—those little colorful plastic swords found in
martinis served in hotel bars and faux restaurants.

The Pope started. He held the top of Chuckie's skull as a platter. The
brain chunks wobbled and danced. He took a toothpick and made a big
show of tilting his head back and thrusting the sword in like a carnival
swallower, removing a slice of Chuckie's frontal lobe from the tiny sword
with his teeth and chewing. "Mmm!! DeLICIous!!!" And wiping the
corners of his mouth with his small paper napkin and folding that small
napkin in half again and half again and wiping his sniffling nose as he
chewed (allergies) and placing it in his pocket.

Rock tossed his portion into his beer and raised his red plastic solo
cup of beer— "Chuck you Fuckie!" He drained the beer instantly and
with it a piece of God's cerebral cortex.

"Would you, Pope?" Dominic asked, teary-eyed.

"OF COURSE!!" The delinquent dilettante squealed and sashayed
over to Sain't Dominic.

Jas took the top of Chuckie's skull from Dominic, removed the
decorative toothpick and held the grey chunk of Chuckie's parietal lobe
and did a sloppy sign of the cross that was more of a circle eight infinity.
Dominic held his hands in prayer, tilted his head back, stuck out his
tongue and closed his eyes. The Pope put the host on Sain't Dominic's
tongue.

I wondered what type of show I would have to put on. I was ninth in line, so I felt pretty good about my chances of being ignored.

Marybeth took the skull top from Dominic and kissed it. She put a piece of Chuckie's occipital lobe in her mouth and chewed. She tilted her head to the right as if to signify *not bad.*

I panicked. I let my geek out. I raised the bitty sword, bisecting a chunk of Chuckie's cerebellum, with both hands above my head and said loudly, "BY THE POWER OF GREYSKULL!" Because I was into He-man and the Masters of the Universe when I was a child and was still a child.

Jas cackled. Some of the Plaguists out there got it and laughed. I didn't really pay attention. I concentrated on trying not to vomit as I hid the pieces of chewed God brain in various places in my mouth. The ceremony continued as I hid the pieces of God's brain between my cheek and gum, a true denier.

While peeing, I spit him out, like a teenage groupie on first knees.

God was dead and no three-day heavenly incubation would bring him back. I had lost a dear friend, a spiritual guru, a political ally. There were so few people who could get me going politically—

Only Chuckie had the non-answers I wasn't looking for. I flashbacked to our many conversations:

How important is the body? Depends on how much fun you want to have.

Where do we go when we die? Nowhere—and in a way you've never traveled.

What's the meaning of life? Hell, I don't man! It's your life!

Is there anything sacred worth a damn? —And his loud laugh and coughing up phlegm—a spit, a swear, a smile and a look hidden behind dark bible-black glasses, his impenetrable eyes for sure taking it all in…

I fit in. It made me feel good to be a Plaguist. I was seduced. I was in. I was with it. I was part of a team of misfits, the most beautifully fucked up group of individuals I'd ever witnessed—glorious-minded deviants with a bent their own. These people didn't get along with their parents, their teachers, their preachers, their sergeants, so many of them were veterans of wars, wars fought in the sand, some old enough to have fought in jungles, but mostly gen-x teens who grew up in an oil-greedy time.

An atom cannot be contained in its current material bond forever. There was no carbon dating for eternity. Your star hydrogen would expel from your body in gas form and evaporate to make new stars. Your bone calcium would decay to neutralize the soil, combining with some of your nitrogen and carbon to make the earth more fertile for growth. Cemeteries should be gardens and tombstones should be walls to keep the coyotes from the rabbits who fed from our tomatoes that grew from the dirt, wet with our decay. Your sulfur atoms returned to their noxious natural state and burned the eyes of passersby. Your iron atoms, too, rested in the soil. Our gardens shall be rich.

Was this how other cults did it? Was the excitement of belonging to the coolest thing ever too much for people to pass up and so Scientology gets taken seriously and teen losers poison their own bodies for a ticket aboard the mothership, hidden behind a comet? What flavor *was* the Kool-Aid Jim Jones served?

There was no escaping the madness—Rock handed me a small plate of Chuckie's ass. It was sliced and served with bourbon-glazed pineapple, and cheddar grit hushpuppies. It was a challenge to fool Rock that I swallowed the meat—making a big show of how tasty everything was to the Chef. I spit chewed-up-God into a half-finished beer bottle that wasn't mine. I didn't know where it came from. I kept it by my side and pretended to drink from it while Rock watched me suspiciously and walked away as if fuming from his nostrils.

I secretly spit out God's ass in an empty beer bottle. I could not and would not partake of this feast. I would deny the final wishes of myGgod. I was a Judas. I was an anti-anti-antichrist.

What did I know about anything?

I didn't want to eat human. That was what I knew. I didn't want to partake in this ceremony. It felt contagious, taking the thing a little too far—like Christ and his outfit—with the drinking of the blood and eating of the flesh and consuming the Lord to be more like him and absolve the sins from the life force.

I became nothing that I didn't naturally manifest.

I consoled no mourner. I sought no mourning. God was dead. Long live me.

The last time I saw God, we buried him in the backyard. He looked like a skeletal zombie, like an extra in Jason and the argonauts, picked to the bone by a ravenous crowd of Plaguists anxious for a taste of the all-mighty. His mouth, cheeks, and throat were missing. His eyes were eaten, his face peeled to skull, he was missing the top of his head also, as his brain had been eaten. He had a hollowed-out head, which was by far the spookiest looking thing about the spectacle.

I was a pallbearer.

Rock and Chef Hiccup took God off the grill and plopped his remains in an old wheelbarrow. The spit slid out easily, wet chipping no bone on its way out. Rock wheeled him to the gravesite, a hole in the ground. Jas, Chef, Tommy, Dominic and I picked up Chuckie from his shoulders. I gripped a greasy bone. My hand tickled from cut tendons and veins and jagged ends of skin.

God's body was remarkably light, the guts removed, the fat burned off, the flesh cooked and mostly consumed, his spine shown from his rib cage to his pelvis—where no meat connected him. He was no more than a messy skeleton with remaining tissue and tendon.

He reminded me of Thanksgiving remains—though there would be no cold sandwiches, no soup stock of the bones, no leftover asshole casserole. The bugs and bacteria could have the rest of him.

We wheeled the wheelbarrow full of Chuckie's zombie-looking corpse to the side of the hole that all the young Plaguists dug—eight feet long and six feet deep. God's been 86'd.

We spilled his charred bones and remaining cooked meat in the hole in the earth, put in a six-foot-tall sugar maple tree. This would be the source of the divine syrup for future generations of Plaguists, be they any.

There was a moment of non-silence while everyone spoke at once creating a cacophony of wails and laughter and screaming and woohooing. Moments of silence were for the soon to be forgotten—but moments of screaming were for the immortal.

The Pope raised his bottle of Colt45. Everyone quieted. "HERE'S TO CHUCKIE!!!"

Jas paused. Insects buzzed loudly in the steamy summer night.

Then a couple dozen of us joined him in loud near harmonious cacophony. "SUUuuucccCKING MyyYYY DICK!!!"

Morning broke. There were only twenty or so of us left: I walked aimlessly around the yard. Everyone else went inside. The light had driven them to the darkness of Plague Central, Rock's place now—now that Chuckie was dead. What would become of his artifacts? I laughed: Artifacts.

I wanted nothing beyond the knowledge I garnished existing in the tone of Plaguism. No souvenir could remind me of that laugh, those snarling, darling, tongue-wagging monologues of most truths that roared from his mouth like dragon fire. God was dead indeed and all the king's horses and all the king's men could go fuck themselves.

I felt strong, a survivor of something—maybe life, having lived longer than God, but maybe not so grand, a kid on the run from the source, searching for a different kind of source. What was I searching for—now that the American dream had been stripped of its stripes and sold off at rock bottom prices? Maybe nothing. Maybe searching for something, anything new...

37.

Splitsville

There were no goodbyes on the road. I had made quick friends with Cannon and talked him into driving to the beach—and heading towards New York. I thrilled him with lies and stories and whatever it took for him to say yes—so that I wouldn't be out there alone.

I needed companionship on the empty stretches of road where it was better to be two than one. Strangers accepted two people easier than one on the road, a solo traveler was often a sign of danger.

Ready, Pookie, and Lingus were on the road, miles out of town, and out of my life. That affair had ended, and what love could've been, wasn't. I wasn't mature enough for any relationship of any kind. I didn't want dates, anniversaries, gifts, and meetings with parents. I didn't want responsible conversations, planning, or discussions about what movie to watch, what restaurant to go to, what friends to invite over... I wanted gross, sweaty attempt to blend the bodies into one, erotic nuclear fusion, releasing enough energy to create a star. I wanted hungry lust and insatiable action. The names of my lovers almost didn't matter. I wanted to lose my body into another body, gone and more.

Jas had fallen in love again with some seventeen-year-old skater runaway boy named Leonard, and that meant I had nowhere to land. I was circling the airport and running out of fuel.

It was truly a blast to be a poet vagabond, friend of the devil, but I was never going to be his lover. What value could I possibly offer if it wasn't love, wasn't physical affection?

God was dead. That was the most surreal of all. The church had lost its head, and with it most of the pizzazz. I waited 'til Jas and Leonard were out of S.P.A.M. Manor and packed up all my clothes, books, and cassette tapes. That was all I had in the world, and it felt like more than enough. The Mystery Ship was packed. All that was left was the not saying goodbye.

Chicago was a bust. We were never getting out of Nashville together. I didn't think The Pope would ever make it out of his fishbowl. It was hard to leave the comfort of the spotlit stage for the unknown shadows.

"You ready?"

"I can't believe we're doing this."

I'd had that conversation too many times in my life to count. But here I was again, stoned, unwashed, and somewhat slightly dazed, alone in my car, listening to Bowie and driving away from one eternity and toward another.

38.

Devangelist

It was late in the evening when Cannon and I arrived in Charleston. We were exhausted from our ten-hour journey and late start. We got a twelve pack of Mickey's wide-mouths and went to the shore. We got high and drunk and danced in the sand with our shoes off. We even took off our clothes and ran into the ocean, to say hello. It was marvelous. We slept on the beach, with lungs full of salt air and skin ready to burn.

On the first day, we played. We swam in the warm ocean. I lay on my back and floated like a well-fed otter, soaking my skin and whiskers in the salty brine. After thirty minutes of this my skin seemed to be in shock. It was the most direct sunlight I'd been exposed to in four months. I felt like a newly freed prisoner.

I imagined what wild sea animals drifted beneath me. I wondered if I was being stalked by the shark—a great white preferably or a tiger— man-eaters with rows and rows of smiling razors and a 2600 pound-per- inch chomp through bone, leaping out of the water with half of me in their mouth—my corpuscles dissolving with salt—invisible pink in the vastness of water—intestines and marrow spilling out into the sunny afternoon for the krill and the shrimp to feast on.

I let myself drift in the ocean, my face burning in the blistering troposphere, my imagination running wild about my death, about the end of material me. All my matter mere food for other life—heart, liver and head swallowed whole by the mighty carnivore, limbs falling useless to the sea floor for the crab and the cuttlefish—my testicles sheared and ripped, sliced through, exploded into the ocean—my semen swimming wildly in the ocean hoping for ovum but withering and drowning within seconds—millions of microscopic progenies evaporating in the primal soup. I stained the coral with my blood.

All they would find of me was a belt buckle and a steel button from my cut off Levis. I drifted in the sea and let my mind wander, not once opening my eyes, which were red before the sun. I didn't care if I drifted to Portugal or Guinea. I contemplated the octopus next—her slithering silk and inch along, a thousand sensitive suckers to feel the complexities with, each sucker equipped with chemosensors to detect the chemical world. I felt a kinship with this type of creature; malleable, valuable, pliable, palpable mind impossible to detect from the moment, like the world's greatest spy.

The cephalopod tasted what it touched—chameleon of the deep, along with the cuttlefish, able to instantly change from one complex pattern to another, not only sensing and recognizing the weird combinations of her purple, brown, and green environment, but mimicking the rocks and the sand and the textures with her skin, her electric shimmering epidermis.

Her entire body undulated and pulsed like water. Patterns of blue and white lines rippled across her body, synapses firing and delicate receptors receiving, a symphony of deceit and camouflage wafting across her intricate skin. I felt like this sometimes when I was having a conversation with some strait-laced person and needed a job, groceries, sex, clothes, or a new place to rent...

The cephalopod slithered and hid, crawled into crevices, abandoned shells and bottles. The octopus was a delicacy, tender and sumptuous, hunted often and torn apart savagely by the predators of the sea, i.e. the bigger fish—limb by limb they were feasted upon until they had lost too much life force and died.

I decided I should return to shore, so I rolled to my stomach and did a gentle breaststroke. Trying to even out the burning red of my skin, I closed my eyes and gently kicked my feet, gently stroking my arms towards the land. The sun crashed down on my back, my neck and legs, all exposed without sunblock. I thought of the blue whale and wondered what it must be like to be the largest living breather on the planet, a monolith, a goliath of the earth, without predator, feasting on plankton and krill, cruising the oceans as if the Earth was no more than a cage in a zoo, a park, circumnavigating the planet often.

I wondered about the sea turtle—two hundred years of life cruising through the deep blue... Would that be more peaceful than boring? I hoped so, maybe a smaller brain helped. I swam towards the shore faster and faster. I seemed to build stamina as I went along. I heard the beachcombers and sunbathers, the Frisbee kids and the adult kites.

Eventually, my toes dragged along the sandy bottom of the ocean, and I stood up. I slowly waded toward the shore, an exhausted Godzilla—too beat to destroy the town now. I needed to rest my fire-breathing rage. What a joy it was to be free. I gave myself time to absorb the spirit of the ocean, the deep, and the beach. I let the aquatic life seep into me. I stretched my legs in the surf and pissed in my shorts. I daydreamed.

I wrestled with the colossal squid and pried its enormous beak open with my bare hands, breaking apart the beast and enjoying a later feast of calamari, enough to feed the entire Polynesian village I now lived on with my fourteen wives and sixty-two children. It took the entire village to chop up the thirteen meters of sea monster, but we had plenty of sharp tools and worked well in the sun, most of us dressed only in loincloths, the women's breasts exposed, brown nipples like doorbells bathing in sunlight.

I grilled the shellfish, flash-caramelizing the skin, leaving it tender and never chewy. The nine hundred pounds of flesh took all day to cook, but I was an expert chef and renowned on my island as a gourmand. I produced a lovely palm wine as well, a drink stronger than vodka and sweeter than rain.

I waded out of the surf and located Cannon. He was asleep with a shirt over his face, and a shirt over his legs, to prevent himself from burning further. I joined him and continued my various beachfront fantasies.

Suddenly, I was ordering raspberry daiquiris under a Cuban umbrella and writing in my journal, another best-selling novel about the seductive Havana scenery—the sooty pillars and macho statues of the Paseo de Prado, the poverty-stricken princesses with their dark island skin and perfect builds, the boys as well, with their daring legs and able swim. I would lead a rebellion against the rebellion and demand to have my pornography published as high art and really cause a great sensation. My home country loved me, but the Cubans were mixed about me. I was a great tourist attraction and a tyrant, bearded now with a large belly, sucking down bottles of rum by the cartful and cigars the same. I did my best to impregnate every beauty on the island. I was an artistic tyrant, a lunatic genius with more cock and balls than sense, but what passed for power these days?

Staring at the water—the hot, twinkling Atlantic Ocean, calm and vast, bigger than anything on earth, except the Pacific Ocean—I thought of Norse Explorers crossing it in the beginning of the Eleventh Century, sons and grandsons of outlaws, in renegade boats screaming across the waters to Newfoundland, one of the most aptly named provinces in the entire world. I thought of the Spaniards and the Italians in their glorious vessels well-stocked with food and wine and fresh water, anxious for new lands, new treasure, new spices, new routes, new discoveries of new ways to express the power of their throne.

Contemplating the first boat builders, I thought of the wild adventurous nature that was deeply seeded in our DNA. How many men perished in the open waters, trying to see how far out they could go? Row! Row! Row! What sort of Ivy League crew could skim across the Atlantic and find new land?

Weary in my thoughts, I stared, observed the evanescent waves baking the gossamer spray of rainbow light—the gentle waves crashing on top of each other, one after another, in rhythm, timed to the great pulse of the universe, the tug of the moon, the rotation of the earth, the bizarre puzzle of gravity. Countless bodies sauntered past my eyes, but my animal-lust was non-existent. I was exhausted from my swim and my mind reeled in every direction at once. I could do nothing but close my eyes and sleep in the waning solar heat.

The sun fell, and the first stars twinkled. I felt refreshed, refurbished, replenished, and new—a phoenix chick from the ashes, a digested Ouroboros, stellar dust thrust through the nothingness sizzling. I was ready for anything. I got Cannon's excitement up I think, with my moxy, my prowess, my proximity to his past. "What do you feel like doing?"

"Let's go drinking."

"I don't have my fake I.D. anymore. It got taken away," I admitted. "Shit."

"You go out drinking—have a good time—meet me at IHOP between ten and twelve."

"Be more fun with you," Cannon contained his enthusiasm.

"Go have fun, meet people. Bring them to me at the IHOP." I laughed, realizing what a Hawaiian King I must've sounded like.

It felt good to sit by myself in a booth, drinking coffee, scratching my bloody quill across a confessional line. I loved dictating my senses in rhyme. This was what I needed—time to sink into the self, the personal link to the omnipotent voice. Everything I wrote had scriptural significance.

I sat alone in the IHOP writing bad poetry and drinking too much coffee. I maybe had fifteen cups. I had diarrhea in the toilet and kept ordering refills because they were free, and the waitress was cute.

Cannon was good at it. He brought in a fleet of rockabilly tarts and stray cats in shiny black shoes, bright red lipstick, and cuffed Levis, Lucky Strike packs rolled up in white t-shirt sleeves and perfectly coiffed slick hair styles. He motioned for me to join him.

I joined them and met them all: Joyce was the matriarchal nucleus of this group—that was easy to see—*flirt with me first by answering my questions before you meander through the rest of the group*—very queen bee—queen vamp—the Vamp of Savannah—the belle of the ball. I took the cue and curtsied my submission to her inquisition.

"Where are you from?"

"Knoxville."

"How old are you?"

"Nineteen."

"Are you gay or straight?"

"Find out," I retorted like Father Oscar Wilde would've wanted.

Everyone in her group laughed and Cannon championed me with a smile.

"We hear you're a poet." The youngest in the group spoke up, the one I had my third eye on the whole time, of course, the quiet, mousy one against the wall, the sensitive fragile indestructible one peering at me from behind obsidian mirror eyes.

I fell in love too easily. I sang old love songs to myself in the mirror. "Vicious rumors," I confessed.

Johnny the Pretty Bass Player inserted himself. "Care to let us hear something?"

"I'd prefer a stage." I said, suddenly out of my element.

"Life's a stage. Read us something," Johnny the Pretty Bass Player said.

I read them (him) something, in fact what I had written minutes before they came in, fresh from the vortex, honey of the words still on my tongue, flow of the music singing from my instrument: *"There exists the possibility for anything in nothing / here lies its perfection and vulnerability to flaw… Fucking with the unfamiliar with a brilliant diligence / youthful and doubtful of anything consistent / forming the laws as they need to be applied."*

I paused and swallowed hard for effect, my eyes on the paper, peripheral on cute and mousy to my left, *"There are those who must tumble down hills and must run up them / those who climb convenient trees and resist no candy / who do not turn down rides from strangers / enjoying the rush and the thrill of ignoring forewarned dangers / who caress their best into play (my favorites) / who savor the evening and waste the day."*

I took a cigarette from my pack while continuing to read, probably coming off more like a moody professor than James Dean. *"Those who bar none and resist not / wick lit and sky high tossed / off getting mythical children tickling the underbelly of a sunburnt heaven with idiot genius silliness / goofing off brilliantly with jelly eyed spheres of looking glass / glued to their own glistening / well felt weapons / tried on sizes / down to the last article of clothing."*

I took a hit from my unlit cigarette like an asshole. *"Pleasurable / incorruptible / rough and tumble stumblers of that eternal somersault / horns over hooves, tail tangled in halo."*

"Oh my god! You're a genius." Fabby Tabby, with marshmallow skin and size, uttered utterly breathless.

"No. I'm a Plaguist." I smiled.

"What's that?" Smart and mousy Daisy Duck wanted to know—and I wanted to know Daisy Duck in the intimate fashion—fleshy tango, sweaty mango ripe with squeezing juice and moist seeds.

Cannon answered for me. "Martin here is The Holy Scribe of The First Interplanetary Church of The Immaculate Deception. He used to be the Angel of Death until people started ACTUALLY dying—and God had to take over the responsibilities of the Angel of Death."

It was comical to watch everyone's head turn from Cannon to me at once.

Johnny the Pretty Bass Player spoke up first. "You guys wanna come back to our hotel and party?"

"Do we have to leave when it's time to go to sleep?" I asked, unashamed.

Johnny laughed. "Of course not—you can crash—there's two beds, neither one of which I imagine you having any trouble crawling into—and places to crash on the floor."

Three girls and one guy? For sure, I'm playing anatomical hide-n-seek with the quietest of the quartet.

All in. "Let's go. I'll follow you."

Cannon informed me on the ride over that he had a thing for Joyce—the singer of Hellfire Kitten Sex—a rockabilly band with stand-up bass and bad ass guitar, the ax-thrasher of which apparently knew someone in town and was out of the picture for the next three nights.

I got the feeling that Daisy Duck was the guitar player's toy—but never inquired or cared. This was a flyby—I was passing through—an inevitable pit-stop on the long and winding road.

Holiday Inn or whatever—Two Queens, chest of drawers with TV and end tables with lamp, phone, and Gideon's Bible—carpet, heavy windows, bathroom—sterile and pungent air simultaneously—a million stale odors eliminated with a million different cleanings.

Cannon bought a six bag of 40 oz Colt45.

There was no real activity, everyone sat down and asked about Plaguism.

"Well, Plaguism is a belief in the teachings of a punk rock guru who recently passed away in Nashville, Tennessee."

"Teachings?" Johnny asked.

"The First Interplanetary Church of the Immaculate Deception," I answered, "was founded on Discordian principles of self-as-god. Prove to me I can't fly, and you can push me out the window." I hit my cigarette while Daisy Duck and Fabby Tabby laughed. I guess they were chicks who got it, or dug me, often hard to tell with fleshy responsive audience. "They've got to run out of Pork-n-beans sooner or later." I laughed and sucked butt.

"What does that even mean?"

"It means that sooner or later—canning pork and beans for nutritious consumption at a profit will no longer be a viable option in our society—already too collapsed to ward off cannibalism."

"That's pretty bleak."

"Well, it is called *Plaguism*," I said with my best Pope imitating God slur and drawl of words.

"Is there salvation?"

"Brought on only by the self—a self-responsive system must be responsible for the self. That's what makes us human—that's what keeps artificial intelligence, artificial, the sense of meaningful preservation."

"God?" Daisy quacked.

"Chuckie the Plague," I answered.

"Plaguism?" Johnny asked.

"Yes. The Belief that our Lord and flavor Charles Theodore Plague is the one true full of shit god meant to be taken as a farcical sacrament. A Plaguist believes that it's not a matter of WHAT you believe but HOW you believe it."

"How do you become Plaguists?" Daisy asked.

"Well, first you have to be baptized by a Sain't or The Pope and you have to write in Plaguist as your religion on any government forms that ask the question—because we're trying to get tax exempt status as a recognized church."

"Sounds far out," Joyce admitted.

"I'm in," Johnny the Pretty Bass Player decided. "What do I have to do?"

"You lie on your back and repeat the sacred oath after me, and I sprinkle some holy malt liquor on you and that's it."

Johnny quickly assumed the position.

I swigged from my 40 and looked down on him. "All right, repeat after me… I once could see but now am blind." And he repeated after me the sacred oath:

"I once could see but now am blind,"

"I once was found but now am lost,"

"T'was disgrace that gave my fear heart,"

"I once was free but now must pay the cost."

What makes an oath sacred was that it would be willingly repeated and treated as holy word. What made a religion work was the need for it to. What made people follow was the forgiveness from responsibility. This was the key—few could handle the responsibility of being the center of the universe, no matter how they behaved in restaurants.

Plaguism offered no eternal reward. The teachings of Chuckie were designed to be absurdist principles of an existential nature—try too hard and your Zen Mojo would go kerplunk—expect too much and you would be left with no funk in your soul, only perfumed fruit in sterile bowls. *Smooth Jazz 101.9* on the radio.

Plaguism was a path for those who wanted to make their own path— and it was seductive—not only to the four Plaguists I baptized in Charleston, but the six I baptized in Georgetown—teenagers—kids tripping on the beach one night—sharing their marijuana and mouths.

We went through cities like a fat kid through cake.

I kissed a seventeen-year-old boy who was prettier than his girlfriend who I was making out with when I met him. I don't remember their names—Slick Black and Rachel Ray—could've been anybody.

"Do you accept the word of Chuckie as the all-mighty full of shit truth?"

I shook up the Colt45 and sprayed the pretty boy and pretty girl and four incidentals. Wet on the beach—let's do it in the ocean—let's intercourse where water and earth meet—let's greet the salty fish with a wave of our own, let's undulate in moonlight—cum in the foamy brine—kiss in soggy seaweed and offer our bodies to the sharks and sand fleas.

I was really getting the hang of being a missionary—a traveler of the land to spread the bad news—There are no selfless martyrs—only supermen—Christs, Mohammeds, Chuckies, Buddhas—be they supernatural or extraterrestrial, son of god or god incarnate, or beer swilling spirituality swindler—they were only men struggling with the divine in a manner most humans can't understand.

Man was a selfish biped with free time and agenda. He needed to erupt as God occasionally, or he stagnated with the decaying social order.

My lessons were simple, mostly stoned and rambling and calling it scripture—it was not a matter of WHAT you say—but HOW you say it.

Everyone wanted to be a Plaguist—no one said no. Once I started proselytizing, I was sure to burn the moths anxious for my flame.

Four more became Plaguists in Myrtle Beach: a spring break paradise city for deviants of all sorts who liked to feast on the flesh of the young—a neon vampire kind of town with amusement rides and boardwalks and decorated piers and tall hotels on the beach with private swimming pools and dirty rooms—a resort playground for business men with an excuse—a vacation destination—Wheels and Deals on every corner—televised sand castle competitions—bikinis, coconut oil—powdery sand, bathwater ocean—sugary fried foods, a tangle of kites and kids screaming.

I couldn't get out of that town fast enough.

We crossed into North Carolina on 17, a beautiful day, whatever day it was, the air was clean. The sky was hot. I saw signs for Cape Fear and honestly didn't know that was a real place—just the name of a movie. I thought I might change my name to Mitchum De Niro and move there. I gave a goofy impression to the rearview mirror, tilted down enough so I could practice facial poses while I was driving a particularly dull stretch of Interstate.

More young people—more Plaguists converted. We seemed to meet the freaks in every town. In Morehead City we got more head from the locals—good-looking dick-suckers who felt the need to impress the new boys in town with their going down.

I felt like a salesman, like I hawked the wares of a dead jester, and it made me feel dirty, like a preacher, like a pastor, like a priest, *like a virgin, touched for the very first time, Like a ViiiIIiiIIiiIIiirgin…*

Put the needle on the record! Put the needle on the record! The drum beat goes like this!

It was fun listening to the radio, turning the old manual dial from station to station and from song to song randomly. We took a ferry to some place called Ocracoke—which I was certain was named after the townspeoples' favorite meal, fried okra and iced cola.

The drive after that was beautiful. I didn't want to stop. We spent all day driving over thin roads and bridges, over the water, gliding like sea birds—majestic in movement. We cruised through Cape Hatteras, Nags

Head, Kill Devil Hills, Kitty Hawk, Whalehead, Corolla, and on into Virginia, both totally out of gas.

I sunk the siphoning hose in the tank of that skylark and sucked and sucked for the liquid to come, but there was none. "This motherfucker must be on empty," I whispered to Cannon, and looked around the lot for another car. It was a curious game to play. It was stealing, in fact, totally against the law, outrageous behavior for anyone to perform, but we were mosquitoes on the community's skin, inserting the antiseptic and the hypodermic simultaneously.

Cannon and I were broke and neither of us wanted to work anymore. We wanted to drive and sun ourselves and drink and listen to the ocean and read. That's what I wanted to do anyway. I wasn't really sure about Cannon. I wasn't quite certain of his trip. But I didn't pay that much mind, being so thoroughly absorbed in my own.

We would take enough from each car, about a gallon or so, half a tub-full—out there in the 2AM parking lots, beneath wet lamps that drizzled a puss yellow mist, the moisture on our faces constant—arms and legs coated in sweat and rain—privates unwashed. We really stank. We hadn't bathed in days and hadn't stopped sweating, most of it alcohol.

I tasted the gas in my mouth and thought I might puke, but I sucked and sucked until I got as much of the liquid as I needed, enough to fill me up—God, I felt like a groupie blowing the whole security team to sleep with Roger Waters. But I wanted to ride, and didn't want to pay. I took the ticket and took the ride. Caution was not a teenager's friend… Into the wind… And so forth…

We wanted to stay on the coast, so we took the Chesapeake Bay Bridge-Tunnel. This was a first for us, driving on a long stretch of interconnecting bridges and tunnels that connected Norfolk and Virginia Beach to Cape Charles, Virginia. I took the lead and drove through the tunnel. I felt like Luke Skywalker in an X-wing fighter zooming out of the death star. Everything was tiled and illuminated like a great space-station in the outer cosmos.

Suddenly we issued forth to the bridge, which was long and straight and over the water. (I imagined murderous housewives dumping their husbands' bodies over the sides here—such a long way from anyone's witness—headlights in the distance, ample time to dump a corpse in five different garbage bags… Jesus! What was I summoning? What horrible scene had happened here? —Certainly, I'm not the only crook in the area with a vision of wickedness.) We glided over the Chesapeake Bay in our individual vehicles and the wind felt great in my hair and the music was perfect—*There's More To Life Than This* by Bjork, and I didn't care about anything other than the direction—the path—the moment—that exact second of that exact minute in the middle of a wayward way.

Everything changed in Maryland. Here was a state of oceanic industry. The beaches here were not destinations for vacations or spring breaks. The beaches here were ports, seaports. These were fishing towns—boats and cranes on every part of the coast—canneries and crab-shacks with excellent food, cakes and croquettes, fresh catches of the day. Here were men prepared for cold weather, able to fish in any climate.

We drove through our acid high and decided to sleep behind some warehouse. We slept only a couple of hours before being awakened by another cop. Same fucking routine as always: license, registration, check us out, everything matches up, okay, "let's see what's in your trunk."

I opened the trunk for the officer, and he nosed around the pile of dirty clothes with his Billy-stick and the stink almost curled my eyelashes as I stood next to him, and it was MY stink. "When's the last time you've done laundry, son?"

"About a month."

"Well, normally I would throw you guys out of town, but since you fellahs are here to start a new career aboard a fishing boat then I'm gonna suggest you either get to a hotel or an all-night diner. I know of a few good ones."

We had bullshitted another copper about the real reason for our journey. Oh well, the only thing to do was to get a cup of coffee and see how much further we could drive. We were in Pocomoke City and why they call it a city I had no idea. We decided to eat breakfast and drive and find a beach. We had crab-cake benedicts which were truly out of this world and drove as far east as we could. Oddly enough, we never found a beach. We kept finding docks, weird marinas that held hundreds and hundreds of boats. It seemed Maryland was not much for sunbathing. Perhaps we were lost.

Tired and exhausted we walked to the edge of one of these piers and collapsed. We were woken a few hours later by some curious fisherman who wanted to know exactly who we were and what we were doing. The sky was magic hour blue, fading the black to yellow.

"You boys are vagrants, are you?" Yellow slicker held a sharp dolly hook, "Look—this is a hard-working community here fellahs—why don't you take a hike—go to New York City or some place, leave our town alone huh? The sea is no place for a boy." Slowly and gradually, one by one, other menacing members of the community joined the angry fisherman.

I was sick of getting run out of town. I was sick of the sun and the sand and the surf, the fish and the seagull, the bikini and the burn. I was sick of waking up in pools of sweat, stretched out across the interior of my compact car. I wanted an air-conditioned room with a bed of my own. I wanted to date and romanticize one woman now, contemplate falling in love again—risk be damned.

We drove north through Delaware and finally decided to find a beach and have ourselves a plunge. It was a warm and beautiful day and already I noticed the way the sand was changing, the way the beach was changing. The sand was coarser, rougher, the pebbles more abundant. The wildlife was different. We found hermit-crabs and starfish by the hundreds. We swam and let the salty water clean our bodies.

We drove to Cape Henlopen and took the Cape May Ferry to New Jersey. We drove our cars onto the ferry and got out, exploring the vast boat. It was a beautiful day. We wore our last clean t-shirts and sat on the upper deck, smoking cigarettes and watching the waves, the gulls and the spray of the wake of the boat. It was a two hour ferry ride.

I asked Cannon how much money he had left.

"Twenty-six dollars. How about you?"

"Fourteen."

He laughed at my smile. "What should we do?"

"I don't know? Bust on through to Atlantic City and gamble our last money?"

"All right!"

39.

Midday Cowboy

We pulled into Atlantic City around seven-thirty. We found a parking lot and filled our tanks up with siphoned gas from a Cadillac and two Subaru's. We walked the boardwalk. They wouldn't let me into the casino.

"What should I do?" Cannon asked.

"Play blackjack, hit on anything under sixteen, but only once. If you get faces or aces split 'em, and don't stop playing until you win a hundred bucks." I really didn't know what the fuck I was talking about, but how cool did that sound?

"Okay."

I waited on a bench and winked at every dirty old man who passed by who had that look in his eye—like he might be cruising, like he might have his bananas peeled for my type, broke and cute, lonely and desperate. I knew I was dirty, unshaven, and rough around the edges, washboard stomach and ham fists, Popeye arms and snarl.

"Do you have an extra cigarette on you, my dear boy?" He seemed like the kind of guy who would put the chalky mark of the rube on the back of his own sports coat, cruise the carnival grounds, and get off on being suckered by the gnarly carnie.

"I certainly do." I even lit it for him.

"What's your name?" The troll asked.

"Plato."

"Funny, you don't look Greek."

"What's your name?"

"Dean."

"Like Dizzy and Daffy?"

"I'm neither of those things, but I see you know your baseball history." He smoked his cigarette with his thumb and his forefinger pointed up and pinching the butt—unusual, no grace or talent about it. He coughed. "I don't normally smoke."

"But you *had* to ask me for one, right?"

"Well, it's the easiest way to engage in a conversation, wouldn't you agree?"

"It is, at that. What would you like to converse about?"

"Well, you look like a young man who's willing to listen to a proposition." He smiled Quentin Crisp teeth at me, delicately smeared with last night's lipstick and Merlot.

"I might be." I was broke, and hungry, hot and horny, and in no mood to work.

"Well, first off, if I might say, you're quite a charming-looking fellow."

"Thank you."

"And polite I must say, willing to take a compliment, even from a stranger, an old biddy like me." He smiled sheepishly, like a fairy past his prime. He wasn't that old, fifty maybe, forty-five, salt and pepper hair, glasses and mustache, thin and sinewy, a runner maybe, totally queer, and probably a serial killer.

"What's the proposition?" I didn't care. I could jerk-off King Kong if the price was right and I would never die.

"How would you like to make two hundred bucks?"

"Doing what?" I asked coolly, not suspiciously at all, knowingly even.

"Well, first, I don't want to fuck you. I mean, I want very much to fuck you, but I can't. My machinery's no longer functioning properly you see, but I do miss the naked male form, the contours and the ridges. I would like to rent you for one hour. I have a room right here at the Plaza, a nice room—room service and everything. You can order anything you want, on me. I would like to… I would like to give you a sponge bath. I can smell that you need one, and for a man of my tastes, it's exciting beyond measure, none of the escorts that advertise ever come so, so, so pungent and delicious." He sounded like a man of experience and wisdom, of unashamed danger and shameless pride.

"You want to give me a sponge bath—like in the bathtub?" I didn't understand what I was hearing.

"Oh no, no, I want you in my *bed*." He said this as lustfully as his pale, wrinkled soul would let him— "the sheets will be off, and I will place towels beneath you. All you have to do is lay there, naked, and let me bathe you. Let me lift your arms, your legs, your testicles and cock and bathe every inch of you."

"Three hundred and you have a half an hour."

"I'll make it three hundred, but you have to give me the hour."

His hotel was nice, and his room was big. I took his money first and shoved the bills into my pocket. I removed my shirt and shorts and lay on the bed, face down like he instructed. He washed my back in slow, concentric motions, moving the cloth lower and lower down my back until over my ass, slowly, slowly—he washed my ass. I felt his grip grow firm beneath the washcloth as his fingers felt over my round curves. He glazed over the crack, sure not to get too intimate, too riley, too much too soon, but close enough. I sensed his face close to my opening. I heard him sniff. He washed my thighs lovingly, reaching deep into the part to find the base of my balls. He washed my calves and my tendons and took delicate time to wash the slimy cheese from between my toes. I felt his warm breath on my feet as he inhaled and exhaled heavily the odor of my foul body before the scrub. He inhaled the dirty cloth and quivered.

He instructed me to roll over. He rubbed my chest with a soapy washcloth, all around my nipples and ridges. He lifted my arms and washed my pits which radiated a hot garlic pepper, locker room sock, marijuana filter. He quivered and sighed as he scrubbed me. His face was red and I could tell that he really relished my stink. He washed my balls and cock quickly and roughly, gliding over them, not really cleaning them, saving them maybe for last. He put the dirty washcloth to his face and sniffed in the fumes as if he was getting high from an ether hit.

He coughed as he exhaled. "My god! You *are* a *dirty* boy!" He washed my legs and when I thought he was finished he found a new washcloth and lathered it a soapy effervescent sludge of suds. He went to work on my balls and cock, my asshole and taint. He relished this activity. I closed my eyes and couldn't help but to become erect, my shaft saluting the eternal ease of youth—hard cement, rigid, and ready like a soldier for battle. He lovingly washed my penis until I came.

I shot thick streams of milky sauce into the air, the tip of my penis oozing final goop from my eruption, white sperm piling up in the blonde tufts of my pubic hair. "My word!" He rubbed a finger across my spill and tasted me. I thought he'd pass out; he was so delighted. He wiped up my semen and let me dress. He gave me a hundred more dollars and told me if I came back unwashed for a week, he'd do the same thing.

Cannon waited for me at the bench where I left him. "I lost everything, man. I was up seventy-five and thought about quitting, and then I remembered what you said and didn't want to stop until we hit a hundred."

I gave him a hundred bucks.

"Wow! Where did you score this?"

"Some old lady gave me two hundred bucks to fuck her."

He didn't believe me in the least. "Get the fuck out of here."

"I'm serious, the rest is in my pocket."

"Bullshit! What are you, some kind of midnight cowboy now?"

"Hell no—I do the blue hair special. I'm a midday cowboy!"

We laughed and went to find food. I still had about a dozen hits of acid left so we dropped two each and found some Hong Kong restaurant. The acid came on before we finished eating. The orange glazes of the breaded meat dishes oozed and bubbled and spilled over our plates. I got the fear something terrible and we had to flee that scene.

We walked along the boardwalk and inhaled one of the grossest populations of people I'd ever been around. They were horribly sad and depressed gamblers and cons feeding off the cesspool of money like roaches—tricks and johns, pimps and whores, two-bit hustlers, obese giants of animal flesh waddling along the boardwalk stuffing their faces with fried food and candy—chain-smoking slot-jockeys with cancer of the imagination staring at the blinking lights and pulling the lever, coin after coin.

We spent the night walking around the lonely ugly town. In the morning, without sleep and still a little high, we drove around to see what we could see. It was devastating poverty—a horrible tribute to American greed. The casinos rose up in the center of this wasteland like a great promise of wealth and decadence, grand and opulent—and once outside the gambling district, it seemed every house was dilapidated. No building rose above two stories—projects and ghettos—vast empty fields of brown grass and broken glass, rocks and graffiti everywhere. We decided to leave immediately. We drove straight for New York.

40.

Revelationships

We arrived in Manhattan early in the afternoon. It was such an awesome sight to behold. We drove I-78 and the buildings appeared like Oz in the distance, the emerald city stacked to the sky with gigantic monoliths of finance and industry, skyscrapers with antenna steeples that reached to the heavens. We entered the Holland Tunnel and emerged at the bottom of the city.

We parked near Washington Square Park. Cannon went to buy us beer and I bought a twenty bag from a Rastafarian who gave me a good deal. We met by the chess tables. I told him of the score and he was very excited. We went to my favorite tree which is on the northeastern side. It had many knots and scars in it, alien bumps and growths that made it look cancerous or imagined by some dark animator. I rolled a joint and Cannon uncapped our pints of Guinness.

We got high and sipped our beers and it felt good to be in the city. There was no other city like New York, not in America, not anywhere. Everything was here, and vertical. Every type of person was here, every race, religion, creed, and color, every fetish, compulsion, and urge. We watched all the young college girls walking to class and all the crazy homeless people feeding the pigeons and begging for change.

We sat on the benches and drank our beer and listened to some young man play 'Dirty Old Town', his sad and lost voice scratching out the vocals and plucking the strings on his acoustic guitar. I gave him a dollar.

We drank more beer and watched as some old man outstretched his arms and let about fifty pigeons land on him as if he were a feeding tree.

We watched a kid set a trash can on fire and then skateboard fast, hit a ramp and jump over the flaming refuse. A crowd applauded and filled his hat with coins and bills and he even had time to put the fire out with his little fire-extinguisher before the cops chased him away. He did a little ollie up on the exit ramp on his way out. He vanished down Sullivan Street at thirty miles an hour, faster and faster. The crowd laughed and cheered. The polyurethane wheels roared up the sidewalk.

We drank more beer and talked about all the crazy shit we wanted to see in the city. By eleven o' clock we were pretty good and soused. I hoped my mother would be home and tolerant of our drunken condition. She was home, but she was not tolerant. There was much screaming and name calling. She threw us out and we slept in our cars again.

We were constantly woken and told to move along. I caught my mother as she was going to work and convinced her to let me sleep it off. I was still drunk from the evening, plus we had had a few more in the angry A.M. She agreed.

When she was on her way, I went and got Cannon. He slept on the sofa and I slept on my mother's bed. We were still asleep when she returned, dreaming sugarplum blowjobs in the nice air-conditioned environment, our first one in states. She screamed and screamed, angry that I had disobeyed and once again we were out on our own.

"Look man, she'll calm down eventually. She—you know—has had her own thing with drugs and alcohol in the past and doesn't want to see…"

Cannon was kind enough to interrupt me. "Look man, I'm not going back into that hostile environment, okay? I have a cousin in Bayonne I can stay with. I think I'm going to give that a shot for a while. I'll meet you in the park tomorrow at around three o'clock, by that cool fucking tree, man. We'll talk about shit."

"All right."

Cannon was on his way to New Jersey.

I settled into the city. My mother agreed to let me sleep on the sofa until I could find work. I was working at Tower Books and drinking less. Sandra, the cute goth chick, was warming up to me and I had found some open mic stages to recite my poetry on—free beer and easy sex… Life was making sense again. I was reinventing myself again.

The phone rang.

His Assholiness The Pope Jas First and Last of The First Interplanetary Church of The Immaculate Deception a.k.a Faggot Hitler was on the phone. "I'm coming up."

"Why?" I asked cautiously.

Sarcasm reflected his charge. "Well, it would be great to see you too."

"Yeah! No! I was wondering if you had a mission," I asked him suspiciously.

"Santagram," he confessed.

He was really going to do it. He was gonna suicide by way of assassinating Macy's prized Saint Nick.

"Rock's coming with me. In fact, he's driving…"

HoLYSHiTohNO. Jas continued to talk but I wasn't listening. The homicidal sociopath known as Sain't Rock was coming to New York. I had nowhere to house these lunatics—Jas by himself was one thing—but with Rock—they would have to be without my assistance.

"Rock says he has a place to stay and that I can crash—but if that turns sketchy can I crash with you?"

"Well, I'm sort of on floors and sofas at the moment."

"No bed?"

"Occasionally, but none with any space—I don't date anyone without at least three roommates."

"We aren't staying long. We both have missions."

"What happened to Rock's mission to eliminate billionaires?"

"He's still on it. There's no higher concentration of billionaires in the world than Park Avenue." I heard him hit his cigarette.

"Aren't you worried about the NSA listening to this conversation?"

"Oh, Martin! I don't care." He exhaled hard into the microphone. "Besides, they're spread so thin listening to the millions of crackpots in the country they couldn't catch fleas."

"Let me know what I can do to aid and abet."

That cackle. I jerked the phone from my ear. "See ya." I hung up the phone.

It was early November, after Halloween, the leaves downtown were brown and dying yellow. There was no delicious deciduous splash of citrus red and sunshine orange. The leaves were sadder here in the city.

I knew what this man was capable of, but I had every intention of encouraging him, anyway. Maybe we could stay at Debbie's. She always had a welcoming couch for lost souls like me. I would have to remind The Pope not to mention his plan.

The Pope told everyone of his plan. I heard it numerous times in bars, in bedrooms, on couches, in cars— "Hey man!" as so many of his sentences start out. "I'm not gonna—*age to death*." His words were fireworks, spit, and apple cider vinegar— "When I know I have some fatal condition—man, I'm gonna deploy Operation Santagram!"

How could you not ask this cartoon doll of dynamite what Operation Santagram was?

"Well!" He was always so pleased you asked. "On Thanksgiving Morning—I'm gonna get all dressed up—you know, real rocky horror—fishnet and lipstick, all pump and corset—with a wig *on* and everything, so that I actually look like a woman in a long dress coat."

Here a break for cigarette suck and perhaps a hand on his chest, so proud of his sentiment. "I'm going to go down to Broadway—and right when Santa Claus is on TV, I'm gonna rip off my coat, storm the float, and put three bullets in that fat bastard's head and neck."

That maniac laugh—joker cackle—madness consumed with self… Ole! Ole! My matador's cape is made of bull hide.

The bastard was coming to New York City. I wondered what would happen. Would he go through with it? Would he even make it to the city? Would he get past security with a gun? Would he be shot in the back by a sniper with a high-powered rifle? Maybe he would get away with it— NYPD too occupied with vagrants to protect good old Saint Nick.

(Note: According to a study by the Rand Center on Quality Policing, the NYPD has a thirty percent accuracy rate while shooting at a target that IS NOT shooting at them. The accuracy falls to nineteen percent when the target is shooting at them. I would be advising Jas to open fire on the cops if he wants to increase damage done. I anticipate a mad cackle of loathsome approval.)

I decided to eat the rest of the acid and walk around my new home, my new streetlight playground in raindrop mist. The streets were slippery and fast, a fog more than a mist, dark, headlights in half mile streaks.

The traffic was a neon grid of glowing umber and amber embers… Bubbling freshness from the sidewalk, fewer people out in the rain— umbrellas and galoshes. Splish-splash taxicab puddles threw off six foot walls of water. The splash of the splash inches from my shoes.

The rhythm of the city got inside me. There was a beat, a pulse, a crazed nonstop guitar solo that at times tried to break the amp, but always finished the song. I walked through Washington Square Park and up Sixth Avenue. Olympic bipeds played slam dunk on the basketball courts and perspired a puss yellow glow in the lamplight rain that made them each look majestic in their heavenly setting. I imagined they shined brighter nowhere else.

I passed coffee shops and antique boutiques, pet stores, wine bars, and blue jean pop up stores where pants are purchased pre-worn by thin boys with no experience but a lust for the look.

I smoked a cigarette and longed for a beer, but kept walking, smoking and grooving on the wet cityscape full of every color, age and size—every fetish, freak, and type. A transvestite Thai prostitute winked at me, I think, but it was blocks before I decided to wink back, and s/he was long gone.

I felt like this was a maze I could really hunt the cheese in.

Drunken young boys swished up the mice-infested steps of Chelsea apartments, undecorated, but full of the best E and a safe place to dose and fuck.

Gaggles of gals galloped past in clippety-clopping high heels and obnoxious talk that sounded painful to emanate… Ugh…

Broadway, Times Square, flashing advertisement to the holy bottom dollar—every neon firework description you've ever read—Bladerunner—bright and ugly—futuristic—a gaudy wasteful display of our powers of seduction, our prowess of destruction: tourists and thieves, businessmen and whores, suckers and their money.

I wasn't hungry, a dieting plus of the acid effect, but I craved chocolate like no one's business. I bought a Hershey chocolate bar and sucked it down square by square, letting the soft sweetness melt on my body temperature tongue and lips. I walked fast and hard around the city, certain to break the concrete open with my steps.

I had nothing to do, no one to be, nowhere to go. I walked and walked all along the crazy city, exploring her little crevices and secrets, taking in the rush and bustle of the hustling avenues and streets.

It got late. The stores shut down and the city gave way to the nightlife. I waited in a line to get into some club and remembered I didn't have an ID supporting my lying age. I got out of line and continued to walk, to explore the majestic scenery of this fantastic town.

I sat outside Central Park and watched the people, obvious drug deals, and secret meetings of undercover lovers, late-night strollers and dog walkers, squirrels and pigeons and rats.

I headed north and walked and walked. I walked through Central Park thinking about Jas coming here to kill Santa Claus. I scratched my eyebrow, which is what I always do when I sense danger. This made me laugh. I had realized that this was something I do, an affectation. Self-Discovery—no one to bother me, I liked New York for this reason, starved for company in the land of good and bad a'plenty.

Was he really going to go through with it? Would I have the pleasure and sorrow of watching my friend being executed on live television? Or would he be drugged and clumsy, too much Percocet and Oxycodone in his system, slurring his speech and wrecking his vision, heavy metal falling from his overcoat, maybe an accidental discharge, brick dust from a building corner and a fat lady screams.

The worst-case scenario I imagined would be Jas arrested with no deaths, a psyche ward, and a burden on me to visit when I can. "I'm sorry dude, they'll arrest me if I smuggle you in cyanide tablets."

The fear was upon me. Impending doom had dialed my number and invited itself for dinner, and a drunken sleepover.

Deny everything. That was it. "No sir, your honor. I had no knowledge at all of this heinous act of terrorism. But it doesn't surprise me. I know this man as a notorious liar and a blasphemous performance artist, a deviant savant not to be trusted with children or firearms."

There was no way they could pin anything on me. I was clean. Maybe a phone conversation… Jesus, could they be listening in on our conversations, the NSA? I could be implicated here… Heard laughing and encouraging the monster. No—paranoia—that was all, let the rain mist and chocolate bar wash away all sense of doom, and enjoy the drug, consider the seriousness later and groove on the surroundings.

I would have to score more drugs—some weed and Xanax, a fifth of whisky and a golf ball of opiated hash—but it was possible. I would have to find a place to stay—perhaps with Cindy and her pretty toilet boy roommate—perfect bait for The Pope. We would have to rage so hard and heavy on the night before Thanksgiving that he would miss his big performance come Thanksgiving morning. Was I saving Santa or saving The Pope? Fuck Santa.

All I wanted to do was walk. I walked east one street and then west the next, curlicuing and zigzagging, ogling and bypassing whatever hallucinated dull moment or exaggerated detail…

Laughter good time drug-high by myself against god-thought and the universe. But seeking unity with both… Ha-ha-ha! I'd lost it and loved it.

No one would sell me beer, so I bought two more chocolate bars and a pack of cigarettes. I continued my walk north, without direction or care in the world. I walked for hours and hours, tireless, inexhaustible, young, wiry, mad at the paternal idea of god and the casual causal self, mad at the happenstance and circumstance, the march without prance, shuffle without dance, stuck in the tunnel trance, and bat shit crazy.

Around 110th street, the sun blazed the blackness away. The city was quiet. The drunks had all gone home. The homeless were sleeping in the cool corners of the city. The businessmen and women still had a few more hours of sleep and the delivery guys were gearing up and loading their trucks.

I found myself at St. John's Cathedral. I walked over to the garden area. I studied the little statues of the zodiac and the little monuments around the church, and I saw it, the most amazing statue ever. It was called The Fountain of Peace. It depicted the decapitation of Satan by the archangel Michael, the triumph of good over evil. It was a beautiful morning, clear blue and sun tattooed.

I lay beneath the bronze giant and watched as the Archangel flapped his mighty and glorious wings above me. I felt the cool breeze of his activity on my face and chest.

I studied the beaten Devil at the foot of the mighty warrior. Oh, obvious subject! The sharpened sword of the hero Michael gleamed in the sunlight. Small giraffes snuggled the angel with favor, as he stroked their long tender necks. They rested on a giant crab. Satan's body forever sinking in the primordial depths, his head dangling lifeless beneath the enormous crab claw…

The statue became illuminated and full of gold. (Note: In fact, later, when I returned to view the fountain again, I was amazed by two things, that it was indeed real, and that two, it was NOT made entirely of the finest gold.) The statue shone a more brilliant light that morning than I'd ever seen. I examined it thoroughly.

I counted nine total giraffes around the statue, each one animate and communicating with long necks. There was an image I couldn't fully understand, that of a lamb lying down with the lion. It dawned on me what kind of message the Fountain of Peace was trying to convey. I'm sure even the artist didn't know that the lion was full from his feast of the lamb's siblings, and that *furthermore,* it was best to keep the meat fresh, and maybe grazing, until the NEXT meal—because the lion that doesn't kill the lamb, is a dead lion.

END